# ALL HER DEMONS ARE BURNING

# All Her Demons Are Burning

### Tess C. Foxes

**Podium**

Podium

# ALL HER DEMONS ARE BURNING

*I will never forget the first time your fire flickered from
my eyes—how my light burned and took shape as your
flames coursed through my shimmering form like blood.
How my wings turned blue as we scattered through gaps
between worlds, burning so hot I could not imagine ever
wanting any other form. Wishing I could hold you to me,
against me, within me. Keep you like this, always,
always—wanting more and more and more of you
and me, just like this, until the worlds ran dry
and crumbled away.*

*I do not know what to say. I only wish I had
one millennia more to give to you.*

*The hunger is taking me, beloved one.*

*The hunger is gnawing away my truth. My resolve.
My being. All that we have done.*

*I can feel you writhing inside me—still, staying with
me—still burning, desperate, frightened . . . and I am
sorry, beloved one. I am so, so sorry. We have lost.*

*This madness is unbecoming, but I swear I will never
forget how all your people and my people burned for the
sake of existence. Even as I transform—the metamorphosis,
the hunger overtaking my every need—even as my
remaining light melts into rotting flesh, even as teeth
blossom in my mouth and I lose my language to a tongue
I do not know—I will not lose you as I lose myself to this.
I may no longer be, but I will always—*

—the final hissings of the fallen angel, name stricken
from destiny. transcribed by Rafa'el, the Scribe

# CHAPTER ONE

# THE PENULTIMATE CLOUD

Jibra'il would be punished, his feathers torn out and nailed to the eyes that covered his back and arms and chest. How was he to face the other archangels? He had failed.

He would be the last to reach the monument. He could sense the presence of the other three above him, yet he slowed his ascent through the clouds, wings flapping at a hesitant pace. In the world of light, he'd reached such altitude that the only remaining light was not the glow of the world but the silver one emanating from his muscular form. His six wings flapped in turn, and the countless eyes that covered his body blinked and wept. Tears fell away like raindrops. His heart was heavy, for he had failed. And his failure would not go unpunished.

One hundred survival challenges had been issued at his command, as they had always been. Every two thousand years, when the worlds stood in order, in perfect harmony, he would rip one hundred puncture wounds in the fabric between worlds. One hundred victors should have emerged, as they had always emerged.

Though all hundred punctures were now closed, only ninety-nine victors had returned to the material world. Only ninety-nine survival challenges had ended.

One challenge remained in effect. This one had reached beyond the Veil and now threatened the very existence of the material world. The proper world. The world in which He was meant to emerge, truly victorious, inheritor of creation, the harbinger of destiny, to bring forth a Golden Age until the sacred trumpet was finally blown and all the worlds would kneel.

But now?

Jibra'il's mighty wings beat nervously as he burst through another layer of cloud and emerged in a spray of glistening moisture. His long dark hair swished, and several feathers fell away, dissolving into vapor; he always shed when he was anxious.

The four archangels had been summoned. They had not met like this in tens of thousands of years; not since the inception of the Great Work.

Time used to roll forward slowly, from challenge to challenge, and Jibra'il had worked his best, instigating messiahs and guiding civilizations and harnessing rulers, but now, for a reason he could not explain or comprehend, he was certain time had accelerated. Time was no longer inconsequential. It was slipping through his feathered wingtips, and he was terrified of running out.

He was terrified the universe would end before the Great Work finished and they'd achieved perfection. It would've all been for naught. But these weren't thoughts he was willing to share with the other archangels, so he prayed instead to Him, hoping He would share some guidance, some adjustment to the plan that would remedy everything. It was easier when orders came from Him; much less worrying on anyone else's part. The Almighty's will was absolute.

As he neared the Penultimate Cloud, the cloud before the throne, it darkened and grew stormy as if it could sense his conflictions. He had another reason to be hesitant; *she* was there. His once beloved. He wasn't ready to see her again.

One hundred thousand years had not been enough to dull the pain, but this was a summon he could not ignore.

Jibra'il retracted his exoskeleton. His was dark gray, metallic in appearance, and as it peeled back from his face, his silver light bloomed. Headfirst, he soared right into the dark underbelly of the cloud, which welcomed him with a clap of thunder.

The raging storm battered him every which way, and he flapped his six wings furiously. Lightning crackled at his presence, curving around him, shooting through him, but other than a slight tickling sensation, it could not hurt him, for how does light harm light? When he pierced the surface and emerged, he came to a stop with one final flap of his wings. Wisps of cloud trailed away from his naked form, fading, precipitation dripping off his light, evaporating in hissing tendrils of steam.

Jibra'il smoothed his long dark hair back away from his face as he took in the awe-inspiring view. The cloud wasn't mighty in size, as Jibra'il could've flown across it within moments, but it was higher than anything else in the worlds save for the throne, so it was called the Penultimate Cloud. The cloud closest to Him, closest to eternal paradise.

At its center stood the monument, a black, box-shaped structure made from a material found nowhere else in any world. It produced no light or warmth and had absolutely no color, so its darkness was rather the absence of any light, any feature. Some called it the nothing box. Others called it the everything box. But most called it the frequented box, as hundreds of thousands of angels made pilgrimage to worship it every single day.

High above, like a multicolored halo, the worshiping angels flew in circles. This was the daily prayer; every day, a new assortment of angels would rise to the heavens and worship Him.

As Jibra'il stepped carefully across the cloud, he could feel their radiating warmth. The vibrations of their prayers, their desperate cries for love and forgiveness, for perfection and glory, offering themselves completely in supplication to Him.

This was once Jibra'il's favorite place. To sit up here by the monument, to bathe himself in the light of countless prayers, to submit himself to prayer. Except now, he knew the other archangels awaited him inside. And *she* was inside. His heart raced at the thought of seeing her again, though a part of him would rather tear his wings off and throw himself from the cloud.

He marched up to the monument and passed through its front wall. The darkness sucked in his light and form, reverberating through him like an echo, scattering him before he emerged, whole again, on the other side. This was a privilege awarded only to the archangels and select beloveds of the Almighty. No one else would survive the threshold.

The inside was an intimate space, small and cramped. Golden circular patterns glistened across every wall, including the ceiling, and they turned rhythmically, thrumming with light as he entered. The floor was the cloud itself, dark and storming.

Standing in the center of the space was a tall, voluptuous figure shimmering with green light. His heart skipped a beat.

She wore a sheer emerald gown, the neckline cut so deep it showcased her pale-green bosom and navel, and there were slits along the bottom that revealed her long legs. She had long, silvery hair, a high forehead, and piercing eyes that were all black, set on a face as green as her gown. She was the Archangel Rafa'el. The Flower. The Scribe. The Trumpet Blower.

**Angel (Stage V - Level 200)**

"You took your time, beloved," she said, her voice as clear and gentle as a ritual bell on an early spring morning. Jibra'il averted his eyes, unable to hold her gaze, and certainly not able to look at her form. Though none of them wore their exoskeletons in the monument, she wasn't like most angels; she preferred human attire and always wore exceptional garments that accentuated her form. It was pleasing, she'd say. For her own eyes and His and, she'd add with a shy smile, Jibra'il's.

On either side stood the other two archangels. The one to the right was Mika'el, who radiated with blue and purple light in turn, sometimes as bright as the sky just before sunrise, sometimes as dark as a bruise.

### Angel (Stage VI - Level 741)

She leaned against a swirling golden pattern, her arms crossed and eyes shut. She was slender and lean, not as tall as Rafa'el, but she preferred to be small. She'd presented as male for centuries until deciding it wasn't right for her, slimming down to a more streamlined presence that was better suited for war. Even her wings were minimal, growing between her arms and her sides like webbing. Mika'el was the Warrior. The Relentless Storm. The Inciter.

On the left was Azra'il, the Angel of Death. His form was muscular and wide; he took up quite a bit of space inside the monument, and his light was charcoal colored, like the ashes after the flames had burned out.

### Angel (Stage VI - Level 332)

Four enormous wings curled inward on his back, countless eyes shining across them. He was the largest of the archangels, with a necklace of skulls over his broad chest, and his hair a colony of miniature red-and-black serpents, each one undulating and moving of their own free will. Their scales shone like rubies stained with blood. Azra'il was the Guide. The Hellfire. And the Warden. Around his waist was a strap of leather that covered his modesty, but the leather was cut from the skin of the tarnished, a new one every day, which Jibra'il had always found unsettling.

Like Mika'el, Jibra'il much preferred to come naked, unashamed, for it was not his body that ever brought him shame. It was his failures. The messiahs he'd failed to save from evil whispers; the challenges he'd overseen.

Neither of the other two angels spoke. They must be furious. They didn't even look at him as he approached, taking careful steps over the cloud floor. It reacted with his every step, electrical energy sizzling up his toes and curving around his silver legs.

"Kneel," said Rafa'el, raising her voice to that grand splendor Jibra'il had once loved so dearly. It was her commanding voice. Her powerful voice. She held out her hand and unfurled her slender green fingers to reveal a bright red fruit.

Jibra'il knelt on the storm cloud, his arms at his sides, lightning tickling his knees. He picked the fruit off Rafa'el's hand with his teeth, unable to stop himself from glancing at her body. It made him jealous, knowing the other two had knelt here as well, had eaten the fruit off her beautiful hand, had seen her chest and hips from this angle, but jealousy was a sin.

Staring into her eyes as she stroked his hair, his lips closed around the fruit and he crushed it between his teeth. Blood—hot and thick—gushed into his mouth and ran down his throat. The heavy fluid spread through his silver body, the redness curling and blooming before fading, and he shuddered as he absorbed it.

"Rise," she said in her grand voice, and Jibra'il stood. He came up to her chest, where her gown split open, and she held him to the green warmth of her bosom. "It has been too long since I've seen you last, my beloved one." This she spoke quietly, in the private, whispered voice shared only between angels who'd known the other's light intimately.

He shut his eyes and sighed, the fruit's blood still streaming from his lips and absorbing into his form as he basked in her glow. She was the light of life itself, he liked to think.

Like the plants that covered the material world, he wanted her to cover him. To grow all over him and into him. Her embrace was so soft, so welcoming, and he longed for the days they'd been lovers. But so many years had passed since he'd held her in the privacy of their cloud chambers—their light blended into one, silver and emerald, like treetops shivering in moonlight—that he felt he had no right to overstay his welcome.

He had loved her more furiously and more passionately than any star in any universe could ever dream of burning. And he loved her still, and he knew he'd always love her, all the way to the end of time, when all the lights of all the worlds had run out of energy, and all that remained was darkness. He would love her through eternity.

But it had been easier to love her before, when it hadn't hurt, when Jibra'il had been Jibra'el, and their eyes and wings would blink in unison, inseparable as salt in the winds of the sea. Then the Almighty had chosen Rafa'el as the scribe, to carve the ruminations of destiny onto the ancient tablet with her ability, Veridian Scripture. She'd been claimed by Him, and they'd realized that they loved each other more than Him. That was the gravest sin of all, so she had made her decision.

In grief, Jibra'el had transformed into Jibra'il, taking the shape of a man, untangling himself from Rafa'el because it only hurt. It always hurt.

Stepping away, Jibra'il took her hand and kissed the fingers that marked down time itself, and she touched his cheek, a longing, mournful gaze in her eyes that asked countless questions. *Are you alright? I miss you. I hope you are well.* But she turned away with a swish of her gown, and he stepped back, the customary conditions satisfied for the discussion of holy matters.

"Have you heard the news?" she asked.

Jibra'il looked at the others. He'd expected admonishment. Anger. They'd already known that a survival challenge hadn't ended. Mika'el sighed and didn't say a word, but she met Jibra'il's eyes and glowered, her skin more purple than blue.

Azra'il picked at the teeth of one of his necklace skulls with a long fingernail. "Mortals have awakened abilities to challenge our own," he said in a deep, gravelly voice. His brows were furrowed. They were serpents too, their heads meeting at the center where their tongues darted between his blood-red eyes. "There were two, in fact."

Jibra'il dimmed with confusion. "The count stopped at ninety-nine. The work has not been completed. Isn't that why we've gathered? I have failed."

Azra'il shook his head. His serpents whisked about. "You haven't failed, dear brother. You orchestrated the challenges as you always do. This crime was the work of interlopers."

"What?" Jibra'il simultaneously felt relief and anxiety. Relief that he wasn't to blame; anxiety for what he didn't know.

"Interlopers," repeated Rafa'el. "The Antithesis has made its presence known." She sank to the cloud floor, her emerald gown spreading like the petals of a flower. She looked so beautiful it ached to stare for too long, but Jibra'il realized it was her way of ordering everyone to sit. She was the weakest in level, but Rafa'el was the closest to *Him*. She held authority over all angels, all creation.

The others slid to the floor as well. Azra'il squatted, the leather cloth flapping between his thighs, his broad chest presented proudly. Mika'el sat with her legs folded beneath her, her hands held neatly on her lap, her webbed wings nearly invisible.

Jibra'il completed the circle, his fingers digging into his palms, his legs crossed beneath him. He saw Rafa'el's gaze flicker toward his manhood, but he didn't move to cover himself. "I thought it was me. I thought my sins . . . I thought my abilities had failed. I thought I had failed."

Rafa'el smiled at him, her green eyes shimmering as she shook her head. "No, my beloved, you could never fail. You have always been dutiful in carrying out His will."

He knew that if she could, she'd reach out and touch him—not in the welcoming way she'd embraced him before but the deeper way, where their lights would merge. He knew that he would let her despite the sanctity of the monument, and he knew that was why she would never.

Rafa'el continued. "The challenge could not conclude due to the actions of two young mortals. Their love . . ." She paused on the word *love* and glanced to the side. "It was their love—foolish and naive love—that bound them together. One actualized an ability to reconstruct reality. The other severed her ties between spirit and form, becoming as the tarnished do. Together, they circumvented the challenge and returned to their world alongside other mortals whose sacrifice was foregone.

"No true victor emerged, and thus, the survival challenge continues within the material world itself. Our guidance system has already responded to these circumstances."

Jibra'il shook his head. His wings stretched by reflex, all his eyes opening and shutting across his body. He saw Mika'el's large eye, the one on her chest, spring open in shock, but she regained her composure quickly, and Jibra'il tried to do the same. He put his face in his hands.

"Do you need a moment?" asked Rafa'el.

"No," replied Jibra'il through his fingers. "I just do not understand. This is not how humans behave. In every survival challenge issued to humankind, they have never . . . They always, without fail, surrender relentlessly to their needs." His wings flickered again, and it took more willpower than he was proud to admit to fold them back into place and shut all his eyes. He knew why she'd asked him and the others to sit. Had they been standing, he would've paced back and forth, and the storm beneath them would have responded in kind.

"It seems we have underestimated them," said Azra'il. He clucked his tongue. "You should see them in Hell. Filthy creatures."

"Hold your tongue," said Rafa'el coldly. "We do not speak ill of the dead. They serve their purpose."

"No, but they speak plenty ill to each other." Azra'il snorted. "Come listen to them when I administer the divine punishments. How they beg. How they scream. They would sell their own mothers, their own children, to avoid it."

As they went back and forth, Jibra'il's mind spun. *Humans.* He'd lived among their kind for so long. He'd watched civilizations emerge and fall. Rulers and ravagers, it was always the same. Brief moments of kindness and love, followed by tremendous strings of tragedy.

Humans always ruthlessly sought one thing: to meet their desires. Whether it was food or rest, mating or violence, humans were ruled by the needs and wants of their bodies. It was why sinful angels were punished, tarnished, forced into physical flesh, forced to succumb to such madness, and prevented from ascending to divinity. To be material was to be sinful, and that was the nature of the Great Work. To eliminate all sin. To eradicate the cravings of the flesh. For all to be clean and holy.

He almost wanted to reject Rafa'el's news, but he knew she could not lie. She was unable to. She could not so much as even bend the truth, for since becoming the scribe, she only spoke of things written on the tablet.

And for the survival challenge to be in effect in the material world . . . effectively Rapture . . . *this* was the final war, whether they liked it or not, whether it had been part of the plan or not, and he knew Rafa'el was shaken by this. It had not appeared on the tablet. It had not been projected. It had not been ordained. She would've informed all His angels if that were the case.

The final war was here, and if they waited too long, there would be nothing left. The material world would devour itself; humankind would end before they could be saved. And if they failed here, it would be the end of the Great Work.

He sat quietly, ruminating, as Rafa'el told the rest of the tale once Azra'il's distaste for humanity had quieted. Mika'el stood once, as if she had something to say, but she just stared at them blankly, crossed her arms, shook her head, and sat back down. Lightning coursed through her blue-and-purple glow, and Azra'il only laughed. Rafa'el squeezed Mika'el's hand, shooting Jibra'il a worried look before continuing.

She explained the ending of the unfinished challenge. Jibra'il was curious. It had been obfuscated for some reason, but he'd sensed something powerful was at play. Which was why he'd fled. He'd assumed he'd sinned. He'd assumed he'd be punished severely, but as Rafa'el explained the details and even Azra'il leaned forward to listen, Jibra'il's feeling of unease grew monstrous.

One of the mortals had slaughtered her beloved in a desecrated state of mind, which confirmed his belief that humans were beyond sense. But the other, the mortal's beloved, had openly sacrificed herself, offered herself to save the desecrated, to absolve her of all sin. And her ability to reconstruct matter had flowed into the severer.

"What of them?" asked Azra'il. His red eyes burned brightly as he raised his voice. "The dead one has been collected. She came peacefully. We should find the other."

"She has moved beyond our view," said Rafa'el.

Jibra'il was speechless. Did the mortal know what she was capable of? Did she know the threat she posed? Despite this, he had the horrible foreboding that Rafa'el had even worse news to share.

"The worst," spoke Rafa'el, lowering her gaze, her hand raised slightly, fingers moving as though she were marking the tablet as she spoke. "The worst is what the severer did upon rejecting victory, rejecting the challenge, and returning to the material world."

They all held their breath, their lights shimmering. The golden patterns on the walls turned quickly, as if they too were disturbed by the news.

Rafa'el took a deep breath, her green light shining brilliantly before fading. "She's become the second Mary and given birth. The Antithesis now has material form."

"NO!" shouted Azra'il. Lightning shot through his enormous form, transforming into vicious red shades before crackling all around him. Every single one of his serpents hissed.

Mika gasped. They had waited two thousand years for a new Mary to birth the Almighty into the world. And now even that was undone. This Mary, this second Mary, had plunged all the worlds into chaos. She'd birthed the Antithesis. The Antichrist. The Unbecoming.

They had known the Antithesis would emerge one day. It had been written on the tablet by Rafa's own hand. The details had remained obscured, but this? This was . . . This was madness. Birthed by a Mary? Birthed from a survival challenge? The Great Plan had always been to bring Rapture about themselves after the conclusion of the final survival challenge. For Him to reawaken in the material world and forge an army of light from the victors so that when the Antithesis arrived, the worlds would be well prepared to protect creation.

But here they were. This was the present. The now. This was what had come to pass.

"Will He see us?" asked Jibra'il in a low voice. He longed to see the Almighty, to stand in His presence, to bow his head in shame and beg forgiveness. To seek guidance. It had been two thousand years since he'd seen the Almighty last, as only Rafa'el was permitted to fly up to the throne. Another pang of jealousy struck his heart. Jealousy that Rafa'el could see Him. And jealousy that the Almighty could keep Rafa'el all for Himself.

Azra'il scoffed. Mika'el bowed her head. It was Rafa'el who answered him. "The Almighty does not wish to be seen until He has procured material form once more and the work is renewed. A suitable candidate must be found, for whom you must be the guide, my beloved."

"A *third* Mary?"

"As it will be," said Rafa'el. She blinked and reached for the air. "It has been written, but the Mary has not yet been decided. Fate seeks her out. And the actions of the mortals . . . Everything is in such confusion, such disharmony."

Jibra'il shook his head. So much uncertainty. Rafa'el only wrote what she saw, inscribing destiny into the tablet, but everything was always shifting, winding and unwinding, until it was done and set in stone. It must be agony for her; here he'd been lamenting his failures and lamenting what was to come without consideration for what Rafa'el must see. What Rafa'el must bear as the ending approached.

"The Antithesis will build an army," Azra'il spoke. "We have always known this. Why are we alarmed? The dead are prepared. Our angels are ready. The humans will fall in line."

"And we shall rain blood and storm on all who oppose Him," said Mika quietly, speaking for the first time. "We shall wage war in His name and bring perfection to all creation."

Azra'il laughed. "You have waited long and patiently for the bloodshed, my sister. It will be glorious seeing you in action again. We shall be victorious, and He will ascend—"

"—for he is the Most Beneficent, the Most Merciful," they finished in unison.

"And what of the severer?" asked Jibra'il after a solemn moment of silence. It was a struggle to even think of such a mortal. The power to sever. The power to reconstruct. Only the Almighty possessed such duality; even Jibra'il himself could only open wounds between worlds. He could not heal them, only shut them once the challenges had ended. He hadn't known it was possible to heal them.

Rafa'el smiled sadly, a smile that made Jibra'il's heart twinge. He wanted to pick her up. Wanted to hold her in his arms and press his lips to the crease in her radiant forehead and assure her that whatever she'd written, whatever she'd foreseen, they would be together.

"That we do not know, my love. She slipped through the worlds, beyond our reach. But she is vital. The tablet has reached its final lines. I can feel the ending approaching, and her name appears so many times I have memorized the shape of her. She will go on to commit such a crime against the Almighty, against destiny itself. But this has not been affixed. It remains in flux, obscured from my sight. The words shift with unease. She must be stopped at all costs. We *must* stop her at all costs."

*A crime against the Almighty?* Jibra'il's wings shuddered, but he managed to hold his composure as Mika'el smacked her thighs with her fists, unable to suppress her rage. Azra'il crushed one of the skulls on his necklace, the bone shards scattering in all directions. The Penultimate Cloud responded with the booming roar of thunder.

"And what is her name?" asked Jibra'il quietly. He couldn't understand how a mortal could do anything against Him. Against destiny.

"Jenny Huang."

# CHAPTER TWO

# AMONG THE PILLARS

*What delusion am I convincing myself of right now to pretend I'm okay? She's dead.*

*I killed her.*

Jenny blinked away tears, trying to stop them, but even with her eyes tightly shut, they kept coming, kept bubbling off her cheeks into the radiant golden light she was falling through. *I'm going to find her. I'm going to find you, Susan.*

*Then I'll be okay.*

*I'll fix this.*

Streams of color swirled around her. She bit down hard on her hatchet as she waded deeper through the light, trying to swim, trying to sink. A river of orange weaved and curled around her body. Dark-blue streams mingled with the sky blue of her new armor, and greens danced across the edge of her hatchet and her face like liquid emeralds. She kept sinking, falling—she couldn't tell which. All she knew was that she had to get away from the school, from the cafeteria, from Susan's cold body.

*I'm okay. I'll find her. I'll be okay.*

*Am I okay? Am I delusional?*

*I'm not. I'm not. I'm not!*

*I KILLED her. I tried to eat her. She's dead. She's dead. She's dead!*

*I'm not okay. I can't be okay. I never have been. How the fuck can I—*

*I'll find her.*

She sobbed, grinding her teeth on the hatchet's handle, and the light responded. Golden ripples reverberated through everything, through her. Her dark hair streamed over her head, and she stretched out her arms. This was Susan's light, after all. Valescent Light. It was Susan's light that had brought them home; Susan's love. But how? How had they accessed this space between worlds?

*Is it 'cause I'm desecrated?*

The notifications from earlier still filled her mind: Severed Spirit. Existential Error. Natural Order Corruption. Rapture.

*I'm broken. I'm broken. I've always been—*

This golden rainbow light was something wonderful. Something miraculous. Something that made no sense. How could light be liquid? How could she wade into it, swim through it, sink deeper and deeper? She knew she was between worlds, but this was nothing like the eerie, sickly glow of the Veil. This was something more . . .

All she remembered was Susan using Valescent Light, and the state Jenny had been in. *I was a monster; I am a monster.* And how the darkness beneath them had reacted, convulsing as though Susan was healing it. Had she healed the wound between worlds? Was that how they'd escaped the Veil?

Wasn't that what Eve had told her?

They'd fallen through the light, the same light the high school and everyone inside had fallen through, to get back to New York. They'd pulled themselves out of hell, but . . .

**Rapture has commenced.
The Final Challenge is in effect.**

All they'd managed to do was throw themselves into another nightmare. And now Susan was dead, and Jenny was . . . She'd run away.

*Why did I leave?*

*I didn't run. I'm going to find her.* The world of death. That's where Susan had to be. Eve had shown Jenny the worlds; she knew the world had to exist, that death couldn't just be the end. There had to be something more, even if it was only something she remembered from her vague memories of Sunday school at her mother's church. Heaven and Hell. The hereafter. The eternal soul. She just had to get there and find Susan and bring her back, and then everything would be okay.

*Why are you deluding yourself?*

*There is no world of death. You just didn't want to stay and fight anymore. You're a coward. You gave birth to that thing. You plunged the world into Rapture, then you ran. You killed your best friend. The girl you love. You ate Miriam alive. You almost ate your brother.*

*You're a failure.*

*You're a monster.*

*You're disgusting.*

*SHUT UP!* She spat the hatchet out of her mouth and stopped trying to swim, stopped trying to move. The lump in her throat hurt so much she swore she would choke. Floating, trying to be as still as possible, Jenny sobbed. The hatchet hovered gently in front of her, twirling slowly as it waited for her. *I don't know where I'm going; I don't know what I'm doing. Can the light hear me? Can it guide me?*

*I want to find Susan. Please help me.*

*Is there a world where people go to when they die? There has to be. Take me there!*

*Please.*

A bright splash of yellow engulfed her, then several blue rings swam around, slowly turning green as they mixed through the yellow. Then came orange. Then red—a dark, crimson curtain that smothered the golden light and swallowed every other color.

Her new armor, fashioned after Susan's favorite color, the one she'd made after sinking into the light, glimmered with the blood-red hue, and she remembered the exoskeleton that had gushed out of her belly button. She remembered how she'd transformed.

Red tendrils of color stretched around her, and Jenny grabbed her hatchet and swung at them.

Her limbs moved slowly; everything was so slow, like she was underwater, underlight. But the red looked like the tentacles she'd had, and when the hatchet's obsidian edge cut through them, they shimmered and dissipated like ink in water. Whatever Susan had done back there, she'd done more than just heal Jenny. Her tentacles were gone, and the exoskeleton no longer grew out of her.

*I'm not a monster. I'm not a monster. I'm not a monster!*

*But I am!*

She flung her hatchet as far as she could. *Get away from me!* She clawed at her face, at her eyes. She could almost feel how empty they were. *Lifeless. Inhuman. Just like the angels.* But even as they burst and gushed beneath her fingernails, as she scraped her sockets, clawed at bone, even as she peeled the skin off her cheeks, the light caressed her like cooling rain. It healed her injuries in seconds, no matter how hard she tried, no matter how much she wanted to hurt.

As if upset by her actions, the light stopped holding her up. A scream tore through the lump in her throat, and she kicked and struggled as she fell, plummeting like a meteor into a golden ocean, burning up a million colors. Then, like an eye closing beneath her, the light and all the swirling colors between worlds snapped shut.

Jenny collapsed face-first onto cold, hard ground. Her hatchet landed beside her.

Something like sand, or maybe ash, tickled her nose when she inhaled. The taste was sharp on her tongue, salty and metallic, and she coughed violently. Everything burned inside. She was exhausted. She was beyond exhausted. She'd been fighting nonstop since the survival challenge began.

Jenny pushed herself onto her knees and looked around. Was this another world? It felt . . . It didn't feel like she was somewhere else. There wasn't that unsettling sensation of weightlessness that she'd felt in Eve's world. And the ground felt like ground. The gravity was the same as Earth's. Heavy storm clouds clung to the sky. It was dark, but there was a soft, pale glow that came from somewhere beyond the clouds, and it was enough for Jenny to make out the crudely shaped pillars that stood in front of her.

They were spread out, about an arm's length of space between them, and they reminded her of trees, like standing on the edge of the woods. She almost thought they were rock formations, but they had to have been man-made. Or maybe angel made. There was something uncanny about them which she couldn't explain; something in their shapes which seemed carefully chipped away to form specific grooves and patterns. These might've been ancient statues of worship, or something like Stonehenge.

As she stood, she realized it *was* some kind of forest. A forest of strange rocks. Countless pillars stood in front of her, and to her right and left, there were even more, spreading like a coastline that seemed to go on indefinitely. Behind her, the world was flat. There was no wind, no hills, no roads or anything. It was a vast, endless expanse of nothing but dark ground with clouds rolling overhead. Jenny turned to face the line of pillars again, and almost right beneath her armored feet, the ground shifted.

The grainy, dark earth cracked. Jenny stepped back, summoning her hatchet with a flash of golden light as something jutted out from the crack, expanding upward like a rapidly growing tree. It took her a second to realize it was another pillar.

She lowered her hatchet, breathing heavily, staring at this new formation standing right in front of her. The rock was dark, almost glassy, and she held up her hatchet against it to find they were very similar. Was it also obsidian?

To her right, another one sprang out of the dirt, slightly different from the one before, a bit shorter. Further along the pillar-tree line, Jenny saw more and more growing out of the ground. They were expanding into the emptiness, like a forest claiming more land. Jenny wondered how far the pillars went, how many of them there were. *Why did the light bring me here?*

Or had she brought herself here?

Wasn't that how they'd left the Veil? Guiding everything and everyone back home? She shut her eyes again and inhaled deeply. The salty air stung, but she didn't care. Everything flashed through her thoughts: from the first angel that had attacked her English classroom—whose head she'd smashed in with a hole puncher—to the desecrated angel and its nightmarish blue light, to Miriam. Miriam, whom Jenny had hunted across the school and ripped apart and eaten. Then Susan.

Susan. How could she have done that to Susan?

*It wasn't me.*

*It wasn't me!*

That's what she wanted to believe. Had to believe. It couldn't have been her. Someone else had been in control. She'd been *Severed*. She'd been out of her mind. An anomaly. *Existential Error.*

Another scream burst out of her throat, and when a new pillar erupted from the ground, Jenny struck it over and over with her hatchet. The impacts drew sparks, and the clinks and clangs rang all around her, echoing, bouncing from pillar to pillar. But each time she struck it, golden light shimmered across the obsidian edge of her hatchet, flashing over and over.

Through her tears, through her rage, she thought she saw something *inside* the pillar. A glimpse of something terrible, so quick she couldn't recognize what it was, but fear surged through her limbs as notifications streamed into her head.

**+100 Energy**

**+100 Energy**

**+100 Energy**

Her angry cries broke. She held her breath, not even daring to swallow as she stared, trembling. She felt her heart pounding in her throat. There was no change in the pillar's appearance, no indication that she'd even attacked it. None of its glossy rock face had so much as chipped. No cracks. No sign of damage. But she was *afraid*, like she'd done something horrible again.

And she'd gained energy. She remembered her hatchet's new ability:

**Hatchet (Tier 3)**

**Your weapon can now harvest Energy**

**with every attack that invokes pain.**

Shaking, she lowered her head and studied her weapon. The obsidian face, dark and metallic and sharp, looked as it had since the moment it'd hit tier three. And the wooden handle, its ridges and grooves where a floral pattern had been, was now stained by dried blood and smudged fingerprints. It had once looked so pretty. But she'd *hurt* the pillar. She'd harvested energy from that pain.

The hatchet dropped from her hand, the edge sinking into the dirt so that its handle jutted out. She stared at the pillar even as two more grew beside it. Was it . . . Could it be? *Alive?*

"Hello?" she whispered, her voice hoarse from all the screaming. What was inside these things? Why was she scared of the answer?

Would the pillars hatch? She could've sworn she'd seen *something* when her hatchet flashed. Maybe these things were like the angels' chrysalises, and she shuddered as more memories filled her head: the angel couple in the stairwell, the boy she'd burnt to death, the blue chrysalis in the chem wing where she'd nearly died, where she'd found Oliver and the other survivors, where an angel had sucked her blood out through her broken nose.

She took another step back, glancing at the other pillars, squinting at them in disbelief, trying to quell the dizziness. They just looked like rocks. What was going on? How could she hurt them? What could be inside them? They didn't even register as anything in her head. There was no notification, no indication that they were anything other than strange rocks that came out of the ground.

Maybe she needed more light. Taking a deep breath, she held out her hand. Her blue armor peeled back from her fingers and hand, revealing pale skin, and with a snap of her fingers, she used Ignite.

Fire flickered across her knuckles. A flame took shape, flickering and growing. Her arm had become a torch, and an orange-and-red glow surrounded her like a bubble of warmth and light. It cast shadows—her own and that of the pillars, tall and looming—but the warmth felt pleasant on Jenny's face, and she felt like the only thing that was *alive* in this eerie, absent world. A thought crossed her mind: if there were predators in this world, they might see the fire and come for her.

*Good*, she thought, her skin prickling. *Let them.* Some part of her still ached with bloodthirst. She really, really wanted to hit something, but she shuddered at the thought of another fight. She wasn't sure why. Maybe her body could sense something. Maybe she was just hungry. Maybe she was just afraid.

As Jenny walked up to the pillar she'd attacked, the dizzying fear response struck her again. It hit her in the chest, harder this time, taking her breath away. Maybe she shouldn't do this; maybe she shouldn't look. She wanted to hide. It would be better not to know.

*But why?*

Her foot had frozen midair, just before the final step. The orange glow of her flames reflected off the pillar's surface, and if she squinted, she could just about see the silhouette of something inside. A person? An insect? What could it be?

Why was she sweating? Her heart stammered. Her knees went weak. Why did she feel like she was doing something awful? As though she were sleeping on the floor again, a kid, praying for God's forgiveness, terrified that she'd done something wrong and would be punished. Praying her mother wouldn't come hit her.

*Fuck this.*

She sucked in a deep breath, trying to compose herself, trying to bury the fear response. She'd fought much worse, seen much worse, and whatever this thing was, she had to know. That was the only way to deal with fear: by exposing it.

She forced herself to put her foot down, forced herself to come face-to-face with the pillar. Forced herself to bring her nose right up against it, her burning hand raised overhead. As the innards of the dark pillar became clear, as her eyes focused on what was inside, Jenny's jaw dropped.

## Death (Level 0)

She clapped both hands over her mouth and stumbled back, choking on a cry as her fire went out. The person inside vanished from view. It was a man. She was sure of it. A middle-aged man trapped inside, his face twisted in agony as he stared back at her with strained, bulging eyes. And his guts . . .

Jenny's stomach heaved. She'd seen so many people and angels cut open, but this? This sight seared itself into her mind. She forced herself to look again, just to be sure.

But without light, the pillar was just dark, just a rock. With a shaky breath, she used Ignite again, but she kept the flame smaller this time, focused on her fingertip, as though she'd lit a lighter. The man came back into view, his wide eyes shining in the firelight; he was so close that it was like he was just on the other side of a window. His face was maybe a few inches from Jenny's, and she had a clear view of his insides.

The man inside the pillar was split from his rib cage to his groin. His arms hung limp, shoulders drooped, and he stood unmoving, as though his limbs were stuck to the pillar, but his eyes followed her. His intestines spilled out like enormous, glistening snakes, latching onto the pillar. *Something* moved through them, bulging up and down the length of each intestine.

She could see his lungs expand and contract, could see his heart beating rapidly, each beat threatening to force his heart out of his exposed chest. She could see the whites of his ribs jutting out like monstrous fangs, and when she caught sight of tears on his reddening eyes, when she realized he couldn't blink and her fire's light must be agony to someone so used to the dark, her entire body convulsed. Jenny stumbled, bumping into another pillar, glimpsing a young girl trapped inside.

She shook out her flame and cried out; she couldn't take it anymore. Was there a person in every single one of these? She doubled over and retched.

Vomit splattered the ground. Chunks of half-digested meat rolled across the salty dirt, and the sight of that, the acrid stench of it, and the ugly realization that she recognized *where* the meat had come from made her retch again.

# CHAPTER THREE

# WHAT AM I SUPPOSED TO DO?

There were no other names for the people encased by the pillars. No other notifications appeared in Jenny's head. It was only when she shone light over them that they became translucent and Jenny could see the whites of their eyes, the notification filling her head.

## Death (Level 0)

Some of them looked to be around her age, teenagers and young adults. Some were older, with gray hair and wrinkled skin. She even found children; the worst were the toddlers and the babies. Their pillars were the smallest, barely coming up to Jenny's shins.

She could've easily mistaken them for random stones, but when Jenny knelt and held her flames to them, she could see the young ones standing just like all the others, their chubby arms and legs, their bellies open with their guts attached to the pillar like umbilical cords. She could see their hearts beating, their organs glistening, and their eyes wide and expressive and so, so afraid and *moving*. Every single one of them was responsive; she knew they could see her.

She was careful not to make her flames too big or too bright, cupping her burning hand with the other to dim it as much as she could. A few of their lips moved as though they were talking, but Jenny couldn't hear them. They couldn't raise their arms or turn their bodies, but their eyes followed her. Jenny tried to smile, tried to reassure them somehow, but what was the use if they couldn't hear her? Could they even understand her?

Her stomach quivered from her retching, and she placed a hand over her navel. The children in the pillars reminded her of the angel babies who had followed her through the school; how they'd imprinted on her. What had happened to them? Were they okay? The last thing she remembered was sending them with Susan . . . They must've tried defending her from Miriam. Had any of them survived?

Jenny sighed and wiped her lips. She tried to relax her shoulders. *Where am I?* she asked with her mind. *System? What is this place? Can you tell me?*

After a moment's hesitation, when nothing responded, she added out loud, "Eve?" It was a faint whisper, a faint hope. But again, there was no response. Eve was gone.

There was no trace of it left in Jenny's head. And why would there be? Eve now had a body, an exact copy of Jenny's; her body, her face, her eyes. And what did Jenny have? She'd escaped the high school and the survival challenge, but what did she have? She was alone, her eyes were empty, and she was surrounded by . . . these *things*.

Swallowing hard to keep from throwing up again, she took a breath, trying to steady herself. But she couldn't stop the scream. *"WHAT AM I SUPPOSED TO DO?!"*

Her voice cracked. Her lungs burned. She dropped to her knees and punched the ground as hard as she could. Tears welled up, and she struck the ground again and again. As the dust clouded around her and she tasted it on her tongue, she realized it wasn't sand at all. It was salt.

*"Is someone there?"*

It was a whisper, a soft sigh moving through the air. Jenny summoned her hatchet back with a flash of light. She was done hearing strange voices, done trying to solve mysteries, but she was sure that someone had spoken. Out loud. It wasn't something else in her head. This sounded like a man's voice.

*"Are you alive?"* came the whisper again, like a gentle breeze. *"Can you help me?"*

Shivers ran down Jenny's spine. She didn't recognize the voice at all. It had to be someone from this world, but why did they need help?

"Who are you?" Jenny whispered back. She wasn't sure why she was whispering. There was no wind here—no warmth or coolness—only the salty pillars and the gloomy sky, but somehow, being alive felt strange and wrong.

*"It's been so long . . . Find me, please. Follow my voice. I will sing for you."*

Sing? Why would anyone want to sing in a place like this? "Why can't you just come to me?" asked Jenny, turning around and around, trying to pinpoint where the whispering was coming from. All she could see were the pillars. "Who are you?"

But as she searched every direction for any sign of anyone, half expecting an angel or a ghost or something worse, she heard humming—a deep, low humming. It was a tune; something sad and lonely. Long drawn-out notes followed by words. But these weren't words Jenny understood. They were in a different language; something ancient or alien. She'd never heard anything like it before.

Forcing herself to calm down, Jenny took a deep breath, shut her eyes, and listened intently to pinpoint the direction of the singing.

She would have to venture into the pillar forest. Jenny glanced behind her at the flat expanse of land again. It was so empty, with not even a hill or a sand dune in sight, just barren flatness as far as the world went. But more and more pillars spurted out of the ground. More and more kept taking shape, and she knew each one had a person inside.

She listened again for the song. It sounded so pained, and a deep sorrow and anguish shifted inside her even though she couldn't understand the words. Touching her hatchet's obsidian face to her forehead and squeezing the handle, she wondered what to do.

She wished Susan were here; Susan was good at languages. Good at helping people. Susan would help whoever was singing, because if they were singing to get her attention, it might mean they were stuck. They couldn't come to Jenny. And they'd asked for help. There was no way Susan wouldn't find a way to help them.

"Okay," whispered Jenny. Then, with conviction, "I'll help you."

Mind made up, she stepped forward, moving carefully and deliberately to sidestep each pillar without accidentally brushing up against one. She didn't generate any flames; she didn't look too closely at the pillars, her skin crawling as she walked. She could almost feel every single set of eyes on her, so she tried to focus on the voice, the ebb and flow of their song. Their voice went low and high and low again, slowly and purposefully, as though they were singing something religious, something from the church. She reminded herself to breathe every time the singer paused to take a breath.

The pillars loomed, and she tried not to study their shapes and ridges. Each one looked like arms wrapped around someone from certain angles. Sometimes, she swore she recognized the outline of someone's shoulders. Maybe their elbows. Maybe their hips. Without any fire or light, she didn't have to glimpse the person inside, but her imagination kept running wild. The deaths inside were just too creepy.

Why were these things even bothering her? Shouldn't she be desensitized to the horror? How many people had she seen cut open and bleeding? How many people and angels had *she* cut open? She'd lost track, but the more she tried to remember, the more she was salivating.

*I'm salivating.*

Jenny paused and sucked in a breath through her teeth, spittle dribbling down her chin. She rubbed her eyes with her palms, her arms itching to try ripping her face off again.

*Stop it. Stop it. Stop it!*

She kept seeing flashes of Susan's face, her smile. Her dust-covered blue hair as she'd held Jenny. As Jenny's teeth had sunk into Susan's throat, and that *taste*. The burst of sweet madness, more delicious than anything she'd ever known before—

*Stop!*

Swallowing hard, Jenny straightened her shoulders and lifted her face toward the sky, as though she was trying to hold back tears. The tears came anyway. Susan had healed her so thoroughly, but what had been the point? Susan was dead, and now Jenny had her ability, Valescent Light.

As if in response, the rainbow of colors shimmered around her arm and climbed her hatchet, reds and purples and oranges curving and forming circles and rings, loops that faded in and out as her arm took on a golden hue.

*Could I open another passage between worlds? Could I leave this place?*

But she grimaced. Her multicolored light revealed the bodies in the pillars more clearly than the fire had, and every single person around her seemed drawn to it, their eyes wide and staring. Jenny felt a strange itch. A strange itch that seemed to shoot right into her mind and get stuck, and if only she could scratch it . . . if she could . . . maybe she could . . .

It was like a thought just out of reach, but with all these trapped people staring and the singing, she couldn't quite grasp the thought. Frustrated, she pressed her glowing hand to the nearest pillar. It was an elderly woman, so ancient her wrinkles hid her eyes, but the light did nothing. The woman stared back, tears streaming down her cheeks, her lips moving silently, her intestines glistening.

*Maybe I'm doing it wrong*, thought Jenny bitterly as she shook her hand free. An ugly shudder went up her spine, and she felt bad for exposing the old woman to more light. Taking a breath, she listened for the song again.

The tune had changed, and there were new lines. These words weren't in English, but somehow, she understood them.

*Save me from this despair,*
*I have been here so long, forsaken.*
*Take me from this wretched place.*
*Such sweet, exquisite pain.*

*Father, make me whole again.*
*Mother, tuck me into bed.*


With a sigh, Jenny continued in that direction. Her heart ached; she wasn't sure why. Somehow, the song pulled on something familiar . . . some horrible, miserable pain.

Flashes of her rapid pregnancy flickered through her thoughts. She remembered how her belly had expanded so quickly, ballooning as the glowing, monstrous baby gushed out of her. The way her ribs had cracked as her insides expanded, and how she could've sworn her entire soul was trying to escape. She shuddered and switched the hatchet from one hand to the other.

*Too many thoughts. I'm thinking too much . . .*

Sometimes, the singing stopped, and Jenny would stop as well, as once or twice she'd tried to keep going but only managed to turn herself around. Then the song would pick up again, and Jenny would course correct. Whoever was singing must get tired. It was better to just wait in the gloomy dark.

She kept expecting something to hiss or leap out from some dark patch of salty ground. Unease clung to her fiercely, and she wasn't sure if it was the world or something from within or both. Salt stung her lips and throat and lungs; she wished she had her tentacles. They would make finding this strange singer so much easier, and if anything else was lurking around, her tentacles would sense it. Sometimes, she reached for them with her mind, trying to flex muscles she no longer had. She swore she could feel them, could feel their thirst. Where had they gone?

She touched her navel, her blue armor peeling away to reveal the pale skin of her abdomen, flat and muscular. The armor responded to her so easily it almost felt like her exoskeleton and not armor she'd created using the system. Blue. As blue as Susan's hair had been.

*Why?*

Jenny had grown so strong, but what was the point? She squeezed her hand against her stomach, digging inside her belly button, scraping it with a fingernail, searching. Where had the exoskeleton come from? Where was it now? She was a desecrated human, so where was it?

*Where is it?*

Was she supposed to build a chrysalis and . . . Well, she didn't know what the desecrated angels had been doing.

*What the fuck am I, guidance system?*

She shuddered as lingering notifications flicked through her thoughts; she'd felt them at the edge of her consciousness. They must've gotten stuck when she'd . . .

**Ranking Bonus!**
**Existential Error**
**Wretched Human → Desecrated Human**

**Congratulations on GUIDANCE SYSTEM ERROR.**
**+50 Stat Points have been awarded.**
**A second Energy Core has been awarded.**

**Natural Order Corruption**
**Awaiting Metamorphosis.**

**You have defeated Wretched Human (Level 24)**
**Experience has been awarded.**
**+1200 Energy**

**You have defeated Human (Stage II - Level 21)**
**Experience has been awarded.**
**+1600 Energy**

Dismissing each notification, trying not to linger on how much energy she'd gotten from Susan, Jenny pulled up her stats, hoping it would give her some answers.

**Jenny Huang**
**Desecrated Human (Existential Error - Level 30)**
**Age: 6,802 days**
**Stats:**
**Power: 35**
**Durability: 20**
**Stamina: 40**
**Agility: 35**
**Stat Points Available: 62**
**Energy Available: 4806**
**Energy Core(s): 2**
**Bloodlust Ecstasy**

She focused hard on the numbers, all her stat points and energy. Everything from Existential Error to Bloodlust Ecstasy . . . She wanted to cry. She wasn't severed; she'd been severed right up until Susan pulled her out and healed her thoroughly. But then? Eve had taken Jenny's eyes and left her desecrated anyway. So, what was she?

How did any of this make any sense? She tapped her forehead with the flat of her hatchet. It felt cool against her overheated skin. She was thinking too much again.

*But I have to think about this, don't I? I have to figure it out.*

*No. I have to figure out where I am. I have to find the world of . . .*

It clicked for her all of a sudden. The notifications for each person inside each pillar was *death*. Slowly, she lowered the hatchet and stared at the pillars again. Were these people's deaths? Was this the world she was looking for?

Was Susan's death here?

An impatient trembling spread down her spine. She wanted to set her entire body on fire and check every single pillar, but then what? She'd be hurting so many of them, and there could be *billions*. And what would she even do once she found Susan? She didn't want to see Susan like that: split down the center with her insides hooked up to the pillar. How was she supposed to get her out?

*What will I even say to her?*

She wanted to scream with frustration. The singing had steadily grown louder and louder, and it was once again in a language Jenny didn't know, but whoever they were, they might know what to do. If Jenny helped that person, maybe they could help her too. Maybe they knew what these pillars were. Maybe the person singing had gotten out of one of them.

Picking up the pace, half wanting to use Instant Acceleration, Jenny ran toward the singing. She dodged and whirled around pillars as though they were enemies trying to attack her, and she focused intently on the song, so intently that she almost didn't notice when the pillars gave way and she stumbled onto flat land. The singing stopped.

"*Here,*" whispered the voice.

The pillar forest was behind her now, and ahead stretched the same empty flatness she'd seen before. To her right and left, more pillars burst out of the ground. She wiped the sweat off her brow and squinted, scanning the view for any sign of anything.

A red burst of lightning drew her attention to a patch of darkness on the horizon. That was when she saw it: an enormous T-shaped, shadowy thing jutting out of the ground in the distance. In the dark, it almost blended in with the flat emptiness and the sky, but when her eyes focused, she could see it.

It seemed so far away. How had the whispers and the singing reached her? She took a deep breath. Since the land was flat now, she could make it across quickly. But as soon as she was about to break into a sprint, the world rippled.

Everything shook, a tremor reverberated through the air, and Jenny felt a strange breeze as the flat ground and the storm clouds seemed to fold inward, almost like an accordion. The distance between Jenny and the shadowy shape closed, as though she were being tugged toward it, and that was when she realized what she'd been looking at. It was a cross.

A cross with a naked man nailed to it, his arms spread wide, nails through his palms. Long dark hair fell forward to hide most of his bearded brown face and cover his bony chest. His body looked sunken, as though someone had sucked out every bit of his insides. His knees were bent slightly, one foot placed over the other, a single nail driven through both. A crown of thorns glistened on his head; there was no mistaking who he was.

But that couldn't be *Him*, could it? There was no notification in her head, just an unsettling feeling of recognition. Besides, Eve had shown her a vision of *Him* already, so who was this? What was this cross doing here?

Jenny had seen so many crosses growing up; she'd seen statues and endless depictions of Jesus, and she'd always wondered what that must've been like. How it must have felt to have nails hammered through her hands and feet. To be left out on display in agony. She shuddered as she stared at the man, her hands shaking, unsure what to do.

"Greetings," whispered the man, his lips barely moving. He raised his head and smiled softly. Up close, his voice had more texture; he sounded so strained, so hurt. "You're not supposed to be here," he said, then he laughed, a gleeful, awful laugh that started small and muffled before bubbling into heavy laughter that became a coughing fit.

His shoulders and his chest shook violently, and Jenny winced, thinking about the nails ripping and tearing through his flesh. Red lightning crackled around his hands and feet before fading away.

"A desecrated human . . ." noted the man slowly, still wheezing. "Level thirty. Aren't you something spectacular?"

Jenny bit her lip. *Why can't I see what he is? What does he want from me? Why does he feel so powerful even though he's nailed up to a cross?* Fire flicked down Jenny's arm as she used Ignite before raising her hand to get a better look.

The man squinted. He was old. Very old. His brown skin was taut and ashy, stretched thinly over his skull, almost like the tarnished angels had been. He was just as fragile, just as delicate looking, like he hadn't eaten in ages and desperately needed medical attention. Jenny got the sense the man had been here for a *long* time.

"Let me see your eyes," said Jenny firmly. *What are you?*

"Do you think I'm like you?" The crown of thorns glistened across his forehead. His genitals were shriveled, like dehydrated fruit clinging to a dying branch. Slowly, he opened his eyes. Brown pupils stared back at Jenny, glistening shiny and bright in the fire's flickering light. "Aren't you just delicious? And you only respond to the language of light. Yet, you question *my* sanctity?"

Jenny's eye twitched. She inhaled deeply. "What do you want from me? Who are you?"

"My name?" hissed the man. Jenny realized he'd just been hissing and shushing this whole time. He'd sung in a different language but spoke with the same sounds as the angels. "My name was . . . I was called Yeshua. And I very much wish to die."

"Yeshua?" asked Jenny, blinking. She'd expected something very different.

"I want you to kill me. Please," he said, tears streaming down his cheeks, getting caught in his dark beard. Then he started laughing, a small laugh that grew louder and louder until he was roaring at the sky. Lightning sizzled across his emaciated body. "You finally sent someone! You finally sent someone to deliver me from this!"

# CHAPTER FOUR

# (NULL)

I'm not going to do that," said Jenny, staring up at the crucified man, eyeing how his chest and ribs jutted out like a fucked-up pair of wings. The cross towered over Jenny, with Yeshua nailed to it several feet off the ground.

"What do you mean?" he asked, eyes wide. He swallowed hard and shook his head vigorously from side to side, straining against the nails, his long hair bouncing in every direction as his shriveled-up balls flapped against his bony thigh. "*No, no, no, no, no!* I prayed so much. So much. For Him to send some-one . . . To come and . . . Why? Why? *Why won't you help me?*"

Red bursts of lightning shivered up and down his body, as though he was statically charged, but Jenny recognized what was happening. She could almost taste it in the air: Yeshua was in a constant state of agony and healing. His flesh was always trying to heal around the nails, always trying to close those holes.

Yeshua started crying and pleading. Or at least, Jenny thought that's what the man was doing because he switched from hissing and shushing to sputter-ing in a language Jenny couldn't understand.

"Wait," started Jenny, hoping to find some answers. Hoping the man would calm down and stop hurting himself. "Can you tell me where we are? What are you doing here? I'm looking for my—"

But Yeshua wasn't willing to listen. His eyes bulged, bloodshot and crazed, and he spat at Jenny, "I want to die. I want to die. Please just let me die. Why else would He send you?"

He screamed and struggled against his restraints, ripping open wounds that healed almost instantly with bursts of red light. He bared his teeth and hissed, appearing completely feral, almost as mindless as the tarnished angels. Spittle clung to his beard as he snarled at her. Yeshua wouldn't listen no matter what Jenny tried to say.

She offered the man water and food, clothes. "I can make you whatever you need," said Jenny, trying to sound calming, trying to sound reassuring. "Let me get you down from there, and then we can talk."

"Just slit my throat. Please. Haven't I done enough? Just do it. I don't want to be here anymore."

It broke Jenny's heart, the sheer desperation in Yeshua's voice, the constant wriggling, the fidgeting, as though he were tossing and turning in bed, desperate to wake up from a nightmare. But this was infinitely worse. He'd been crucified. "I don't want to kill you," replied Jenny. "I thought your singing was beautiful. Please let me help you."

Yeshua let out a pitiful cry, raising his face up to the clouds as a sob broke into a deafening cry of anguish. It echoed all around the flat, salty lands. Then he slumped forward so that his brown hair covered his face and chest, and he went still.

Jenny held her breath, expecting Yeshua to have another outburst, but the man seemed to have fallen asleep. Exhaling loudly, exhaustion tugging on the edges of her thoughts, she figured it would be a good idea to get some rest as well. It didn't seem like any other creatures were alive in this world. Besides, what was the worst that would happen? She'd get killed in her sleep? At least that way, she'd find the world of the dead right away.

*That's silly,* she thought with a grimace, but Yeshua's screaming words kept echoing through Jenny's mind: *I want to die. I want to die. Please just let me die.*

Her head ached with questions, with fears and thoughts. Where was this place? What was Yeshua doing here? And why did he think Jenny had been sent here to end his misery? For a moment, Jenny considered getting the man down while he slept. *Maybe I can pry the nails out; maybe he won't be as frantic once he's free.* But exhaustion made Jenny reconsider.

*He needs serious help, and he wants to die. I can't help him like this.*

*And what if he's dangerous?*

*What if there's a reason he's contained here?*

Her head spun with gruesome images: the angels, Miriam, Susan, Oliver, everyone. She waited a while to make sure the man was actually passed out. It might've been a dozen minutes or so, but then, Jenny sat down and raised her hand to make a bottle of water.

But that energy . . . She'd gotten so much of it from Susan, from Miriam. Was it right to use that? She'd already used some to make her blue armor, but . . . she'd done that almost instinctively whilst in the light. She hadn't wanted to go somewhere else naked, and her first thought had been the color of Susan's hair. But was it alright to use the energy now?

*Of course it is. You have to survive. You have to find her.*

*I don't know if . . .* She stifled a sob and slammed her hand against the coarse ground. It was like sitting on the beach, except the air burned slightly and everything tasted like salt. There was no breeze. She stared at Yeshua's body, the steady rise and fall of his chest, and wondered how he'd folded the distance between them. It almost reminded Jenny of her Instant Acceleration, but this seemed to warp everything around her, and . . .

"Are you there?" whispered Yeshua in angel tongue.

Jenny nodded awake. She must've fallen asleep, her chin resting on her hands, her hatchet flat in front of her. She cleared her throat. "Yeah?"

Yeshua's eyes remained shut, his head raised. "Oh Lord, deliver me from evil. Guide me. Preserve me, for I take refuge in you . . ."

Brushing the salt from her armor, noting how it seemed to drain color from the blue scales, Jenny stood and approached Yeshua again, cautiously. *How long was I asleep?* She felt somewhat rested, but now, her stomach rumbled with hunger. A rumble that went straight to her throat; she didn't want to throw up again.

Red lightning flashed around Yeshua's palms and feet. His gaunt face relaxed as though he were asleep, but his thin lips moved. He was singing again. This one sounded like a hymn, and Jenny was about to sit back down and try resting some more when his eyes flung open.

"*Which one are you?*" he hissed menacingly. "An angel? What do you want from me? I have nothing. Nothing! *WHAT MORE DO YOU WANT FROM ME?*"

"I'm not . . ." started Jenny, blinking at the sudden enraged outburst. "I don't want anything. I'm human, remember? A desecrated . . . human."

"A what?" spat Yeshua before unleashing a tirade of words in another language. These sounded vicious and ugly, as though he was cursing Jenny up and down. Then he fell quiet again. His body shook; he was crying, sputtering, "Please, my Lord. Please, deliver me from this. Please, just . . . They're coming. They're coming. Just *kill* me. I can't do it again, please . . ."

"Who's coming?" whispered Jenny, glancing around. It was nothing but flat ground as far as she could see. In the distance, she could barely make out the pillar forest, and the sky overhead rolled with the same storm clouds. Was it just her imagination or had everything become darker than before?

"My children," said Yeshua, his eyes glazed over. He looked right through Jenny, staring at the ground, eyes darting from side to side as though he were searching for something, some possible way out of this. "I died for their sins," he continued. "I died for their sins. This is my body, given to my children . . . I died for your sins. I died for your sins. *I died for your sins.*"

He repeated it again and again, over and over, his voice rising in pitch, in franticness, until it was a shrill screech. Red lightning snapped and popped, this time around his throat too, and he slumped forward again, breathing heavily.

*He died for our sins?* Jenny started forward to soothe the man somehow. *Maybe I can take the thorns off his head. Or maybe I should just make a water bottle and force him to drink. Can I get those nails out?* But Yeshua's head snapped right to Jenny, his brown eyes piercing and bright, and Jenny froze, shocked by the abrupt motion.

"Don't move," hissed Yeshua slowly, emphasizing each word. "Don't make a sound. Don't move a muscle. Don't even blink. Let them come. My children always come. But I do this for you. For you. For them. So don't move. Don't even breathe. Don't do anything. It will be over soon. My Lord will protect me."

Something sickly warm, like a stranger's breath, crawled across the back of Jenny's neck. She whirled around, ready to face whatever had Yeshua terrified and out of his mind, but there was nothing there. Just the salty, dark flatness of this world. Was she imagining things? She rubbed her neck and wondered if she should just get Yeshua down and figure out the rest later. But when she turned to face the cross again, she saw the ground around it shifting and bubbling, coming alive.

Round white shapes surfaced from the salt, wriggling and gelatinous in the same way the exoskeletons of the angels were before hardening. Thin limbs stretched out from the shapes, like creatures unfurling, and then, there were their heads. They expanded like balloons until the creatures resembled bald, genderless humans. Except they were all white—ghostly white—with no discernible features other than five-fingered hands and five-toed feet.


## Ghoul (NULL)


*Null?* Each one was roughly the size of a small adult, each the color of exposed bone. Their bodies jiggled and wiggled as countless more ghouls surfaced from the ground like bubbles rising to the top of a glass of water. They stretched their limbs and shook their heads. A few brushed up against Jenny's legs and sides as they stood, just a few inches taller than her, and a cold, ugly sensation traveled up her spine. She didn't move, remembering how intently Yeshua had asked her not to. But she was surrounded. She felt like she was in a crowded train, holding her breath, the underground closing in.

The creatures' eyes opened. Jenny expected them to be like the angels, white and empty, but these weren't just blank. They were *hollow*. It was like staring into holes in the ground. Smoke or vapor, she couldn't tell which, swirled inside the sockets. They had two narrow slits for noses, and then, the ghouls opened their mouths and *spoke*.

They spoke in shrill, high-pitched voices, in languages Jenny recognized: Spanish, Cantonese, French, and even English. These were human languages, and even though she didn't know them, she recognized what they were doing: the ghouls were crying for their fathers.

"*Otōsan!*" one of them screamed.

"*Ég er hrædd,*" said another.

"*Dios mío, condúceme a tu luz.*"

Every single ghoul turned their round white heads toward the cross, and as they spoke, Jenny noted their mouths were too big for their faces. Drool, glistening, spilled down their chins as the flurry of languages swirled around her.

"*Father! Father, save us!*"

"*Babā, āmākē bām̐cā'ō!*"

"*Ich habe zu viel Angst, Papa!*"

The words grated the inside of Jenny's head; she wanted to cover her ears, but she didn't want to move. She almost *couldn't* move, because Yeshua was laughing.

He was roaring with laughter, his head thrown back, his shoulders shaking, drawing the attention of all the ghouls. Tears streamed from the corners of his eyes as his laughter died down. He shook his head and whispered, "Don't move, desecrated human. Don't move at all. Or they will come for you too."

The ghouls, some of them shrieking in high-pitched voices, some of them muttering, all of them begging for their father, moved in unison, rushing toward Yeshua like a nightmarish stampede of mannequins. Their round heads bobbed up and down; they looked so much like cartoon creatures that Jenny didn't know what to even expect until they reached the cross and began to climb. One latched on to Yeshua's feet, stretching up to grab on to his ankles as it sucked his toes into its oversized mouth.

With a series of ugly *pops* and *cracks*, blood sprayed all over the other ghouls, staining their pristine bodies. The first one tore off his toes, and Jenny almost cried out. But it was the look on Yeshua's face that kept her frozen; the grimace, the sadness, the way his lips were pressed so tight, his eyebrows squeezed together. He was used to this. The only indication of pain was the way his thin body stiffened against the cross. *I died for your sins.*

The blood sent the others into an even more crazed frenzy, and Jenny knew exactly why. She could smell it, could taste it in the air: His blood was *delicious.* The metallic tang, that sweet promise of warmth, the taste of fresh blood in the air.

Another ghoul climbed onto Yeshua's thigh, where it bit into his brown flesh and tore away a chunk, revealing glistening bone. This time, Yeshua howled in pain, and the ghouls howled in solidarity around him as they continued. More and more climbed up his legs and found new places to bite. Some nuzzled against him, as though seeking warmth, as though seeking nurture, but then, their teeth found his skin. They bit into his sides, his ribs, his shoulders. Some climbed onto the top of the cross and chewed on his fingers. Some clung to his elbow and ripped into his armpit.

Some made it to his face, where they cut their hands on the crown of thorns and cried as he cried.

*"Father, I need you."*

*"Je t'aime!"*

*"Anqithna min hatha al-makan al-raheeb."*

Red lightning sputtered and sizzled each time, sometimes muffled by the wriggling bodies of the ghouls but always present. It repaired Yeshua's body so that after every bite there was always a new place to bite down on, new skin to tear off, new flesh to rip away.

The first ghoul let out a shrill cry. Blood ran down its white chin, and its round head seemed to have swollen. The smoke in its eyes stopped swirling, and, with a heavy sigh, it fell away from Yeshua's body, bounced off several ghouls, and lay trembling on the ground.

As Jenny stared, it melted into a puddle of white and pink liquid that the other ghouls mindlessly splashed through. More joined the first one, splattering on the ground, and slowly, the liquid seeped into the salt and disappeared. It was like the ghouls were returning to the dirt.

Did they die once they got their fill? Jenny stared at the entire ocean of ghouls that now covered the flat land; they came from every direction, like some brutal pilgrimage. How long was this supposed to go on?

How long would Yeshua scream and suffer? And hadn't he called them his children?

Jenny held her breath when she could, trying not to inhale too deeply, the scent of blood almost intoxicating, but she listened as Yeshua cried. As Yeshua screamed. As Yeshua sang until a ghoul bit through his bottom lip and chewed off his beard. Lightning flickered and flashed so often that Jenny felt like she was staring into the heart of a demonic thunderstorm.

*What do I do?*

*Why am I hesitating? I need to help him. But how?*

*Why did he ask me not to move? Are the ghouls that dangerous?*

*The lightning.* The healing ability . . . Jenny swallowed hard. Something was clicking into place, and maybe it was part of the answer as to why Yeshua was here, nailed to a cross. The world of death. The man on the cross. The ghouls feasting on him . . . Yeshua had to be important, had to be powerful, had to be. How else could he heal like this? Jenny inhaled deeply, loudly, expanding her chest and making herself feel bigger.

A ripple moved through the crowd of ghouls. Their white forms paused in unison. Yeshua looked up, blood streaming from his torn cheeks and exposed teeth, and shook his head. He must've tried to talk; Jenny could see the man's vocal cords glistening and moving.

She raised her hatchet slowly and cocked back her arm. The ghouls responded in unison, all of them falling quiet, their round heads turning to face Jenny, to stare at her with those smoky eyes. The entire world was suddenly silent, the mass of creatures standing still. She exhaled slowly through pursed lips, eyeing the ones nearest to her. They were slumped forward, arms swinging, but they weren't attacking. Maybe they were confused.

"I told you to kill me," hissed Yeshua weakly as light traveled up his neck and his mouth healed. "Don't pity me now. This is my purpose."

"I'll do you one better," said Jenny, sliding one foot back till it bumped against a ghoul. She grimaced, but when it didn't react, she figured it was now or never. She took aim, stomped forward, and launched her hatchet as hard as she could. *Savage Throw!*

With a satisfying *clunk*, the edge cut through the ghoul holding on to Yeshua's arm and sank into the wooden beam of the cross, completely severing his wrist from the rest of him. Blood sprayed horribly from the wound, but Jenny had freed that arm.

Just as the ghouls started screaming, an enormous bolt of red lightning, far stronger and brighter than any of the lightning before, sparked out of the bloody stump. Jenny caught a glimpse of his widening eyes, his blood-and-spittle-soaked beard, and then, all the ghouls leaped into the air.

Summoning her hatchet back, she threw herself into the fray, praying desperately she'd made the right decision by freeing that man.

# CHAPTER FIVE

# I HAVE REDEEMED YOU

Like water balloons, the ghouls burst into liquid as soon as Jenny struck with either her hatchet or her fist, it didn't matter which. She just had to hit them hard enough. But the hatchet's edge cut through them swiftly, so she swung it repeatedly at each creature that rushed her with their arms outstretched, mouths open in wide grins.

The ghouls had little resistance; it was like their entire body was an empty shell, a white casing that splattered as soon as it was compromised. It didn't matter where she struck them—their arms, their sides, or their head. As soon as anything cracked, their entire bodies turned to liquid and splattered. Jenny didn't know what to make of that, so she did the only thing she could do: relentlessly attack.

*Kill. Kill. Kill.*

She moved quickly, darting backward and forward, sidestepping the ones trying to grab her. They were slower and clumsier than wretched angels, but they had her completely outnumbered. Fortunately, the ghouls kept tripping over themselves in their mad scramble. Their legs tangled, they grabbed one another by mistake, or two dove for her at the same time and their heads clunked together like two coconuts, and Jenny would finish them off with a rapid strike.

Many kept losing their footing, falling face down on the ground while the others trampled them. Jenny stomped *hard* on their heads, splashing from body to body in her efforts to dodge. The only thing she had to watch out for was their hands. They had virtually no defenses, but their blows cracked her armor, and the impacts *hurt*. But the worst was their grip. It was viselike, impossible to slip out of.

Catching her arm, a ghoul forced her to the ground by throwing its weight at her. Fingers dug into her armor, and Jenny nearly dislocated her shoulder trying to break free. Another one slammed into her chest and clawed at her face, but she punched it square in the chin, cracking it open so that the ghoul burst right on top of her. Its remains—that thick white liquid—tasted almost like salty milk.

Trying not to swallow, trying not to gag, Jenny let go of her hatchet, caught it with her other hand, and chopped off the hand threatening to break her arm. Without skipping a beat, she buried the weapon in the next ghoul's head. Its smoky eyes went wide, its grin faltered, and the creature exploded into white droplets. Before another could jump her, Jenny rolled away and got to her feet, huffing for breath, already sweating way too hard. She wiped the milky substance off her face and spat.

### A Reinforced Helmet will cost 400 Energy.
### Sufficient Energy.

*Susan would approve*, thought Jenny as golden light swirled around her head. The light made the ghouls pause, and they blinked in confusion, gasping and making sounds of amazement like children at a fireworks show.

A blue helmet materialized on Jenny's head, metal curving forward to protect her face, a horizontal slit in the front to see through. But before the light faded away, the ghouls snapped out of their daze and rushed her again.

She glanced at Yeshua, who was still on the cross ogling his new hand, that arm no longer stuck to the wood. He turned it every which way, inspecting his palm and knuckles. He licked his forearm. All the while, he kept laughing and crying even as the creatures ripped away chunks of his legs and bit into his stomach. One even clung to his chest and suckled on his shoulder. His old hand remained nailed to the cross, blood dripping from where the hatchet had severed it, and several ghouls waited below, mouths open expectantly.

Now, if only he'd *do something*. The ghouls kept coming, kept swarming, and she lost sight of the cross in the gaggle of salivating white bodies. With a shout, she used Savage Throw again, launching her hatchet into the crowd.

*Pop, pop, pop!* A row of them burst into liquid, raining down all over her and the others as Jenny kicked and punched the ghouls closest to her. She struck one in the stomach and another in the eye, but one managed to grab her arm again, nearly snapping her elbow. She grimaced and summoned her hatchet back, slicing the ghoul's head open with a flick of her wrist. It burst into liquid as Jenny spun away.

They were easy to kill, but they gave her no energy, no experience, not even a notification. Her hatchet didn't flash with light to indicate any pain; she wondered if their being *Null* was the reason. Maybe that was why they didn't have a level or anything. But then, why were they so strong? They could rip her limb from limb if she gave them the chance.

Fingernails chipped off scales. Punches and smacks left cracks and dents, impacts that rattled her bones. One even managed to peel away a chunk of armor, exposing her back. She buried her hatchet in the creature's chest and rushed out of reach, gasping for breath. She was sweating profusely now, her head pounding with exhaustion. Whatever nap she'd taken before hadn't done anything, and she cursed herself for not assigning her stat points sooner. Having a boost in stamina or durability would've been perfect right now. Maybe she could make a potion.

*Fuck it, I need space.* Jenny inhaled deeply and roared, "*Ignite!*"

Flames streamed from her throat and out of her armor as she turned herself into a walking bonfire. The ghouls raised their arms to shield their faces from the sudden brightness and heat, and they all stumbled back, clumsily bumping into the ones still trying to come after her. Their mad rush cleared enough space for Jenny to—

Beneath her, on the ground around her, she saw the salty surface bubbling. Puddles of gelatinous white liquid glistened in the orange-and-red glow of her fire. They were all the ghouls she'd cut down. All their liquid was still on the ground, bubbling and merging back together, taking shape again, much more quickly this time. Hands reached out from below to grab her, and she hopped back to stay out of reach.

Jenny shut her mouth in frustration, extinguishing her flames and the light. She thought she'd been killing them, but they'd just been reforming this entire time. Then she had a sickening thought: Was feeding them the only way to stop them? The ones that turned pinkish red after feasting on Yeshua's body had drained into the ground. The white ones seemed to get stuck on the surface.

*I need to get out of the crowd. Maybe if I run as fast as I can . . .* Jenny dashed forward with Instant Acceleration, bursting through another row of ghouls, her hatchet extended to catch as many as she could. Their hands kept reaching for her, kept trying to grab her no matter how many elbows and throats she cut through. She needed to breathe. She needed to get away from the milky stench, the suffocating air. She needed *space*.

She paused for a second to catch her breath, dropped down to dodge a swinging arm, and slashed one of the creatures in the stomach. There were still

too many. She couldn't even see the edge of the crowd. With a cry of frustration, she used Instant Acceleration again, but she *tripped*.

There was a sudden jolt, a horrible *crack*, and she was flung forward onto
her face and arms. She bounced off the ground before crashing forcefully into
a pile of ghouls, kicking up clouds of salt.

Some burst upon impact. Others she knocked down, their teeth gnashing, their arms scrambling, but there were so many of them that they grabbed
onto one another, grabbed onto her, and it was a suffocating, screaming mess
of limbs.

She had to blink away tears. Salt had gotten through the slit in her helmet,
which had come askew, but it was like all the strength had left her body. Pain
surged up her left leg. Grunting, she elbowed one of the ghouls in the teeth
and glanced back, trying to see what was wrong.

She'd left her *foot* several paces behind her.

Blood squirted out of the stump of her knee, and she cried out. The sight
of it was somehow so much worse than the pain. Ghouls were already pouncing on her foot, pouncing on the splattering of blood she'd left in her wake,
pouncing on her.

She summoned her hatchet back, but powerful hands clamped down on
her arm. Several creatures pinned down her legs, teeth sinking into the
exposed flesh of her leg. Some of their white heads turned pink. They sighed
in relief as a scream tore through Jenny's throat, lighting her entire body on
fire again. *Ignite!*

Flames blossomed from the wound, tears running down her cheeks as
her blood sizzled. But the sudden light had shocked the ghouls off her. The
ones that had gotten bites in were already melting into the ground.

Jenny sat up, breathing hard, staring at the flickering fire rising from the
stump of her leg and trying very hard not to think about how she was running
out of fuel. *I'm going to pass out.*

*But I can't. Not like this.*

*They'll rip me to pieces.*

Pain shot right up to Jenny's throat, closing around her windpipe like the
hand of a ghoul. Exhaustion pinched the corners of her vision. She just wanted
to sleep. *I just want to rest. Just for a little bit.* But even though her fire kept
them at bay, she could see the ground bubbling around her, could see the
creatures trying to reemerge from the salty ground. Even the puddle she'd
splashed into was starting to move beneath her.

A hand reached up and coiled around her thigh. A head rose right beside
her. Jenny jammed her burning fingers into its eye sockets and pulled up her

stats quickly, preparing to pour all her available points into stamina. Another dove on top of her burning leg, as though trying to snuff out the flame, and shoved its face into her stump. Teeth made contact with her torn muscle, but before Jenny could react, a furious drumroll of thunder shattered the entire world.

It sounded like the sky was coming apart. As soon as it settled down, ringing in Jenny's ears, the ghouls stopped what they were doing and stared up at the sky.

Lightning struck. An enormous red bolt zipped straight down from the storm clouds, crackling and splitting into several trails before crashing right onto the cross with another thunderous roar.

The impact was like a bomb going off; a violent gust blew the ghouls away, many of them crying out as they burst into vapor. The winds blew out her flames, rattled her helmet, and threatened to blow her away too. In the center of the red glow, as more and more bolts of lightning rained down onto the cross, she could see Yeshua.

All the ghouls on and around him had completely vaporized. He was tugging on his other arm, trying to rip it free even as the lightning healed his palm around the nail. He jerked with his entire body, ribs and shoulder bones threatening to burst out of his skin, until finally, with a cry of anguish—his face red, spittle flying from his mouth—the nail tore through the gap between his fingers, and he yanked his arm off the cross with a spray of blood.

Shouting with triumph, he held up his freed hands, blood streaming down his arm as the lightning worked its magic around his fingers and palm. Then, panting for air, he knelt forward so suddenly Jenny thought he'd passed out. But he clung to the cross with one arm and reached down with the other to yank out the nail holding his feet in place.

But his fingers must've slipped or something, or maybe his strength had given out, because Yeshua collapsed forward while his feet remained stuck to the cross. His face hit the ground, legs outstretched, his flat ass in full view as lightning rained down on him.

Jenny adjusted her helmet and tried to get up. Clearly, she had to help him. He was powerful; he had to be. That lightning was insane. But she needed to help him up. To get his feet free. Then maybe he could fight and put these creatures down permanently.

But she could barely move. The ghouls were reforming around her and scrambling back now that the wind had died down. She had to be quicker.

Gritting her teeth, groaning from the pain, she grabbed her injured leg and squeezed it as hard as she could. Golden light shimmered out of her hands, and blood gushed between her fingers as she used Susan's ability, but something was stuck. Her mind lurched away from Valescent Light, and the ground seemed to spin. Rainbow light crackled across her wound, but she didn't have enough stamina for something like this; she was losing too much blood. Her head felt too heavy for her shoulders.

A white hand grabbed her shoulder and *squeezed*. The scales of her armor cracked as the ghoul yanked her to the ground. Another grabbed her helmet, and she struggled to get out of their grips, but it was no use. She risked breaking her neck. Breaking her arm. But they were going to eat her alive.

Just then, a shout echoed, and the ghouls stopped trying to peel off her armor. The winds stopped blowing, and everything went still. It felt like even the sky was holding its breath.

One by one, the creatures let go of Jenny and straightened up in silence. They stood around her, ignoring her, staring at a source of golden light that seemed nearly as bright as the sun. Jenny felt it too. Deep inside, an immense sense of *holiness*. A gravity she'd felt a few times before, crying in prayer, begging God to help her. A solemn stillness; a reminder that she wasn't alone.

Her bones aching, Jenny dug her elbows into the ground and lifted her head, trying to see between the ghoul's legs, trying to find the source of this feeling. It was Yeshua.

He stood in front of the cross, shining so brightly he was like a beacon in a storm. His long brown hair and beard billowed as another, gentler breeze stirred, and he spread his arms wide. Behind him, nailed to the cross, were what was left of his torn feet, blood dripping from the mangled flesh and bone.

"Behold!" he shouted. Lightning raced up and down his emaciated body; he looked so much like a tarnished angel. He bared himself completely, shriveled and bony, his face sunken in. A purple robe materialized around him, and he inhaled deeply before bellowing, "I . . . AM . . . *FREE!*"

Another burst of wind blew through the world, and another giant bolt of lightning flicked down from the sky and erupted around him, into him. The ghouls stumbled forward, arms swinging, all of them muttering. Smoke swirled in their eyes as they bumped into one another, but they seemed hypnotized. Completely taken. Like a crowd of people consumed by worship.

"*Father,*" whispered a ghoul behind her. Its foot struck her elbow, but it didn't seem to notice. They marched right by Jenny, their voices growing louder and louder, filling with desperation and need.

"*Tunapenda wewe, Baba!*"

"*Ham āpkō pyār karte hain!*"

*"Jiù wǒmen tuōlí xiōng'è!"*

"Come to me!" called Yeshua, his booming voice echoing all around. Golden light shone even more brightly from his body. Red sparks crackled, curving and twisting around him.

He stood nearly as tall as the cross. He raised his skinny arms, the sleeves of his robe falling away, to grasp the crown of thorns. Raising his chin, chest expanding with a deep breath, he lifted the crown off his head. Another bolt of lightning shivered across his forehead, healing the patchwork of wounds.

"Come to me," he repeated in a gentle voice that Jenny felt rumbling deep inside her chest. She felt a *pull* on her heart, and if it weren't for the agony of losing her left foot, she would've gotten right up and marched toward him. But why? Something about his voice, something grand and immense and powerful . . .

## Human (Stage V - NULL)

*What?* She squinted at him, trying to make sense of the notification in her head. What was he? How was he *stage five*? What level did he need to reach . . . *Why is he NULL like the ghouls?*

"I am reborn," said Yeshua, raising his voice again. "Come to me, my children. Find salvation in my arms, for I am nearer to you than your soul." He was grinning, a wide toothy grin, his beard, his hair, his purple robe flowing in the wind.

*"Hallowed be thy name . . ."*

*"Elthéto ē basileía sou . . ."*

*"Metool ddeelokhee malkootho . . ."*

Despite her exhaustion, despite the agony, Jenny sat up, staring, her heart pounding. She couldn't believe what she was seeing. Could he really be who she thought he was?

*No. He couldn't be. He can't!*

She'd fought against her mother's faith for so many years, rebelled against the stories, the lectures, the nonsensical rules that always seemed to put down girls in favor of men . . . but here he was, glowing with golden light. He'd been crucified, and yet, there he stood, alive and powerful, and Jenny had set him free. He even *looked* like Him too. There was a firm, powerful kindness about him, an aura she couldn't explain, and Jenny found herself completely baffled. Should she be praying too? Was everything her mother tried beating into her true? Was that man really . . . ?

Once one of the ghouls had gotten close enough—the rest surging forward, each of them trying to be the first, their arms outstretched as if coming
in for a hug—Yeshua lunged. He grasped one by the sides, fingernails digging into its white flesh. He scooped it into the air.

"I have redeemed you," said Yeshua with an enormous grin as the ghoul
kicked and struggled midair, squealing as it failed to escape his grip. Lightning
sparked around his hands, around the creature, and his golden light seemed
to envelop everything. The other ghouls stood frozen, all of them staring
silently, while Jenny held her breath.

Yeshua pressed his lips to the ghoul's face, and Jenny heard a wet, *sucking*
sound she'd never wanted to hear ever again.

*SHLURP.*

# CHAPTER SIX

# FOOT

The cries for "Father!" quieted as a hush shivered through the crowd of ghouls. Hundreds of them stood—seemingly dumbstruck—around Yeshua as he pulled deeply from the one he'd captured.

Jenny stared through their legs, through the entire crowd of them, at the source of golden light as unmistakable sucking and slurping noises cut through the air. She couldn't see Yeshua clearly, just his silhouette in the golden light holding on to the ghoul. The robe fluttered around him. She pictured him either kissing the creature or sucking from its eyes, and she couldn't decide which was worse. Maybe he was just biting its neck like a vampire.

One of the ghouls let out a choked cry, and all at once, chaos erupted.

Sobbing and screaming, they rushed away from Yeshua, hundreds of white mannequin forms scrambling, their toothy grins erased from their faces, their wide eyes trailing smoke.

She curled up into a ball as they stepped all over her in their mad frenzy to escape. Several of them fell, hands reaching wildly for anything to grab. Their palms slapped her helmet, fingers cracked the armor around her arms. Several stomped on her injured leg and slipped in her blood. She clenched her teeth to keep from crying out, hugging her knees to her chest.

A shout came from Yeshua's direction, and another massive bolt of lightning struck the ground. Everything shook as thunder rolled violently across the sky, across the world. Through the chaos of rushing ghouls, through their white limbs, Jenny caught glimpses and flashes of Yeshua snapping from one creature to the next. He was like a bolt of golden lightning zipping through the crowd, pausing every time he caught one, making that horrible slurping noise again.

With his flowing long hair and beard, he reminded Jenny of a lion hunting down a pack of beasts, all of them too frightened to make a stand or fight back, running mindlessly in every direction as he picked them off one by one. All the while, he was *laughing*.

Laughing loudly with manic glee—a deep, booming laugh—his purple robe billowing behind him as he ran. Milky liquid dripped from his beard, and his chest seemed to be widening, shoulders and arms filling. He was growing bigger. The ghouls he attacked didn't burst into liquid like the ones Jenny had cut down. These clattered to the ground, lifeless and limp like mannequins tipped over at the mall. After a while, piles and piles of them spread all around Jenny as Yeshua bolted back and forth through the crowd.

Once most of the ghouls had gotten away, another lifeless white corpse falling from Yeshua's embrace, he faltered like he was drunk. He swiped his hair back with both hands, sighing deeply, and Jenny wondered how long it had been since he'd touched his hair, his face. Then, hunched over and wiping his lips, Yeshua turned his head and looked right at her.

Panic struck her chest like a drum as she blinked away the salt the ghouls had kicked up, trying to clear the cloudiness that blanketed her thoughts.

*I need to heal. I need to use my stat points. He's going to . . .*

Yeshua sauntered toward her, his body swaying left and right. He was shaky on his feet, but golden light bloomed and radiated from his skin. Jenny's vision kept blurring in and out of focus; he looked like a star had taken the shape of a man and was coming for her.

She released her injured leg, flinching from the pain as she summoned her hatchet back. Light flashed, and she blinked away tears, trying to keep her focus on Yeshua, trying to slide away from him. But even that took more strength than she had left, and her hatchet, now too heavy, slipped out of her hand, bounced off her armor, and landed on the salty ground. What was the use? Even if she poured all her stat points into power, there was no way she'd keep up with someone two stages higher than her.

In the blink of an eye, Yeshua towered over her, breathing hard. His chest, though fuller than before, was still scrawny, and she could see his ribs jutting out when a breeze swirled around him. It ruffled his long hair and beard and the purple robe so that she could see his thin thighs and his sunken belly; he was clearly still hungry.

Was he going to suck on her too? Was he going to drain her just like the ghouls? Was he a monster too?

*Should I pray to him?* she wondered as he stood there, catching his breath, his golden light brightening and waning. No. The ghouls had been praying to him this entire time . . . or had they? She couldn't tell. But they'd been eating him, they'd been hurting him, and it's not like she'd done anything to hurt him.

*Well, I did cut off his hand.*

She was trying to be brave, trying to brace herself to fight back, but when Yeshua took another step, when his bare foot landed inches from the bloody stump of her knee, she almost choked on a scream. Her lungs twisted like wet towels.

*Don't come near me. Don't!*

*No, no, no, no!*

Her insides rebelled; she kept flashing back to the chemistry wing, lying immobile on the table in too much agony to fight back, and how that wretched angel had knelt over her, pinning her down with its weight as it pressed its lips to her broken nose and . . . *Shhhlurrrp.*

The sound still snaked through her ears and filled the inside of her skull with fear. Not again. Never again.

*No!*

*I'd rather slit my own throat.*

But Yeshua held out his arm, palm facing down, over her. She looked up at him, tears streaming down her face. *Don't cry*, she told herself. *I deserve this. I deserve this. I killed Susan. I killed Miriam. I deserve this.*

*He'll grab my hair and lift me off the ground and—*

Several small bolts of red lightning shot out of his hand. Crackling and snapping, they rained down on her injured leg. A furious hot pain once again tore through her leg, and this time, Jenny couldn't hold back the scream.

Agony seared across her like a ferocious gale. If she'd had the strength, she would've chopped off what was left of her leg, would've attacked Yeshua, but pain wracked her body, and she writhed on the ground, twisting, her arms and legs jerking involuntarily as she screamed into her helmet till her throat was about to collapse.

Then, all at once, it stopped. The bolts of lightning blinked out of existence, the pain vanished, and Jenny collapsed, breathing hard. Her insides felt scraped out. Yeshua stood over her, smiling kindly, his arms folded in front of him.

She saw flashes of imagery: paintings and statues and stained-glass windows, all of them depicting Jesus, his kind eyes and smile, his powerful presence.

Coughing, Jenny slowly pulled off her helmet and turned to her side to push herself up. Both her feet responded.

Wide-eyed, Jenny glanced down to see her foot had grown back, pale and brand new and coming out of her armored knee as though it had always been there. She shot Yeshua a look, then slowly lowered her head and stared at her new foot. She wiggled her toes; it felt like her foot. She tried to get up, but her elbow gave way, and she almost collapsed again.

Yeshua knelt. "You need to rest," he said. In her exhaustion, all Jenny heard was a series of hisses and shushes until Yeshua repeated himself.

She shook her head, but she couldn't bring herself to speak. There was a lump in her throat, but now that the pain had subsided, now that someone else was holding her, maybe she could rest. Maybe she could allow herself to rest. And Yeshua wasn't just anyone. Though she'd just witnessed him butchering a bunch of ghouls, their lifeless bodies left scattered around the flat land, she found herself trusting him. His aura, menacing and imposing as it was, was kind.

Bracing her back with one hand, Yeshua raised his other arm and shook it free of his robe. He presented it in front of her face. "You should eat," he said. "You need your strength. You have to maintain your *blooded* status, or it will consume you."

Saliva flooded Jenny's mouth as she stared at the fleshy bit of forearm. It was inches away from her teeth. She could smell him: sweet with a hint of savory, salty. Drool spilled over her lips. His soft, light brown skin . . . It would be so nice to sink her teeth into it. To feel the burst of his blood in her mouth. The delicious warmth. And he was just offering it to her! For free! All she had to do was put him in her mouth and—

It had to be a trick. She'd already been tricked once.

It wouldn't happen again.

"Eat," repeated Yeshua, making a fist to flex his muscles. "It's alright, my child. This is how I saved my people once. My flesh is yours. My blood is the covenant, given willingly for the forgiveness of sins."

His voice was too reassuring, too warm. Jenny grabbed his arm, digging her fingernails into his wrist. Red lightning flickered across, as if promising that no matter what she did, what she ate, he would heal right away. Her heart pounded; she could feel it pounding in her jaws, in her throat. *Just one bite. Just press my lips to his skin and feel his blood pulsing and . . .*

Her breath came short and quick. Hunger clenched her ribs like a roaring beast. The taste of him was so close she could already feel his skin tearing open, could already feel his flesh moving down her throat as she swallowed.

The warmth that would fill her belly would radiate through her. The strength that would return to her limbs. She would feel whole again; she would feel alive again.

Then she remembered the last time that had happened, and more tears welled up. Tears of hunger and anguish as she pictured Susan's warm smile. Susan had welcomed Jenny into her arms, and she'd . . .

*I have to maintain my blooded status, so I have every right to eat. That's what he said.*

*But what does that mean? How does he know about that?*

*I'll become that thing again . . . But I am already . . .*

## Desecrated Human

*Susan healed me. At the cost of her life. I don't want to lose control again.*

*But what about the fights ahead? What about stronger and stronger enemies? Look how powerful Yeshua is.*

*I need to get stronger. And besides, I don't have to kill anyone for this. Yeshua can regenerate. I could eat as much as I want!*

*But that would make me no different from the ghouls. And what if Yeshua is playing me? Just like Eve . . . Eve promised me victory and power, and in the end . . . ?*

*I won't squander Susan's sacrifice. Not over this.*

Her stomach growled, threatening to rip through her skin and latch on to Yeshua, but Jenny shook her head firmly and released his arm. The movement made her head spin, and she lurched to the side.

Yeshua caught her. "My child," he whispered soothingly. "Perhaps, then, it's time to rest. But know this: you are forgiven."

She squinted at him, struggling to stay awake, raising her head to ask him what he meant. But his hand hovered over her, and his fingers gently touched her forehead. There was another burst of light, and then everything went dark.

Jenny awoke beneath the cross, eyes opening to see the severed hand and torn feet still nailed to the wood. Dried blood stuck to the skin. For a dizzying, horrifying second, she pictured herself crucified, her arms spread, the pain of it all as she bared herself to the world. Then she lurched back into her body and sat up, gasping. She felt as though she'd been underwater, and she stared at her fingers and palms, peeling her armor back just to make sure there weren't any holes in her body.

Then she grabbed her feet. The armored one was still intact. The new one, smooth with pale skin, was bare. When she touched it, she shuddered, and her toes curled. She slid her hand down and squeezed her calf muscle, peeling the torn armor back further up her leg, looking for a scar or any indication that her leg had been ripped off. The only difference was the new foot was lighter, cleaner. The rest of her was filthy.

To her side lay Yeshua, facing away from her. She noted that he didn't have his golden aura while he slept, but he'd piled several more bodies around them. Jenny's nose curled. Liquid leaked from their empty eyes, and their slack-jawed mouths were left open, their heads cracked at the cheeks. Yeshua must've been sucking their juices out through their eyes. She shuddered again as she got the ghost of a feeling: his teeth scraping her eyelids as he sucked and sucked . . .

"Gross," she whispered.

*How long was I asleep?*

She rubbed her face with her palm before looking around for her hatchet. The sky seemed brighter, or so she thought. It wasn't sunlight or moonlight; did this place even have stars? There was no way to tell what time of day it was.

Her hatchet was right beside her. The dried blood had been cleaned away, and the flower pattern inscribed into the wooden handle looked beautiful again. The obsidian face almost seemed to shimmer. Her helmet, dented and cracked, rested on the ground next to it, but something else caught her eye. Her severed foot lay waiting behind her helmet.

Armor clung to it, the scales chipped and broken in several places where the ghouls must've chewed. A mangled bone jutted out the top; the bone that had once connected to her knee. She suppressed the strange twist of disgust as she stared at her old foot. She was no stranger to having bits of her restored. Jenny flexed her fingers. An angel had chewed them off once, but Susan had grown them back for her. She touched her chest and her side. She'd been impaled by a steel rod then later eaten alive by Miriam.

She shut her eyes and sighed, remembering the dumb philosophical dilemma Oliver had once told her about. It had been an excuse to engage her in conversation, and it had worked on Susan, but Jenny had ended up ignoring them both while half listening. She didn't remember it exactly. Something about a boat and all its parts being replaced over the years. The old parts were then used to build an identical boat, and the riddle asked, which one was the real one?

*Am I still the real me?* Jenny tried not to think about that. *Don't we lose cells and stuff every day? We grow back every day. Every day, we are someone else . . .*

She bit her lip to keep it from trembling. *All I ever wanted was to wake up feeling new.*

All she'd ever wanted was to get away from home, to get away from her mother's clutches. She'd wanted to figure out who she was, but now? The only answer she'd found through this nightmare was that she was a bloodthirsty, flesh-eating monster so consumed by her inner ugliness that she'd killed Susan.

With the weighted feeling of having slept too much dulling her head, Jenny reached over and grabbed the severed foot. It was cold and clammy. The armor had turned gray, no longer blue, and some of it curled back. Scales crumpled from her touch, reminding her of dried, dead plants in autumn. She remembered something Dr. Lee had said about their armor being organic, but that all seemed like a lifetime ago. And what about her exoskeleton? That had been organic too, hadn't it? It had come right out of her.

She peeled and brushed away the dead scales, flakes drifting down like ashes, until a dirty, blood-smeared foot remained. She forced herself to look at the exposed flesh on top, the spiky remains of her bones. Her toenails were too long. The big one had chipped, and she smiled, remembering that she'd bumped it on her dresser table the day before . . . Her smile faded. It had been the day before the earthquake.

She rubbed her ankle, taking note of the brown patch of skin, darkened by endless hours of sitting on her bedroom floor. It was dry and as dark as the bark of an aged tree, and when she ran her thumb over it, the skin seemed to slide right off. *Taste yourself,* urged something inside her, and Jenny realized she was salivating again.

Her new foot flexed involuntarily, toes digging into the salt, and she glanced down. The new ankle wasn't dark at all, but pinkish. The nail wasn't chipped. Even her toes seemed better, less crooked, no longer misshapen from years of walking. Her skin was pale and soft, and there were no dry patches on her sole.

But the foot she held in her hand? Its sole felt plump and tender, and she scratched at the nearly hard-as-a-rock dead skin, already picturing herself biting into her heel and . . . With a frustrated cry and activating Savage Throw, Jenny threw the foot as hard as she could, launching it through the dark, miserable world until it vanished from view.

"Probably should've eaten that," said Yeshua from behind her. She nearly jumped, turning around to face him, ready for a fight. He was sitting up, one arm resting on a knee as he stared intensely. "You are hungry."

Anger crackled up Jenny's spine. She knew she should be grateful. He'd gotten rid of the ghouls and healed her leg, but she couldn't help it. She forced herself to take a breath, to lower her arms. "Who *are* you?"

*As if I don't already know.*

Yeshua stroked his beard. He seemed so different from the desperate, shriveled-up man she'd found nailed to the cross begging to die. He smiled warmly.

"I am who I am," he replied after a weighty pause. "He who takes the sin of the material world."

# CHAPTER SEVEN

# FEET

*Get away from him,* was Jenny's first impulse.

*Get away. Get away.*

*Leave me alone.*

Thoughts bubbled up the back of her head, each one worse than the one before. Flashes of Sunday school, of sermons and being told who to worship and how to obey. Of her mother slapping Jenny's face and telling her that Jesus would be ashamed. Of those miserable nights where she'd prayed on the floor till her knees hurt, begging the lord for forgiveness, terrified of what sins she might've accumulated by accident, terrified that she was being punished already. After all, good people were rewarded, and she would get punished by her mother, would have to go hungry, would cry herself to sleep.

She'd begged the Lord to save her. Studied and read verses from the Bible. Kept trying to find the strength everyone kept saying would be there. She knew the words, or at least once knew, and now, here this guy was. A guy she'd found nailed to a cross in another world, looking the part and saying the things she'd grown up hearing. The one who took the sins of the world . . .

He'd said she was forgiven.

Jenny inhaled deeply, her fear response making her head spin. She didn't know what to say. She felt young again, standing in a church that felt like a palace, her small footsteps echoing as she turned around to admire the tapestries above. It had been the middle of the night, and her mother had been hoping to find shelter, and . . . Jenny had walked up to the enormous statue of the man on the cross and felt this sense of awe, this tremendous fear that her younger mind couldn't figure out, a pressure that a foot was hanging over her head just waiting to come down and crush her like a bug.

That same feeling came back to her as she looked at Yeshua. That was how she knew who he was.

"May I ask you something?" he started, one leg folded beneath him, his arm resting on the knee of the other. "Why didn't you kill me?"

Jenny bit down on the inside of her lips. "I don't know. I figured if you wanted to die, you could die after you got off that thing." She remembered her decision. Throwing her hatchet. Slicing through Yeshua's arm. The red bolt of lightning. Why had she set him free?

Wasn't it to save herself? She'd been surrounded by the ghouls, and she'd figured he was powerful. And that healing ability . . . Was that where the stories came from?

Could he . . . resurrect the dead with that ability?

She smushed her new big toe against the sand, bending the toenail, feeling the flex of her muscles. Was this how he'd done it? In the stories? Healing the ill, restoring the disabled, giving strength to those who couldn't walk or take care of themselves?

Ideas and memories spun. Stories from the past. Readings of the Bible. The fish and the loaves of bread . . . Had he just been using the system to produce mass quantities of food? And what about walking on water? Did he have a skill which allowed him to cross over the waves without sinking? But most importantly . . . healing and resurrecting the dead?

Susan.

Yeshua was quiet. It was a solemn, weighty quiet.

"I am glad to be alive. Being alive is a very good thing." He shut his eyes, raised his head as though in prayer, and swallowed hard. Jenny saw his Adam's apple moving up and down. Then he straightened up and walked over to the cross. He touched the feet he'd left nailed to the wood and glanced at Jenny. "Are you sure I can't interest you in something to eat? You and I . . . We have to eat a different kind of food now. And the system can no longer create the sustenance we require."

"What?" asked Jenny, squinting at him. Her stomach twisted and rumbled with furious hunger as she watched him touch his torn feet. It was like he was inspecting vegetables growing on a vine. "What do you mean?"

He shot her a tight-lipped smile before turning back to his feet. It was one foot over the other, both of them ripped at the shins, almost exactly where Jenny's foot had broken off earlier. A nail with a round head driven through the center of each foot held them in place. Dried blood stuck to the skin; blood from when he'd struggled to break free.

Yeshua grabbed the cross with one hand and braced himself. Then, with a grunt, he grabbed his feet and yanked them upward.

There was a gross tearing sound, a series of cracks as the nail moved through a series of bones. Then, with a final soft cry of effort, Yeshua popped his feet free.

Thick, dark blood oozed from the gash between his toes where the nail had ripped through. He separated the feet, toes and loose skin flapping. Jenny couldn't help but be reminded of jelly-filled donuts.

Something flickered in Yeshua's expression. Hunger. A fierce, violent hunger that Jenny recognized. But it vanished as quickly as it had appeared, and he smiled at Jenny. "Go on," he suggested. "Give the system a try. Make some food. Anything. The only way to learn is to try."

The sight of the feet made Jenny feel weak. She wanted to snatch one from Yeshua's hands, wanted to bite off the toes one by one, wanted to sink her teeth into the wrinkled pink flesh of the heel. His feet looked so much more appetizing than Jenny's had; they were larger, fleshier. More of a meal. More meat. Yeshua wanted her to create food using the system, and she . . . she wanted the foot, yes, but what had he meant before? *The system can no longer create the sustenance we require . . .*

*What does that mean?*

*I can't eat . . . normal food?*

She placed one hand on her stomach, trying to quiet the restless hunger, holding out her other hand in front of her, palm facing upward. She kept reminding herself she wasn't a monster anymore. She didn't have an exoskeleton. She didn't have tentacles. She wasn't . . .

*Give me a banana or something*, she thought, turning away as she focused her mind on the guidance system in her head. A shudder of uneasiness crept up her side; she kept expecting Eve to respond whenever she used the system.

**A Banana will cost 100 Energy.**
**Sufficient Energy.**

Golden light shimmered on top of her palm, blossoming and stretching, elongating and curving like a rounded crescent moon before hardening. The light remained yellow and bright, and after a moment, it faded away, leaving Jenny holding a perfect banana in her hand, just waiting to be peeled.

"What a strange looking fruit," said Yeshua over her shoulder. Jenny flinched.

Before she could snap at him, she caught sight of him chewing, the blood oozing down his chin and into his beard. That queasy twist of hunger wrung out her insides, and she swallowed what she was going to say.

"I wonder where that might have grown," he said thoughtfully before putting the big toe in his mouth. His teeth connected with a crunch, and she watched him chew and swallow. Then he nodded toward her fruit. "Tell me how that tastes. I hope it's good."

*Is he . . . Is he antagonizing me?*

Saliva gushed in her mouth. She tried to convince herself it was because of the banana. She could smell its sweet, fruity aroma, and she hadn't eaten in so long . . . Why shouldn't she be salivating?

But that wasn't true, was it? She'd eaten Miriam. She'd taken a chunk out of Susan. She'd eaten angels. She'd eaten plenty, yet she was *starving*.

*Desecrated human . . .*

She punctured the top of the banana with her fingernail before pulling the peel down. Strands of fibers stretched as she turned the banana around, peeling carefully and slowly to reveal the curved white flesh of the fruit. She fought the urge to shove the entire thing in her mouth, her hands shaking as she stared at it, white and creamy, the fruity scent so strong in her nose. She tore a sizable chunk off the top.

The banana felt cool between her thumb and fingers, and she held it in front of her, her eyes flicking toward the half-eaten foot in Yeshua's hands, the toes now gone, the bones exposed in a grisly sight. Again, saliva filled her mouth, and she met Yeshua's intense gaze.

"Eat," he said. "Then you will know."

*Okay, okay.* Jenny forced herself to relax her jaws. What was going on? Her entire body was hesitating, and a ballooning feeling of dread filled her chest as she brought the banana chunk to her lips. Tingling raced up and down her legs. Her lungs contracted. *What the fuck?*

As soon as the banana touched her tongue and she closed her mouth, she understood. The rest of the banana fell from her shaking hand and landed with a soft splat on the ground.

It tasted like vomit. It tasted foul and bitter and rancid. The squishy texture felt like a chunk of mucus. Her bottom jaw ached. Her entire body convulsed, every signal firing: *Spit it out!*

But Jenny's trembling fingers kept her lips shut. She was trying to force herself to eat. She looked up at Yeshua, who smiled sadly before turning away, as if averting his gaze to give her privacy. Jenny took a shaky step forward, still trying to keep the banana down, trying to swallow.

She glanced at the cross, hopelessness welling up inside her like a cavernous beast as she fought against the terrible feeling. She was shaking. Tears streamed down her cheeks as she shut her eyes and clenched her fists. And then, when she couldn't withstand it anymore, she threw up.

She dropped to her knees, clutching her stomach as she heaved again. There wasn't much left in her stomach—mostly water and blood and bile—but it splashed onto the sand, and in the middle of it, sat the glistening chunk of banana, her teeth marks visible in the gooey white flesh.

When it was over, when her body had calmed down enough, Jenny flopped onto the ground, breathing hard as spittle stuck to her chin. Her mouth tasted acidic, bitter and burning.

*I can't eat normal food anymore . . .*

"I am truly sorry," spoke Yeshua gently. His voice drifted down to her as though he was speaking from the sky. "Once we become *blooded*, even if the status disappears, our internal systems are forever changed."

*Blooded.* That notification . . . Jenny remembered when she'd first gotten it: When she should've died as countless angels pulled her battered, falling-apart body toward the desecrated angel. She'd taken a bite out of one of them, desperate to fight, desperate to get out of their clutches.

She remembered how wonderful it'd felt. The way flesh had given way to her teeth. Saliva gushed in her mouth even though her tongue burned from the banana she'd tried to eat. It overflowed, escaping her lips and running down the sides of her face toward her ears. She sat up quickly and wiped it off.

Yeshua placed the foot he hadn't eaten in front of her. "For when you are ready," he said, sitting beside her on the ground. "I would like to hear about how you came to this world. How you became desecrated, especially when you are so against consuming flesh."

Wanting to cry, Jenny reached for the foot. Her fingers closed around what was left of the ankle and she brought it toward her, holding it as though it was a sandwich and not a man's foot. She couldn't look at Yeshua; couldn't take her eyes off the meal. Her stomach felt twisted and gross from throwing up again, and her throat felt scraped raw, but she knew beyond a shadow of a doubt that Yeshua was right. She would have to eat; she so badly wanted to eat.

Turning the foot over and bringing the heel to her lips, she braced herself. It was cold. Cold and bumpy, and she held her lips against the weathered skin for a while. The metallic sweetness of dried blood rose from the torn skin and exposed muscle and bone. The scent filled her nose and her lungs; she inhaled deeply. Thumbs pressing into the sole, she sank her teeth into the heel as fresh tears slid down her cheeks.

*This is my body. This is my blood.*

She'd been so hungry. She'd been so, so hungry. "Thank you," she whispered, shoulders shaking as she ate. As the word filled her mind again.

### Blooded.

She expected her exoskeleton to burst out of her belly button, red and viscous and thick. She expected the tentacles to surge from her back, transforming her into an uncontrollable monster again. But after the first bite and the second, after she'd nibbled on the heel and flesh filled her stomach and nothing changed, her shoulders relaxed. She shuddered and stifled the urge to cry. She ate more readily, snapping and cracking through the elongated bones of the toes.

*Maybe I have more control over it than I thought . . . Maybe there's still hope for me.*

She wiped away the tears. And then, she told Yeshua everything, starting with the earthquake, the first angel she'd seen, and ending with the rainbow light that had brought her to this bleak world.

# CHAPTER EIGHT

# EEMA

The bottom of the cross dragged along the ground, the scraping sound a steady constant as Yeshua carried it over his shoulder. One end of the crossbeam stuck out like a shark fin, and Jenny followed quietly, feeling as though the dark emptiness of the world had brightened immensely since she'd told him everything.

Hissing and shushing in the language of angels, she'd spoken at length about the survival challenge. About the angels she'd fought, the people she'd seen die, the nightmarish scenes she'd stumbled into. She'd described the blue-colored angel who'd become desecrated, and talked about the babies that had followed her around. She'd spoken about her brother, about Mrs. Monique and the others, and Susan. She'd said a lot about Susan: her kindness, her bravery, her abilities, her sacrifice. Yeshua had looked a little amused when Jenny had described Susan's blue hair.

"A girl with blue hair? I've never seen such a thing among humans," he'd said. He'd spoken as though he was trying to lighten the mood. "You must care greatly for this friend."

"Yeah . . . as a friend," she'd replied, unsure how to explain how she really felt. She'd been about to let it go and carry on describing her tentacles, but she couldn't help herself. "I think . . . I think it's more than just as a friend."

"I see," he'd said, stroking his beard. Jenny'd thought he'd admonish her, denote her feelings as sinful and condemn her, but he'd been smiling. "Love is truly a radiant thing," he'd said after a moment. "Blessed are the ones who love, for they bring warmth to the worlds and shall receive love in return."

His words had resounded like a prayer or a sermon or something—something more than just a mere phrase—and Jenny had felt a sense of weightlessness. It'd felt good. It was nice listening to him speak, but the feeling had faded as quickly as it had come. Jenny had fumbled her next words as she described everything else. She'd told him about Eve and the promises it had made, how she'd used Severed Spirit, and about Miriam.

She'd described the weird memory of life as an angel, the darkness on the cafeteria floor, about how she'd pulled everyone through the light. How they'd avoided the end of the survival challenge. How there was no true victor. How she'd brought about the apocalypse.

Then she'd told him about giving birth to Eve, and Yeshua had gone quiet again. For a while, the only sounds had been Jenny's chewing, finishing up the foot he'd given her. She'd crunched through bones and toenails and veins, not wasting a single bit of flesh, and it wasn't till she'd finished that she realized she'd eaten *all* of it. Her hand had gone to her stomach, thinking she'd be sick, but her body had made good use of the meal. Strength had returned to her muscles and limbs, and she'd felt satisfied. She'd felt restored.

She'd eaten.

That was when Yeshua had stood up, his purple robe billowing about him as he twisted from side to side. He'd looked at her, a faint smile on his face, and said, "Follow me."

He hadn't said another word since. Jenny trailed along, sometimes a few paces behind him, watching the wooden beam bounce along the dark sand, watching the muscles of Yeshua's broad back roll as he lumbered forward. He kept a steady pace despite the apparent weight of the cross. Jenny wanted to help him, but he'd given her an intense look earlier when he'd struggled to hoist it over his shoulder. It was a look that said: *This is my burden to bear.*

Sometimes, she walked beside him, thinking about all the stories and sermons she'd heard about "walking with Jesus." How Jesus carried people during their hardest times even though most people assumed they were alone. Forsaken by God.

She wasn't sure where they were headed, but she didn't mind the quiet. She'd spoken for such a long time that her throat hurt. With a small flash of golden light, she made a water bottle for herself. *Don't forget to hydrate.* Susan's voice floated through her thoughts, and it brought her warmth.

*Love is a radiant thing*, he'd said. Why wasn't that in the old texts? Why wasn't that written and expressed everywhere?

After a long while of walking, the pillars came into view, and Yeshua spoke in a strained voice. "I have been thinking very hard about what you have shared with me. I would like you to know that I am very sorry for your loss. I too have lost many, and it was my fault, for I had asked them to follow in my footsteps." He kept walking forward, his sweat-drenched hair bouncing, his robe fluttering around his knees. The cross only seemed to get heavier, and he hunched forward a bit more.

Jenny didn't respond. She knew all the stories of the apostles and how they'd died in horrible ways. She knew of the persecution, and then she thought of how their words had reached the eastern edges of Asia. How there'd been turmoil as her ancestors either rejected the faith or embraced it, and the bloodshed that had followed. She didn't know what to make of that.

Yeshua continued. "My *eema* liked to say that all things have their time. And then she'd say, 'If not now, when?' And for a long time, I did not understand. But she was a very strong woman, and I think you are like my *eema*."

"*Eema?*" echoed Jenny. This word wasn't spoken in angel tongue. It wasn't hissed through teeth. It was said lovingly in a language she'd never heard before, but even though she'd asked, she already understood what it meant.

"My mother," he said. "My mother, Myriam. The first Mary."

At his words, a shiver tangled itself around Jenny's spine. *Miriam?*

"Myriam was a common name in my time. I had many friends who went by that name, and they even adopted the name Mary." He chuckled a little bit, pausing to catch his breath. A raspy, wheezing sound had snuck into his voice. A bead of sweat trailed down the side of his head, clung to his beard, and dripped off. His arms and legs were shaking, but he turned to smile at her over his shoulder. "It was the cause of much confusion. But *Mary* wasn't just a name. Mary was a title bestowed upon my *eema*. Mary, Mother of God, they called her. But as you can see, I am just a man."

He fell quiet again. Jenny got the sense that a lot of heavy emotions and memories were going through his mind, and she felt similarly. Questions burned holes in her thoughts, but she listened patiently, just as he'd listened to her.

"My *eema* was the victor of a survival challenge. Like you, she was sought out by a voice. Ushered. Guided. And she slaughtered endless numbers of angels and humans alike. She was young too, and she recognized who the voice belonged to. Whose will had taken root in her mind."

Yeshua sighed deeply. "At first, as many of us would be, she was ecstatic to be host to the Lord. After all, how many generations of her family had prayed to Him? Had begged Him for guidance? And now there He was, in the midst of hell, guiding her. Granting her the strength to fight. Pushing her forward when she wanted to collapse. She believed she was chosen. Blessed. Acting out the will of Adonai. El Shaddai. Elohim."

Jenny slowed her steps. She remembered that train of thought, remembered how she'd felt when Eve had shown her visions of powerful people.

Victors of past survival challenges. Of gods and goddesses and their many powers. Eve had promised her that strength. It had fueled Jenny with want. With need. If only she could be so powerful, then she'd solve all her problems.

But Eve had only used her. She'd just been a means to an end. And as Yeshua went on, she learned that his *eema* had been similarly used.

"Why she was chosen, we will never know," continued Yeshua, sweating more and sounding upset. "But in the blood and horror, as she herself became powerful, she realized what He was. He wasn't a force for good. He wasn't what her fathers and mothers had prayed to. He couldn't be. He wasn't love. He wasn't truth. He was nothing but despair and anger.

"My *eema* made many mistakes. She hurt people. She slaughtered so many . . . Because of His presence and promises, she'd prioritized victory and His will over all else. He'd declared everyone else as sinners, and that she was exacting divine justice."

He stopped, breathing hard. He gently straightened up, placing the cross down before letting it go. She wasn't sure if it was an ability or something, but somehow, the cross stood on its own, and Yeshua stumbled forward.

Ahead of them were the pillars, the misshapen things that stuck out of the ground like a bizarre forest. Was this the same area Jenny had been in before Yeshua pulled her toward him? She wasn't sure. All the pillars looked virtually the same. *Does Yeshua know what they are?*

"The deaths," he said as if reading her mind. He wiped his brow and bowed his head, his wet hair falling forward. "This is the world where it all began. With death. This is why my *eema* made her sacrifice."

Jenny tried to speak, but the words felt too thick. She cleared her throat, unease slowly unraveling in her belly as she eyed the pillars. "What happened to her?"

"My *eema* had a very powerful ability," he said, straightening up and raising his face to the sky again. Red lightning flickered across his arms and down his legs. "A healing ability that even *He* could not stop. She emerged from her challenge after seven nights, returning to her home covered in blood, her belly swollen." He turned to face Jenny and held out his hand.

She blinked at it in confusion. The sheen of sweat had vanished from his face. The strain of carrying the cross was gone, and he had that healthy glow about him again.

"Take my hand," he said. "Allow me to show you my *eema.*"

"*Okay?*" whispered Jenny. She hesitated, but that earnest expression on his face made her want to trust him. Besides, if he'd meant harm, he wouldn't have let her sleep in peace earlier. She reached out and placed her hand onto his much bigger one.

He closed his other hand over hers and shut his eyes. For a while, nothing happened. She only felt the warmth of being encased in his hands, but then, he uttered one word.

*"See."*

Everything—Yeshua, the pillars, the dark sand, the cross—faded away from view. A series of images filled Jenny's mind, reminding her of the visions Eve would show her, but this was different. She lost all sense of self. She was a disembodied viewer observing as a young woman with brown skin and long dark hair stepped into view.

The girl wore red-and-golden armor. She carried a helmet in one hand. A long feather stuck out of it, and as she stumbled forward, the cracked parts of her armor—around her legs and her shoulders—broke away and fell. She was covered in dried blood, and she looked like she hadn't slept in days. She was Mary.

As people in flowing robes rushed to help, others pointed and shouted at the cluster of collapsed houses behind her. Her challenge must've involved a bunch of homes, not just one building like Jenny's high school. But Mary fell to her knees, her eyes wide with fear, and a bloodcurdling scream tore through the vision.

The imagery stirred, and Mary was in a private room, lying on a bed on her back, her belly so big it looked like a whole person had crawled inside her.

Women fretted all around. Rabbis in dark robes chanted as Mary shrieked at the top of her lungs, clawing at the sheets and the blankets, kicking aimlessly with her feet. Her legs were spread open, her tunic stained completely with blood. Red lightning flashed violently between her thighs, flickering over and over as the midwives and other women cowered, as the rabbis tried chanting louder and louder, shaking sprigs of various herbs and sprinkling holy water.

But the lightning, red and intense, only lashed out more dangerously. It flickered across the entire home, and Jenny thought it would shatter everything around them. That it would leave scorch marks and burn the women and the rabbis to ashes, but there was no fire, no damage, nothing. And it went on for what felt like forever, all while the woman screamed, her eyes bloodshot, her face ghastly, sunken in. She almost looked like a tarnished angel.

The midwives fled. The other women ran away. The rabbis cowered outside the home where a desperate-looking man paced back and forth. He was angry and terrified and shouted at them. He was the only one brave enough to go back inside. He held Mary's hand and stroked her sweat-drenched face as her body convulsed. As her legs kicked. As more red bolts of lightning erupted from between her legs. She only slept when she passed out, but the lightning continued to work.

The man, who must've been her husband, brought her water and bread, holding it to her lips, trying to get her to eat. Lightning sparked up and down her entire body, and Jenny understood what was happening.

Mary was refusing to give birth. She'd emerged from her survival challenge, victorious and powerful, and she'd become pregnant just as Jenny had. But Mary had been stronger. She'd held on, using her ability to heal herself continuously, refusing to give birth to Him.

The images flickered with the light, and Jenny got the sense that days were going by. Weeks and months and maybe even years. All the while, Mary struggled on the bed, screaming and screaming. Red lightning danced, her face contorted in pain, her legs kicked. She remained bedridden the entire time, her swollen belly rippling as the creature inside tried to tear its way through. The screaming. The crying. The pleading.

She could've given in. She could've just let it end. But she'd held on.
*Why?*

One night, Mary stopped screaming. She rose from the bed as though something had grabbed her by her swollen torso and lifted her up. The lightning flickered softly, and her husband called for the rabbis and the healers and the midwife. Anyone who might be able to help. But all they could do was watch as Mary's body levitated. Her eyes rolled back into her head. Her belly rippled violently. It almost looked like she'd give birth, but something smoky, something shadowy, plumed out of her belly button instead.

It gushed out like the smoke billowing from a volcano during an eruption. Lightning crackled and sizzled and popped, and a face appeared in the smoke. A face that screamed and howled as though trying to escape the smoke, but a wind blew through the home, and the smoke dissipated. The face faded away, and all at once, everything stopped.

Mary collapsed on the bed. There was no more lightning. The rabbis and their dark robes looked in awe. The midwives rushed to her side. She cried out again as a deluge of blood gushed between her legs.

And there, curled up and red faced and still attached to his mother by the umbilical cord, was a baby.

The images started fading as an exhausted Mary struggled, her eyes flickering to stay open, her body ragged and worn down and broken, her swollen belly deflated as more blood gushed from her insides. She held out her hand. One of the women wiped the baby down with a cloth. It wasn't crying. It looked bright and alert, its little hands and feet kicking as it turned its head every which way.

Mary nuzzled the baby into her arms. Wrinkles had formed deep grooves on her face. Her hair had turned gray and ashy. And even though she was bleeding, her lightning no longer worked. She held the baby to her chest and spoke in a raspy, choked whisper, "Yeshua."

With a shudder, Jenny came out of the vision. Her hand slipped out of Yeshua's, and she took a step back, tears spilling down her cheeks.

Yeshua was smiling. "My *eema* was a strong woman. The first Mary."

"Did I make a mistake?" whispered Jenny. She was shaking. "Did I make a mistake by giving birth to Eve?"

"I do not think so," replied Yeshua. "Eve and Adonai are not the same. Opposite forces, maybe, but . . . we shall see. Our actions are irreversible. Right or wrong isn't the question anymore. We must focus on what we can do now."

Jenny sniffled, her heart torn by what she'd seen of Mary. "Does this make me . . . the second Mary? I don't know what to do."

"You want to find your Susan, yes?"

She nodded, not trusting her voice.

"Then help me, Jenny Huang. Help me save Death, and I will help you find your Susan."

"How?" She looked at the pillars behind Yeshua; she couldn't look him in the eyes. Her mind still swam with images of Mary, pregnant and engulfed in red lightning. It was the same lightning that Yeshua had. And what was that shadowy face that had come out of Mary? Was that . . . *Him?*

*And am I really the second Mary? What does that mean?*

Her hand went to her belly, her fingertips pressing against her skin through the chips and cracks in her armor.

Yeshua took a deep breath. "You have told me of an ability; an ability so rare that I believe it is unique in its expression. Unique in the woman manifesting such power, for I have never seen nor heard of such an ability in the hands of a mortal."

Jenny wiped her nose and sniffled. "Do you mean . . . ?" She raised her hand and used Valescent Light. Colors flared to life around her fingers. A golden aura emanated from her skin, and Yeshua looked at it with his eyebrows raised.

His lips twitched with the hint of a smile, but he shook his head. "While that is a very beautiful and warm blessing, something I have not seen in such a long time, it is not the ability I am referring to. This power is all your own."

She shook her hand free of the light. She knew which one he'd meant, but she'd hoped she was wrong. Her insides twisted. Fear crawled along the back of her neck.

"I believe you called it *Severed Spirit*."

# CHAPTER NINE

# CRACKS IN THE SALT

Place your hand on the pillar," called Yeshua from somewhere behind Jenny. He was keeping his distance. Not much, but there was enough space between them to make her worry. What was he expecting would happen?

She stared at the pillar. It was dark and glassy, its edges and faces sculpted to encase a body. She wondered who was inside. Were they an adult? A teenager? Old and wrinkled? It didn't really matter. Whoever was inside would register as "death" and they'd be terrified, their guts twisting out of them, attached to the pillar.

What was she even supposed to do? Yeshua had noted her Severed Spirit, and she'd tried explaining that all it did was turn off pain. Well . . . she'd fumbled the explanation, as she hadn't completely understood what it did, only that she didn't feel anything. And that she stopped being a normal human. And that no matter how much damage was done to her body, she could keep moving, keep fighting. It was just a monstrous defense mechanism.

Except she was already a desecrated human. What would the ability do now?

"You'll understand once you try it," was all Yeshua had said. "Push the usage *outward*. Beyond yourself. Sever something other than yourself, and let's see what happens." He'd been so determined she couldn't even snap at him. There was an almost childlike hope in his eyes, and the wrinkles around them, the smiling wrinkles . . . She'd almost forgotten the emaciated man who'd begged her to kill him on the cross. He'd stepped away and motioned for her to approach a pillar as several more burst out of the ground.

She got the sense that Yeshua enjoyed teaching. He'd rather watch people try things than tell them outright, like how he'd told her to attempt making food with the system instead of simply explaining.

*That way, you can't deny what happens.*

*It's a trick.*

Jenny clenched her jaws and shut her eyes. Her thoughts were spinning and spinning, and fear flickered between her lungs like a breath of cold air. Her palms were sweating; she didn't want to touch the pillar.

But that was all she had to do. She didn't need to use light or fire; she didn't have to see what was inside. It would just be like touching a rock. She inhaled deeply through her nose as Yeshua called encouragingly to her. Again, she wondered why he was so far away. Why not come and watch? This was his idea, after all.

*Is he afraid of something? Is this a trap? Why am I listening to him anyway?*

*He promised to help me find Susan.*

Jenny raised her hand, her arm trembling. She stared at the cracked blue scales covering her forearm and shoulders, chipped and dirty, patches of pale skin poking through. She reached for the pillar.

"You have to use both hands!" called Yeshua. "Place both hands on either side of the pillar and cast yourself *out* of your body."

She dropped her arm and looked back at him. "If you know so much about this, why can't you do it yourself?

"My healing ability—my *eema*'s gift—while powerful, cannot do what you can. But I promise you. You can do this."

"Why are you so far away, then?"

"Death is a scary thing!" he called back.

*Is he . . . Is he making a joke at a time like this?* Jenny bit her lip and turned to face the pillar again. Another one burst out to her left like a swiftly growing tree made of dark rock. *Just get it over with.*

She stepped forward and brought both hands to the pillar's sides. It almost felt like she was touching someone's face, cupping their warm cheeks. She tried to picture Susan, her blue hair and her soft smile, but all she saw was Susan's corpse lying lifeless on the cafeteria floor. Jenny recoiled and stepped back.

Her hands shook as she stared at her fingers. They tingled with warmth; the pillars had that strange warmth that made them feel alive.

"You're doing great," called Yeshua.

She knew he was trying to be helpful, but his words were not helping in the slightest. Fear unfurled in her belly. She couldn't shake the memories of looking inside the pillars, using her light, and seeing the deaths. She couldn't get Susan's body out of her head. But she'd *felt* something when she'd touched the pillar. She was sure of it. Trying to tune out all her thoughts and Yeshua's voice, Jenny tried again.

She placed her hands on the pillar again, this time determined to hold on and try what Yeshua wanted her to try. Her armored foot slid back so she could brace herself. Salt crunched between the toes of her bare foot, but she tightened her core and held on to the pillar. She shut her eyes and concentrated.

This time, she didn't picture Susan. Instead, Jenny visualized the person inside. How they must feel. Alone, trapped, and miserable. Feeling completely stuck, with no chance of anything better.

Jenny knew those feelings all too well. "I'll help you," she promised softly. "I don't know how, but I will." She leaned forward and rested her forehead against the pillar. She wasn't sure if that was instinct or some subconscious thing she wanted to do, but she relaxed. Warmth radiated through her, and she sucked in another deep breath before reaching for the skill she never wanted to use again.

Last time, she'd snapped. She'd completely lost control of herself. Something had burst open inside her and taken over, and all she could do was surrender to bloodlust. Would that happen again?

*No*, she assured herself. Not this time. It was just like with Yeshua's foot. How she'd gotten the *blooded* status again. How she'd loved the taste of flesh. She was desecrated and didn't have an exoskeleton. She didn't have those tentacles. She didn't have to lose control. Didn't have to be a monster.

*It won't happen again.*

*This time . . . This time . . .*

She remembered Yeshua's words. To focus outward. Project her Severed Spirit outward. *But how?*

*How?*

For a long time—maybe it was only a few minutes, but it felt like hours and hours—Jenny kept her forehead against the pillar, her hands on its sides. Her palms and fingertips hurt from how hard she was gripping it. And then it came to her. How to do it. How to use it. How to set the death inside free.

*Severed Spirit*, she thought with a quiet sigh. Her focus shifted to the tactile senses of pressing against the pillar, the warmth of it.

*Out of my body*, she repeated under her breath. *Out of my body.*

It started as a tingling sensation, as though she'd been sitting on her hands for too long and they'd fallen asleep. She didn't make a sound. She maintained contact, maintained focus. An ache formed between her eyebrows, like someone was trying to shove something sharp into her skull.

Then it spread. She was cracking. Her face was cracking open, and she was terrified of what would come out. But she inhaled deeply and tried to maintain composure. Yeshua said something, but the sensation was overbearing. Her brain felt like a wet towel being wrung out. Her mind twisted. She got the horrible sense she was cutting something *ancient.* Something sacred. But it was an easy movement. It was something *natural.* Something that longed to be separated. Something that was never meant to be *stuck.*

And then, the sensation spilled outward. Her knees almost buckled. It came out of her, flowing into the pillar, and bright light blossomed inside. She could see the light through her eyelids, but she didn't dare open her eyes. Didn't dare lose concentration. Whatever this was, it felt fragile and delicate. If she stopped focusing for even the slightest moment, it would reverse and shatter her instead.

**Severed Spirit (Tier 2)**

**System Warning!**
**Severed Spirit (Tier 2) is a Restricted Skill.**
**(Guidance System Error)**
**Existential Error**
**Existential Error**

**Severed Spirit (Tier 2)**
**Sever the metaphysical bonds—**
**Existential Error**
**Natural Order Corruption**

A shudder went down her spine so violently she almost collapsed. A whimper struggled in her throat. Her thoughts filled with a series of notifications, but she'd had something like this before. Back when she'd lost herself. Back when she'd become desecrated. Back when she'd . . .

*CRACK!*

It sounded like a tree splintering. Like the earth splitting open. But it brought her back to focus. The notifications faded away. Her breathing came quicker, shallower. Her heart pounded in her chest as sweat trailed down the sides of her temples. Then she felt warmth, a strange, jubilant warmth concentrating right above her eyes.

Her forehead was pressed against something warm. It wasn't as hard as the pillar, but there was a fleshy kind of firmness . . . She knew without looking that it was someone else's forehead, except it was too hot. It was burning hot. Did they have a fever? Did *she* have a fever?

The pillar cracked and fell away from her hands. After another series of cracks and the sounds of falling debris, Jenny opened her eyes to find the pillar had opened. Half a person stuck out of it, their lower body still encompassed by the dark rock, but their intestines no longer stuck out. They were whole. Jenny's forehead was pressed against theirs, and she looked them in the eyes.

## Death (Level 0)

It was a girl. Older than Jenny, and with dark-brown skin, her eyes swimming with tears. Her lips quivered as though she so badly wanted to speak. Their noses touched, and Jenny blushed, stepping back as the rest of the pillar fell away from the girl's hips.

Jenny's forehead throbbed. Her nose stung. Her fingers and arms ached as though she'd been hanging from a pull-up bar for too long. The girl stood in the crumbling pillar, breathing hard, not even trying to cover her nudity. She raised her tear-stricken face to the dark sky and let out a wail before sinking to the ground.

Grasping a fistful of salt, the powdery salt that had once encased her in a pillar, she slumped forward. Her long hair hid her face as her bare shoulders shook, as she clutched her stomach and cried.

In a hoarse voice, a voice that sounded so torn and pained, the girl whispered, "*Thank you,*" before breaking down into loud, gut-wrenching sobs.

Yeshua bounded toward her, kicking away a few large chunks that remained of the pillar, disintegrating them with each blow. Then he knelt beside the girl, placing a hand on her head. He shook his other hand free of his sleeve and held out an exposed forearm, the same way he'd offered his flesh to Jenny before. "Eat," he whispered in a gentle voice. "Eat, and you shall be free once more."

The girl looked up, tears streaming down her face. Her bottom lip wobbled as she clutched Yeshua's arm with both hands. She glanced at him again, as if asking permission, and when he nodded, she sank her teeth into his flesh as though she was biting into a corn cob.

Jenny turned away, hugging herself. She was shaking too, the urge to cry simmering beneath the surface of her thoughts. She didn't want to just cry. She wanted to *scream.* She wanted to wail and lash out and destroy everything around her, but tears didn't escape her eyes. She bit down on her lip.

Something felt *wrong* inside her. Or did it feel *right?* She couldn't tell. Something had changed when she'd used Severed Spirit like that. All those notifications . . . The skill had even reached a new tier. She'd gotten . . . stronger? Was this strength? And what had she severed? What was it that she'd felt between the pillar and the girl inside?

*To sever metaphysical bonds.*

Jenny pulled up her stats, trying to see if anything had changed.

**Jenny Huang**
**Desecrated Human (Existential Error - Level 30) (Blooded)**
**(Awaiting Metamorphosis)**
**Age: 6,802 days**
**Stats:**
**Power: 35**
**Durability: 20**
**Stamina: 40**
**Agility: 35**
**Stat Points Available: 62**
**Energy Available: 4706**
**Energy Core(s): 2**
**Bloodlust Ecstasy**

Nothing. It was the same except now she had the *blooded* detail. She hadn't changed at all. She was still a desecrated human.

But she'd hoped. A small part of her had hoped that this would've reversed what she'd become, and as she struggled with that hope, there was a flash of golden light behind her.

She turned back to find Yeshua helping the girl to her feet. She wore a purple robe of her own now, and her brown face seemed to shine with warmth. A trickle of blood ran down from the corner of her lips, but she either didn't notice or didn't care. She was smiling. "Thank you, Mother."

"I'm not your—"

"She means your title," said Yeshua gently, placing a hand on Jenny's shoulder. "You are the new Mary. And notice now you are not speaking the language of light."

Jenny was about to respond to the Mary thing, but she sputtered. She licked the back of her teeth. She touched her throat. He was right. She hadn't been hissing. Neither had Yeshua or the girl. But what language was this?

"This is the language of death," explained Yeshua. "As the angels have their language, so do the deaths."

"What are they?" asked Jenny, cutting him off. "What is she?" She almost apologized for being so blunt when the death looked up, but the girl bowed her head.

"I am death," she replied.

"I know that," said Jenny, trying to remain patient and not snap at the girl who'd been trapped inside a pillar for an eternity. "But . . ."

"Perhaps I can shed some light on that," Yeshua spoke up. "What is it that people—our people from our world—fear the most?"

Jenny bit her lip. How was he answering her question with another question? She watched the girl move around. She was trying out her legs, swirling her purple robes, and then hopping in place. Jenny rubbed her forehead. "I guess people are afraid to die. They're afraid of death."

"Very much so," agreed Yeshua. "And what is the promise of faith? Of obedience?"

"That . . ." Memories of Sunday school flooded her mind again. "That we will be rewarded with an eternal life. Paradise."

"Exactly," he said, an intensity shining through his voice as he raised a finger to highlight his words. "Eternal life. That is the false promise made to those who believe His will. But do you know what I say to that? Folly. Folly upon those who accept such foolishness as an antidote to their fear. And what do they fear? Death is not something to fear. Death is a part of who we are. Why are our people taught to fear themselves?"

Jenny stared. Her mother would hate this guy. Everyone at her parents' church would hate this guy.

Yeshua was about to speak again, but light drew both of their attention. The girl knelt by a shorter pillar. She pressed her brown hands to its sides and pressed her forehead against it, just as Jenny had done earlier. And the salt began to glow.

It brightened the same way her arm did when she used *Valescent Light*. Streams of reds and yellows, vibrant greens and purples seemed to shiver through the pillar, and then there was another loud *crack*. A series of cracks, and with the light, Jenny could *see* inside the pillar, could see the little boy whose intestines curled back into his body. As the salt crumbled away, as the skin across his belly healed, he leaned forward, pressing his forehead to the girl's, and started to sob loudly.

Jenny shuddered as the girl hugged the boy. She remembered how hot the girl's skin had been. Was the boy just as warm? Were all the deaths this warm? For some reason, she thought they should've been ice cold, like the ghosts she'd always hear about in stories.

"Humans are beings of three parts, Jenny," continued Yeshua, rolling up his sleeves. "Our vessels, which contain our beings in material form. Our deaths, through whom we return to the source. And our souls."

"Souls?"

"Our souls," he said, walking over to the boy. "Our expression of self. What makes us people. That is what they've stolen from us. And that is what we must fight to reclaim."

# CHAPTER TEN

# ENHANCED ARMOR

As deaths awoke other deaths, golden light blossomed around Jenny, brightening the gloomy world. Tendrils of colors—bright reds, vivid blues, yellows and purples and greens, and every color in between—unfurled from each pillar and reached toward the sky. They then crumbled and fell away, and one by one, deaths stumbled out from their containment, crying and shouting and needing to be consoled.

Jenny couldn't keep watching. Her mind spun with what Yeshua had said about deaths and souls, and the light made her heart ache.

Why? She didn't really know. Why did she want to cry? Why did she want to scream? She thought it might've been because she'd used Severed Spirit again, but this felt deeper. A primal urge to claw her emotions out of her chest and . . . Was it the light? Was the light making her feel like this?

It was similar to Valescent Light, but that couldn't be the reason. There was something else to it. Something that called to every single hurt Jenny had known since she'd been born. It called to the helpless feeling a baby might have, crying and screaming into the unknown, hoping someone would pick it up.

Jenny turned away from the spreading light while Yeshua fed each newborn death. Her shoulders were trembling, and there was a feeling in her throat she didn't like. A salty bump she couldn't swallow.

She decided it would be a good opportunity to finally go over her stats and apply her awaiting points. Why she'd been procrastinating on them, she didn't know, but she supposed she'd always been like that. Playing games on hard mode. Playing life on nightmare. Waiting, waiting, waiting. Saving up potions or points or whatever so that by the time she got to the final bosses, she'd have way too many things and nothing to really show for it. Even Eve had called her out for it.

She'd gone through her entire life with a voice snarling in the back of her mind: *Why try? Look at you. Why try?*

And now, that voice had a face. It was her own. A monstrous, ugly face that only wanted to consume, consume, consume, and she swore she wouldn't let that come out again. She'd been afraid of that happening, losing control, and . . . But she'd eaten the foot. She'd used Severed Spirit. She'd set free a death.

Why had she been able to do that, anyway? The death had woken another pillar. And then each death had gone on to wake up another. How were they doing it? They couldn't also be using Severed Spirit, could they? Or was there some similarity between Severed Spirit and something that came naturally to deaths? Or was it because she'd been so close to death herself?

*Let's not go there.*

*Focus on the numbers.*

*You have sixty-two points waiting.*

*Sixty-two.*

That number seemed way too high, but she'd leveled up several times, and she'd ranked up. Or at least . . . she should've been human stage three. What would the notifications have looked like if she'd reached that level without Severed Spirit? Things would've been clearer. Easier. Jenny sighed.

*Fifteen into each stat.* That seemed like the most even way to split everything. That left her with two remaining points that she could use later. Remembering how it'd felt when she'd added a large number of stat points, she braced herself for the changes this time.

**Jenny Huang**
**Desecrated Human (Existential Error - Level 30) (Blooded)**
**(Awaiting Metamorphosis)**
**Age: 6,802 days**
**Stats:**
**Power: 50**
**Durability: 35**
**Stamina: 55**
**Agility: 50**
**Stat Points Available: 2**
**Energy Available: 4306**
**Energy Core(s): 2**
**Bloodlust Ecstasy**

Her muscles flexed; her entire body clenched. A tingling sensation shot up from her fingers to her elbows as though she'd hit her funny bone, and warmth blossomed across her back. What felt like a cramp ignited in her sides, and she cried out softly. But then, her toes readjusted on the salty ground, her stance shifted slightly, and she stood taller. This wasn't the dizzying, intense reaction she'd experienced before when increasing her stats.

As quickly as it had started, the tenseness faded away, and she exhaled. Maybe she'd gotten used to it. Or maybe the changes would be more subtle now. She placed her hand on her stomach, feeling the taut firmness of her abs. Then, after taking several deep breaths, she opened her eyes to find the world even brighter than before.

It felt like the sun was rising behind her. Golden light made the dark, barren expanse seem much less imposing, and her shadow stretched far ahead. It was strange seeing her shadow and all the light behind her, the darkness ahead. It finally hit her that she was in another world. She wasn't on Earth.

She rubbed her face, her armor responding almost instinctively. The dirty blue scales rolled away from her knuckles and her wrists, revealing her dirty hands. Salt and dried liquid and blood stuck to her skin, but she didn't care. They shimmered in the golden, colorful light. She let the armor peel away further, exposing her pale forearms and elbows. Ever since she'd had an exoskeleton, it felt like she had better control over the things she made. All she had to do was picture it, and it happened.

Looking down at her arms, she brushed aside the bits of dead armor—and it *was* dead, she realized, remembering how the armor was organic. The parts that had been cracked and broken by the ghouls had died on their own, losing their blue luster and feeling like crumbling autumn leaves.

She peeled the armor off to admire the outline of her muscles. Her forearms, her biceps, even the way her arm moved in her shoulder socket felt so strange. She remembered nearly failing gym one term because her class was doing weight training and she couldn't do a single pull-up. Her gym teacher had been so disappointed. Jenny shook her head, balling her fingers into a fist and staring at the way her tendons moved.

She didn't feel much of a size difference, but she was definitely stronger. Standing on her tiptoes, she stretched out her arms and rolled her head from side to side. She straightened her shoulders back and focused on her breath. Away from the hell of the high school and the nonstop chase by the angels, she could appreciate how her body had changed. Had she ever felt this good? Had she ever felt so capable? When she took a step, everything just felt *right*. Like she could be more purposeful. Like she could do anything.

Her skin was tougher. Her flesh firmer. Her body felt light and free. *Maybe if I'd been this strong earlier, everything would've ended differently.*

*Maybe if I'd just listened to Eve and . . .*

*And what? Killed the other kids? Got more experience by hunting other people? Like Miriam?*

*No . . .*

Groaning, she rubbed her face. Her breathing had quickened; her head was hurting. Something felt wrong inside of her, but she didn't know what. It'd started when she'd used Severed Spirit while fighting Miriam. When she'd lost control. She'd felt it the entire time, hadn't she? That urge to kill.

*Kill. Kill. Kill.*

A shudder twisted its way up her spine, and Jenny tried to shift her thoughts. She had to make new armor. She'd been hesitant to address the system this entire time, to use her stats and energy. They felt ill-gotten, like she'd stolen them or done something worse. But Yeshua had pushed her to try making food, and the memory of that made her want to wretch again.

She couldn't keep wallowing in the despair. She couldn't keep feeling sorry for herself. If the ghouls attacked again, or whenever something attacked again, she didn't want to be caught off guard once more.

**An Enhanced Armor will cost 1500 Energy.**
**A full-body armor that mitigates impacts and is resistant to pressure.**

"Sounds good," she whispered as more sobbing and crying erupted in the distance behind her. How many deaths were they going to set free? There must be millions—*billions* of deaths. Could Yeshua feed them all?

Golden light of her own shimmered around her limbs. It sparkled and shone, enveloping her torso and her chest, spiraling down each of her legs. The crumbling blue-and-gray armor dissolved away, and light danced across her pale skin. She glanced down to see she hardly recognized her body.

She couldn't see her ribs anymore. Her legs weren't thin and fragile looking. Her shoulders felt wider, her hips looked wider, and her muscles glistened with strength.

It made her head spin to see herself like this. She had the body of a movie star or a model; it felt unreal. How many times had she promised herself she'd eat better? Cut down on the chips and chocolate. Go for more walks. Work out. She'd been saving all that for when she moved out on her own, when she got to university. There, away from the suffocation of her home life, she'd be able to progress. That was what she'd told herself.

If there was any good that had come from this whole nightmare, at least she'd finally gotten into better shape. The light hardened, flashing with green before turning blue, a darker shade than before. Red mixed into the color, and Jenny wondered about her exoskeleton. It was still there. When she focused on her belly button, she could just about *feel* a strange tickle, as though it was just waiting to burst out.

### Activate Exoskeleton?

The notification made her want to spit. *No.*

She pushed the thought away and continued forming her armor, imagining it firmly in her mind, bringing it to life. How the red would go beneath the blue armor, giving it an almost purple look. How the scales would be smaller but layered, the entire armor streamlined.

Another memory surfaced: Why Eve had found her in the first place. How Jenny had created half a minor potion to heal Susan's leg when she hadn't had enough energy for a full potion. Eve had said that had been remarkable, bending the system to her will, but she hadn't really done anything like that since. Unless . . . Unless she counted Severed Spirit. That skill had triggered such a bizarre response from the system, after all.

### Natural Order Corruption

But she didn't feel as though this was something special or even unique. If the system could create anything that could be imagined, then why couldn't anyone imagine half of anything? Why couldn't they create any kind of skill or ability?

Or was it just that most people didn't bother trying?

Blue scales spread across her skin, covering nearly her entire body, coming up to her throat and the bottom of her jaw. It reached her ears and went up the back of her neck, then came down to her fingertips and her toes, fitting snugly around her legs and between her thighs. It hugged her waist and ribs tightly. The armor almost felt like a layer of thermals, except it was dense. Dense and solid, and it reminded her of that desecrated angel's exoskeleton. That bluish metallic thing that she'd had to break through before she could hurt the angel.

When the light dimmed, Jenny turned to see a small crowd of people gathering. Well, her first instinct was to think they were people, but their notifications—each one the same: Death (Level 0)—gave them away.

Looking at them now didn't give her that frightening, *run away* feeling anymore, but it was still odd. Some of the deaths were on the ground naked, crying and sobbing, while others held them as Yeshua went around offering his arm as sustenance. He created purple robes for them to wear as he went from death to death, reminding Jenny of a hummingbird flitting in a flower garden.

But something about him felt off. He didn't bound across the ground anymore. He was limping.

Jenny took a few steps closer, aware of the clearing they'd made in the pillars, aware that more were rising around them, but something about Yeshua was wrong. And when she got close enough, she saw what it was.

Yeshua was shrinking. He was losing weight, deteriorating with each death that he helped. His face was gaunt again. His eyes had sunken in, and bags weighed down on his cheeks. But he smiled when he noticed her.

"I like the new look. It suits you." He sounded breathless.

Jenny nodded, feeling a tiny bit bashful. The new armor was darker, more conforming to her body. This one had been designed with less emotion and more tact. It hugged her muscles tightly, making her feel like a spy in a big-budget movie, and the new color was sleek. "Thank you," she said, but she was more concerned about him. "Are you okay?"

"Me?" He pushed back his sweaty hair. "I am exactly where I want to be, and this is all thanks to you, Jenny. For freeing me. For freeing death. Existence owes you a debt it cannot repay with a thousand worlds. I should very much like to see the look on Azra'il's face when he realizes what has happened."

"Azra . . .'il?" The name sounded evil to Jenny, like it was something she ought to know, and a weird, creepy sensation crawled along her sides. It was the same feeling she'd get when looking at skeletons: disturbed.

"Azra'il is the archangel in charge of the afterlife," explained Yeshua, his lips curling. "He is the reason deaths have been sequestered to these pillars of salt. He rips souls as they pass from the material world to the Garden, ensuring that the cycle of our lives can never reach completion."

Jenny's head was hurting again, and fear laced her every heartbeat. The *archangel* of death? There was an angel assigned to death? And something about the way Yeshua spoke of him made her think that this Azra'il was *powerful*. "Is he, like . . . Is he what comes after a desecrated angel?"

"No," Yeshua replied, shaking his head. A death came up to him, a young girl, and pulled on his robe. He smiled kindly at her, lowering his shaking hand to pat her head. "He's much worse. The tarnished angels are distortions of their true selves. True angels cannot advance in stages like you or I through trial and triumph. They are light. They are not meant to grow. So, what do they do?"

Jenny didn't need him to explain. She knew by the sick feeling in her gut. "They eat people."

"They eat people," he repeated solemnly. The young girl dashed away, her purple robe billowing. "But this way, they can maintain control over their minds. They can harness the ability of their light and the energy of the worlds, and . . ." Yeshua slumped, teetering like he was about to collapse, and Jenny dashed forward. She placed her hand on his chest to catch him.

He seemed even shorter now, only a bit taller than Jenny. He looked ill. Jenny tried to steady him as she glanced at the deaths. A crowd of them, maybe thirty or forty people, stared at Yeshua with concern on their faces. There was a cost to this. That was why they'd stopped. Yeshua couldn't go on feeding them forever without rest. His healing ability wasn't free. How had he fed so many already?

Jenny helped Yeshua sit down before conjuring a bottle of water. He blinked at it, his eye twitching, and she realized he'd probably never seen plastic before. What had they used to carry water back in his day? Did that really matter now?

"Drink," she said, mimicking how he'd commanded her to eat before.

He smiled gratefully, the wrinkles around his eyes so deep the expression looked like it hurt. He drank deeply, the bottle crinkling in his grip, and Jenny took the pause to ask the question burning a hole in her mind.

"Will I find Susan's death here?"

Yeshua lowered the bottle, water dribbling into his beard. He nodded as he swallowed. "Yes," he replied. "She has died, so her death is here somewhere. But her death will not recognize you."

Her heart sank at his words. "So I have to find her soul?"

"Her soul houses all her memories," he said. Once he'd finished the water, he remained seated, taking in a deep breath. Color returned to his skin, but he still looked hungry. Weakened.

Should she . . . *Should I offer a bit of my arm? Would that help?*

"Azra'il is the one collecting the souls. We must find . . ." He trailed off. Before Jenny could ask what was wrong, his eyes went wide, and he grabbed her arm. The bottle fell to the ground. "They're coming."

"What?"

"Again! They're coming again!" He snapped his head toward the deaths as he used Jenny to pull himself up. "Nobody move! Don't move one bit. Just stand still! Just stay right there, and they won't harm you. Let them come to me. I will . . ." His voice broke.

He turned to grab Jenny, dropping his voice to a horrible whisper. "I can't protect them all like this." Saliva flicked out with his words. He looked crazed.

Upset. He wasn't blinking at all, and redness spread across his eyes. A sob had snuck into his voice.

He sounded the way he had when she'd first met him on the cross. When he'd begged her to kill him. And she knew what was coming. The ghouls.

Jenny swallowed hard. She glanced at the deaths, who were exchanging frightened glances. There were too many of them. Some of them old. Some of them just kids. One even was a toddler, held in the arms of the first death that Jenny had freed. They looked helpless. And all of them were level zero. They wouldn't be able to fight.

The ground began to bubble. It was frothing and rolling, like an angry ocean on a stormy day. There must be more than before. Everywhere around her, the white liquid seeped out; it would be a matter of moments before those bubble-shaped heads emerged with those empty eye sockets and high-pitched voices.

She shook Yeshua. He was still holding on to her, his fingers curled tight around her armored arms. "Can't you frighten them off again?" she asked. "Can't you just . . . drink them?"

He shook his head; he was trembling. But he released her arms as the liquid bubbled around both of their feet and pointed toward the sky with one finger.

Looking up, Jenny's hopes sank. The clouds were bubbling too, almost mirroring what was happening on the ground. But instead of white liquid, this was red—dark red. The sky bubbles ballooned and expanded and burst, then they began to fall as rain.

The deaths cried out while Yeshua splashed through the bubbling white liquid now churning pink as the rain grew heavier. And this rain wasn't anything at all like rain. It wasn't water.

It was hot and sticky, with a thick metallic stench to it, and Jenny knew what it was with each heavy breath she took, each beat of her heart. It was blood.

It was raining blood.

# CHAPTER ELEVEN

# IT'S RAINING BLOOD

The blood was hot and sticky, and the downpour was relentless. Thick globs soaked through Jenny's hair. It ran down her face and new armor in ribbons. Every breath she took was stained with its heavy metallic stench, and she felt like she was drowning.

It coated her lungs, her insides, and she felt the blood with every pulse of her heart. Shielding her face with one hand, she tried to blink it out of her eyes, to keep it from dripping down her face. She really wanted to swallow; she could tell just by the scent, by the aroma, that the blood was *delicious*. That it would hit better than any meal, any drink. She wanted to stick out her tongue and catch every single drop. She wanted to cup her hands and gather a mouthful and slurp it all up and—

Unable to resist, she stuck her tongue out and lapped up what she could off the sides of her mouth. The flavors, rich and savory, coated her tongue, and she felt a wave of dizziness as her body adjusted. No new notification came up. Nothing changed. Of course it wouldn't; she was already blooded.

The ghouls hadn't come out of the ground yet, but everything was bubbling. It felt like they were taking their time; or maybe the blood was making them thicker, heavier . . . She splashed through some of the liquid, blinking over and over to clear her eyelashes, too aware of the blood dribbling down her back and down her arms. Yeshua was urging the deaths to gather.

"Stay close!" he shouted. "Stay near me. I will protect you." He was gesturing wildly with his arms, like he was trying to herd a flock of sheep, and the deaths—all their faces frightened and covered in blood—did as he instructed. But as the rain grew thicker, as the blood fell heavier and wetter, it grew increasingly difficult to see.

Jenny fashioned new headgear, dark blue to match her new armor. It covered her hair and the sides of her head. Blood dribbled down behind her ears, and she suppressed a shudder. She'd included a raised visor to keep the blood out of her eyes, to keep the blood from filling up her nose with every breath. And it was done just in time.

Hands reached out from the frothing liquid. Arms stretched upward and out, fingers curling as though the ghouls were in agony, as though they were drowning in their own substance. A rounded head emerged amidst all that, the two eyeholes filling with vapor, filling with blood. One by one, more heads appeared, looking like pinkish-reddish flotation devices bobbing on the sea; their limbs could've been pool floaties.

But there was something wrong with them. Something different. The first head that appeared was the first ghoul to fully form. On all fours, it rose from the bubbling water, blood streaming down its entire body, staining its once white coloring. This creature wasn't like the ghouls she'd fought before; it was as red as the blood, darkening with every drop of rain.

## Blooded Ghoul (NULL)

*Blooded?* It didn't cry out. It didn't call for its father. It didn't say anything. All it did was groan, moaning and mumbling incoherently. If it was trying to communicate, Jenny couldn't understand what it was saying over the drumming pitter-patter of blood splattering her armor, splattering the ghouls' heads and shoulders, and running into their empty eye sockets. Several of them turned their heads upward with their oversized mouths open even as they struggled to fully emerge. Their teeth glistened as their throats collected blood.

Steam swirled out of their eyes. She hoped they would collapse the way the ghouls who'd eaten from Yeshua's body had fallen to the ground, becoming pink puddles that drained away. But more and more crawled out of the bubbling puddles instead. More blooded ghouls stretched their limbs and turned their empty eye sockets toward her.

This was going to be a fight, messier and uglier than before. The first ghoul opened its mouth to reveal two rows of stained teeth, blood running down its chin. She half expected it to say something, to call out for its father again, but it scrambled toward her, batting away reaching arms and legs, kicking its fellow ghouls; it was coming straight for her.

Her hatchet flashed to her hand. More and more ghouls climbed out of the frothing liquid; it now felt like she was wading through a flood that came halfway up to her ankles. The first ghoul stumbled, reaching for her, eyes swirling with steam that trailed behind it. Jenny sliced through its elbow with one swing. There was a muted flash of light which made all the rain-drops around them glisten, which made the ghoul's grotesque face shine for a quick second.

**+64 Energy**

It didn't burst into liquid. Instead, there was a *crack*, and the arm splintered like wood. And this time, she got energy from the attack. She was causing pain. The ghoul slipped, clutching its arm and howling, howling so loudly that Jenny wanted to cover her ears. But she was already stepping back, sloshing through the liquid, trying to keep out of reach of the other hands climbing out of the ground.

A wild thrill flickered up to her throat. This was what had been missing during her first encounter with these creatures. With a renewed wild frenzy, she struck over and over as more ghouls got to their feet and came after her.

**+64 Energy**
**+64 Energy**
**+64 Energy**

Were there more ghouls this time? She couldn't tell. Their bodies glistened like shiny red plastic, and in the blood rain, she could hardly keep track. Each of their faces looked the same: Hollowed out eyes; large mouths filled with blood. Their moans and whimpers swirled around her as she struck, but this wasn't like before at all. She'd rested. She'd eaten. And she'd invested her stat points. She wasn't going to be on the defensive this time.

But too many bodies crowded between her and Yeshua and the deaths, and no matter how many she struck down, more ghouls kept coming, all while the relentless rain pummeled her with blood, making her feel sticky and bogged down. It thickened the air in her lungs, her breath burning with the metallic aftertaste of blood. But the scent egged her on; she wanted more.

The ghouls shrieked like banshees every time she struck them down. They didn't die, but they'd clatter to the ground, clutching their wounds and wriggling and screaming. She'd wince if they were too close to her ears, but even then, their sounds of agony felt justified. Rage thrummed through her limbs: Rage at how they'd feasted on Yeshua for who knows how long. Rage at what the deaths had felt trapped in their pillars. Rage at herself. Rage at the worlds. Rage at everyone and everything.

This was almost therapeutic, beating down on the blooded ghouls without a care. Their bodies didn't have bones or flesh or veins. If there was any more liquid coming out of them, it was meaningless in the rain. And they didn't even die. It didn't matter if she slit their throats or left a deep gash in their faces or lobbed off their arms. They didn't die. Most of the injured fell to the ground, others stood helplessly in the swarm, crying like children lost in a crowd before another ghoul knocked them over. It was pathetic. And all the while, she harvested their pain through her hatchet.

**+64 Energy**
**+64 Energy**
**+64 Energy**

She punched one in the face, her armor-covered knuckles making a satisfying *thwack* as the ghoul's face caved in. It collapsed to its knees, fingers digging into its new orifice, and Jenny spun to attack the next one with her hatchet. This was almost too easy, she thought. Was she really that strong?

As far as she could tell, the only difference between the ghouls and the blooded ghouls seemed to be their dark-red color and that they no longer burst into liquid when struck. But how was that an improvement? Now, they writhed in pain and *felt* pain.

She'd been afraid they'd advanced to a more powerful form, how the angels had gone from tarnished to wretched to desecrated. But the more she fought—as the ghouls closed in and bumped into her shoulders and arms and back, as they threatened to suffocate her—she realized what the issue was.

Before, she could strike down several of them with a Savage Throw or Instant Acceleration and make space. But now, she had to be even more careful when she dodged. The ground was cluttered with fallen bodies shrieking and wriggling. If she fell, the ghouls would pile on, and she'd never get back up.

Hands grasped her shoulders. Red fingers curled, and she felt a few of her scales crackle, but the new enhanced design held up a lot better than her previous armor, and the blood rain made her slick and wet. She slipped out of their grip and shoved her hatchet into the ghoul's chest. It fell away with a gasp, the steam swirling violently in its eye sockets.

Another creature's fingers curled around her leg, and she fought the urge to kick it off. An elbow struck her in the back, and hands grabbed at her helmet, trying to yank it off. It forced her head back, causing blood to rain down on her face. Jenny used Ignite.

Flames roared to life from head to toe, boiling the blood dribbling down her armor and scorching the ghouls who'd grabbed her. She seized the opportunity, flipping her hatchet as she turned, striking them down in a wide crescent, each one lighting up with a brief flash of light. She then shook her leg free, a hand still curled around her calf. She'd cut the arm off.

Jenny was stronger now. Their grips weren't as painful or effective, and with her increased power, each strike cut through the ghouls with ease, each one giving her more energy. Slowly, she found her rhythm, slashing off their arms or their heads, letting their bodies topple to the ground. She stomped on them like she was crushing red pots of clay, whirling around, slashing and shoving, swiping arms that reached for her when she didn't have an easy swing, punching faces or throats.

Screams and groans assaulted her ears, but her enhanced armor—her tougher body—took their attacks like they were nothing. In the frenzy, she'd almost forgotten her plan to fight toward Yeshua and the deaths, but then, a powerful gust blew away the ghouls swarming her. They rolled by, arms and legs flailing like they'd been sucked up by a tornado. The rain curved and flicked around Jenny, swept away in the same direction, giving her a brief break from the downpour before the blood came pouring down again.

Red lightning ignited the sky, illuminating the rain and the roiling clouds, and Jenny saw Yeshua standing in front of the deaths, his soaked robes billowing, his hair stuck to his face as blood ran down his forehead and cheeks.

But he also stood behind them, as well as at their sides. Seven or eight of him in total, all wearing the same purple robes; they all hunched and looked exhausted, but he'd formed a perimeter around the deaths as they huddled in a compact circle.

Each Yeshua punched and kicked the ghouls that swarmed them, but when their hands and feet made contact with one, the creature completely disintegrated into a fine red mist, and the impact blew away the surrounding ghouls.

He must have had an ability that let him duplicate himself. Jenny rushed toward them with Instant Acceleration, taking advantage of the momentary cleared space to catch her breath. She caught up to the crowd of deaths, blood dribbling down all their frightened faces and soaking into their robes. They all looked almost as red as the ghouls.

"This won't end," said the Yeshua bodies in unison, his voice echoing and booming all around. "They will come endlessly. They are the world responding to change."

Jenny held her breath, trying to ease her heart rate and watching as the ghouls struggled to get past the many Yeshuas. He struck them over and over, using his fists to generate enough wind to disintegrate the closest creatures and push back the rest.

The younger deaths were sobbing as the older ones tried to console them. But the rest of them were crying too, frightened and meek, and Jenny didn't know what to do. She remembered Yeshua's warning that he couldn't protect them all, and judging by how weakened he looked, how the ghouls kept coming despite how afraid they'd been earlier, she wasn't sure how long this would hold out.

As she prepared to jump back into the fight, one ghoul slipped past a Yeshua to her left. Its red limbs flailed as it leaped toward the deaths, teeth gnashing, empty eyes swirling, vapor trailing behind its head. Jenny turned on her heels and ran toward it, pushing through the crowd of deaths. The ghoul had grabbed the little girl, the one who had come up to Yeshua before. It was holding her in the air as she kicked and cried, rain battering her face.

The closest Yeshua turned, his face strained, teeth bared. But several ghouls grabbed him by the neck and shoulders and brought him to the ground. Neither he nor Jenny were going to make it in time.

Just then, the girl squirmed out of the ghoul's grip.

*How?* Jenny barely registered what had just happened. Was it just because of the rain? Had that let the girl slip away? The ghoul scrambled before grabbing her again, this time pinning her to the ground as it bared its teeth, ready to take a bite from her shoulder. But that had been enough time for Jenny to catch up, and she didn't bother slowing down. At full speed, she kicked the ghoul in the face.

The tip of her armored foot connected with one of its eye sockets. There was a hideous *crack*, and the top of its head flew off as though she'd just popped the lid off a jar.

Its body fell limp to the ground as the girl wriggled out and ran into the arms of one of the other deaths. Jenny turned, tossing her hatchet with Savage Throw to strike down the ghoul chewing off Yeshua's nose.

But more creatures broke through the line of defense, and despite Yeshua's multitudinous cry telling them to stand still, the crowd of deaths scattered. They ran in every direction, and in the frenzy, in the bloody downpour and the ghouls swarming, everything became a mess of red limbs and screaming. Shouts and cries erupted all around her, and she knew neither she nor Yeshua could attack with ease. They'd risk hitting a death.

Red lightning surged as Jenny used the flat side of her hatchet, parrying blows and trying to knock creatures away from her. She saw the Yeshuas splitting, each one separating into three or four more, but the new ones looked even thinner and weaker. Strained. They were being overrun, and in every direction, there were only more ghouls, more blood-colored mannequins moaning and whimpering and scrambling over each other. And the screaming!

Shrill screams of agony that she knew were the deaths'. She found the girl, the first death whom Jenny had freed, lying on the ground, wriggling and shrieking as three ghouls feasted on her arms and legs, splattering blood and flesh. With a scream of rage, Jenny lodged her hatchet into their heads. She beheaded one. She snapped through another's skull. She kicked one off the girl.

But before she could help the death up, several more grabbed at Jenny. Fingers curled around her wrist. Hands latched on to her sides. Something struck the back of her head so hard she saw sparks.

*What did they want?*

*What did they get out of eating the deaths? Could the deaths even die?*

*What do I do? Ignite? Savage Throw? Instant Acceleration?*

*Valescent Light?*

*That's it!*

She elbowed a ghoul in the face and struck down another. She pushed a death, an old man, to the side and struck down the ghoul that had nearly gotten him. Her mind spun, trying to connect thoughts as she evaded ghouls and blinked blood out of her eyelashes.

She could open another portal. She could get everyone out of here. But how? And where would they go? She didn't know how she'd opened it last time. She'd just made use of what was already there.

*How did I do it?*

An arm grabbed her shoulder, and this grip felt too firm, too powerful. She swore out loud, twisting her body to attack, afraid her arm would pop out of her shoulder. But it was one of the Yeshuas. He'd had the same idea as her. He shouted in the chaos, blood dripping down his face and beard.

"Open a passage! Open a passageway to the world of demons. We can lead these abominations right to Hell!"

# CHAPTER TWELVE

# OPENING

**B**efore she could register Yeshua's words, a hand smashed into her face. Jenny couldn't tell if it was a ghoul or another Yeshua or a death, but fingernails scratched her lips, scraped her teeth, and she reacted. Her hatchet swung, and the hand was separated from whomever it belonged to.

She stumbled back, yanking the hand out of her mouth, unable to tell if it was bleeding in all this terrible rain.

**+64 Energy**

It was red all the way through and felt like plastic. It was a ghoul's. She hadn't hurt one of the deaths. But her momentary relief was cut short. Another ghoul rammed her side, clawing at her scales. Two more grabbed her shoulders and tried to pull her down, but she turned her heel, grounding herself firmly, and swore loudly as she tried to shake them off. Her joints ached from their grips, but she wrapped an arm around one's head, its jaws snapping against the armor that protected her armpit, and struck another in the eyes with her hatchet.

But more hands grabbed onto her legs and waist. Blood rain splattered over everything, and the ghouls' whimpering and moaning were making it too hard to think. With a cry of rage, she used Ignite again.

Fire burst out of her shoulders almost like two wings unfurling. The ghouls cowered, the sudden brightness shocking their systems. Every single drop of blood around them glistened tantalizingly, hissing as they struck Jenny's burning body and evaporated.

The ghouls recovered almost immediately, swiping at her face, but that split second was all she needed. She swept around quickly, slashing through each ghoul before sidestepping their collapsing bodies. They fell to the ground, screaming and clutching at their wounds, while Jenny twisted her arm, snapping the head off the ghoul she had in a headlock.

As she moved away from them, she expanded her helmet, stretching the metal forward to shield the front of her face, leaving only a slit for her to see through. This limited her visibility, but it was better than having her mouth ripped open. Her lip bled from where it'd been scratched, and she licked at her own blood. It tasted sweeter than the blood rain.

The Yeshuas shouted around her, and a thunderous burst of wind blew past, knocking away the rain and an entire group of ghouls and deaths alike. Jenny managed to stay on her feet, but she could tell this blow was weaker than his earlier attacks. He was worried about hurting the deaths; they couldn't fight like this.

"You must hurry!" shouted the Yeshuas in unison. Two of him were wrestling with ghouls, while another one was twitching on the ground, crying out in agony as ghouls snapped off his limbs and one chewed a hole through his side as yet another Yeshua helped one of the deaths up.

She didn't know whom to help. The deaths were in the same situation, being eaten alive. Teeth gnashed. The ghouls moaned and whimpered and ate, and the deaths screamed and cried out helplessly. Jenny kicked ghouls in the ribs. She slammed her hatchet down on their heads like she was splitting firewood, elbowing and punching and roaring flame, but it didn't matter. For every ghoul she disabled, two or three more took their place.

What had Yeshua said? This was the world responding to change?

Jenny had started this. This was her fault. She'd set Yeshua free. She'd awakened the first death. And now, all of these poor people—A ghoul tore the head off one of the younger deaths, swallowing it whole. Jenny screamed, using Instant Acceleration to burst through the crowd. She punched the ghoul so hard the scales covering her knuckles cracked. It spat out the head, which rolled across the ground spraying blood as the ghoul collapsed.

Jenny then grabbed the death's headless body, shaking. This one was just a kid. A little boy. But even as she held the body, a warm light seeped out of the gruesome neck and solidified into a new head. A new face with clear skin and pretty hair and big brown eyes. The boy blinked at her for a moment, then the rain splattered his face, and Jenny couldn't tell if the kid was crying or not. She wasn't sure if *she* was crying or not.

Two more ghouls leaped toward them, and Jenny thrust the boy away as hard as she could before another ghoul struck her in the face with its arm, its hand rattling her helmet. More grabbed her, and they piled on top, wriggling, teeth scraping against her scales, palms striking her helmet and her back over and over.

She twisted carefully to avoid dislocating her shoulder or leg, then swiped to the side, burying her hatchet in one ghoul's hip. Another leaped right onto her head, knocking her forward and down, her face smashing into a bloody puddle.

With a muffled scream, she tried to crawl out of the wriggling pile. She couldn't help but swallow blood as more ran down her face and dripped from her helmet. She slammed her hatchet into the ground, trying to will herself to get out, trying to focus on Ignite again, and that was when it came to her: that eye-shaped pool of darkness back at the school, like a wound in the cafeteria floor.

That was the opening which had allowed the angels to come through, and she and everyone else had only been able to get back because of . . . because of Susan's light.

The healing! The light had healed the opening between worlds, and that was what Jenny had done later, when she'd wanted to leave. She'd reopened it with light. But for her to use Valescent Light like that, there needed to be a wound in the first place. A tear between worlds.

Her heart pounding, aware of all the horror around her, Jenny stopped struggling and tried to relax. A foot struck her helmet and smashed her face into the puddle again. Teeth and fists and screaming pummeled her as blood rained down on everything. She touched her fingers to the ground—*Concentrate*—with both hands, even as fingers curled around her forearms, even as the ghouls tried to pry off her helmet.

She touched the ground the same way she'd done with the pillars, and she realized that Yeshua had also been showing her how to do exactly this. It had to be beyond her body. Something outside of her.

*Severed Spirit.*

Immediately, the ground responded. She felt it *open*, felt something shift. A horrible feeling coiled around her stomach and squeezed tight, then it kicked, like a baby kicking inside of her. It spurted out of her belly button. Her exoskeleton.

A scream tore through her throat, gurgling in the blood she'd swallowed. The armor on her back cracked and split. Her six tentacles burst out of her flesh and—

**You are overjoyed. You are reborn. You are alive again. The blood! It's raining delicious, precious blood. You can feast all you want.**

**You don't have to stop. These creatures can feel pain, and you can harvest every last drop of Energy.**

**Look how powerful you can be. Look how powerful you are.**

**You don't have to be alone anymore.**

**Your tentacles whirl about, soaking in the rain, slapping the ghouls into dust with a single blow. They are nothing creatures. Empty. Hollow. Your tentacles crush them. Curl around them and fling them into the air like dolls.**

**They're not on top of you anymore.**

**You can get up.**

**You can feast.**

**Yeshua has already offered his flesh. The deaths don't die either. They grow back. You can eat all you want. How delicious will they be? Your mouth is already watering. Your stomach is already grumbling. All you have to do is—**

With a violent shudder, Jenny snapped out of it, breathing hard. Everything was dulled. Everything had slowed down. She was lying in the puddle of blood as it bubbled and churned, but the bubbles burst in slow motion, and the rain was gentle. The ghouls moved in slowly, running toward her. People were screaming—shouting—but their voices were faint and far away. Her vision felt faded, like she'd just woken up.

She was lying on the ground, but her arms, stretched out above her head, were covered in red. It was her exoskeleton, covering her belly and her sides, coming up to her jaw. It was growing over her armor, but it hadn't grown completely. It hadn't covered her completely. And her tentacles.

She could feel the precise location of every drop of rain falling from the sky, soaking into the ground, dripping down the bodies around her. Her tentacles ingested as much blood as they could, but she forced her attention away, down to her chest, her body. To her hands and fingers. To where she was touching the ground.

It was almost like instinct, or like sticking her hand out the window on a freezing day just to feel the biting chill of the wind while the rest of her was safe and warm inside. *Focus. Breathe. Swallow.*

*I want to leave this place.*

*I want to take the deaths away from here.*

*I want to save them.*

She pictured Susan again. It wasn't like last time, when she'd thought of her and lost focus while trying to sever the death from the pillar. This time, it was memory. This time, it was longing, as though Susan were her guiding force. As though the hurt of what Jenny had done could push her forward.

*Open me up!*

*Cut me open!*

*Get it the fuck out of me!*

A silent scream blossomed inside Jenny, rising, slowly and slowly, as everything around her shifted into motion again. Her tentacles swirled. The ghouls grabbed and tore at the deaths. Yeshua struck blow after blow. And all the while, the blood rained down on everyone and everything.

She kept her mind on Susan's smile. On when Susan had still been alive, standing on the darkness in the cafeteria, her arms outstretched to welcome Jenny. She'd run toward Susan. She'd run right into her arms, the hunger uncontrollable, the *need* beyond any urgency she'd ever had before. Jenny felt Susan's throat between her teeth. The squish. The crunch. The burst of flavor. The warmth she'd always wanted.

She saw Susan's corpse. Her lifeless eyes. And the hurt. The heart-wrenching, rib-shattering hurt that made her want to bury her fingers in her belly button and claw herself completely open so that all that pain, all that self-hatred and disgust and hurt could burst out of her and break free, shoot from her fingertips into the fabric of the world itself.

And everything ripped open beneath her.

It felt like she'd punctured something. Darkness gushed out from the ground, swallowing the bubbling liquid and the rain; it was the same horrid darkness she'd found on the cafeteria floor where the angels had surfaced from. The many Yeshuas yelled something, the ghouls screeched in unison like a thousand fingernails scraping her ears, and the darkness *tugged* on Jenny. It tugged on her exoskeleton, drawing out more of her monstrous side.

**You must give in to yourself.**
**You must break free.**
**You must—**

Jenny knew what to do next. How to make it work. She kept her mind on Susan, kept her focus on how she felt: Hurt. Regret. Love.

Want. Need. Hope.

*I'm going to find you.*

Golden light surged from her hands. Colors, all the colors of the rainbow, flowed into the light like ink bleeding into a page, and warmth radiated from her hand. All the darkness shimmered away, turning golden and colorful, illuminating the world just as the deaths had done before as they'd woken each other up, just as Susan had done when she and Jenny had left their survival challenge.

Jenny stared into the blinding light, tears streaming from her eyes as she sank like a stone. A sea of golden light welcomed her. Streams of color—swirls of glistening reds and threads of vibrant greens—curled around her limbs like tentacles or underwater plants, tangling her, pulling her further into the depths. Jenny relaxed all her muscles. She let go. She surrendered to the light and felt all the others—the many Yeshuas, the deaths, and the ghouls—sinking in with her.

*Where am I going?*

# CHAPTER THIRTEEN

# SEEKING THROUGH THE LIGHT

Her breathing eased. The aches from the ghouls' attacks faded away, and when she blinked, tears bubbled off her cheeks alongside the blood from the rain. Her sweat, the salty dirt of the world, all of it was washed away. In a few moments, her enhanced armor, which had several cracks and many scales missing, was clean. The light cleansed and healed her, but it did nothing for the hurt that filled her heart to bursting.

The front of her body was covered by her red exoskeleton—her chest, her arms, her navel, and most of her thighs. Rough and uneven, it jutted out in every direction like a strange rock formation. It hadn't even settled completely; she'd stopped it before the gelatinous substance could completely spread, but it covered her arms up to her wrists, and a bit even covered the underside of her jaw.

As she sank through the light, she touched the covering on her chest. The sensation shuddered through her; it was like touching the salt pillars, like touching someone else. A strange warmth. A misshapen hardness. At least the exoskeleton hadn't completely taken over her face, and it hadn't made it all the way around to her back. She tried to tell herself she hadn't reverted back to her monstrous form, but she could feel the tentacles swirling behind her.

She turned to look at them over her shoulder. They'd grown. They were thicker and fleshier than before, partially covered with the dark blue of her enhanced armor like a thin layer of fish scales.

All sorts of colors swirled around them: greens and oranges, purples and pinks, silvers. They formed floating rings that spiraled along the length of each tentacle before fading away and coming back.

Jenny turned slowly as she sank through the thick golden light to see hundreds of bodies trailing behind her. It reminded her of a school trip to the aquarium, the dark underground room with the glass ceiling. She remembered looking up at the beautiful sea creatures and plants above, wishing they could all be free. Wishing they weren't trapped in a glass cage for people to come see. How was that fair?

The blooded ghouls looked like red mannequins. They clutched their heads, wriggling and struggling as though they had piercing headaches. No color reached out to them. No swirls of light enveloped them. And no sound escaped them; she couldn't hear their moaning or screeching.

The deaths fell almost gracefully, their arms spread wide, their torn robes fluttering in the light as purple-and-pink streams curled around their waists and limbs, enveloped in oranges and yellows. Some of them held hands, and to Jenny, they looked more like the angels she'd grown up always reading about and picturing whenever she prayed—they looked perfectly at ease in the passageway.

And then there were the Yeshuas. All of them had their eyes closed, their beards and long hair drifting, their robes billowing. Every one of him seemed like they were resting, and all signs of damage were gone, healed away by the light. He was still emaciated. Too thin, too tired looking. But just like with the ghouls, no colors encircled him. She wondered if that had to do with him being NULL too.

*Where am I supposed to go?* she wanted to ask him, but when Jenny opened her mouth, air bubbled out, melting into the golden light. Panic didn't strike her. She didn't need to breathe. This was the air she'd held in her lungs. Spittle floated away from her lips. Spittle and blood, and she let go of whatever bit of stale air she had left.

Her mind emptied. She tried to concentrate on the colors, on the light. Turning away from the falling bodies, maneuvering with her arms, she caught sight of her hatchet floating nearby and swam toward it. Once she had it in her hands, she held it to her exoskeleton-covered chest, her tentacles reaching in every direction, trying to sense, trying to make sense of things.

She was leading the others. Taking them somewhere. Yeshua had mentioned the world of demons; he'd called it Hell. But she hadn't been thinking about that when she opened the passageway. All she'd wanted to do was *open* it, but now that it was open, how was she supposed to decide where to go?

*Think.*

*How did I get to the world of death?*

By wanting it. By wanting to find Susan. She hadn't known of deaths and souls or anything like that; she'd only wanted to find Susan. She'd focused on the thought of death, and the light had guided her through it.

She shut her eyes, trying to ignore the pressing worry of what had happened when she'd used Severed Spirit. When that *voice* had taken over.

Had it been a voice?

Or had it been her true self?

She'd felt so *separated* from her body, like she'd been watching herself through a movie screening; like she'd been feeling everything through a story she was reading. Like she wasn't real.

*Doesn't matter.*

*Find the demons. The world of demons.*

*Find Hell.*

Suddenly, Jenny felt it. A gentle push, like the light was pushing against her, like feeling a breeze nudging her from behind, pressing her away.

And something else pulled, as though trying to reel her in. It reminded her again of fish; something from biology about how fish had a strip of special organs along their sides. That was how they sensed movement and currents around them, and that was how they truly "saw."

She kept her eyes closed, focusing on the pulling and pushing sensation. *Guide me. Show me where to go. Please.*

There was a current to the light. No, *multiple* currents in four distinct directions. Her heart skipped a beat as recognition filled her chest. The biggest pull was toward what felt like a center. A core. The sun of a solar system. Her body turned toward it.

This pull felt familiar. It felt right. It was . . . That was the world she belonged to. Earth. What had Eve called it? The material world. That was at the center of everything.

From above came a push. It was pushing her down, away from it, deeper into the light. That was the direction she'd come from; that was the world of death.

If she'd wanted to, she got the sense she could kick, swim, or fly upward and break the surface again, returning to that bloody rain and bringing everyone with her. That wouldn't do much good. And she couldn't go to Earth. Something told her it would be a mess to bring deaths to the material world, a violation of natural order.

Ahead of her was . . . light. It was cool and misty, and she'd felt this world before, too. This one pulled, tugging on her; she'd seen this world when she'd lived through the eyes of that orange-covered angel. She remembered the clouds and the shining towers and the flocks of other angels.

There was something dark there. Not just in her memory of the world but right now. Something horrible and heavy; something she didn't want to see.

Something she didn't want to be found by. And even if that *thing* weren't there, even if that thing weren't trying to invite her, she couldn't take the deaths there. She wasn't sure if there was any land; would they all plummet to their . . . ? Well, she didn't know what would happen if the deaths fell.

Jenny turned away, toward the remaining pushing/pulling sensation. This one was tugging on her tentacles but pushing against her body, like it couldn't decide what it wanted. It was cold—ice cold—and a shiver spread through her. If she'd had breath, it would've taken it away, like she'd been splashed with ice water.

But it felt right somehow. It felt like the world she was looking for. Besides, process of elimination ruled out all other directions she could go. That left this icy world, so Jenny opened her eyes, grabbing at the light—fistfuls of it— and tried to propel herself and the hundreds she was dragging behind her.

*What'll happen to the ghouls?*

She didn't care. At least in another world they would have more space to fight, and there would be no more blood rain to fuel the blooded ghouls, no more bubbling liquid for more creatures to emerge from. Was that what Yeshua had had in mind?

Did he know of the other worlds she could've gone to?

Why had he been so specific?

The colors responded. The greens and blues faded to pale white and silver, and the golden light shimmered around her, drawing her in. She'd found the current. The pushing sensation gave way to a fearsome tug, sucking her forward.

She flowed into it, moving without kicking her legs or flapping her arms, letting the light guide her. She trusted it. She surrendered to it. And this time, the light didn't just snap shut below her. It parted in front of her, and Jenny stepped through.

When her armored foot touched down on the other side, it crunched on ice. A cold wind blew through the gap in her helmet, and when she exhaled, steam rose from her face.

With a shudder, she stepped into another world. Something inside her relaxed, and her tentacles wriggled violently, swirling as they emerged from the colors and light, snapping back into Jenny's shoulder blades and spine with a *shlurp.*

Like a rubber band snapping, she cried out and fell forward onto the snow, a cramp burning a hole in her navel as her exoskeleton retreated beneath her enhanced armor. It drained back into her belly button, returning back inside her, and she coughed violently, spitting blood as the trembling eased.

Freezing wind blew through the gap in her helmet. Her armor protected her from the worst of it, but the cold seeped right into her bones. As her vision adjusted to this new world and she blinked away tears from the biting cold, she saw in front of her another empty wasteland, though instead of salt and gloom and blood rain, this one was bright blue and white, icy snow stretching as far as she could see through the steady gentle snowfall.

It was silent. This world was completely silent, everything muffled by the snow and ice. There were no trees. No rock faces. No pillars. Only the gray-white clouds above, the snow, and the ice-covered ground.

Behind her, the opening she'd made hovered in the air. It blurred in and out of focus, a rippling, elongated oval. Colors leaked out—tendrils and beams of reds and yellows that surged as though the opening was spitting them like solar flares. Most of the light evaporated into the world.

Jenny hobbled around the opening, wondering what it looked like from the side or the back. But it didn't matter how she circled or moved, the gash always looked the same: a wound in the air. Where was everyone else?

She reached for it, willing them to come out, and in response, the passageway pulsed. It shone brighter and brighter, so bright that Jenny had to raise a hand to protect her eyes.

Screams and cries and moans filled the air, and Jenny blinked as she found piles of ghouls struggling over one another as frost spread across their red limbs. Their teeth gnashed as their fingers reached for her, reached for the deaths. Their eye sockets were wide, as though they were shocked, and then, the vapor swirling inside their eyes came to a standstill, and the ghouls froze like ice sculptures dyed red, freezing in their piles—some half standing, some crawling, most grasping onto other ghouls or deaths.

The deaths' breaths clouded around their faces as they scrambled away from the frozen ghouls, and the many Yeshuas were standing up to their feet, shaking off their robes. They snapped frozen limbs off ghouls who'd managed to grab a Yeshua or a death, and Jenny sank to her knees as the rest of them huddled for warmth and safety. Coldness crawled up her spine as she allowed herself to feel the wave of exhaustion and relief. She needed to lie down for a while.

As the passageway closed and the golden light faded, one of the Yeshuas approached her, concern on his strained face. Snowflakes clung to his beard and eyelashes. "Hell has frozen over."

Jenny opened her mouth to respond, to ask if they should go somewhere else, but she didn't know if she could open another passageway so soon. She felt drained. Her heart squeezed empty. But then, Yeshua stumbled—all of them at once.

Face twisting in pain, he clutched his chest as the other Yeshuas shimmered, disintegrating into light that beamed toward the Yeshua in front of Jenny. He was breathing hard, his face red. Each light splashed onto him, outlining him brightly before fading, but it didn't seem to be helping him at all.

"What's happening?" Jenny stood quickly, reaching for the system, wondering what kind of potion she should create for him. Was he injured? Exhausted? Did he need a bite of her arm?

He shook his head, the artery on his forehead bulging as his eyes turned red. She could see the one on his neck bulging too. "The cross," he hissed through his teeth. Then his eyes rolled toward the back of his head and he faltered, reaching out with a hand as if trying to grab something for balance, as if hoping Jenny would catch him. But as she rushed toward him, Yeshua disintegrated into vapor.

For a moment, his silhouette lingered, made of misty air. Then, he faded away.

Jenny was breathing hard, not sure what to do, staring at the spot where Yeshua had just been. She glanced at the deaths as though they might know what was going on, but they looked just as frightened as Jenny felt. They were all shivering and crying, rubbing their arms or holding on to each other for warmth.

Yeshua was gone.

# CHAPTER FOURTEEN

# A FROZEN WORLD

Steam clouded the inside of Jenny's helmet; she was breathing too quickly. Yanking the thing off, she tossed it aside, blinking repeatedly at Yeshua's footsteps in the snow. Already, the steady snowfall was filling them in, erasing them just as Yeshua had disappeared.

"Yeshua?" she called out, glancing around, half expecting one of his bodies to stand up from the pile of ghouls or emerge from the crowd of deaths. She walked briskly, trying to figure out what had happened, and made her way to the frozen ghouls.

Her heart was pounding. Hundreds of blooded ghouls were covered in a layer of snow spread out as far as she could see. There might've been even more, but the falling snow limited visibility, and Jenny got the sense she was standing on the edge of a mass grave. There was a solemnity, a blanketed quietness, as she stared at all the frozen figures, who looked too much like people.

Most of them were still on the ground, stuck to one another like victims of a natural disaster. A few had gotten to their knees or a halfway standing position. The ghouls' red color looked foggy pink.

Some of them looked like they were reaching for her, and she imagined it must've been horribly painful to freeze to death. Their empty eye sockets glared as if accusing her. Was this her fault? Had she messed something up? Was Yeshua dead?

Yeshua had said something about the cross before he'd vanished, and she remembered how he'd dragged that thing across the gloomy world to the pillars. As if he couldn't go too far without it.

Did that mean he was bound to it by more than just flesh?

She dug her nails into her palms, trying to search her memory. She'd been so focused on opening the passageway, of getting out of that nightmare, she hadn't even thought to bring the cross with her. Why hadn't she noticed?

But how was that her fault? She couldn't have known.

Yeshua should've told her. Or had he tried to? He'd shouted several things, but she couldn't have understood him in that mess of blood and teeth and desperate hands.

Jenny tried to find the spot in the air where the passageway had hovered. She felt around, turning this way and that, trying to remember where she'd been standing in correlation with the ghouls, but everywhere looked the same. It was snowing, gentle but relentless, and it was already tucking away the footsteps and disturbances in the snow.

The deaths muttered and whispered, and she heard echoes of their questions. *Where is he? What is she doing? It's so cold. I'm hungry.* She wanted to tell them to shut up, to be quiet. She needed to think. Gentle trails of steam rose from where the snow landed on their bodies, a little fog gathering around them.

Jenny was breathing hard, voluminous clouds of breath escaping her lips. It was cold. Too cold. And the deaths were huddling for warmth. But she figured they'd be okay for now. When she'd freed the first death, that girl had felt so hot to the touch, like she'd been on fire. They could keep each other safe from the cold; Jenny had to figure out how to help Yeshua.

She couldn't bear the thought of him stuck in that world again, back in that storm of blood with more and more ghouls crawling out of the ground to feast on him in his weakened state.

Or would he fight better now, without any restraints? He wouldn't have to worry about harming one of the deaths, and he might be able to feed on the ghouls and grow fuller and stronger again. She tried to calm her breathing, reminding herself that he was several magnitudes more powerful than her and that he could handle himself. Panicking wouldn't help.

But it wasn't just fear for his sake that was making her head spin. Slowly, she turned to the deaths. There were about thirty or forty of them huddling close together so that they looked like a blob of torn purple cloth and fog. Snow stuck to their hair and melted down their faces. That wasn't going to help. That would make them feel even colder. What was she supposed to do with them? How could she help them?

She did not want to feed them with her own flesh.

Her teeth started chattering, her shoulders trembling as the cold seeped through her armor and into her bones.

*Okay. I can open the portal again, then I can go see what's happening to Yeshua. Maybe I can bring his cross over too. Then he can come here and explain things, and we can figure out what to do next. How to find the world of souls. How to help the deaths. How to get to Susan.*

Trying to stay calm, she reached out again with one arm, armor peeling back to expose her knuckles and wrist to the cold, as though that might help. As though more sense data could activate what she needed.

Turning slowly in every direction like the needle of a compass trying to find north, snowflakes tickling her nose, she deepened her breath, taking her time, trying to keep the worrying thoughts at bay. And after a few turns, she felt it. A slight, magnetic tug, which she stepped toward.

There was a slight gelatinous pressure in the air, like she'd found something gooey and invisible. The air felt thicker. Bumpier. Like a scab. A tremor radiated through her chest; she was feeling the healed wound between the worlds. It was similar to how the cafeteria floor had felt after she and Susan had brought the school back.

How did it work? Once a passageway was cut and then healed, would it always be there? Like scar tissue between worlds? Or was this some aspect of Valescent Light which allowed her to open the passageway again without creating another wound?

Sucking in a deep breath of cold air, she activated Valescent Light, and a golden aura enveloped her palm and fingers. Colors skipped up to her fingertips before fading away, and a wave of dizziness hit Jenny so hard she stumbled back, losing her balance. The light blinked out of existence.

"Gah!" she spat, breathing even harder than before. Sweat beaded down the side of her face before the frigid air sent shivers crawling across her body. She leaned forward and grabbed her armored knees, trying to steady herself, spitting onto the snow.

This was more than exhaustion. More than a lack of stamina. Pressure gathered behind her eyes, and her brain felt wrung out. She remembered the gaunt expression on Susan's face after using Valescent Light to heal Jenny from the brink of death. How tired Susan had looked. How sunken her eyes had been. A potion couldn't restore her.

The skill drew on something more than physical exertion, and Jenny had the sneaking suspicion that it had to do with her own death or soul or something. She squeezed her knees, her hair falling forward to cover her face. "Fuck."

She couldn't use it again. Not now. Not for a while. She had to rest, like the ability was on cooldown. Slumping to the ground, her knees hit the snow with a crunch. Her ears were freezing, the tip of her nose was freezing, and she was sure her snot was turning to ice. Were her lips turning blue?

What the fuck was she supposed to do?

*Ignite!*

A roar of frustration tore through her throat, and a stream of fire billowed out of her mouth, melting the snow in front of her before she raised her face to scream at the cloud-covered sky. Snow hissed and evaporated, and when she snapped her teeth shut, she closed her eyes. The warmth faded as quickly as it had come, sapped away from her face and her insides by the freezing wind of this world.

*I'm in Hell.*

What was it that Yeshua had said before? Hell had frozen over? Wasn't that just an expression? Something people said? So, if this was Hell, why was it snowing? Why was the ground frozen? And where were the demons?

**We are right here.**

Her eyes flew open. "Who said that?" she demanded, standing and taking a menacing step toward the deaths. "Did you hear that?" It had almost sounded like static. Like a voice crackling over an old-timey radio.

They shook their heads, their torn robes fluttering as another breeze swept by. They all looked ragged and cold. Jenny searched for the first one, the one she'd freed, the brown woman. Her eyes were wide and frightened. She was hugging two of the younger deaths to her, trying to keep them warm.

**Your warmth has guided us to you.**

The voice rattled through her head like a distorted phone call, as though someone was about to lose connection.

"Hello?" said Jenny in exasperation. She summoned back her hatchet, light flashing as anger burned inside her throat. A tense pressure pounded behind her eyes. "Who's talking? Where are you?" She turned around and around before snapping at the deaths. "You guys seriously can't hear any-thing?" She jabbed her hatchet accusingly in their direction, and they all stepped back, blinking at her like she'd gone mad.

She almost apologized, but she couldn't stop shaking. Something was reading her thoughts. Reading her mind. Something was talking to her from inside her head again.

**You are not going mad. We are not speaking to the deaths. We are speaking to you, strange human.**

She clenched her teeth so hard she thought they'd shatter in the cold. She whirled around, scanning the snow for where she'd dropped her helmet, seeing nothing but snowfall and the crowd of deaths and frozen ghouls. She couldn't stop shaking, couldn't stop the boiling-hot rage from taking over. She was done with invisible beings talking to her like this. "Who the fuck are you? What do you want?"

**You are intruding on our home. Perhaps you should answer these questions first.**

"Okay . . ." The voice was right. She *was* the one intruding. She didn't really have a right to make demands, but she still had another question. "Why can't I see you?"

Light shimmered in front of her, over the field of frozen ghouls. Many lights sparkled and sizzled, ranging in color from red to yellow to blue, like a swarm of bioluminescent insects all buzzing their wings.

Jenny stepped back, holding her hatchet defensively with both hands, trying to figure out what was coming. Was this some new monster? Some other creature that would try to eat her? She was so sick and tired of fighting for her life. But if these things were going to attack, why communicate? Why give her any warning?

The lights rained down on the ghouls, sparkling and glimmering, like shooting stars concentrated in one area. When a light splattered on a ghoul, its body began to glow. The snow melted away from its head and limbs, and with several cracks, the frozen creature's joints moved, returning to life.

Its head turned. Blue flames alighted in its eye sockets, as though someone had just turned on a gas stove, and Jenny gripped her hatchet tight, ready to strike it down. Was this some new form of ghoul? Would it try to eat her too?

**This body hungers . . .**

She bit her lip, trying to keep her teeth from chattering. Every instinct in her body told her to attack before the creatures got up. Before they were fully awake.

But it was *communicating*. It wasn't a mindless monster. It wasn't like the angels.

The ghoul's limbs twitched, and it stood, head lolling back, chest protruding forward as its arms swung uselessly. It moved unsteadily on its feet like a puppet held by strings. With a shaking step forward, it righted itself, and more blue fire spilled from its eyes, rising upward so that they looked like two flickering horns jutting out of the ghoul's head. Jenny couldn't help but stare. In the empty eye sockets sat two balls of flame, like miniature blue stars.

## Demon (Stage IV) (Vesseled)

Jenny's heart sank. The demon was stage four. It didn't have a level, but it wasn't NULL either like Yeshua had been. Cold sweat ran down her back. What did *Vesseled* mean? Was that referring to the ghoul's body?

The other ghouls were standing as well, some with orange flames, others with red or yellow or white. They ranged from stage one to stage three, but there weren't any other stage fours or anything higher. None of the others had blue flames.

Within moments, there was a small crowd of them. Their heads lolled like they were too heavy for their shoulders, but the one in the lead, the only one with burning blue eyes, managed to take another shaking step toward Jenny. Its head swerved back before falling forward, chin bumping its chest as its arms waved back and forth, trying to find its balance.

Her body twitched, ready to run away, ready to fight, but unable to decide. Were they a threat? The ghouls already had cartoonish features, with those bulbous heads and thin limbs, but as the demons stumbled around, struggling to right themselves, she wasn't sure how to respond.

Their eyes burned brilliantly, and the bloody-red sheen of the ghouls' bodies faded away, returning back to white so that they blended in with their surroundings. If it weren't for their fiery eyes, Jenny would've lost track of them.

## What are you?

The first demon's mouth opened and closed, teeth clacking in a repetitive pattern, like watching a low-budget animation where the audio and the lips were out of sync. The voice was still inside her head. Was the demon moving its mouth to pretend it was talking? Or was it imitating her?

She took a step back, trying not to appear afraid. Trying to stay calm. She glanced back at the deaths then back at the demons as more frozen ghouls came to life, their eye sockets filling with flames. A strange sense of panic clung to her limbs, and more snow continued to fall.

Was this going to be another fight? If they were limited to their ghoul bodies, then all she had to do was strike them down. "I'm human."

**A strange human.**

The demon's mouth opened and closed again as it spoke. Snowflakes touched down and melted all over its bulbous head, sizzling and evaporating where it reached the blue flames of the demon's eyes.

**We seek your light. You have a gift.**

"My light?" asked Jenny. Other ghouls shook themselves free of the ice and stood with burning eyes. There could've been a hundred of them by now, standing behind the demon with blue eyes, gathering like an army rising out of the snow. "What do you want with my light?"

It seemed to be glaring at her, the blue flames growing larger and larger. Then its teeth clacked, its static voice flitting between her ears.

**Restitution.**

# CHAPTER FIFTEEN

# A WARM BODY

Restitution?" she whispered. She got the sense it wanted something from her.

**We require more bodies.**

The demon took another shaky step toward her, foot sliding on the frozen ground. Snow blew into its flames and evaporated, droplets running down the sides of its oversized ghoul head, glistening. It almost looked like a jack-o'-lantern, except instead of a pumpkin, it was made out of snow.

Jenny glanced at the fields' worth of frozen ghouls. "Well, you've got plenty to pick from. So how about you leave us alone?" She chewed on the inside of her lip, blinking snowflakes from her eyes.

The demon didn't waver.

**We require more.**

"What? How's that not enough?"

**We number in the billions.**

It cocked its head as if to size her up, the flames seemingly turning as it did so.

She shivered. She told herself it was due to the cold, but when the demon took another step, she stumbled back. Jenny hadn't meant to; she didn't want to appear weak or frightened, but she couldn't help it. She knew what the demon wanted. What they would want.

**Your body is so warm.**

Its mouth clacked open and shut.

**And the many behind you . . . So warm. They will suffer in this world without our flames.**

"Suffer?" she repeated, swallowing hard. "You're just going to possess us, aren't you?" *Shit. Shit. Shit.* Her mind raced, trying to figure out what to say or do. She couldn't open another passageway again. Not yet, at least. She'd have to fight them.

Could she even fight them?

The demon straightened its head.

**You cannot defeat us in battle. You cannot escape. There is nowhere to run. Submit, and your bodies will be of use. Your bodies will be relinquished when we are restored.**

"No!" shouted Jenny, throwing her hatchet as hard as she could in the freezing cold. *Savage Throw.*

It whistled through the snow and struck the demon on its bulbous head with a *thwack,* snapping its head back. The long, white arms flailed like the creature was trying to find its balance, but then, it slid on its heel and landed on the ice with a hard thud.

*Did that . . . get it?* Her lips stung from the cold, and she balled up her fists, willing her armor to grow back over her fingers and cover them. It didn't help much, but at least the wind wasn't directly hitting her skin. She only wished she could go back and fetch her helmet.

Flames still flickered from the ghoul's eyes, and there was no notification of having defeated a creature or of energy gained. She hadn't hurt it. The other demons, nearly two dozen of them, stepped forward in unison.

Their eyes burned in various shades. Two of them were red; they were stage one. She wasn't afraid of them in the least, but some were yellow and white—stage two and stage three respectively—and flames flickered all over their ghoul bodies like they were charging up for an attack.

Before they could make their move, the first demon's arm shot up in the air, fingers stretched out.

**Refrain from attack! We require her light.**

Jenny grimaced as the demon got to its feet, her hatchet's handle sticking out from between its burning eyes like a bizarre unicorn horn. With a flash of light, she summoned it back, wishing the ghoul body would just disintegrate from the blow.

There was an ugly gash on its head, cracks stretching away from the point of impact. But it was glowing with something . . . It was liquid. It looked like glowing blue liquid that flowed thickly inside the creature like gelatinous blood.

**I will retrieve her light.**

Its blue flames pulsed, growing larger and larger with every flicker, and Jenny couldn't help but remember the bright blue light emanating from the desecrated angel she'd fought nearly to the death. She thought back to the blue of Susan's armor, of Susan's hair. The blue of the sky on a sunny day. Then, the flames went out, as though the demon had been a strange candle and someone had blown it out.

The ghoul, now free, stumbled forward, shivering, its mouth wide open as it tried to stand. A scream formed at the base of its throat, but even as it straightened up, frost spread across its limbs, and the creature froze, the ugly crack no longer filled by blue light.

Before Jenny could respond—she wanted to hack the ghoul into tiny bits so that the demon couldn't get back inside—she saw the sparkling, hovering array of lights again. Shimmering like little blue stars, they rose over the frozen ghoul before shooting toward her.

She swung her hatchet. The edge sliced through the air, doing absolutely nothing to the sparkling lights that zipped past her weapon. For a second, she saw the brightness up close: a flash of blue dots, the ghost of an outline, like a blueprint of what almost appeared to be a person. The silhouette of a hand reached for her, and then it struck her in the face.

The force knocked her onto her back, and she could *feel* the demon. A wriggling, crawling sensation burned into her face, as though the light was climbing up her nose or burrowing into her pores or dissolving into her eyes.

*Wait, wait, wait!*

She wanted to shout, but she could only think the words. Her body wouldn't respond. Panic surged through her limbs, but she couldn't even curl a finger. No matter what she tried to move, all she got was a tingling feeling, like pins and needles when her foot would fall asleep. It spread through her chest and up into her brain.

A choked breath slipped out of her throat as her lungs relinquished control to the demon. And then, as though someone had plugged a cable in, a jolt of electricity shot through her. She swore it flashed between every wrinkle of her brain, and she could see *it*. She could see the demon.

*A demon!* It was humanoid with long arms, but instead of flesh, it was made of rippling blue flames that curled and billowed inward and upward. Burning wings spread from its back; this was a creature of fire.

*Get out*, she whispered silently. A tear slipped out of the corner of one eye, trailing down her face. Her body remained still on the ground, unmoving; she wasn't even blinking. She stared up at the clouds as snowflakes stuck to her eyelashes, as they landed on the fluid of her eyeballs. Snow tickled her nose and lips, and the coldness of the ground threatened to consume her.

Her eyes burned. Her lungs burned. She needed to blink. She needed to inhale. She needed to swallow the saliva pooling at the back of her throat. *I'm going to drown!* Her body was shutting down; did the demon want her to die? If it was possessing her, then shouldn't it be doing all these things?

*Blink! Swallow! Scream!*

Then, realization struck her: The demon wasn't in control.

It couldn't completely take over; all it had done was block her off. It couldn't operate her body.

**Surrender!**

Its silhouette emerged in her thoughts again, flames curling upward over its head. Its eyes were two bright dots of light, its face a mask of fury.

Jenny almost laughed. She wasn't sure where they were; it seemed like some strange space inside her head. A dreamscape? Her imagination?

She felt disconnected from her body. From the world. From the pain.

*I'm dying.* She could see that through her open eyes, could feel it through her aching limbs. Her body was dying. She was sick of dying.

**You are not human.**

The demon's voice burst with static, its form flickering. She could feel its rage, as though she'd done the demon dirty, tricked it somehow.

*I guess not*, thought Jenny, wanting to berate the demon further. *We're both going to die in here*. But then, she realized what had happened. Why the demon couldn't take complete control.

*I'm desecrated.*

Something screamed inside her. Cold wind sent an involuntary shudder up her spine, something neither she nor the demon could control. She'd felt this before. When she'd been trapped within her own flesh, confined to some corner of her mind while something else took control. While that something else surrendered to her darkest desires.

But this time, there was nothing. Nothing was in control. The demon couldn't take over, and she felt an odd sharpness, like a dagger cutting into her thoughts—it was cutting through the *demon's thoughts.* The demon was afraid!

If her body died while it was inside, it would die too, and a part of her thought this was her chance to defeat it, to take it with her. But she didn't want to die. She had to live. There was work to be done.

*Just concentrate. With thought. With intention.* The same way she'd used Severed Spirit on the pillars, the same way she'd cut through the fabric of the worlds—she concentrated and reached for the demon scrambling to seize control of her body. She hadn't decided whether she wanted to push it out—to force it out of her like a breath of foul air—when her mind made contact with the demon's, and sparks ignited. As lights flickered through her mind, Jenny saw into the creature's soul.

**No!**

The demon cried out, its blue flames rippling all around the thought space as its wings spread. But Jenny's arm twitched. Her toes curled inside her armor. She closed one eye and opened it again before doing the same with the other. After a small gasp, a tiny inhale, the pressure eased off her lungs, and she could breathe. Ever so slightly, but she could breathe. Warm air escaped her lips.

The other demons lurched closely, standing over her, waiting. Orange and yellow flames spilled out of their eyes, but they didn't speak. Could they speak?

**No, they cannot. Demons are not creatures who speak in words. Demons communicate through fluctuations in temperature, through presence. Demons don't even have a concept of language. No societies. No genders.**

These words weren't spoken. The demon wasn't speaking to her . . . No. She was *inside the demon's mind.* She was reading its thoughts as though it were an open book.

And she realized how the demon had gotten inside her: fear. It wanted her to be afraid. Her fear, her worries, her emotions had given the demon an opening to access her. All demon communication *was* that. Emotions. Temperature. Light.

Another scream. A pained scream—she was falling through the demon's mind. Blue flames and fear and *rage*. There was *so much rage* inside the demon. Another inhale. A shudder. She wasn't sure who was shuddering, but images flashed through her mind.

It was the demon's life.

It had been born a tiny dot of darkness, no bigger than a speck of dust, floating through emptiness for countless years, slowly growing larger, heavier, denser, soaking up the light and warmth around it until it folded into itself, until it compressed and compressed, vibrating with an intense desire to unfold, to express itself on the space around it, to know, to feel, to understand—it exploded in a burst of brilliant colors, a supernova. Thus, the demon hatched.

# CHAPTER SIXTEEN

# BURNING MEMORIES

Pinks and blues. Swirls of bright red and whites. Clouds of purples and greens scattered the demon's growing body far and wide in the darkness. For a long time—for centuries, millions of years, for so long that time was no longer consequential—it existed as a mass of dust and warmth.

But bit by bit, with each passing century, it began to converge, reconstituting itself, forming around twin cores of light. Two bright spheres gathered all that substance, all the clouds of dust and matter, and the silhouette of a body shimmered into shape. It was almost humanoid—or perhaps it preceded the human shape. Long and slender, with two limbs extending for legs and two more for arms. And once it finished its celestial metamorphosis, it descended from the heavens, falling out of the sky like a shooting star.

Jenny saw the demon world—this world—before the ice. It was a landscape of rocks with pools of lava and fires that burned like forests made of flame. A clear sky sprawled overhead; a sky filled with enormous stars—No. They weren't stars. They were incubating demons born in the sky, waiting to go supernova.

**THIS IS NOT FOR YOU TO SEE!**

The radio static voice of the demon crackled, trying to take over her body. It scratched through her mind, and the memories faded as the demon's burning blue-and-purple eyes rose from the darkness.

A burning-hot rage filled her chest. Jenny sucked in a deep breath, expanding her diaphragm completely—No, it wasn't her taking the breath. The demon was inhaling with her body. A burning feeling climbed up her throat and through her skull to alight on her face. Her vision flashed blue, burning, and she didn't need a mirror to know that fire was streaming out of her eyes just as it had done for the ghoul.

*Not again*, she swore, trying to reel in her mind, trying to root out the demon. But she could feel it digging, burrowing. Every time she tried to catch it, it slipped out of her grasp and struck deeper. It was clawing through her fears, trying to pry her open, forcing itself into every orifice of her thoughts. Visions of Susan flashed. Her smile. Her hair. Her corpse. Her glowing hand. Light.

The demon's static voice came at that, higher pitched than before.

**The light. Give me the light. Open the worlds again. My people cannot survive here. My people need warmth. My people demand salvation.**

*Yeah?* Jenny forced her body to take the next deep breath. In the split second of the demon's excitement at seeing the light, its stranglehold had relaxed. Jenny's eyes shut and opened. She squirmed on the ground, but it hadn't been enough. The demon still rooted through her life.

Her childhood memories blew through the mind space. The demon saw Jenny's desperation to leave home; it saw her mom. It felt her crying and sobbing as she was screamed at, as she was hit, as she was trying to hide under the bed—Jenny threw herself back into the demon's memories. She didn't need to relive any of her life, but if she could find something, *anything*, that would help her win control of her body, if she could distract it from opening the wounds of her own life, maybe she could—

Flames, orange and blue, erupted from her body. From her skin. From her armor. It was using Ignite, mixing her flames with its own.

Her eyes burned furiously, and any snow that drifted onto her melted away. Steam rose from the ground around her, enveloping Jenny as it hid the world away. She could no longer tell what was inside her head and what was in the world. Choking sounds filled her throat as she rolled over onto her stomach, wriggling and struggling, splashing in the water as she continued to burn.

A wind blew, clearing the view, and she looked up to see the crowd of deaths. The girl that Jenny had woken up moved toward Jenny, eyes wide, wanting to help.

"Stay back!" she gasped, but then, another voice—deeper and uglier—tore out of her throat.

**"Do not interfere!"**

Her body turned over again. Her head snapped toward the demons who'd been closing in, their ghoul bodies sauntering, arms swinging. Their eyes burned.

**"Do not interfere,"** rasped the voice from her throat again. **"We need this body. We need its light."**

The light! That's what it wanted more than anything. The demon's desire was the way out. That was its weakness.

They both pictured the light of the passageway, golden and bursting with colors, and how Jenny had opened it. She showed the demon the exact memory, the exact hurt she'd used to tear the worlds open before healing the wound. And that gave her just enough access to the demon's emotions to slip through.

Her body went rigid, back arching as she cried out. If it was a cry of triumph or the demon's cry of fear, she couldn't tell. But then, she was freefalling again through the demon's memories. Its own hurt. The desperate reason it wanted her light.

Battle spread all around her. Was this a survival challenge? Some other kind of fight? She couldn't tell, but she was sure it was grim.

Countless humanoid silhouettes made out of flame were present, the fires of their eyes rising like enormous flickering horns, their wings—magnificent and wide—feathery and burning, with little bits falling away to fizzle out. They had fearsome burning claws extending from their hands: the army of demons.

Angels swooped down from the sky, brilliant bursts of colorful lights and white wings flapping powerfully. In their hands were shining swords and glassy spears.

The collision was cataclysmic.

Burning claws melted through angels. Weapons made of light sliced demons in half. Bodies exploded. Fire and lightning and wind blew around every single one of them as the elements raged on as well.

Fierce gusts blew away weaker demons and angels. Rivers of water gushed through the air, and geysers of lava burst from the ground. Some demons flew into a group of angels and exploded, lighting up the sky in a show of color and light nearly as bright as the sun. And there was so much color—reds and oranges and blues. So much light, and they were so beautiful, Jenny swore the stars were battling.

But the memories were hazy; she was in the demon's body, looking through its memories with its own eyes.

It felt responsible for the massacre, for the dead on both sides of the war, demons and angels alike. It had been chosen to lead . . . Not *it*. A *he*. He identified with masculinity, something he'd adopted for himself after observing the angels. And this demon identified as Iblis, a name given to the demon by an angel called Sat'en.

Iblis had loved Sat'en.

A weighty feeling surfaced through these thoughts: longing, duty, responsibility, regret. Iblis had led the other demons in rebellion, following in the footsteps of the angel he loved. Fighting against an enemy they didn't have much hope in defeating, but a burning desire for change had fueled Iblis. They'd had no choice in the fight.

Through his eyes, Jenny saw the other demons floating in circles around Iblis, so that everywhere he turned, shimmering silhouettes with burning eyes looked back at him. They had chosen him as their leader.

The next memory shifted like smoke. Iblis's wings spread and flapped, the burning feathers generating heat and lift, and he looked down at the world as he flew through the sky. Volcanos dotted the land as far as she could see. Rivers of lava thrummed across the land like veins. And above shone the stars, each one burning brilliantly.

Iblis loved the stars; they were his birthplace; they were his children. But they reminded him of the angel he loved.

Jenny couldn't see that angel no matter how much she searched. She tried to root deeper through the demon's mind, but those memories were blocked away.

No, it was worse than that. Most of the memories of Sat'en had been forgotten.

Through Iblis's eyes, she saw the sky rip open—a deep gash between the stars, like a jagged wound, as though someone had taken a knife to a painting of the night sky—and from that horrible darkness, poured out the angels.

Tarnished angels plummeted from the wound. Unable to fly, their thin arms and legs flapped and kicked uselessly, their gaunt faces screaming as they dropped like stones. Some landed on the molten ground, breaking apart into burning bits upon impact. Some landed on demons, dragging them down, flames billowing behind them.

Flying gracefully between the tarnished angels were the natural angels, holding swords as brightly colored as their bodies.

The memories came distorted and quickly. At first, she was in Iblis's body, his burning claws raking a purple wretched angel. He tore a tarnished angel in half, guts and blood splattering on the rivers of lava. A spear made of green light flashed through his arm, but his burning body regenerated as quickly as the blow. The green angel didn't even get to respond; Iblis clawed its head off, and the angel disintegrated into vapor.

She couldn't tell who was winning. She saw angels sucking up demons, inhaling the glowing flames that seemed to comprise the demons' silhouetted forms. But she saw just as many angels struck down, cut into pieces or scorched to ashes. Iblis cut open desecrated angels, blood bursting in every direction. He flew through the battlefield like a bullet train, and corpses rained down—angels and demons alike—as the demons rose higher and higher, trying to get to the gaping wound from which the angels kept pouring from the darkness.

She could feel Iblis's determination. His desire for victory. For freedom. But a ghost of a face appeared, burning red eyes and an evil grin that was too wide. A large shadowy hand curled into an enormous fist and struck Iblis down from the sky.

A name popped into Iblis's mind, into Jenny's: Azra'il, the Angel of Death.

A shudder rippled through the mind scape—the enormous angel flapped four hideous batlike wings and rushed down. Azra'il's wide, muscular frame seemed to take up the entire sky, and as he closed in, reaching for Iblis with one hand, she saw the angel's face. The look of sheer glee as Azra'il's fingers closed around Iblis' throat—around Jenny's throat, as she was seeing through Iblis's eyes, feeling through Iblis's body.

A part of her wanted to feel happy watching the demon lose, but she felt his pain and anguish, and beyond the pain, a deep, cutting feeling of regret. The burning feeling of regret that she knew all too well.

Iblis the demon, chosen by his people, had done something horrible, something dreadful. Something that had cursed his entire people.

He had fallen in love. He had led his people into a war they could not win. He had—

There were gaps in Iblis's memories. Flashes of Azra'il's dark-gray face. She noted he was the only angel wearing cloth. It looked like a loincloth made from leather. A necklace of skulls bounced all over his broad gray chest as he punched Iblis repeatedly with fists the size of boulders. Snakes lunged from his head and snapped at Iblis's wings.

The demons had lost. Everything blurred. Jenny was falling, the dizzying sensation of tumbling from a great distance—No, the demon was falling, burning up in the air, losing its silhouette as it crashed into the desolate rock below. All around her, the other demons fell from the bursting stars, and the shadow above, the darkness, started sizzling away.

Snow began to fall. Gently at first, but with every passing second, the storm picked up, and a furious blizzard enveloped the world.

The flames of the demons rippled. Iblis's blue fires struggled as the ground froze, as the warmth and heat faded away. He and his people succumbed to the cold, their bodies slowing down to a standstill—and he/Jenny looked up to see Azra'il towering over it all, a cruel fist raised to the sky. The angel was draining all the heat from the world, and he was laughing, laughing so loudly that his laughter became thunder that rolled across the sky, fading only as Azra'il vanished in a flash of darkness.

Cold became the only memory, spreading like frost across a windshield. It was all Iblis felt. It was all he'd known. The coldness that sapped all his strength, his ability to maintain form. He and his demons drifted across the frozen world, moving gently with the wind, with no care for self, with no desire for self.

Without warmth, they had no *idea* of self, and nobody could tell him apart from the others—and he was grateful. The sense of responsibility dulled. His regret dulled. His broken heart faded away.

Centuries curled up and crumbled away; millennia passed by. How many oscillations around the material world? They lost track of all meaning, but the demons didn't die.

They couldn't die. Billions of demons languished in their world, stuck in place, all of them still and calm, comatose, like fish asleep in a frozen lake. With no thoughts to be shared, no emotions whatsoever, a quiet world where the only sounds were the muffled softness of snowflakes landing on piling snow.

But burning discreetly, hidden away, a familiar desire to break free. For revenge. For love. A nurtured, secret want.

Iblis's buried wants: To live his life. To escape from this frozen, cold world. To rise up to the heavens and tear the angels down from the sky. Something he kept hidden away, lamenting and lost, drifting through the snow and blinking away centuries of sleep, until one day, the snow parted.

The wind curved, and *temperature* rippled through the world. A little opening appeared in the air, and golden light bloomed. Colors and heat spread across the world, chasing the wind, fading, but it was enough.

Iblis shifted from the snow. His fellow demons began to move again, their particles, their sparkling essences growing excited. They rushed over to the parting in the air, sensing the warmth of the other worlds, a warmth they had not felt in so long that it stung, it burned.

He wished so desperately to slip through this gap and leave this frozen hurt, but then, a *human* tumbled out of the light. A girl with swishing tentacles and a partial red exoskeleton and the blank white eyes of the tarnished ones.

# CHAPTER SEVENTEEN

# BURNING THROUGH HER THOUGHTS

It took Jenny a second to recognize she was watching *herself* emerge into the world. She'd nearly gotten lost in Iblis's memories; his astonishment at seeing someone of material form became her astonishment as well. Ages spent frozen, without feeling, without change, and suddenly, here was a human with tentacles retracting into her back and an exoskeleton bubbling back inside her.

The heat of it. The heat emanating off her body, off the rippling light behind her. Warmth radiated, awakening the demons, bringing them back to life, inviting them to the source. More and more bodies tumbled out of the light to collapse on the snow, each new one burning with life.

She felt Iblis's surprise as the ghouls froze in place, then at the intense heat radiating off the deaths. He recognized them. There were flashes of memories, of people trapped in pillars of salt, screaming and crying—of the ghouls marching across a desolate land. Jenny slipped deeper into the demon's psyche almost by accident as more memories tumbled out—

Fear shook the mind scape so violently that Jenny lost her grip. Her hold on the demon's mind loosened, and Iblis tore to the surface in this strange mental space they shared. The demon was shocked. Furious. Ashamed.

**You are not human.**

His static echoed around her as though countless echoes were clashing inside a cave.

**But you are not properly desecrated! Your mind is still intact. What are you? How can this be?**

*I DON'T KNOW,* Jenny screamed back, and all the horrible, twisted feelings surfaced all at once. The mind scape vibrated violently, shattering like a mirror, ugly cracks running along every edge of this invisible space. *But get the fuck out of my body if you want to talk.*

The demon didn't respond right away. It floated aimlessly inside her, watching. Observing.

**I cannot fail my people again.**

And with that, it struck again.

Radio static pierced through her anger, forced her from the demon's memoirs and back into her own. Iblis burrowed inside, and Jenny's body shook. Fire streamed from her eyes. Cold air stung the back of her throat.

Internally, she was trying to kick, trying to struggle and resist, but her body would not respond. Iblis was in control, trying to take control, and her body hunched over. Warmth spread through her limbs. Her fingers twitched.

The demon had tricked her. He'd wanted her to see all those things, just as Eve had once shown her so many things—it had all been a distraction to rile up her emotions, to make her understand the demon's plight.

But she could do the same.

*You wanna see hurt? You think you're the only one who knows what it feels like to get away from something so desperately?* Spittle dribbled down her chin as her body convulsed. *Then here!*

Her memories bubbled to the forefront of her mind. Visions of Yeshua, how Jenny had found him on the cross, begging for death. She brought up the ghouls, watching them bite and chew through Yeshua and the deaths.

She showed the demon what it was like to *have* a body. To hunger, to feel disgust, to *bleed*. To never feel comfortable even just having a body. The awkwardness of it all—to love someone, or think you love someone. To feel alone and miserable. To never having clothes that fit perfectly. To questioning how you look everywhere you go. To questioning how everyone looks at you, and how silly it all feels because in the grand scheme of things, who gives a fuck?

She showed Iblis her life in high school, rifling through classes and homework and crushes. Gaming late into the night with Susan. Wanting to tell her how she felt. Wanting to say so many things that she never could. Crying. Sobbing. Feeling empty on the train. Hiding grades and things from her mother. Dealing with her expanding family. It felt so stupid that she'd cried over these things, but they'd hurt. They were *her* hurt. And she wanted the demon to see, even as the memories shifted into the survival challenge, even as nightmares tried to eat her.

She showed the demon all the tarnished and wretched angels she'd fought. She showed the demon what she'd become. *Severed Spirit.* How she'd fought and eaten angels. How angry she felt. Then she showed Iblis the thing she feared the most: what she'd done to Susan. Susan's final moment. How the light that the demons wanted so badly belonged to Susan.

How she'd killed Susan.

*I HATE THEM TOO!* she screamed silently from the imprisonment of her worst memories. She wasn't even sure *what* she hated. Just *them.* The idea of them. The things that had taken everything from her, that had never really let her have anything. Even if that was her fault. There was something beyond the world that had always kept the world miserable; she was sure of it. And she was sure it had to do with the angels and demons and deaths and all these stupid, horrible things that kept happening.

Her memories went on: from Susan's lifeless corpse on the cafeteria floor to the sunlight streaming in through broken windows, to the moment Jenny's stomach rippled and stretched and that glowing *thing* squeezed out of her and grew into a copy of her—and feeling that, feeling the pain of giving birth and feeling the pain and regret and anguish of what she'd done to Susan and watching Eve take shape—*that* made the demon finally relent.

Everything went quiet inside Jenny's head, like a storm ending abruptly. The winds stopped. The battering chaos eased. The assault on her body faded away as Iblis retreated.

Her body convulsed. Her back arched. And then, with a scream she wasn't sure if she was screaming inside her head or out loud, blue fire rose from her body, spilling out of her face, from her eyes and nose and lips, billowing and bubbling as though something inside of her was boiling away.

It took a while for the steam to clear up. Cold air enveloped her again, and the water turned to ice beneath her. A cough racked her lungs, and she spit bloody phlegm before wiping the hair out of her face. She'd been sweating profusely, and now, all that sweat was freezing. The cold sank deep into her bones with a horrible ache.

A shimmering form hovered in front of her as she shivered. Tears had frozen on her cheeks; she couldn't tell who'd cried them. Iblis shrank, the humanoid form fading away until all that remained was a small group of sparkling blue lights.

**I apologize.**

Jenny swallowed hard, forcing out a breath that clouded away from her lips. Her fingers curled in the snow. "You're only sorry 'cause you didn't get what you wanted."

The sparkles floated away, back to the ghoul body lying in the snow with an ugly crack in its skull. The lights shot down into its face, sinking beneath the frost, and a moment later, the blue flames roared back to life in its eye sockets. The body stood, its mouth opening and shutting, and that gooey blue glow seeped out from the cracks once more.

**I am apologizing for my rash actions.**

"Like I said, you're only saying that 'cause you *failed*. You couldn't take control, and now you need me. You need *this*." She held up her hand and used a little bit of Valescent Light.

Immediately, the dizzying sensation of exhaustion struck her, but she clenched her chattering teeth and shook the light away, not wanting to show any weakness in front of the demons. What would happen if she passed out and couldn't consciously fight the possession? Would they just wait till she collapsed from the cold and take over? What if she fell asleep?

But the burning blue eyes brightened, and the flames grew larger. The other demons clacked their jaws and stepped closer, and Iblis turned to face them. She couldn't see or hear anything, but she felt waves of warmth fluttering around the air; little pockets of warmth that faded into the freezing wind.

Then Iblis turned back to Jenny, lowering his bulbous head, the two blue flames curling over it.

**Very well. I felt that you had many questions. That you are lost in this grand drama. May I explain what you glimpsed? May I explain my actions? And may I offer a suggestion on how we can proceed?**

Jenny couldn't stop shivering. Her eyes watered, and she blinked several times to keep from crying, to keep her eyes from freezing. She used a small burst of *Ignite*, letting the flames flicker down her arms and legs, then glanced back at the deaths. Some of them had collapsed. Others stared helplessly. And she decided she didn't care what the demons had to say just yet.

She turned her back on them.

It was a risky move, but she knew they wouldn't attack her. She'd felt Iblis's desperation, and they'd played their one card: they'd tried to control her and failed. Would they go after the deaths? They might, but the deaths didn't have the ability they wanted. Deaths couldn't open passageways between worlds. They needed her, and only her.

Maybe she could use this to her advantage. She finally had the upper hand; she could finally get some answers. And maybe, she could even help . . .

*Help them? WHY? They wanted to possess me! Why would I ever help them?*

*It's what Susan would do. It's the right thing. They were just desperate, and maybe we need them on our side. We don't know what's even going on.*

*Susan's not here. She's dead.*

*YOU killed her.*

*I fucking know!*

She approached the trembling deaths, trying to put on a brave smile, trying to assure them everything would be okay. Then she focused on the system.

### A Pile of Wood will cost 100 Energy.
### Sufficient Energy.

Jenny squatted in front of the deaths, wary of the demons staring at her. Were they angry? Insulted? She didn't care. They were the ones who'd attacked her when they could've talked this out from the get-go.

Holding her hand out over the snow, she felt that familiar shudder as the system responded.

Golden light swirled around her fingers and arm. The deaths stared with intense curiosity, and she inhaled deeply as the light slipped gently off her palm and onto the ground, glowing brighter and brighter as it turned solid.

After a moment, a pile of crudely stacked wood lay on top of the snow, just as she'd pictured it. It was nearly identically to the firewood she'd once chopped and gathered in front of her stepdad's cabin. She made two more piles, spreading them out so the deaths would have enough space, and with three uses of Ignite, lit them up. Three bonfires on a frozen world flickered with orange warmth as the grateful deaths gathered around them, murmuring their appreciation and gratitude toward Jenny.

She wondered if the demons longed to be near the flames as well. Deciding to keep with the camping vibe, she created several large logs. She'd always liked sitting on fallen trees; she didn't know why. Something about being in the woods, away from the bustle of civilization.

Jenny made several logs and dragged them into place around the fires. This way, the deaths could rest and wouldn't have to sit on the frozen ground. Susan had once told her that when making shelters for the alley cats behind her apartment building, they had to make sure the small structures were raised. If they were on the ground, all the body heat of the cat would seep into the cold ground, and they would never be able to get warm.

Once that was prepared, she conjured a fire for herself. Then another log. Then, finally, she turned to face the demons, sitting down to rest her legs. *Breathe. Inhale and exhale. Relax your body and mind.*

She couldn't handle any of this—deal with any of this—if she responded out of fear, out of desperation. She was worried about Yeshua, terrified of having to look after the deaths and keep them safe from the demons. Terrified still of losing control of her body. She didn't want anything controlling her like that ever again.

But if she didn't relax, she wouldn't be able to figure out what to do. The demon had inadvertently taught her that: fear made an opening; fear allowed them to enter.

She didn't know what to do. But that was okay. Her plan had been to rest, anyway. To gather her strength and open the passageway back to the world of the dead so she could retrieve Yeshua. That plan hadn't changed.

But maybe . . . maybe the demons could help her in return. Iblis had recognized something before he pulled away; she'd felt *recognition*. It had been when she was pregnant, when she'd given birth. That had to be the key to this. Did they know Eve?

No. It was deeper than that. They knew *betrayal.* That angel named Sat'en . . . Why was that so familiar? Was that . . . Satan?

And why was there such a deep sense of betrayal? A wound so deep that Iblis had rid himself of those memories?

Love. There'd been such an intense love—but what did all that mean? What did it add up to?

Once the tension in her body eased and her lungs stopped feeling like someone else's and the heat radiating from the campfire had soothed her stinging nose and brought sensation back to her face, Iblis approached her.

He could read her thoughts; she knew that. It wasn't an exact read, but he knew that she would be willing to talk now. And she knew that the demon knew she would help, but that she had questions.

She straightened her shoulders, trying to appear confident now that she had a fire going, now that she'd bested the demon in maintaining control of her body. "Go on, then. Tell me why I should help you."

**I believe we are on the same side of this war.**

# CHAPTER EIGHTEEN

# WHAT THE DEMON HAS TO SAY

**Long ago, everything—matter and nonmatter, darkness and light—existed in chaos. A mass of tangled fabrics, nothing recognizable, nothing distinct. A precursor to energy.**

Jenny sat and listened as Iblis spoke, clacking the ghoul's jaws, the crack on his head glistening with blue light. The flames rose up like horns, and it was weird that he was just standing there. It made her feel self-conscious, but she was thrilled to finally have some answers to all this. To existence.

He explained where the demons had come from. At the beginning, there was only one world, and the demons were the embodiment of the first substance, the source of energy. And from that energy came light. Light was the second substance. The third substance was matter, coming into existence as energy was spent, as energy cooled.

Over billions of years, these substances separated, each one acquiring different needs, different wants, existing at different levels of reality. And at the start, the demons ruled, taking on a parental role in the expansion of the worlds. Their leader was a primordial being without name, an entity that drew itself across every world, guiding and shaping, seeking to understand—the entity that Jenny had come to know as Eve.

It . . . *She* had birthed the stars and all the planets, and she'd so desperately wanted to be material. There was a holy trinity, a balance to it: Energy, Light, Matter. Jenny had a flash of the three-headed figure, shining so brightly, shifting, always shifting.

Iblis's static voice dropped low as he took a break from his storytelling.

**In your languages, we called her "Parent." But you might translate it more accurately as "Mother."**

"And I finally gave her what she wanted . . ." whispered Jenny with a shudder. She'd given birth to their mother. Did that make her Iblis's grandmother? But what did Eve want? "So, was she the first demon?"

**She was the first everything. But she did not communicate with her children. She abandoned us for a different world, as we could not give her what she wanted.**

That other world . . . Was that where Eve had taken Jenny? With the pool of water and the forest and the stars? She remembered the stars, shining so brightly in the night sky, much larger than any star she'd ever seen in any night sky. Had Eve constructed it to be like that? Or was that Eve watching over her children?

Iblis continued with his explanation. Neither he nor the other demons knew what Eve wanted, so he spoke of the angels.

**Angels were beings of light. They were the second beings to come into existence, life pouring from the glow of energy. But they were limited in their capacities for growth—they hungered for growth in the same way Eve had. Wanting to be more, wanting more substance. And no matter how fast light may shoot across the heavens, it could never catch up with its own desires. But one angel discovered that it *could* grow. It *could* change. It could be more than itself by feeding on other angels.**

Jenny shuddered, staring into her little campfire as the possessed ghoul stood on the other side. Its jaws kept clacking. The other ghouls stood a distance away, but the snowfall got heavier, and most of them faded into the blanketing softness, the glow of their eyes blurring.

Iblis maneuvered its body to sit down by the fire, its legs crossed. Jenny had the sense it'd picked up on this sitting position from rooting through her memories, and the ghoul—with its oversized head and lanky white limbs—looked rather odd in a seated position. She'd gotten too used to them desperately trying to rip her to shreds.

The blue flames in the ghoul's eyes flickered, and Iblis continued.

That angel declared himself ruler of all angels, the master of everything. It used its tremendous strength to bend the other angels to its will. It expanded its power, taking over the world of light. And as it fed, as it learned of even more worlds beyond the world of light and the demon's world, the world of flames, the first angel's hunger only grew. It discovered the most important world, the largest of all: the material world. And subsequently, the world of death and the world of soul.

On the material world, something was taking shape. None of existence knew how or why, but something new emerged from the third substance. From matter came matter that inherently had energy and light.

Iblis lifted the ghoul head to look right at Jenny.

From matter came you. The humans. And the angel who could not exist in material form watched with increasing envy—seething jealousy—as you conquered your world. As your people expanded and grew from the dirt. As your people could *create*. As your people experienced all the pleasures and hurt this angel wanted for itself. It abhorred the thought that it itself had been created, and it was consumed by its envy of whatever had created your kind, and how your kind itself could create in turn.

The angel even adopted your ways, declaring that angels would now distinguish between male and female forms. The males would adopt names ending with 'il, and the females would adopt names ending with 'el. This way, the angels could be closer to their ultimate desire: to be material.

But this angel did not accept limitations on himself. He wouldn't just take a male identity and a male name. He would be titled. He would be *Him*. He called himself Adonai, Master of All Creation. And he convinced the angels that he had created them—and who could deny him when he had such power? Through his messengers to the material world, he convinced humans that they and all living things and everything else in existence had been created by Him. He crowned himself as master of all creation.

Iblis's flames seemed to diminish. A cold wind blew through the fire in front of Jenny, and a chill went down her spine. How many times had she heard sermons, preachers, her mother going on and on about the one who'd created them, the one who'd died for their sins, the all-powerful, the all-loving—that it was through Him that everyone would be saved.

Iblis continued.

**And still, Adonai was jealous of the beings he'd now claimed ownership of. For he was not yet whole by his definition of whole. He could not be happy with what he'd worked so hard to achieve, and he found it even more frustrating that those who could create, those of the material world, were mortal.**

**So, he set about with his grand plan. Drawing around him five angels of the highest order—beneath him, of course, but far more powerful than any other angel—he taught them his secrets. Enlisted them into his cause.**

**He wishes to have true dominion over all of existence. He wishes to conquer the material world. He wishes to *BE* the material world.**

**And he found his entry point: a strange crack between the worlds, a rift, something so ancient that he only found it more offensive—what you call the survival challenge.**

**It began with the birth of the material world. No living being understands why, but evolution is inherent to that world. Change. Growth. The strong and capable overtaking the weak and vulnerable—an idea that Adonai was obsessed with. But he also recognized that some other force was at play, something beyond his grasp of existence. It filled him with want. With rage.**

**So, he infiltrated the survival challenge, recognizing that it took place in the space between worlds, enabling him to intercede with his angels. An invasion of the material world.**

"You mean the Veil?" whispered Jenny before exhaling deeply. She could still picture that pale, pasty, gross world the high school had gone into. The strange emptiness that had stared back at her when she looked out the window. The sense of deep gloom. The snow around them now was white and pristine, and even with the possessed ghouls standing like ghostly figures on a haunted night, this world wasn't anywhere as unsettling as the blank emptiness of the Veil.

**The Veil. It exists between the worlds. Nobody knows why the survival challenges take place there. Perhaps it's due to the nature of material life, being both matter and spirit, but Adonai**

and his angels infiltrated it using a power he had to physically cross between worlds, something unlike anything anyone across the worlds has ever seen before.

The way Iblis said that made Jenny shiver. She could almost hear the underlying *until now*. But she wanted to remind him again it wasn't even her power. It was Susan's. Or was it a composite of both?

**But Adonai's power wasn't perfected.**

The ghoul body looked up at the sky, and snow fell into its glowing blue crack, melting down its cheek and giving it the odd impression that it was crying.

**His power converted light into matter by force, thus creating the tarnished creatures you have come across. Their minds reject their transformed bodies.**

The horrible darkness. The empty eyes. The desperate hunger that promised if you just ate enough, if you got enough life into your belly, maybe you could be whole too. Jenny remembered that all too well, digging her fingers into her palms and trying to suppress the ugly hunger roiling inside her. Her tentacles remembered. Her exoskeleton remembered. The taste of blood, wet and hot on her lips. The delicious, satiating warmth.

"But what's different about what I can do?" asked Jenny, though she was already starting to suspect.

**You can open passageways between the worlds that do not trigger transformation. They do not tarnish. But that also means that any angel moving through your passage would lose form in the material world.**

*What?* Jenny blinked. "So they'd have form in their own world and this world, but not in mine?"

**Yes. In the outer worlds, the six worlds beyond the material world, energy and light are defining factors of existence. Matter is secondary.**

"But what am I sitting on, then? Isn't this ground? How does that make sense? How can I be here?"

Iblis didn't respond right away. She heard the deaths stirring, and another wind howled across the land. The snow felt the same as the snow back home. The ground felt the same as ground. So what did it mean to be part of different worlds?

Finally, Iblis spoke.

**For you, it is of no consequence. As a human, you are both matter and nonmatter. Solid energy is indistinguishable from matter but isn't truly matter—**

"Oh," whispered Jenny, suddenly understanding what Yeshua had meant. The food they created with the system didn't have *life* in it. It would never satiate the hunger she had. Sure, they could create all the meat or vegetables or whatever they wanted, but it would never come from a living thing. And as Iblis explained more, about how matter was energy in a different stage of being, Jenny shut her eyes and finally understood what all this was about.

"So you're telling me there's a crazy-ass war across all these worlds because God is jealous of us?"

**And he set about to bringing all the worlds under his command. We do not know all the details of his grand plan, but as you can see from the world of demons, he means to assert dominion and control over all creation. And they came for our world first. For millennia, my people and the angels went to war. We fought not only for our sake but to maintain balance between the worlds.**

Memories—Iblis's memories—flashed through Jenny's head. "So where does Eve play into all this?"

**That story, I'm afraid, is forgotten to us. She is as ancient as Adonai, and the role she plays, we do not know.**

"I gave birth to her. That's what Adonai wants too, right?"

**Verily. And we cannot allow that to happen. But now that you are here, we have another chance to win this war. The war they are so sure they've already decided. They call it *destiny*.**

"Okay," said Jenny, deep in thought, trying to make sense of all this. "So where do I come in? What will you do with these passageways?"

Iblis's mouth clacked.

**Us demons, before the Great Freezing, were able to project ourselves into the material world.**

"To possess people?" she asked accusingly. Was that where all the horrible stories came from?

**To disturb the angels' plot to shape humanity's ascension to their will. To guide. To redirect. But that was all we could do—and that was all the angels could do too. Project themselves into the material world.**
**The angels, however, under Adonai's guidance, mastered physical mobility between the six worlds. And that was how we came to war. But we were at a disadvantage. While light can travel between worlds, us demons required a vessel to do so. To be physically present. Our projected selves were powerless, and once humanity began to reject us, once the angels led them astray and they lost their faith in the world around them—we were doomed.**
**We lost the war.**
**We were frozen.**

Jenny sat quietly for a long moment, thinking. Thinking. As the fire crackled. As Iblis stared at her. There were other questions she had—about Adonai. About the greedy angels. About how human history had been shaped. And about the angel called Sat'en that she'd seen in Iblis's memories, but even she knew not to go there. She got the sense that Sat'en to Iblis was what Susan was to her. Something heartbreaking.

She couldn't understand Adonai's thinking. Why did he want so much power? What was he after?

And there was something else in Iblis's explanations that was bugging her. She'd thought Adonai and the angels were at fault for the survival challenge that had ripped her school out of New York, but Iblis seemed to imply it was already a thing long before the angels got involved. So what did *that* mean?

"Earlier, you said you would help me find Yeshua. How?"

**I was within your memories. I know your limitations. But if I should possess you and you use my energy—my essence—to fuel**

your light, then perhaps we can open a passageway sooner rather than later.

Jenny's teeth clenched. She curled her nose. "I don't want you to possess me."

**I will not seize control. I will not overreach your autonomy. You will remain in charge.**

"So, you want to be inside my head and work together?" She'd heard that before.

**Yes.**

"And you're asking for consent this time?"

**Yes. I believe it will be mutually beneficial.**

"And what will you get out of this?" She swallowed, staring hard at the unmoving ghoul. It looked like something out of an animated movie—the bulbous head, the burning blue eyes, the gentle snowfall around it.

**We ask that you help us in return. In the war against destiny.**

# CHAPTER NINETEEN

# POSSESSION

And what about the rest of you guys?" asked Jenny. She was still apprehensive about letting the demon back into her mind, but then, as she looked at the silhouettes of the possessed ghouls, an idea struck her.

If the demons could possess ghouls . . . and they needed bodies to move between worlds . . . and there were more ghouls in the world of the dead . . . maybe she could bring a lot more ghouls back with her. There was a deal to be made, some kind of cooperation that might finally put Jenny ahead of the chaos for once.

She blurted out her next thought before Iblis could respond. "I want more," she said. "You're not just helping me save Yeshua. I want to find someone else too and help her if I can." Her heart raced, thumping inside her chest as she realized what she was doing. What if the demon said no?

But why would the demon say no? Jenny held *the* card the demons needed. And they couldn't possess her. If there was ever a time to barter, if there was ever a time to stand up for herself and fight for what she wanted, to fight for her own needs, it was now.

Iblis cocked his head, the flames flickering up its side.

**What do you want?**

"You told me about the worlds before. And Yeshua told me about how deaths are only *one* part of us humans. That humans are three parts. You called it energy, light, and matter." She swallowed, trying to put everything together. It all sounded like the Holy Trinity. "I guess that translates to our living bodies, right? Our deaths and our souls being the other parts?"

**Yes.**

She leaned forward. Fire crackled as she stared intently at the demon. "Then I want you to help me find Susan's soul. You'll help me save Yeshua. And then, you'll help me find Susan. I need to save her too. I need—" She stumbled.

She knew the demon knew what she'd done. The horrible thing she'd done.

When Iblis didn't respond, Jenny licked her lips, ignoring the biting wind. She had her idea too, something that would bolster the demon's numbers if they all worked together. But again—that was also up to her, wasn't it? She had to drag all those bodies through the Valescent Light to bring them between worlds.

"If you help me, I promise to help your people get as many bodies as they need." Just saying that out loud gave her a strange chill. It was something out of a horror story. A nightmare. And even though the ghouls seemed to be mindless, she felt bad. She was signing over their bodies to the demons.

*That's what happens in a war.*

**Very well. The souls you speak of are indeed the light of humankind. And we believe they are a vital part of Adonai's plans; seeking that out will be mutually beneficial.**

"And one more thing," she added, feeling bolder now. "I want to stay in control."

For a long moment, there was nothing but the stillness of the snow and the crackling flames and Iblis staring back at her.

**We accept your conditions.**

"That's that, then," she whispered. *I am trusting someone else.*
*Can you trust them?*
*I don't have a choice!*
*You can wait.*
*Then what? Go back to the world of death alone? Leave the other deaths here to the demons? Isn't it better to make an ally?*

Her thoughts spiraled in several directions. Would this be like what had happened with Eve? But she hadn't really had much of a choice that time. And Iblis couldn't quite lie to her. She'd seen inside Iblis's head too. And Iblis had sat down and finally explained things to her.

She decided she trusted the demon. And she had to, didn't she? To let him into her body. If she was afraid, if she was mistrusting, there would be too many cracks, too many openings, and she'd lose control. There was a thin line between control and loss that she had to navigate. *And this will work*, she told herself. This was going to work.

**I must warn you, human. Possession can be very taxing on the vessel. Especially vessels with developed minds.**

"Are you kidding me?" said Jenny. She almost burst out laughing. "So, you were just going to take over my body, use me to open the passageway, and then burn me up?"

**No. We would have released you upon fulfilling our needs. Prolonged exposure is what leads to deterioration.**

She wasn't sure if she should feel better about that or not. Was this really the best way to do it? Should she just rest and do it herself?

As if reading her mind, Iblis spoke up again.

**You will have our support in fighting the blooded ghouls. We will protect you against their hoard as you assist Yeshua.**

She inhaled deeply, shutting her eyes and standing from the log she'd been using as a seat. "Alright," she said, making up her mind. If Iblis tried to take complete control, she'd vanquish him again.

Jenny even wondered what would happen if she used Severed Spirit while the demon was trying to possess her. She took another deep breath, too many horrible thoughts spinning through her head as she braced herself to allow another being to enter her mind again. "Let's do it."

She swept her hair out of her way and straightened her shoulders. This time, she was prepared, she told herself. This time, it was her decision. *I will stay in control.*

The blue flames went out in the demon's eyes, and the ghoul awoke. It was still seated. Its mouth opened as it cried out—a choked, pained cry that made Jenny wince. Was it in terrible pain? Did it hurt to lose its autonomy? But as it tried to get up, as it tried to clamber to its feet, reaching for Jenny, ice spread from its fingertips across its arm.

In a moment, the ghoul was frozen, its limbs awkwardly in the air, ice glistening all over its body, shining brightly in the flickering glow from her campfire.

Above its frozen body hovered a sparkling blue light. All of a sudden, the light flashed toward her, and Jenny sucked in another deep breath as it shimmered at the tip of her nose. Then, like water splashing her face, she felt the demon, felt Iblis, enter her body again.

She didn't struggle, but her core tensed like she was bracing for a punch to the gut. She forced herself to unclench her fists, trying to be at ease, trying to focus on the warmth from her crackling campfire, trying to ignore the sensation of a foreign mind pushing against her own.

A different kind of heat spread into her bones. Thoughts that weren't her own swished around in her head, and she figured this wasn't that different from having the guidance system or Eve. At least there wasn't a headache this time. It wasn't an assault. She could feel Iblis's presence, but it was more like a faint tickle.

Then Iblis's voice came from inside.

**Allow me to show you something. As you have shown me your hurt, allow me to show you mine; then perhaps we can reach a greater understanding of one another.**

*What? I . . .*

But Iblis's memories flipped open before she could say anything. They were fragmented, disjointed, like watching someone else's dreams. These were the remnants of the memories Iblis had forgotten. The memories of Sat'en.

She saw an angel made of pink-and-purple light. This angel had once taken on a male identity and was called Sat'il. He had beautiful wings of pink-and-white feathers, and his glowing hands were on Jenny's face. No. Not Jenny's—it was Iblis's face. These were the demon's memories.

**Not every angel wanted to fight for Adonai. One angel rejected Adonai's decree, and many followed their lead. They rejected Adonai, abandoned their name, and became Sat'en, they who lead rebellion against injustice.**
**They gathered the other likeminded angels, connected with the demons—with me—and war grew to a scale that shattered many worlds.**

Jenny's chest tightened. Her breathing quickened. And with each quick breath, she felt the pain like a knife lodged between her ribs. Iblis had loved Sat'en, but he had never been sure if Sat'en had loved him back. But for Sat'en, Iblis had led the demons to battle over and over.

The memories blurred. There were some flickers of Iblis pressing his inanimate self against Sat'en's light. There were moments where their wings touched, and warmth—such warmth—would flow through Iblis. It was hotter than any supernova. More brilliant that any galaxy. But these memories were disjointed and incomplete. These memories were lost. And then, there was anguish. Heartbreak. A ripple in the fabric between worlds.

She saw Sat'en sinking into the darkness, as though the angel had been trapped by quicksand, wings beating furiously, struggling to get out. And had the angel been rested, had they not been battered and bruised by the towering figures standing over them, Sat'en might have escaped.

Iblis threw himself into Sat'en's body, trying to give his beloved the strength they needed, and now, Jenny was also inside Sat'en. Another mind. A grand, unfathomably scaled mind full of memories and dreams and—New chunks of memory hurtled through Jenny. And this part, she was familiar with. This part, she understood.

The wings tore away, disintegrating into nothing. Skin stretched over the angel's light as bones and muscles took shape. Veins and arteries snapped into place, tangling and expanding, and the pain . . . the sheer hunger. The uncontrollable appetite that made her want to rip out of her stomach and never feel hunger again—

Sat'en emerged in a dark world, clawing at their own face, ripping off their own skin, pulling on dark hair. This new mind was tearing itself apart, shredding, pulling—they couldn't stand it.

And Iblis, desperate to take over, desperate to stop the self-harm, flailed, tossed around the newly tattered mind like a rowboat in a storm. And other angels, other tarnished beings, their teeth glistening with blood and want, leaped onto Sat'en as their eyes flickered with blue flames that kept going out. Iblis couldn't take over Sat'en. And Sat'en's teeth sank into flesh, and an overwhelming joy ignited in their belly.

But it wasn't enough. It would never be enough—

Iblis remained inside Sat'en for a long time. So long that the memories blurred. But Jenny watched Sat'en grow. They became wretched, covered in pink-and-purple exoskeleton, continuing to feed their insatiable hunger.

There were humans too, and Jenny realized the world was Earth—a prehistoric Earth, with early humans attacking with spears and rudimentary tools. Some even started to pray, designing religions that depicted the tarnished angels. Some begged. Most were eaten, villages razed to the ground, populations wiped off the face of the planet.

And still, it wasn't enough. Sat'en buried themselves into the Earth as Iblis watched, a cocoon of glowing pink light, until eventually, a desecrated

Sat'en hatched. Pink beams of light radiated from their enormous body, blue-and-purple bubbles of energy bringing pyramids down to rubble. And as Sat'en hunted, the memory faded away. Iblis didn't know when he left his love. Perhaps Sat'en died. Perhaps Sat'en's body remained in the mortal world somewhere.

But there were no memories of Sat'en left, and Jenny straightened up, returning to the present, blue flames now spilling from her eyes.

She blinked several times, even waving her hands in front of them. Energy flared up inside her, more flames spreading across her armor, and she clenched everything, shutting her eyes as her body adjusted. A notification appeared.

### Desecrated Human (Vessel)

Heat pumped through her blood. Gushed into her muscles. She clenched her teeth tight to keep from crying out as Iblis spread across more of her—and everything seemed to expand, like she was growing, inflating, like a car tire being pumped with air. It was oddly familiar, like the first time she'd applied a bunch of stat points too quickly, which prompted her to pull up her stats.

**Jenny Huang**
**Desecrated Human (Vessel)**
**Level: N/A**
**Age: N/A**
**Stats:**
**Power: 50 (+200)**
**Durability: 35 (+200)**
**Stamina: 55 (+200)**
**Agility: 50 (+200)**
**Stat Points Available: 2**
**Energy Available: 3232**

Jenny felt as though she could shatter the world with one blow. Trembling with raw power, she looked up at the falling snow, at the stretch of white clouds.

*+200 to each stat?* That was mind-blowingly powerful.

**Direct possession lends the vessel my power. But it comes at a cost. Your body will burn if we maintain this for too long.**

"Got it," whispered Jenny, wishing there was some way she could harness this, wishing she could keep this. Maybe she could make something with the system which would allow her to continue? Like a stamina potion or—

**There is nothing. This is overheating your spiritual being and will consume your material form. A potion might prolong it, but it cannot sustain you long-term. We should not waste time.**

A memory was pushed to the forefront of her mind. She could feel Iblis making the suggestion as the demon showed her the light, the glowing hands, Severed Spirit, and the hurt she needed to open a passageway, and she got the sense that Iblis was asking her to use his hurt too so she wouldn't have to shoulder the burden alone.

She faced the deaths, the crowd staring at her from the comfort of the logs and campfires she'd made for them.

"Stay here," she told them. "I will return with Yeshua."

Then, in another voice—a deeply layered voice that startled her—she spoke to the demons.

**"Do not harm the deaths. Vessels, to me. We take our first step toward salvation. And this time, we will prevail."**

But it wasn't exactly with words. She wasn't even sure what sounds were coming out of her mouth, or if this was just how her brain translated what Iblis was communicating to the other demons, who bowed their ghoul heads, flames streaming upward from their eyes. The possessed ghouls stood at the ready, waiting for her to open the passageway.

For a second, she marveled at the new sensations. Every step made her feel like a giant. Her limbs felt powerful, brimming with raw energy, and she could feel Iblis inside her head like a blanket wrapped tightly around her. Like a second suit of armor. She could feel every shift of the wind, could feel the slight differences from demon to demon, which was strange.

It wasn't like names, but she could differentiate between their temperatures. She could sense how hot they burned, and though they didn't have age the way humans did, it was through these temperature fluctuations that they measured themselves. And as she focused on that, she realized it wasn't as simple as that; even the various ways they shifted in temperature mattered, like a fire burning hotter on the inside with a cooler flame on the outside.

It was completely bizarre to her, but to the demon part of her mind, it was very much normal. She wondered if it was similar to how scientists measured stars. Gravity and light and the color of the flame and . . . she could feel the air too. And it was much easier to find the strangely warm gooeyness of the passageway.

She walked up to it, steam rising from her body, the flames in her eyes brightening everything around her. Her fingers reached out, and she touched it, touched the slight thickness in the air before whispering, "Valescent Light."

# CHAPTER TWENTY

# DESECRATED HUMAN (VESSEL)

The passageway felt different this time. She felt different. She still couldn't wrap her mind around the power boost possession gave her, even with Iblis's warning that it would lead to her burning out. It was exhilarating. She couldn't wait to *punch* something, and that familiar desire welled up inside her: *kill, kill, kill.*

She floated through the light with ease, searching by feeling the currents around her. The demon part of her mind was far more in tune with this than she'd been—and she got the sense that the substance she was moving through was similar to the substance demons were made from. Iblis didn't deny nor confirm her theory.

He didn't say anything while in her head, as though he was buried in her subconscious, since Jenny had control. She drifted along, moving her arms and legs gently, colors ranging from purple to orange to green spiraling away from her movements. She pushed from the world of demons, the world she was leaving, and ignored the immense pull of the material world trying to swallow her up. It was almost like a gaping black hole in the center of the light. If she let it, it would reel her right in. From above came the pull of the world she was looking for: the world of death. But ahead of her was something new.

This had a different kind of pull; one that coiled around her throat and sank hooks into her heart, yanking so hard that breath bubbled from her lips, and she opened her burning eyes. Blue light like ribbons drifted around her face.

*What is that?* she wondered. *Why does it . . . hurt? But in a good way?* It felt pleasant. Peaceful. Promising.

**Your senses are more highly attuned due to my presence.**

The small thought came from the back of her mind. It was like distant static, muffled inside her head.

**That is the world of souls.**

Souls. When she shivered, bright blue light fizzled around her. A trail of orange floated through her chest, leading toward the pulling world. That was where Susan's soul would be. That was where Jenny had to go.

She almost grinned. She was getting closer.

**That is where Azra'il reigns.**

The static voice cut through her happiness. A warning.

**The world of souls will not be a pleasant place. He is the cruelest of the highmost angels.**

Her heart constricted. What was happening to the souls there? Would they be suffering somehow too? The way the deaths had been encased inside pillars with their intestines attached to the rock? What was happening to Susan?

She couldn't bear to think about that world, so she turned, wading with her arms to see the hundreds of pale-white ghoul bodies and their burning eyes floating with her. Now that they were possessed by demons, they didn't struggle in agony like the blooded ghouls had before. They drifted along, limp, their arms swaying at their sides like bodies underwater.

It was unnerving, but Jenny kicked with her feet, propelling herself up toward the world of the dead. Colors gathered, forming a ceiling of rainbows spiraling and rippling as though it were raining. Then, with a splash, her head broke the surface, and hot, sticky liquid struck her repeatedly from above.

Blood rained down more furiously than when she'd left, and in the bright golden light of the passageway, she saw endless blooded ghouls stretching and hissing and clambering over each other to get to something that towered over the world in the storm.

It was the cross. And nailed to it, once again, was Yeshua, naked and thin. His head, crowned again with thorns, hung limp.

His beard flowed in the breeze of the blood storm as ghouls scrambled all over the cross, biting down everywhere, peeling his skin off with their teeth, chewing through muscle and bone and everything else they could reach. And all the while, red lightning snapped around his arms and legs, around his face, healing him endlessly as ghouls fought over which one would get the next bite.

## Blooded Ghouls (NULL)

These ghouls didn't splash away once they'd eaten. They kept going for more and more. They kept wanting more—biting off Yeshua's arms and legs, fighting each other for each limb that fell to the blood-soaked ground; a feeding frenzy as more leaped onto the cross to chew at the regenerating flesh.

Anger roared to a scream as Jenny waded out of the pool of light and slapped the nearest blooded ghoul with so much force the creature disintegrated into a cloud of red vapor and a burst of blue flame. The ghouls responded in sync, all of them turning to face her, moaning and whimpering, gnashing their teeth.

She'd left her helmet in the frozen world, but with her heightened stats, she didn't care. They couldn't hurt her. And she was too quick.

Running between them, she dodged attempts to grab her, avoiding teeth, punching and elbowing. When she attacked a blooded ghoul, blue flames erupted from her fists, from her blows. She struck them with enough force to shatter their bodies, disintegrating heads or chests and leaving the rest of the body to collapse. Some, like the first ghoul she'd struck, she hit hard enough to completely destroy, but she was trying to be quick—and she moved so freely! So easily. She felt like the wind.

Not a single bit of her seemed to tire. She could go on forever, she thought, but she knew Iblis was counting down the time before she would burn herself out.

The demons in ghoul bodies emerged from the golden light behind her, dozens at a time. They clashed with the blooded ghouls, who seemed to realize there was something wrong with them. Yellow and orange flames lit up the blood rain around Jenny. Some of the demons tried to drag the blooded ghouls, kicking and screaming, back into the light with them, but it looked like once they emerged, they couldn't go back inside.

Iblis's static moved between her ears.

**We cannot return with the ghouls.**

"I think I have to take everyone back myself!" she shouted as she punched another ghoul into oblivion. Blue flames kept leaking out of her as she fought her way toward Yeshua, glimpsing his struggling form every time she punched away the ghouls. He was crying, screaming in a language Jenny didn't know, gurgling when his throat or lips were bitten away. But she didn't need to understand him to know what he was trying to say: he was begging for death again.

**We are running out of time. You are burning out.**

*Help me free him, then*, she gasped. Just as she said that, she felt Iblis stirring, coming forward from her subconscious. More flames shot out of her back, the same way her tentacles would, but these were orange and curling, feathery, not the same hot blue as her eyes or her attacks.

She kicked off the ground.

The ghouls stared up at her as blood dribbled down her face, dribbled down her *wings*. She had wings made of fiery feathers, but as much as she wanted to admire them, to study them, she knew there wasn't enough time. The fire was turning orange: she was burning out. Orange flame was weaker than blue.

But she could fly! With a flap of flames, she rushed over the ghouls leaping into the pouring blood to try and catch her. She swerved, kicking with her leg, motioning with her arms as though she was swimming. For the demon mind, flying would be natural, but she wasn't made of energy like Iblis was. She had a material body. She had weight. Rain splattered over her face and pelted her sides.

With a flash of golden light, she summoned her hatchet to her hand and flapped hard, snapping herself back midair. She took careful aim in the split second she had before she'd drop out of the air and aimed for the cross, launching her hatchet at Yeshua with Savage Throw.

Blue-and-orange fire glinted brightly around the hatchet as it spun through the air like a shooting star. It smashed through Yeshua's right wrist again, separating his hand from the arm and freeing him from that nail—then it went further, cutting through the wood of the cross and bursting through several ghouls on the other side. Yeshua looked up, his eyes widening as Jenny met his eyes.

Flapping her burning wings again, she kicked away a ghoul that had leaped to try and grab her legs. Her foot dislodged its skull, and then she was up in the air again.

Yeshua let out a wild cry as a huge surge of red lightning snapped down from the sky. Jenny recalled her hatchet and threw it twice more with two more flashes of light, freeing his other arm and his legs, and Yeshua fell from the cross as the largest bolt of lightning yet seared a path down from the sky. It seemed to snake down in slow motion, as though it were an enormous serpent unhinging its jaws to swallow Yeshua whole.

When it struck, everything exploded with crackling red light. Yeshua bellowed loudly, just as he had when Jenny had first freed him. His arms were outstretched, but he didn't announce his presence again. Blood ran down his shining form, still fragile and bony and thin, and he didn't create a new set of robes.

Instead, he grabbed the nearest blooded ghoul, palming its head like a ball as its arms and legs kicked futilely. Yeshua pressed his lips against the creature's eye socket, ignoring the other ghouls tearing and biting his arms and sides and legs. Even over the loud drumming of the rain and the endless moaning and crying, Jenny heard the unmistakable *shllluuurp*.

Dropping out of the sky, Jenny landed beside him, cutting down several blooded ghouls. Her orange wings shone bright and wide as she played defense while Yeshua drank, as his body restored itself.

"I found the demons!" she called, sounding out of breath as she whirled around and punched another ghoul in the face. "The deaths are okay. I made a deal with them, and—"

But Yeshua must not have heard her over the storm. He grabbed her arm violently, his eyes manic and wide and bloodshot. He snarled, "Demon! I sense you within that body!"

He raised his other hand as though he was about to strike Jenny with his palm. Anger flashed in his eyes as blood streamed down his bearded face.

She tried to push him away, holding up her hands. "No! No, wait! It's—"

But it was too late. With a bellow that sounded like someone had rung an enormous bell inside Jenny's head, Yeshua shouted, "BE GONE FROM HER!" and slammed his palm against her forehead.

# CHAPTER TWENTY-ONE

# BE GONE FROM HER

B E GONE FROM HER!"

As though a sudden burst of wind had slammed through her, Jenny felt the words ripple through her entire being. The shock forced the air out of her lungs, knocking her off her feet and away, her hair swirling, her arms spreading. The orange flames of her wings snapped out of existence, and blue flames billowed out of her every orifice, streaming out of her eyes and mouth, out of her nostrils and ears, floating above and away, and try as she might, she couldn't hold on to Iblis's mind as the demon was expelled from her body.

She landed in a heap of blood, the liquid on the ground bubbling and frothing in the rain. Ghouls scrambled over, grasping at her arms and shoulders and hair. Suddenly, their attacks hurt. Suddenly, they were a threat again. Blood splattered her face and soaked through her armor, and without Iblis's power burning inside her, Jenny felt heavier and weaker than ever before.

"No!" she shouted as fingers and hands grasped her all over, as teeth flashed inches from her ears. She swerved and struck blindly with her hatchet, cutting off limbs, trying to clear some space so she could breathe. But in the mess of blood and bodies, there was no escape.

Through the ghouls, she saw Yeshua had collapsed to his knees. Creatures bounded onto his back and forced him to the ground, their teeth sinking into his shoulders and back.

"NOOO!" Jenny screamed again till her voice went hoarse. Teeth cracked through the armor at her elbow. She felt so weak—so pathetic—now that the demon was gone. She cried out again, punching a ghoul away, kicking one before it could bite her foot. But these blows weren't as powerful as before. The ghouls didn't disintegrate, and there were too many to fight off. She roared to the sky, wondering why Yeshua wasn't still fighting. Had he used too much energy to expel the demon from Jenny?

She swore loudly and used Ignite. Blue fire erupted from her skin, hotter and fiercer than any flame she'd produced before.

The ghouls smoldered, their plasticky red skin melting and sliding off their faces as they screeched and rolled away. But as powerful as her flames had become, they cost more stamina to burn at this temperature, and within a heartbeat, the blue color faded to white then orange. But they'd done the trick; the flames had cleared enough space for her to run toward Yeshua.

Striking quickly with her hatchet, she lobbed the head off the ghoul biting Yeshua's neck. She kicked another one and shoved a third off him before using Ignite again, roaring as she exhaled blue flame in a circle around her to force the ghouls back. Blood evaporated all around in a hiss of steam as the ghouls scrambled, clutching melting body parts and screeching.

Yeshua wasn't moving. Jenny looked up at the sky, blinking through the blood splattering her eyes, trying to find any sign of Iblis, any sign of his sparkling lights. She spotted the other demons in their ghoul bodies, now colored red by the storm. They were only distinguishable by their burning eyes, and they rushed over to Jenny, forming a perimeter around her and Yeshua and the cross.

Blood coated her throat, coated everything. It made her senses spin. Jenny forced Yeshua up as red lightning crackled across his body, patching his torn flesh back together. She saw a glimpse of his exposed shoulder blade. He was too skinny. Too weak. She had to get him out of here.

"We have to move," she shouted at him over the relentless rain. "To cross the light again."

"Demons," muttered Yeshua, his eyes barely opening. "Demons haunt the Earth; we must be rid of them. We must not let them into our hearts."

"No," said Jenny firmly. "I made a deal with them. They're helping me. You. They're helping us."

"A deal? A deal with the devil? No, no, no!"

She grabbed his face, digging her fingers into his beard. She pulled the crown of thorns off his head with her other hand, and his eyes finally opened as little bolts of lightning went crisscross around his head. She didn't know what to say to him. They hardly knew each other, but he was . . . he was *Him,* wasn't he? She'd prayed to him all her life without him ever knowing. She needed him to trust her.

"If it weren't for the demons, I wouldn't have been able to get back here," she said.

"You can't trust them," he whispered. "They're . . . They abandoned the light."

"No," said Jenny again, growing frustrated as blood rained down still. "Look, we can figure all that out later. Right now, we have to get out of here, yeah?"

Yeshua nodded like he was drunk, and Jenny spit in frustration.

"I'm gonna drag the cross over, okay?" She made to let him go and move toward it, wondering how she'd drag that thing through the crowd of ghouls. And where was Iblis? She could use his help right now.

But Yeshua shook his head, gasping for breath as blood went down his chin. He was trying to stand.

"What do you mean *no*?" she almost screamed.

He grabbed her arm. "Only I can bear it. Only I can. It has to be me."

"Then get off your ass already!"

But he was struggling to right himself, barely functioning. He groaned as he held on to her arm for balance, his head hanging low, his wet hair sticking to his face. "I need . . ."

Jenny looked around in desperation. The possessed ghouls had sprouted burning wings, and she saw some of their bodies crumbling away to ash. But they needed the extra firepower to keep the blooded ghouls at bay.

Iblis's voice crackled through her ears.

**I am still with you, but the passageway will not remain open for much longer. Your body cannot tolerate that strain.**

The passageway! It was still open; she hadn't closed it. She wiped blood and wet hair out of her eyes; she hadn't noticed how much that was eating up her energy when she'd been possessed. Her breathing quickened, and she knew how to fix Yeshua, who'd collapsed back to his knees, clutching his bony chest. She peeled the armor away from her fingers, away from her wrist, all the way up to her elbow, then Jenny presented her forearm to Yeshua, smashing her pale skin against his lips.

"EAT!" she shouted.

Yeshua's eyes went wide. Blood splattered right into her arm, but he didn't blink, only shaking his head fervently. But that movement caused his teeth to brush her skin, and she saw his eyes dilate, felt him shudder. And then, he grasped her with both hands, just as she'd once grasped his limb. His fingers curled around her wrist, his other hand on her elbow, and Jenny braced herself, determined not to cry out.

His teeth sliced into her arm. A scream filled her lungs, but she swallowed it, muffling the whimper as pain radiated from where Yeshua was chewing. Teeth snapped through her muscles, scraped her bone, and he slurped, drinking her blood. Swallowing. And when he slurped, she shuddered, feeling a *tug* on all the blood in her body. Wasn't there enough blood in the rain?

But he wasn't growing . . . he wasn't filling out again. He was still too thin, too painfully weak.

What was wrong? He released her arm, shaking his head, his entire body trembling.

"Desecrated . . ." he whispered, his breath hot against her exposed flesh.

*Shit.* It wasn't going to work.

Jenny whirled around, the ghouls and demons fighting furiously in the mess of blood. Yeshua slumped, retching loudly, but whatever he was throwing up mixed in with the pouring rain, and Jenny didn't care.

"Iblis!" she called as loudly as she could, ignoring her burning, aching arm, ignoring how the rain felt dripping into the missing chunks and running down her bone. "Come back to me!"

His voice crackled.

**I cannot. Not with that man's presence. His power is still active.**

"No," she whispered, breathing hard, her arm hurting so much she wanted to rip it from her shoulder. *What do I do?*

In the distance, she could see the last glimmers of Valescent Light, waiting, draining her. She didn't have much left, but if Iblis could get back inside her . . . she'd have more stamina, more energy, more everything. *Fuck.*

If only there was a way to open another wound, to open a new passageway. But could she even do that? Open another wound while the original was overflowing with Valescent Light? She was terrified of deactivating it—terrified that she wouldn't be able to use it again for a while.

Her mind spun. Her body wavered, the throbbing pain of her chewed-up arm proving too much. Blood squirted out of her, mixing with the blood of the storm. What was she supposed to do? She needed to move the cross to the light and . . .

What if she could bring the light to her?

*Bring it to yourself.*

*Will it. It's yours to command.*

Jenny reached out toward the pool of light with her good arm, its golden aura shimmering brightly even with the pouring blood rain. When she'd used it before, she hadn't just taken herself to another world but she'd carried all the deaths and ghouls and demons too.

*You can do it.*

*You are strong enough.*

*This is Susan's light.*

So Jenny shut her eyes, emptying her mind, freeing herself from the pain. The rain faded away. Yeshua's whimpers became background noise. Everything emptied.

This wasn't Severed Spirit; it was something else. Almost like someone else surfacing to the top of her consciousness. It reminded her of Iblis pressing against her mind. It reminded her of Eve. She was so sure someone else was there, inside her body. Operating her thoughts. But it was just her. Just Jenny.

*Just me.*

*Are you sure?*

Shivers ran down her spine. Goose bumps spread across her arms, and when she opened her eyes, tears ran down her face. "Who said that?" she whispered, but already, a notification was surfacing in her head; already, she could feel the squishy, gelatinous thing in the air that showed her where to open the passageway.

She could feel it pulsing, moving, climbing along what felt like threads that reached in every direction, connecting her to the pool of light, and connecting the pool of light to everything else. She pulled the light toward her, elongating it, opening it. It bloomed furiously, growing with the warmth of the sun, and the ground beneath her unzipped.

The blood and the dark sand gave way, and she was sinking again—she and Yeshua and the cross, and all the demons in their ghoul bodies and the countless blooded ghouls that had been swarming all over them.

**Valescent Light (Tier 3)**

# CHAPTER TWENTY-TWO

# STAND CLEAR OF THE CLOSING DOORS

## NANCY

The underbelly of New York City was filthy. Maybe that was why Nancy preferred praying in the subway. She'd tried the church, the library, and even near the crater where her children's school once stood, but underground was the only place she felt safe enough to pray. It was the only place she felt like God might hear her. Or maybe it wasn't God she was reaching for; she didn't know anymore.

The subway felt suffocating with its retched odor, the bustle of busy people, and the screech of metal every time a train roared in and out of the station. It was difficult to breathe too deeply, and the stench of piss or trash or rot clung to everything.

Nancy clutched her purse, her jaws clenched, her eyes on the dirty tiled wall. A homeless man lay beside her on the bench, covered in a filthy brown blanket. Beneath him were piles of dirty clothes and shoes of all sizes and colors. She'd sat down and counted the curious stains on his brown blanket—twenty-four. Some she'd identified as food stains, and a good wash or two might get those out. Some of it was dried blood or smeared dirt. Other stains were things she'd rather not wonder about.

People kept shooting her concerned or curious looks as they walked by. She couldn't blame them. After all, who would purposefully sit beside a vagabond whose stench surrounded the bench like a toxic cloud? Nancy would; she deserved it. She inhaled sharply through her nose, a miasma filling her lungs. Her stomach tried to compress and contract, to force her to expel this rancid odor. *Throw up*, said a voice in her head. *Throw up*, urged her body. *Just get up and move somewhere else.*

But where? Every inch of the station was filthy, and it wasn't like this was the homeless man's fault. Maybe he had debilitating medical issues. Maybe he'd been dealt a bad hand in life. Maybe he'd gotten cheated. Or maybe he was evil, and he deserved this. Wasn't that what her parents had raised her to believe? What she'd tried to instill in her daughter? That the sinful were punished.

And all Nancy had ever done was sin.

She buried her fingernails into her palm and squeezed her eyes shut as tears trailed down her cheeks. *I lost my children. They're gone. They're gone. God took them from me. I'm a bad mother. I'm a terrible person. It should've been me! God, please, take me. Take me! Bring them back. Please!*

"Lady," grumbled the homeless man, lifting his blanket to squint at her with sleepy eyes. Her sniffles must've woken him up. He had terrible bags beneath his eyes, bags that matched Nancy's. A scraggly beard crawled over his chin and cheeks; he was bald beneath his wool hat. "What's wrong, beautiful? You're really good looking. Do you have any food?"

Nancy reached into her purse, heart pounding. Her fingers closed around her pepper spray, but the man wasn't trying anything. He wasn't being weird. He smiled almost apologetically, or maybe he was just grateful someone would sit next to him.

She returned a strained smile and pulled out a wad of cash. The man's face lit up, and he flashed a toothy grin as he reached for it. But his hand came too close to her navy-blue skirt, and Nancy stood abruptly before placing the handfuls of fives and tens on her seat and briskly walking away. She kept her eyes on the tiles beneath her sandals as the man praised her from behind.

She didn't glance back, instead waiting by the yellow line at the edge of the platform. The yellow line meant danger; anyone standing on it risked getting hit by an oncoming train, risked falling into the tracks. A rat skittered across them, and she stared at its long pink tail before it vanished into a drainage pipe.

A short while later, the station rumbled. A train screeched out of the dark tunnel and rushed in front of her, a violent gush of wind lifting her hair and ruffling her skirt; windows and flashes of all the people inside went by, and Nancy grimaced. She must look like a mess.

With a shaking hand, she tried to smooth down her hair. How long had it been since she'd washed it? She hadn't washed her face in a while either. No makeup. No moisturizer. Not even lip balm. She forced herself to smile as the train slowed to a stop and she caught sight of her distorted reflection in the doorway window. Three days. It'd been three days since that earthquake, since God had taken her children away, since she'd last eaten. Her stomach had no space for food; it was too filled with worry and disgust.

Once the doors slid open, she flowed inside with everyone else and grabbed a pole. A moment later, the announcer came on. "Stand clear of the closing doors." The doors shut, then the train groaned back to life and pulled out of the station. Through one of the windows, she could see the homeless man counting the money she'd given him. He looked like he was about to cry with joy.

She studied the ads splayed across the train's sides. There was something for breast surgery, something for trade schools, something for designer watches. There was a sign saying, "If you see something, say something" in bold white letters. "New Yorkers keep New Yorkers safe."

Her lips twisted. She was aware of people moving away from her, avoiding eye contact. They got up from their seats to find another place to stand. They leaned against the door. They didn't want to be near her. Nancy sniffed her armpit—she reeked. Maybe she'd sat too long on that bench, or maybe it had been too long since she'd washed. She didn't care; she got to sit down. A bench had cleared out in front of her.

Nancy sank into the seat and rested her head back as the train bumped and jostled. She looked at the other passengers as they side-eyed her.

They seemed nervous. On edge. The city was haunted; nobody knew what to do about the buildings that had vanished. So many people were gone, and almost everyone knew someone who'd disappeared. The news had run the list every single hour. The first night—and for most of the second day—Nancy had sat on the living room floor reciting as many names as she could, hoping, praying, even as Henry tried to pull her away, to kiss her and give her food, that Jenny's and Oliver's names wouldn't appear.

*Please, please, please, please.*

Just before she'd left the apartment this morning—after telling Henry she didn't want any breakfast, that she didn't want anything but her children— she'd punched the television. The screen had cracked, and she'd stormed out. And now, she sat on a train staring at the red patches of skin. Her knuckles were already bruising; she could barely open and close her fingers, but she forced herself to do so anyway. Just to feel the pain radiating into her wrist and climbing the veins right into her brain. Oh, it felt *good*. It felt really good, and she deserved so much worse.

Why was she on the train? She'd gotten out of the apartment; she'd had to. She couldn't stand going up and down the stairs anymore, hoping to hear Jenny's voice, her biting sarcasm, or Oliver popping his head out of his room to ask what was for dinner. Her husband, Henry, had become a shell as well.

He wasn't eating much, but he kept cooking. Kept making breakfast, lunch, and dinner, and setting the table for four. Except now, he kept his handgun on the counter. "Just in case," he'd say.

"In case of what?" Nancy would ask.

He'd look at her with those sharp, brooding eyes that had won her heart over and say, "I don't know."

His ex-wife would call sometimes; Oliver's biological mother. She'd screech on the phone about her precious boy, about how Henry was a failure, about how she would kill Henry for failing. She was a horrid woman; Nancy had always wondered about her. Jessica Spencer. She'd kept Henry's last name, but it was all a strange mess, something Nancy was afraid to untangle.

Henry had been adopted from Korea. He'd grown up in the Midwest, and he'd tell Nancy about how he'd constantly felt like an outsider, constantly bullied for being different. He'd joined the navy to see the world and find his purpose, and Nancy hated all the things he'd suffered through, all the racism and toxicity.

She'd tried her best to make his son, Oliver—who was her son now, too—feel welcome and loved. His shock of red hair was from his mother, but his face and soft skin came from his dad. And his kindness, his sweetness, that was all Oliver's. So, she didn't care what features came from where; she just loved him as her own. *But I couldn't love Jenny like that.*

*I tried my best!*

*I should've done more; I could have.*

More tears slipped down Nancy's cheeks, and she licked them off her face. The train rattled through tunnels. Small lights flashed by the windows. At the next stop, more people piled in, took one look at the sobbing mess she'd become, and scrambled away from her. She didn't care; the world was broken, falling apart. How was everyone else so normal? How could everyone pretend things were okay? Everything was crumbling, and all it had taken was a few buildings going missing.

She could've laughed. The news that day when she'd come home, her feet bleeding, her heart broken, had been all about the stock market crashing.

*Who gave a flying fuck about the economy? The world was ending!*

She'd collapsed in Henry's arms, and all they could do was follow along as people and news outlets and social media twisted this in every way possible as they tried to make sense of it: The reckoning. The end of times. Sinkholes. Rapture. Sin. It had to be aliens. It's because of the gays. It's because of the immigrants. It's because of the monsters in power. Everyone found someone to blame, even Henry, who blamed God. But Nancy blamed herself.

That first day, it'd felt like the world stood still. People had held their breath, waiting for the sky to burst open. But by the second day, the trains and busses were running again with reroutes and delays. Coffee shops reopened. The business district filled with men in suits. Everyone was expected to go back to work; it was a bizarre nightmare that made no sense.

Riots broke out in the evenings. Marches and violent protests. But what were they for? What did they expect would happen? A curfew was instilled. Everyone was to be home before 9:00 p.m. Anyone caught outside without permission would be arrested. But Nancy didn't care about any of that.

"Oh, that's right," she said out loud. She laughed and touched her injured hand to her forehead. "I'm going to their school."

Several people glanced at her. One asked if she was alright. Nancy smiled and shook her head. She was on the N train. A few stops more and she'd arrive at Jenny's and Oliver's high school, to the crater in the ground that had filled with muddy rainwater. She'd have to walk back later. She'd given all her money away, and she hated using her credit cards at the kiosks. Maybe she'd call Henry. Or maybe he'd come looking for her again.

She tried to relax. She straightened her blouse and smoothed her skirt. She wasn't sure why she was trying to make herself look nice for a hole in the ground, but she ran her fingers through her hair and dabbed her eyes with her sleeve, and just as she was about to fish for deodorant in her purse, the train *bounced* violently, throwing Nancy forward onto the floor.

Everyone who'd been standing got slammed against the windows and the doors and each other. Several bumped their heads on the seats and collapsed. A roaring scream of people and metal whirled around her; the lights flickered, the ground shook violently—rumbling and shaking—while everything bounced as though the train was trying to vomit them all out. But Nancy recognized these tremors, recognized this chaotic rumbling of the world: it was the same earthquake that had taken her children away.

It was the same. Much stronger, and much more impactful, but it had to be the same. She wasn't sure how she knew, but she felt it in her bones as someone's boot struck her ribs and her knee banged against a pole. The train screeched to a halt, sparks flying and flashing by the windows, and then, the earth stopped shaking.

After a long, quiet minute, one of the lights flickered, but most of the train was stuck in near darkness. Someone turned their phone's flashlight on, and light glistened across the mess inside.

Everyone was a pile of limbs. Many were bleeding, and people kept asking one another if they were alright, helping the elderly stand and get to a seat, trying to assist the unconscious.

Static blared over the intercom as the conductor's voice crackled through. Nancy could barely understand him. It was a mess of white noise, but she caught a few words. "Remain calm . . . don't move between . . . inspection . . . wheels and rails . . . emergency services."

Nancy felt herself all over. She'd hit one of the seats with the side of her face, and her cheekbone was sore to the touch. She was sure one of her ribs was broken, and she winced when she tried to extend her leg. But she grabbed the nearest pole and forced herself upright, groping around for her purse. A man was lying on top of it; he was out cold but still breathing. Shaking, Nancy yanked her purse free then pulled out her phone.

Would she even have a signal this far underground? She typed in her PIN, and *yes!* She had a bar! They must be close to the next station; she could access the internet. Her heart pounding with adrenaline, the threat of several prayers on her tongue, Nancy flicked to the news as someone tried to wake the man beside her. She ignored them both as she scrolled through reports of the earthquake, tapping her phone hard enough to chip her nails. The connection kept dropping, but finally, a site loaded.

There, on the front page, was the headline she was looking for. A video tried to autoplay, but her signal was too weak. and it couldn't load. Fresh tears streamed down her face. A cry of happiness and hope broke free of her throat. She'd been right. "Breaking News: The missing buildings have returned!"

Something wet and hot ran down the side of her head. She scratched it absentmindedly, her fingers coming away with blood. It glistened in the tunnel lights. She was dizzy. Someone knelt in front of her, a face full of concern, mouthing something. Nancy just shook her head. It took her a few moments to understand; they were asking if she was okay.

"I have to call my children," she said in a choked voice. The person gave her a strained smile and moved on to check on someone else. Nancy shut her eyes. She couldn't stop shaking.

The school was two more stops away, and the train seemed to be upright. Maybe they could get moving again. Or maybe she could run to the next station and get back to the surface. Slowly, she became aware of the other passengers helping one another up, crying, calling loved ones, calling for help. As she searched for Jenny's name, her screen lit up with a call from Henry, and her heart lurched. For a moment, she thought it was Oliver's face in the icon.

"Hello?" It was Henry's voice, but the line dropped, and she couldn't hear what he said next.

The train announcer came back on as well, his voice crackling overhead. "Emergency services are en route to escort everyone out. Please remain where you are. Nobody should move between . . . between . . ." There was a burst of static. "What the fuck is that thing?"

Nancy blinked at the ceiling. Then she glanced at the other passengers, who were staring up in confusion at the intercom as well. Another light flickered, and they heard more static. There was a shout then a strange hissing sound, almost like a snake or a radiator, but it triggered every danger-sensing cell in her body.

It was followed by a thud. The intercom cut off abruptly, and the train fell silent. Nobody spoke a word or made a sound. Her phone crackled.

"Nancy? Nanc . . . are you . . . ?"

"I'll get off at the next stop," she whispered into the phone. She was trembling, but she told herself that was just 'cause she'd hit her head. "Emergency services are on the way."

"They're not . . . pick . . . up, Na . . ." he said, breathing heavy. "The traffic's so . . . run . . . ning, and . . ." The line cut again, and when it came back, Nancy couldn't understand what he was saying.

Before she could whisper frantically, a strange sensation, like a headache, moved through her head from behind her left eye to just inside her ear, and a shudder went down her spine. Someone cried out. Words appeared in her head:

**Rapture has commenced.**
**The Final Challenge is in effect.**
**The faithful shall be rewarded. May His light guide your way.**
**Humans remaining: 7,885,246,104**

Her phone fell from her hand. Her breath caught in her throat.

*Rapture . . . Humans remaining? The final challenge?* She could hear something faint, something echoing down the tunnels. Was it sirens? The wind? Was it the emergency services coming to help them?

She reached for her phone, but her injured hand found her purse instead. She grabbed her pepper spray and remembered what Henry had told her about his handgun. *Just in case.*

Then the door on the far side of the train car slammed open. Nancy flinched. People rushed into their car, scrambling over one another, the flashlights from their phones bouncing all over the place. Countless shadows flicked across the train, and as they rushed toward her, as she caught the glimpses of sheer terror on their faces, Nancy realized what she'd been hearing. It wasn't sirens or the wind. It was screaming. It was people screaming.

# CHAPTER TWENTY-THREE

# PEPPER SPRAY

### NANCY

Nancy didn't know if she should scream too, if she even could. The train car, mostly dark but with flashes of light from people's phones, had erupted into chaos. It was almost like another earthquake. She stood in the midst of the stampede as elbows and shoulders knocked into her, as someone screamed into her face to run, surrounded by the thunderous roar of footsteps.

As though the fear was infectious, people left the injured behind and followed the panicked crowd through the exit behind Nancy. That door led into the next train car, where she imagined the panic would swallow up everyone in there as well. How many cars till they reached the very last one? Where would they go? What were they running from?

Was it a fire? It couldn't be a fire, she reasoned. If it were a fire, then there'd be more light in the dark tunnel. Everything seemed dark outside the cracked windows. Why had the conductor screamed?

She held on to the pole with both hands, standing as still as possible as the stream of people raged past her, eyes wide with confusion and terror, sweat glistening in the bouncing phone lights. Most of them were adults; some were teens with their headphones around their throats and oversized bookbags. There were even children, crying as their parents held them close or tugged them along by the hand.

Nancy got shoved and tussled, but she held as firmly as she could. Nobody glanced at her twice. This was worse than the crowded subway stations on busy summer morning commutes, with people in a rush to pack themselves into a train, desperate to get to work on time.

Sweat drenched her back. Her blouse was torn from the earthquake, and blood ran down the side of her face. She wiped it with the back of her busted hand. *Should I run too?* Her lips trembled; Jenny and Oliver were ahead. Their school was two stops ahead; why would she turn back and run now?

Besides, where were all these people going? Once they scrambled out of the last car, they'd be stuck in the dark, disgusting tunnel between stations, and it was a long way back to the previous stop. If help was going to come, it would come from ahead.

She wasn't the only one waiting. There was a kid, a dark-skinned boy in a bright orange jacket, who was clutching the handrails of a bench tightly. An elderly woman lay on the floor beside him, her head beneath the seat, unconscious, blood pooling from her mouth.

There were others sprawled across the floor, some of them groaning, most of them quiet. She wondered how many had been injured during the earthquake and how many had been trampled in the mad rush. Screams still echoed all around, drifting up and down the tunnel outside, and a stale breeze blew through the shattered windows. Nancy hobbled toward the boy. He'd started prodding the woman; she must've been his grandmother.

Nancy's legs nearly buckled as she moved from pole to pole, eyeing some of the unmoving bodies, stepping over one or two until she could lean against the door beside the old woman. Words filled her thoughts like a notification when she looked at the boy.

## Human (Level 1)

But there wasn't anything like that for the woman, and her head hurt too much to figure out what it meant. There was just enough light to see them both. Someone's phone had been left behind on the other side of the bench, its flashlight still on. Nancy knelt, half collapsing on her knees, to press her fingers to the woman's throat. There was no pulse.

"I'm sorry," she whispered, looking up at the boy's wide eyes. He might've been three or four, she wasn't sure. His orange jacket was zipped halfway up, and the colorful T-shirt underneath depicted some superhero blasting a beam of light. Oliver would recognize the character; she had no idea.

"Nana?" the boy asked, his busted lip moving slowly.

She didn't know what to say; her empathy was all burned-out, but when the boy pointed at the woman again and said something that sounded like "hospital," Nancy nodded. "Yes, hospital. People are on the way. They'll help us."

"It's going to be okay," said the boy, eyes quivering with tears. He rubbed his lips, smearing blood across his face. "My dad is in the hospital."

"It's going to be okay," repeated Nancy. Did the boy's dad work at the hospital? Was he a doctor? Or was he a patient and they'd been on the way to visit? Her heart broke imagining that, and she reached out to wipe the boy's chin, but then noticed her own blood smeared all over her hands and thought better of it.

On the opposite bench across the aisle, underneath a wide window that had remained intact, lay a man about Nancy's age. He was on his side, clutching his ribs and glaring at her. He had unruly long brown hair and a mean look, and he puffed out his sweaty cheeks with every shaky breath. His black shirt was torn, revealing a round, hairy stomach. "This is all our fault," he wheezed. "All this nonsense with phones and money."

## Human (Level 1)

Nancy didn't know how to respond to that. "It's nobody's fault," she replied. "Help is on the way."

The man closed his eyes and coughed, his entire body jiggling. "Immigrants," he said. "Always asking for help. You know? Those other folks who dress wrong. Them queers. Illegals. Dirty people. God is angry with us. He is punishing us."

*Okay, there's no point talking to this man.* Nancy pressed her lips tight and leaned back against the door. The boy still clung to the chair; he was holding his grandmother's hand, and he kept looking at Nancy like she might stabilize him somehow, might save him from this. The echoing screams grew quiet after a while, and Nancy wondered if that entire crowd had gotten away. And if there was a fire, what would she do? She'd pick up the boy and run, too.

"Help me," she whispered, blinking away tears, trying to ignore the pain, trying to pray. *Help me.*

Unless *this* was God taking her away. She'd asked for this. She'd gotten her children back, after all. Wasn't that the bargain she'd made?

*Not till I can see them*, she thought furiously. *Not till I can hold them. Only then can you take me.*

She knew she was being greedy, but she had to be sure. Were they safe? Were they alright? As if in response to her prayer, a shrill scream sounded way too close for comfort, raising the hairs on her back. This one didn't sound human. It almost sounded animal, like something enormous and hungry.

One of the phone lights flickered out, casting the far side of the train car into darkness. Even the bigoted man went quiet, and the little boy cried out and rushed into Nancy's arms. Her ribs cracked and popped, and she grimaced, but she held him tight, one hand on his curly hair.

"What's your name?" she asked, trying to keep the boy calm. "My name is Mrs. Huang." It was a trick she'd learned dealing with young children at one of the old restaurants she'd worked at. If you made yourself sound like a teacher, sometimes they listened.

"Amir," said the boy in a muffled voice.

"We're going to be alright, Amir," whispered Nancy.

The man made a gagging sound. He looked disgusted, his face half lit as he muttered about the ethnicities he couldn't stand, how morally corrupt society had become, how the Rapture was finally here to purge—A hand smashed through the window over his bench, and he erupted into squealing as shards of glass rained down.

Nancy held her breath, squeezing Amir as a skeletal arm reached into the train car. It was so thin, just bone with skin stretched over it. A face emerged next, a shock of white hair and sickly skin. There was just enough light to see it had no pupils. Its eyes were empty and white. Looking into them sent shivers of fear through Nancy's chest, and all she wanted to do was scream. It was some kind of monster, like something from those violent video games Jenny played all the time.

The creature pulled itself through the jagged glass of the broken window and coughed up blood, spraying the man crying beneath it. With a hiss that sounded like a snake, it pulled itself over and collapsed right on top of the kicking, crying man as words filled Nancy's head:

**Tarnished Angel (Level 5)**

"*What?*" whispered Nancy as the man wailed, struggling to push the creature off.

"Not me!" he cried. "Not me! You don't want me! Take them! *They're* the sinners!" He pointed at Nancy.

The angel grabbed the man's head and slammed it against the bench. A choked cry escaped the man's lips, who looked utterly shocked. Blood ran down from beneath him onto the floor.

Nancy held her breath as the angel hissed, revealing stained teeth. It looked like a person, someone whose body had been dug up after months of rotting. Its skin clung so tightly to its bones that even though its body was poorly lit in the dark, away from the phone lights, Nancy could see every bump of its ribs, the ridges of its hips. Long white hair bounced as it knelt forward, as its teeth found the man's throat. He was still crying softly that he'd always been a good servant of the Lord, that he'd gone to church as often as he could, and that he'd always—His desperate pleas ended with a *crunch*.

The angel chewed through the man's neck, and Nancy shut her eyes, unable to watch. The sounds were even worse—the chewing and crackling of bone, the wet, sloppy smacks of flesh, the blood splattering the floor as the angel grunted and slurped and swallowed. Wet, hot droplets landed on Nancy's face. The angel was making a mess. She flexed all her muscles, going rigid as she held the boy tightly, keeping him from turning around, trying her best not to flinch or make a sound of dismay.

More glass shattered around them. Nancy opened her eyelids as little as she could, trying to see in the dark, wishing one of those phones had slid down this way to light up the space. Or maybe it was better not to look. Did she really want to see these people-eating creatures so clearly?

The angels threw themselves into the car one after another, their skin scraping on broken glass. Nancy tried to count how many bodies she heard bounce off a bench or land on the floor with a thump, but the stench of death, the metallic stench of blood and meat, filled the entire train car, overwhelming her senses. She held her breath. Slowly, as slowly as she could, she reached into her purse with one hand, holding the boy with the other. Her fingers curled around her pepper spray.

Once she had that, once she'd thumbed the cap off, Nancy sat as still as possible, thankful that Amir wasn't moving much either. Every time he tried to turn his head toward the sounds of footsteps and hand steps, Nancy held the boy's head tight and kept him against her chest.

She didn't dare whisper to him. Didn't dare breathe too loudly. The creatures moved on all fours, from body to body, sniffing and chewing and tearing off limbs. A few people cried out, but that was followed by a hiss and a choked scream, and then the disgusting sounds of feeding. It reminded her of pigs on a farm, lapping up wet food from a trough.

Above, thuds and scrapes and dragging sounds went along the ceiling. The angels must've climbed on top too; more screams echoed up and down the tunnels and into the train car. The hissing cut sharply through her thoughts, leaving her with nothing but gut-wrenching fear. Nowhere was safe.

Wanting to throw up, Nancy forced herself to look. She counted four shuffling bodies moving. Four, counting the angel chewing through what was left of the horrible man. The angels looked so painfully like people; it confused her. She'd never imagined angels like this; she'd always pictured them as beautiful beings of light and brilliance, shining servants of God with gorgeous feathery wings. That was how she'd imagined them all her life; standing beside her, protecting her.

These creatures looked completely wrong. Extremely underweight, moving as though they had no minds, almost animallike, sniffing and eating, like vultures or raccoons. Their bodies glistened from the phone lights, and their shadows crawled all over the walls. Then one of the angels *screeched*, and this time, Nancy couldn't help but flinch. She banged her head against the train door, and Amir wriggled in her arms.

The angel was clawing at its eyes, wailing as it scrambled over a body. It spat blood and hissed as its foot kicked a phone. A flashlight bounced all over, causing one of the other angels to hiss in pain too. It smashed itself against a seat, and the entire train car jolted.

The other angels shuffled around, hissing and crying, and Nancy squinted at the first angel that screeched. It was on its elbows and knees, almost like an injured dog. As it clawed its face, blood dripping from the scratch marks on its forehead and cheeks, Nancy realized what had hurt it.

*The light.* Someone's forgotten phone, still beaming its flashlight. The angel had walked over it and looked down, and that must be their weakness. Direct light. *Their eyes can't handle the light!*

Hope clawed its way down her throat. Shaking, Nancy let go of the pepper spray. It took tremendous effort to release her fingers. She had to shut her eyes and inhale slowly to relax. She felt around carefully, sliding her palm over her purse's velvet lining. Her fingernails bumped against some cards, some cough drops, and the wrapper of some candy bar she'd forgotten about. She winced as it crinkled, but the sound was muffled inside the purse. *Where is it?*

The first angel finished feasting on the man across the aisle, his wide-eyed face frozen in permanent horror. His throat and chest had been hollowed out, and his ribs stuck out of the fleshy red mess. Bits of him slid off the seat and landed *splat* on the floor. Another angel came from Nancy's left, sniffing the air, its empty eyes scanning the bodies and searching.

**Tarnished Angel (Level 3)**

Glass crunched beneath its hands. Its shoulder blades moved grossly as it crawled closer to her. It'd caught her scent. Hers and Amir's; she was sure of it.

*Come on. Come on!* She couldn't find her phone; she was trying not to panic, trying not to let it overwhelm her, but her breath came shallow and brisk. Her lungs refused to work. She couldn't tell if she was shaking or if that was the boy.

This angel had short hair. Nancy couldn't tell its gender in the dark. It was thin like the others, hunched over and hissing softly. Then its eyes met Nancy's. It locked onto her. She felt it in every single one of her bones.

Baring its teeth, the creature hissed sharply and launched itself, arm outstretched, grotesque fingernails reaching for her.

Nancy gave up trying to find her phone. She grabbed the pepper spray and, with the scream she'd been forcing down this entire time, sprayed the angel right in the face.

The burning mist caught it straight in the eyes and mouth, and the creature's head bounced off the arm rail with an ugly thud. It collapsed to the floor on top of Amir's grandmother, its skinny, horrible body wriggling in agony as it clawed at its eyes and screeched at the top of its lungs. Its feet jerked blindly, catching Nancy's wrist and knocking the pepper spray from her grip as she slid across the floor to get away, holding the boy tightly.

There was another *thump* as the angel that had eaten the man slumped onto the floor, glistening blood rushing down its throat. It opened its mouth and burped, then cocked its head, sniffing.

## Tarnished Angel (Level 6)

Its number had gone up. It had eaten the man, and its level had gone higher, and now, it was eyeing her like dessert. She glanced quickly for the pepper spray; it was rolling away from her as the other angel thrashed in agony, but its thrashing had knocked her purse in her direction, and she could see the glossy casing of her phone sticking out.

The angel pounced. She grabbed her phone. Her fingers trembling, panic shuddering through her every movement, she tapped the screen furiously. She found the button for the flashlight and, just as the angel yanked Amir from her embrace, just as the boy cried out and grabbed her blouse, tearing the cloth further, just as the angel's reeking breath wafted over Nancy, she flicked her phone up and aimed the sudden burst of brightness into its face.

For a horrid, twisted instance, she got a clear look at the angel: the taut, stretched-out skin, the red strands of meat stuck between its decaying teeth, the glossy emptiness of its all-white eyes, the thin hairs of its eyebrows. It released Amir and fell away, screaming in agony. It writhed and splashed in a pool of blood.

Nancy stood, shaking, adrenaline pumping through her injured body. She had a way to protect herself. She shouted for Amir to get behind her as she held the phone in front of her, armed with light. The other two angels moved closer, perched on a bench, grasping a pole and hissing at her. She shone the light in their faces, and they scampered back, arms raised, hissing angrily. They couldn't attack her as long as she had light, but where was she supposed to go?

She figured the footsteps above meant the angels were working their way down the train. They must've come from ahead, so they'd be going after that crowd of people earlier.

*What the fuck is even going on?* How had she fallen into a zombie horror movie? Was this a dream? A stress-induced nightmare? No, it couldn't be. She was awake. She was sure of it. Everything hurt, and the stench of blood was too thick in her nose. She had to focus right now. She was breathing too hard, trying to calculate, trying to figure out her next step. What were these angels doing here? Were they connected to the earthquake? Were Jenny and Oliver alright?

That message in her head . . . it had said *Rapture*. Was this it?

*Is this Rapture?*

She bit her lip. That didn't matter. She had to get to the surface. If the angels couldn't stand a little flashlight, then surely she'd be safe aboveground. At least until nighttime.

Amir had scampered behind her legs, staring wide-eyed at the angels. She almost told him not to look, but there was no point. He'd already seen them all, and he was shaking too much, clinging to the back of her legs, crying silently. She had to get him out of here, but they were stuck in a stalemate. A stalemate that would end violently once her phone's battery died.

"Okay," she whispered as the angels hissed. The first two she'd blinded had recovered, but they stayed back, like alley cats on high alert, waiting for an opening to pounce. The one she'd sprayed was bleeding profusely from its eyes, its face red and blotchy. "It's going to be alright," she said loudly, for her own sake as well as the boy's. She tried to sound confident. "We're going to move to the front of the train."

The boy whimpered, but he didn't protest. She'd done the math quickly. She'd been on the train for a while before the earthquake, and they had to be closer to the next stop than the previous one. Everyone who'd run back was probably doomed. Going forward made the most sense, and if help was coming, she could meet them before they got to the train and warn them about these monsters. She swallowed hard, her mind made up.

She stepped back, knelt, and picked up her pepper spray. The boy grabbed something from his grandmother's body, and after a moment of tapping, another source of light shone from it too.

"Good," whispered Nancy. "We have to hold them back at all sides, okay? Just like a video game. The flashlight keeps us safe. We'll go to the hospital and find your dad."

The boy nodded fervently, his brows furrowed, an intent expression on his little face. He held the phone with both hands, turning this way and that, and the angels hissed and screeched and scrambled out of their way, bounding across the benches and running into poles with hefty thuds to escape the light.

One brushed right past Nancy in its mad rush, and she cried out and stumbled back. But it didn't have a chance to hurt her; the light had flashed in its eyes, and the creature bolted to the far side of the train car. Breathing hard, Nancy led Amir slowly up the aisle until they got to the heavy door.

She told him to keep his eyes and the light on the angels as she struggled to slide the door open. Beyond it, through the cracked windows, she could see the bloody mess in the next car. One of the overhead lights was flickering, and she grimaced at the sight, but at least there weren't any angels in there.

"Okay," she spoke, turning back and making sure none of the angels had gotten too close. "We're going to cross over into the other car."

"Nana says we should never do that," said Amir, clutching his phone with both hands. His back was to the angels, and she clenched her teeth out of fear. She stifled the impulse to snap at him. That wouldn't help.

"This is an emergency," she said firmly. "Nana wants us to do our best, right?"

He nodded.

Keeping her light on the angel, Nancy motioned for him to go across. "Watch your step. There's a small gap."

She hurried after him, glancing at the train tracks below before shutting the door. All the angels screamed and bolted toward them. Just as she opened the next door, just as they managed to get inside, she heard a series of thuds and shattered glass. She looked back to see two angels struggling to crawl through the door's window, their heads and arms thrashing against the other.

# CHAPTER TWENTY-FOUR

# THE NEXT STOP IS…

### NANCY

Every ounce of instinct in Nancy's body was screaming at her. This couldn't be real. This couldn't be happening. But even as her muscles and limbs refused to accept the bodies and blood, the broken glass crunching beneath her feet, she felt a strange, cold sharpness. A clarity she'd never felt before. There was no anxiety, no panicking, just a burning desire to get to the front of the train while keeping Amir safe, and getting outside.

She wanted to get to her kids. Jenny and Oliver. Were they safe? Were they in danger? The earthquake had to have brought them back. This was an act of God. But what were these angels? Were these things attacking her children too?

And her damn phone. It didn't seem to be connecting now. She'd gotten a warbled call through before, had heard Henry's voice. But nothing would load now. No texts would send. She couldn't call for help. There was no more signal. Was that because of the earthquake? Was there a power outage on the surface too?

But these worries wouldn't help her, so she didn't worry. Her mind emptied of everything but her surroundings, and she put one foot in front of the other.

She tried not to slip on blood. Tried not to notice the carnage. Opening the heavy doors at the end of each train car was painful; it took too much arm strength to slide open, then she had to hold it for Amir to get out, and her hands were injured already. The crossing between cars wasn't easy either. Once she'd shut one door behind her, they were stuck in between cars, in the sweltering heat of the underground tunnel, darkness surrounding them, as all the train lights had finally gone out. If it weren't for their phones, they would be helpless.

There was a tiny gap between each car that they had to step over. She'd been worried about Amir's legs being too short, but he crossed them well enough, though he kept looking down in fear. After the second car, an angel tried to attack from above as they moved into the next.

Nancy spritzed the creature in the face with pepper spray then ducked as its arms swung blindly, the hissing and screaming hurting her ears as she pulled the next door open, hurried Amir inside, and followed as quickly as she could. Each breath was strained. Her ribs hurt so much, she was barely upright, but there wasn't a moment to rest.

An angel was already in this train car, feasting on a man crying softly for help. Amir flashed it in the face with his phone's light, and the creature scrambled to the far side, screeching in pain, moving on all fours like some sort of demented zombie. It crawled out through a window, glass cutting into its hips and thin legs.

Footsteps followed along the metal ceiling. More hissing noises echoed around the tunnel as Nancy stepped over the bodies, making sure not to trip. If she fell again, she wasn't sure she'd be able to get back up. She ignored the man, who was crying softly, and told Amir sternly to keep moving. The man wore a dress shirt and tie, and was lying on his side, eyes glossed over. The angel had torn into him, exposing much of his guts, and Nancy knew he didn't have much time left. There was nothing she could do for him.

She tried to move quickly, but there was too much blood, too many bodies, and Amir was struggling to keep up. Their lights shone on torn chunks of flesh, teeth marks, and exposed bones, on streaks and handprints of blood on poles and door windows and benches. But that wasn't even the worst part. No, the worst part was the eyes.

People's eyes stared at nothing, glistening with every flicker of light. And the *smell*. It smelled like metal that had been sitting in the sun for too long. She got the sense the angels had attacked quickly and suddenly, but there had been too many people, too much prey, and they'd pounced from one to the other trying to gorge on as many as possible. Or were they just hunting for sport? Killing just because they could?

Some bodies had been trampled to death, shoe prints on their backs or faces. Others must've gotten hurt in the initial earthquake, easy targets for the angels when the onslaught began. She wished she could cover Amir's eyes. She wished she could scoop him up and carry him out of this nightmare, but she needed his set of hands. They both had to be alert with their phones. That was the only thing keeping the angels at bay, and her pepper spray was almost out.

She wished Henry was with her. Henry and his gun. Was this the "just in case" he'd had in mind?

It helped that Amir was quick. Even though he trotted along slowly behind her, whenever a ghastly face appeared in a broken window, he'd cry out and shine the light right into their eyes. The angel would tumble off in a fit of screaming, shards of glass raining down in and outside the car.

The boy didn't seem too bothered by the bodies. Or if it did bother him, he didn't say anything. Maybe he thought it was a video game. Or a movie. Kids grew up watching much worse these days, she told herself. Or was she just trying to convince herself that things weren't as bad as they were?

What would happen once their phones died? Batteries didn't run forever. And what if the angels realized they could just shut their eyes or cover their faces? In a face-to-face fight, those things would tear Nancy apart.

*Don't worry about that now. Calm. Stay calm.*

They made it to the last train car, the very front of the entire train. But this final door wouldn't open no matter how hard Nancy shook the handle and yanked. It was locked from the inside. She shone her light through the window. This one was denser and darker than the other windows on the train, but Nancy could see the conductor.

A uniformed body lay slumped against the controls. He was missing most of one shoulder and arm, blood dripping from the wound. Nancy grimaced. Beyond him was the shattered front glass of the train; she'd been hoping they could get into the conductor's room then out through his door.

Exasperated, she tried turning the handle again, but it wouldn't budge. She glanced to her right and left at the sliding doors. Could she pry them open? With her hand as injured as it was? With how weak she was? And all that noise would surely attract the angels right to them. She bit her lip hard enough to draw blood. Her plan had come to a dead end, and her clarity was falling apart. It was too hard to think.

She was too aware of the footsteps above and the hissing echoing around the tunnel. At least the angels weren't inside the car with them, but . . . She wondered if she could crawl out through a broken window. If she could get the boy out that way. But it was no good. The glass would cut into them, and they'd be an easy meal for the angels.

Did she really have any chance of surviving this? She squeezed her phone and glanced around the train car again, trying to find any possible escape route. They just had to get to the station ahead, then they could get to the surface, to sunlight. And there'd be more people there. Police officers. Firemen. Rescue operatives. Maybe even the National Guard. She just had to get there.

*Maybe . . .* An idea lit up Nancy's thoughts as her light shone on the opposite side of the train car. Between each car was that tiny gap, and there was a little more of a gap on either side of the hooks that connected the cars. There were large cables that prevented people from just stepping off the sides, but that space beside the hook . . . They'd have to squeeze through, but she was sure she could fit. She was thin and small, and the boy was even smaller. That was their best hope.

"C'mon," she said, hobbling briskly back the way they'd come. Amir hurried after her, one hand on her skirt, the other aiming the phone behind him. A hand emerged from a window and squeezed jagged glass, drawing blood. The sheen of a forehead appeared next, but Nancy put it out of her mind. Her heart was pounding so hard, she felt it in her throat, and she focused as intently as she could on the door. *Get to the door.*

She slid it open, forearms straining, just as that angel climbed into the train car and went sprawling over a bench. "You first," she whispered, holding the door for Amir. Once they were in the gap, she shut the door before the angel could realize where they'd gone. She held her breath.

Amir looked up at her with wide eyes. He puffed out his cheek and glanced at the doors. "Are we moving back to Nana?"

She shook her head. "We're going to drop down here. See the gap?"

She shone her light on the space between the two cars. A large metal hook and binding went across the center, but on either side of the hook was a space. Glass clinked in the train car, and she hoped more angels had gone inside. She nudged the boy forward with one hand and gave his shoulder a squeeze. In the sweltering heat, it was difficult to breathe, and Amir kept clinging to her leg. He glanced down at the dark tracks below and shook his head.

"It's going to be alright," she said, trying to stifle her own pounding sense of dread. She scanned the ceiling of the tunnel, keeping the light focused on the floor. That gave her enough visibility to make sure nothing was above them. Nothing would pop out from the train tops. "Okay, I'll go first. We're going to duck down under these cables, see? Then edge along the tunnel."

The gap looked even tinier now. Shaking, she lowered herself till she was sitting on the metal ledge, lowering her feet into the space below. She ignored the horrifying image of getting stuck halfway, her head and upper body a buffet for the angels as her legs kicked uselessly.

*Are there rats down there? Filthy, disease-ridden rats?*

*Do rats really matter right now?*

She sucked in her belly, wincing at the sharp pain in her ribs, then glanced assuredly at Amir. Holding on to the train with her good arm, she lowered her hips through the gap. She went lower and lower until her shoe felt the metal hardness of the railing. *Never touch the third rail,* she remembered. That's where the electricity ran. But she had no way of knowing which one was the third rail, and either way, nothing responded to the bottom of her shoe. Slowly, she let go of the train and stood on the rail.

She tried to smile encouragingly at Amir, most of her body beneath the train now. He shone his light into her face, and she squinted.

"Don't look," she whispered, holding out her hand. "Come on now. Nearly there . . . Yes. I got you." He sat down on the edge just as she had. But instead of letting go, he held on. And she realized he couldn't jump. He was too short. He'd trip on the rail and . . . She repositioned herself so he could slide off the train and onto her.

But as he threw his arms around her, his phone slipped from his grip and clattered down to the bottom. She clutched his head to her chest as she knelt into the dark space, her heart pounding so hard, terrified the angels had heard the noise. The phone had landed face down, its light shining upward and illuminating the metal underbelly of the train. She kicked it away so that its light wouldn't be as visible, then she ducked beneath the cables, suppressing a groan as her bones protested, making her way to the side of the train.

She wished there was enough space for them to crawl beneath the train, even if it meant being on her hands and knees, crawling over the filthy railing. But there was no time for what ifs, and she slipped into the gap between the side of the train and the tunnel wall.

"I'm setting you down," she whispered as quietly as she could. The boy shook his head, but she had no choice. They couldn't move in this space if she was holding him; they had to flatten themselves against the wall.

Once she'd set him down, she showed him her plan. She tucked her phone into her coat pocket, obscuring the light so that only a soft glow illuminated the metal skin of the train in front of them, and flattened herself against the tunnel wall. She ignored the crawling sense of filth, how dirty it must be, how she was ruining her hair and the back of her coat, but what did that matter. She stepped forward, the train in front of her, its unmoving metallic body looking like a gigantic insect.

Sucking in her breath, she heard a soft crackling in her lungs. Her knees burned as she extended her leg to the side before sliding her body forward. She motioned for Amir to follow, and he did the same as her, flattening himself against the tunnel and moving sideways, shuffling his feet with careful steps.

If there had just been a bit more space, the two of them could have walked facing forward, but at least the windows were too high up for them to peer into the train car. She could hear angels scrambling inside. Could hear them hissing and sniffing.

Could they smell her? Could they smell her fear?

She heard a loud *thud* somewhere behind them. It must've been two train cars down. Were the angels leaving? Had they found someone else to eat? That didn't matter.

They moved slowly. Carefully. Continuing their sideways shuffling. One step to the side before the other foot slid over. The movement made her hips ache. Her hamstrings tightened. Her ribs were ready to pop out of their cage. But bit by bit, they made their way.

The angels must not have known the two of them were off the train. Maybe they didn't understand. Or maybe the thick, disgusting stench of the tunnel, the sickly hot air, was masking them. As long as Nancy and the boy remained quiet, they could go. They could slip away unnoticed!

Her back and hips ached from their awkward movements. Her lungs burned. But they got to the front of the train car, right below the conductor's window, and the tunnel opened ahead of them. They could face forward again and move . . .

She held her breath, too afraid to step out from their little compact space between the train and the tunnel wall. It was claustrophobic, but at least it was safe. The empty space ahead looked daunting. It was hardly visible, and the darkness opened like an enormous mouth. The tracks led to nothing.

But with every passing moment, every bead of sweat dripping down her back, she knew her phone was running out of battery. They were down to one phone now. They had to keep going.

She reached for Amir's hand, wincing as she tapped the tunnel wall twice before finding Amir's sleeve. Pulling him with her, she stepped out into the open space and sped away from the train without looking over her shoulder. She was careful to step between each of the tracks so there would be no tapping sounds against the metal, and she hobbled as quickly as she could, forcing Amir to keep up.

His breaths came quick and shallow, and he was half running, but adrenaline pumped through Nancy's limbs. Her exhaustion and pain faded to a dull throbbing. They were going to make it. They were going to be just fine.

A short while later, after they'd put five or so minutes of distance between themselves and the train, she heard a hiss that sent a chill shooting down her spine.

Her hope fell apart, and she froze. Amir bumped into her leg. This hiss was coming from up ahead.

Then there was another. And another. Nancy pulled her phone out from her coat pocket, careful to cover the flashlight so as to not give away their position. She shook her pepper spray gently, trying to measure how much was left.

Not enough. There wasn't enough. Amir clung close to her, and she dragged him along, holding her breath as the hissing sounds grew louder, as another sound became terribly clear.

Chewing. Chewing and tearing and swallowing.

A dim, eerie glow came into view. She'd hoped the station would be more brightly lit, but it must've lost power too. The rock face of the tunnel walls gave way to cold, white tiles. A strip of green tiles ran along the center stating the station's name in big, bold letters. *57th Street, Lexington Avenue.* Her phone vibrated, and she almost dropped it as her eyes went wide. Her heart pounded in her ears as she realized she had a connection again.

She tapped on the screen, struggling to unlock it as the notification bar kept popping up.

*Where are you???*
*Are you okay?*
*Nancy!*
*Nancy pick up*
*What ix going on:?*

There were dozens of texts just like that from Henry. But then, the worst notification came, and it flashed by so quickly she wasn't sure if she'd seen it: *Ollie's at the hospital. Heading there right now.*

*The trains are stuck. The mta's not updting shit.*
*Nancy!*
*We're at Mnhattan hope fgeneral*
*NAncy, please respond*
*They wn't let me insde*

There were endless missed calls from Henry, from coworkers and friends and family, from numbers she didn't recognize. But tears filled her eyes and blurred her vision, and the light and colors on the screen blurred into a meaningless blob.

She blinked them away. *I can't cry yet. I have to get out of here. Oliver's safe. And Jenny . . . Jenny. Where's Jenny?*

Trying to recompose herself, she lowered her phone, ignoring the vibrations and the oncoming notifications, ignoring the desperate need to call Oliver's number and then Jenny's and then Henry's. She stepped forward.

As the station came into view, she spotted an angel on the tracks ahead. It was on all fours, feeding on someone. Two more angels were on the station platform.

Blood dripped steadily onto the tracks, but Nancy eyed the little service stairwell on the side. They'd have to climb that, cross the station platform, and get through the turnstiles. Then they could bolt up the main stairs to the surface. She could almost *feel* the sunlight on her skin. The lungful of fresh, clean air. Then she could respond to her messages. Then she could call her husband and her children, and she could help Amir find his family.

They were so close. So close that it ached.

She took Amir's hand and whispered, "We're gonna run for the stairs."

He nodded, looking determined. *If only he had his phone*, she thought.

She swallowed hard and went up the steps, counting each one to keep her mind focused. *One . . . two . . . three . . .* At twelve, as soon as her feet were on the platform, she shouted, "Hey!"

The angels whipped their heads around, most of them on all fours, the whites of their eyes focused on her. They bared their stained teeth and hissed, all attention on her. Perfect.

She raised her phone, bringing the flashlight up, shining it right into all those bony, blood-covered faces.

The result was immediate shrieking. Hissing and screeching echoed all around as the angels scrambled to get away. Nancy led Amir up the stairs, picking up her pace, keeping her light pointed forward. Two of the angels ran up the tracks to the safety of the darkness ahead. The other went for the turnstiles, spilling over them and onto the other side.

She swore silently; it was blocking off their exit. Its thin limbs flailed as it ran headfirst into the metro card kiosk with a loud *crack*, scrambling away on all fours, clawing at its face, nearly tripping as it bounded over several bodies before hitting the stairwell.

A shout came from above—a human shout.

Three shots rang out, nearly in unison, sounding like claps of thunder, and the angel screamed. Nancy dropped down and pulled Amir against her, holding him tight until her ears stopped ringing. She glanced behind her, making sure nothing was sneaking up on them, then glanced at the angel that had tried to go up the stairs.

It lay on the steps, a bullet hole in its forehead and another in its shoulder, oozing blood.

Hope, warmer and more powerful than before, filled Nancy's chest as she stood up, still holding Amir. Adrenaline surged through her legs as she ran for the stairwell. She could already hear hissing echoing in the tunnel behind her, but that didn't matter. There were people up there. People with weapons. They were safe.

Amir shouted something she couldn't fully hear as she ran as fast as her legs could go. She stepped over the bleeding angel and was looking up at the long flight of stairs to the top, where sunlight was leaking through the entrance, when another shot rang out.

"Hold your fire! Hold your fire! She's a civilian!" roared a voice. Everything blurred and echoed around her. The light dimmed. Shadows darted around her. She turned instinctively to the side, trying to shield Amir with her body.

Nancy felt like she'd been punched in the thigh. Amir cried out, and she fell to her knees, still holding Amir. Something hot and wet ran down her leg.

*I've been shot . . .*

*I've been shot!*

Something grabbed her foot and yanked. Nancy let Amir go as her chin and elbows bounced on several steps and she screamed, trying to grab onto something, the pain in her leg feeling like something was ripping her in half. Amir reached down and grabbed her arm as she screamed at him to run.

The shadows from above swarmed closer and closer. Blue uniforms. Frightened faces. Flashlights. More shots rang out, like cannon fire echoing in the stairwell. The static of walkie-talkies rang through her head like electricity. Crackling voices. Urgent callouts.

Whatever had grabbed her foot let go, screeching and hissing and shouting erupting at the foot of the stairwell; she couldn't tell what was human and what was angel, but she grabbed the collar of the nearest officer as they tried to help her.

"Manhattan Hope," choked Nancy. Her vision faltered. Her ears throbbed from the loud shots. She wasn't sure if she was screaming or whispering. She wasn't sure if her leg was still attached. "My son . . . *Take me to him right now.*"

# CHAPTER TWENTY-FIVE

# WHAT JENNY HAD TO SAY

When Jenny opened her eyes, it was snowing, snowflakes tickling her eyelashes as she blinked. She rubbed her nose. A fire crackled beside her, and she was lying on one of the logs she'd made. Yeshua sat beside her, one arm resting on a raised knee. He was wearing his purple robes, and he looked much healthier again. Towering over him was his cross.

Jenny raised her arm, remembering how he'd chewed through it and not gained anything. She turned it every which way, but there wasn't even a scar. He must've healed it. Or maybe the Valescent Light had . . . She shuddered. It had gone up a tier. It was tier three now, and she kept picturing herself stretching the light open, expanding it . . .

Wait. She could still feel it.

She could still *see* it. Jenny bolted up, her armored feet slamming onto the snow as she stared over the flames at the floating gash in the air, glistening with golden light.

"It's still there?" she whispered. But it wasn't draining any more of her stamina. She felt well rested. She felt just fine.

But she couldn't remember bringing everyone into this world. Couldn't remember anything after she'd pulled on the light and saw that her ability had grown stronger again. She looked at her pale hand as snow landed and dissolved on her skin. It was like she'd gone into autopilot.

*Are you sure?*

That's what the thought had said. And it hadn't been Iblis. She knew it wasn't Eve, so who else was in her head? *Was* there someone else in her head? Or was she just imagining things?

"Hello?" she said out loud accidentally, and Yeshua raised his head, his eyes opening.

He smiled at her, but it was strained. The wrinkles on his face deepened. "You're awake."

"What happened?"

"You saved me," he said. "Again."

A ghoul, white colored and with familiar burning blue eyes, shuffled toward them. Jenny reacted out of instinct, drawing her hatchet back to her hand with a flash of light, then she remembered who it was. "Iblis, is that you?"

Yeshua grimaced. The demon nodded. It had better control of its body now.

**I am relieved to see you have recovered, but we have an issue.**

"What is it now?" she asked, glancing at Yeshua, who wouldn't meet her eyes, then back at Iblis.

**The passageway you opened only connects to the world of death. We cannot travel to any other worlds.**

"And why would you want to?" snarled Yeshua, rising to his feet with a swirl of his robes. He towered over the possessed ghoul. "Haven't your kind done enough?"

The demon didn't back down. He fixed his smoldering look on Yeshua.

**We will not rest until we have torn *him* down. We wish to be free of this frozen world.**

"This is your *home*," spat Yeshua, his voice dripping with distaste. "This is where you belong. You sacrificed your world, and for what? You couldn't even get past Adonai's guard dog."

Jenny sat quietly. Though she was rested, her head still felt woozy, but she wanted to know more. It seemed like Yeshua had some history with the demons, and she wondered what that was about.

The radio-staticky voice crackled louder than usual.

**I don't know what issue you take with my people, but I assure you, we have no ill will toward humankind. We mean the material world no harm.**

Yeshua glowered. "Demons have plagued my children for countless generations. Lurking in the dark. Taking advantage of the vulnerable. What do you have to say to that?"

The demon didn't back down, its ghoul head staring steadily at Yeshua.

**My people have been sequestered in this world for time immea-
surable. How could we have done this harm to you?**

"Yeah," said Jenny, recalling the memories she'd seen from Iblis. "They've
been trapped on this world, stuck here. Barely able to move. Barely alive."

But Yeshua didn't seem convinced. "I know the stories; I know what happened. How your kind would eavesdrop on my world. How your kind only
made things worse, leading members of my flock astray."

Iblis's flames burned more brightly. Maybe it was because their minds had
been so connected, but Jenny could tell he was mad, even though the ghoul
face showed no emotion.

**Renegades. There are always those who seek selfish desires, act
with ill intentions. But is that any different from the angels? From
the humans? Can you truly blame all your people's misgivings on
my demons?**

Yeshua raised his arm as though he was about to yell again, his purple
sleeve billowing, but Jenny threw her hatchet into the fire. Sparks shot out,
and they both turned to face her. She was younger than the both of them by
far, but she wasn't going to waste time squabbling. She was tired—so tired—
of all this. "We have the same goals. We can work together."

"How?" asked Yeshua, crossing his arms.

Iblis answered.

**We aspire to dethrone Adonai and free the worlds. You know the
damage he has done. The crimes he has committed.**

"Yeah?" Yeshua turned again. "You already failed once. How do you pro-
pose you'll win this time? March into the world of light with those useless
bodies and lose again? It will be the same result as before." He exhaled through
his teeth. "I wanted to bring the ghouls here as punishment, to watch them
burn, not to be wineskins filled by your kind."

As they continued their back-and-forth, Jenny's eyes went up to the cross,
the symbol that seemed to tower over the world, snow drifting gently around
it, piling on top of the wood. She closed her eyes, thinking about what Iblis
had said just a few moments ago. The passageway only went to the world of
death now. That's what he'd said. But what did that mean?

It was still open, still hovering in the air and expelling light and emanating warmth—and it looked like Iblis and the others could use it without Jenny needing to guide them. Had she locked it into place somehow? Made it a fixed thing that would always work?

She got up and walked toward it, ignoring Yeshua and Iblis. They stopped arguing and watched as Jenny touched it, the light shimmering and responding, thin tendrils of color reaching out to envelop her hand.

The light felt different now. Not as gooey; almost spongy. Something with a slight bit of resistance; more physical.

Ignoring what they were saying, Jenny stepped forward. She didn't need to activate any skill or do anything; the light parted for her like a curtain, then she was inside, surrounded at once by the warmth of golden light and swirling colors.

"Why don't I remember what happened?" she whispered. "Why don't I remember what I did?" Her breath bubbled away, and blues and reds stretched out and wrapped themselves in circles around her arms and thighs before fading away. A splash of green light broke against her chest.

She didn't remember pulling everyone into the light, didn't remember bringing them all out. Had she lost consciousness? Had she done all that on autopilot? There had been a voice. In her head. Someone had spoken; she was sure of it.

A shudder traveled up her spine, and wavy purple lights rippled around her. She tried to focus. There wasn't any pushing or pulling now; it wasn't like before, when she'd felt so many different paths. That was all gone. Even the enormous pull of the material world—her world.

No. She only felt two directions now. The first led back the way she'd come, a gentle push from behind. Above her was a gentle pull, and she swam toward it, her head clearing the surface of the world of death. But only her head. The rest of her waded inside the light.

Immediately, she was greeted by a splatter of hot blood. It was still raining, pouring, and she could see the ghouls moving aimlessly between the pillars, their red limbs glistening in the glow of her light. They could see her. Their moans and whimpers and mutters reached out to her, pleading with her to feed them. She could feel their hunger.

But she didn't care. Jenny sank back into the light and turned. This time, the slight push came from the world of death, and the pull came from the world of demons. There were still no other directions to go. It was a two-way passage now. She swam slowly through the light, trying to relax her mind, trying to think.

When she returned to the snowy world, and the bitter cold stung her nose and lips, she stepped out and surveyed everyone around her. Yeshua and Iblis stood on opposite sides of her campfire, watching her. The deaths sat on a neater row of logs by their much larger fires. Yeshua must've added more things for them to sit on.

And beyond them, like a mass of giant statues, stood a large crowd of demons. She almost felt like she was back in the city, having just surfaced from a train station into one of the busiest parts of midtown. But the demons didn't move. They were statues with burning lights in their eyes, watching her and the others.

She scratched her chin then looked at Yeshua and Iblis. "Okay," she said. "What do we need to do?"

Iblis spoke first.

**We require more bodies if we are to invade the world of light. I am sending groups of demons to grab more ghouls and drag them back here, but it is slow, and we lose and injure as many bodies as we replace.**

Jenny nodded before turning to Yeshua.

Yeshua gestured toward the deaths. "We must still free the remaining deaths. I want to take a few and return to that world to free more. If we move in and out, then we can fight off the ghouls, get some rest, and continue saving the others."

She licked her lips, trying to do the math of what they were saying, her brain turning over the data. There was something obvious they hadn't figured out, but she still had so many questions. What were the ghouls? What were the pillars? And would Yeshua ever accept the demons? Could *she* trust them?

Her face reddened when she remembered Iblis could read her mind. The ghoul didn't turn its head or anything, but she pointed apologetic thoughts in his direction. *I do trust you.*

And she did. She'd *felt* the demon's mind, lived through some of the demon's memories. She knew his hurt.

Then she realized what the plan was. It was so obvious, she almost slapped her forehead. There were still things to figure out, but they had to work together.

She squeezed and opened her fists, then spoke. "I think I have something."

Yeshua stroked his beard thoughtfully. Iblis stood still as snowflakes drifted by, his eyes smoldering.

"Okay. I know this is going to be a bit weird, but what if your people possessed the deaths?" Before Yeshua could interject, she held up her hand. "Only momentarily. They need a vessel to move through the passageway, right? So, the demons can go along with the deaths, and you can go with them too, Yeshua. This way, we can help free more deaths from the pillars, and the demons can possess more ghouls . . ." She stumbled for a moment here, unsure about that. Was it right to subjugate the ghouls?

**The ghouls are a byproduct of Adonai's desire to control matter. They are ancient creatures born of his attempts to create a body.**

"That's why they're always calling for their father," replied Yeshua, walking over to the log and sitting down with his hands on his knees. A dark expression flickered across his face. "It was Azra'il who thought it would be poetic justice to crucify me to that world and leave me to the failed sons."

"So, what's the blood rain?" asked Jenny. "What's with the blooded ghouls?"

"That world was reformed to be a prison," he explained. "A prison for deaths, so that they cannot go on their journeys and fulfill their lives." He raised two hands, holding them together before separating them.

"When we are born, you and I, humans, we have three parts. Our body, our soul, and our death. And when we die, when our bodies no longer can contain us, our souls and deaths leave the material world and are reborn into their respective worlds: the world of death, known as Hades by many, and the world of souls, known as the Garden."

Jenny almost felt like she was in Sunday school again, but she listened closely. The Garden. Hades, the underworld. "And this world was called Hell?" she asked, glancing at the demon to make sure it wasn't insulting.

**Hell. *Hell* is an ancient term for punishment. I believe it was called so because of our suffering.**

She grimaced, remembering their pain and anguish, remembering how the demons had existed in a comatose state for all those years in the cold. She shuddered. "So, what do you think? Are we good with my plan?"

"The deaths can't fight," said Yeshua, scratching his beard again. "But the demons . . ." He tried to hide his scowl as he turned to Iblis.

**We will pass quickly from the deaths to the ghouls, ensuring that no deaths are harmed.**

Iblis bowed his head

Yeshua nodded solemnly. "And this will be perfect. By freeing more deaths, we are weakening their machinations."

"The pillars, you mean?"

"Yes. They are entrapment devices which harvest the connection between deaths and souls for infinite energy." He turned to face Jenny. "Deaths are manifestations of energy, and while the souls are alive, while the souls are forced to remain alive . . ."

**I am sorry. They could not harvest us, so they have chosen to harvest your people.**

Jenny exhaled a long cloud of air. She could tell there was still animosity between Yeshua and the demons, but something seemed to have given way. They looked prepared to work together.

She wondered if the deaths would have any issue with this; someone had to go explain to them what was going on, but Yeshua would be the best one for that. And she didn't want to be a part of this plan. She'd made the passageway, made it permanent—for now, at least; she wasn't sure yet how it worked. And while they dealt with freeing more deaths and securing more bodies for the demons, Jenny wanted the second part of her agreement with Iblis.

"I just want to find my friend," said Jenny after a moment of heavy silence.

"Your 'more than a friend' friend?" asked Yeshua with a small, understanding smile.

"Yeah," Jenny replied. "I just want to find her. And I guess that means going to the world of souls, right?" She stared at her hands as she used a little bit of Valescent Light. At the golden light shining from her palm. At the streams of colors. "I will find her. And then . . . I don't know what'll happen after that, but I swore I'd kill God if I had to."

She took another deep breath, allowing the cold air to fill her lungs before exhaling slowly. She had more to say. Jenny found herself wanting to speak more; she wasn't really sure why.

"We've all been so trapped by all this. By fear. By other people's control. By people thinking they know better. I don't know what this Adonai wants or what the angels want, but I know what *we* want. Iblis, you want your people to be free. The deaths want to fulfill their purpose. Yeshua, you want to help them. And I want to . . . I just want to be okay, and I want the people I care about to be okay. And I want everyone to be okay. I know that's naive."

The deaths moved closer to listen. To watch. The demons did as well. They were all listening to her. Watching her. She didn't know how to feel about that, and she wavered until she caught sight of Yeshua's encouraging smile.

And it was all the same, wasn't it? Everything she'd ever gone through. Growing up struggling with her mother. Getting through the awkward years of middle school and high school. Exams. Bills. Strangers on the train. And what the angels were going through . . . what the demons had suffered through . . . It felt like life *was* the survival challenge. And maybe it shouldn't be.

"It's not fair, and I know you guys have been through a lot too. All of our people. Humans and demons. I also don't think every angel is on board with whatever is going on. You showed me that yourself, Iblis."

Jenny bit her lip, remembering his pain and sorrow and anguish at losing Sat'en to the hunger. How much had they all lost because of a few power-hungry people? "So, what we need to do . . ." She looked up at everyone in the cozy, calm ambience of the gentle snowfall, feeling so fired up her eyes might as well have been on fire. "What we need to do now is stop their bullshit and free everyone. And then, we can decide what's important and what's not."

# CHAPTER TWENTY-SIX

# TO ANOTHER WORLD

With everything decided, Jenny sat alone in the snow, poking the flames with her hatchet. She loved the way the flickering orange light caught on the obsidian edge, and sometimes, when she stared closely, she thought she could see the flame turn blue. Or was that just a trick of the light?

She sucked in a deep breath, holding it; it was cold and refreshing inside her lungs. The conversation with Yeshua and Iblis, and what she'd said loudly to everyone else, bounced around her head like a tennis match. She also kept thinking of Azra'il, the Angel of Death; the enormous angel with an evil grin and snakes for hair. Yeshua had told her the loincloth he wore was cut from the skin of tarnished angels. She shuddered and rustled the flames again, sending up a spray of sparks, lost in her thoughts.

She was preparing to open another passageway to get to the world of souls. Neither Yeshua nor Iblis could tell her what to expect, only that it was known as the Garden, where souls went after death to contemplate their lives. Then, once they were ready, once they'd made peace with themselves, they set out on a journey to reunite with their deaths. Yeshua wouldn't clarify what happened next; she got the sense he didn't quite understand. But it was evident that whatever was supposed to happen naturally had been corrupted.

The pillars were prisons that siphoned energy from the deaths, somehow turning them into infinite batteries. Neither of them knew what was happening to the souls, but Iblis seemed adamant that they were trapped in the Garden, forced to work for the angels' great plan. That they'd been rounded up and collected and enslaved, and that was how the angels had gone around subjugating the worlds. Enslavement. Punishment.

"What about you and the demons here?" she'd asked.

**Our punishment was helplessness. Abandoned here to waste away in eternity.**

Jenny had nodded. She'd felt that pain. She'd known it long before all this, stuck in her home, wondering if she would ever amount to anything. Everyone always said you could do anything if you put your mind to it, but she'd put her mind to everything and anything—writing, music, sports, math, science—and she'd always struggled. In the end, the only thing she seemed to be good at was letting people down. And now, Yeshua and Iblis were looking to her as though she'd done something important. Like she was someone important.

But all she'd done was give birth to some ancient being, then free Yeshua from the cross. And the only reason she had this world-traversing power was because she'd killed her best friend and—*Ahhhh!*

She wanted to scream, but the deaths had taken a liking to her. The demons stood by, rows of ice statues with fire in their eyes. She didn't want them to know anything was wrong, that she was deathly afraid of what they'd find in this Garden world, and what would happen once she found Susan, and what might be happening *to* Susan, and . . . The list of things she dreaded went on and on.

Possessed deaths—who now read as *Death (Vessel)*—marched into the Valescent bridge alongside groups of possessed ghouls. A short while later, they returned with even more ghouls and even more deaths, sobbing and weeping. Yeshua greeted them as they arrived, offering his arms and creating for them purple robes. If it was still storming blood on the other side, Jenny couldn't tell. None of the blood came back with them.

Once she felt rested, once she felt prepared, Jenny stood, brushing the snow off her hair and armor. Yeshua and Iblis stepped toward her.

"I'm ready," she said, trying to sound confident. She slung her hatchet through a loop on her waistline and pulled on her helmet, covering her hair and most of her face.

**I am prepared to leave as well.**

Jenny nodded. She was glad the demon would be tagging along; she didn't really want to go alone, even though they were concerned about avoiding detection. They wanted to be quick. The mission was to collect information, find Susan, then get out. Reconnaissance and rescue. With Iblis by her side, she didn't worry too much about the fights that might be ahead. Not even the desecrated angel that had nearly killed her in the high school would stand a chance against her and the demon teamed up.

"Remember," said Yeshua, "you are only looking for your friend. Do not fight Azra'il alone, and come back right away if there's any trouble." He looked at Iblis, the wrinkles around his eyes deepening. It was a look of warning, which almost made Jenny smile. She trusted Yeshua. She trusted Iblis. It was nice having them both on her side, being part of a team.

The flames went out in the ghoul's head. Its empty eye sockets stared at Yeshua then at Jenny, and a sound escaped its throat as if it was about to say something. But then, the cold overtook its body, and within a few seconds, the creature was frozen, its open mouth making it seem like a strange snowman. The blue sparks shot toward her, and she welcomed him with ease this time, as though she was taking a breath.

Light and warmth shivered through her face, and then Iblis's mind pressed against hers, and he was inside. Steam curled away from her lips. Flames didn't sprout from her eyes, and she blinked at Yeshua as Iblis explained.

**I will remain dormant until necessary to avoid any harm to your body. This will also help us remain undetected by Azra'il and his forces.**

That made sense, she thought. She smiled at Yeshua, who nodded slowly in return, then she turned away and reached for Severed Spirit. Should she touch the ground? Some point in the air? There was no storm of blood this time, no ghouls trying to tear her apart, but she also didn't know what would be waiting on the other side.

*Breathe. Concentrate.* Severed Spirit hurt to use, but again, she wasn't using it on herself. She wasn't cutting some connection with herself. It was external. *The worlds. Feel the worlds.* She licked her lips and straightened her shoulders. Cold air blew in through the gap in her helmet as she concentrated on the tip of her fingers, pretending they were claws, like when she had her exoskeleton out and she could cut through anything. *Severed Spirit.*

It felt like she was cutting through a sheet of cloth, like she was in elementary school, anxiously parting the auditorium curtains before the start of the school play, peeking out at the crowd, hoping she wouldn't spot her mother's face.

Jenny split the air, and darkness blossomed, unfurling with countless tentacles before golden light shone bright and clear. It hadn't hurt this time; all her fears and anguish hadn't come spilling out, and she'd used Valescent Light in tandem.

It was becoming easier. It was becoming instinct. Sever the space, then use Valescent Light. She wanted to experiment more with this, wanted to learn everything about it, like why did the darkness transform angels into tarnished angels? Why couldn't she pass through the darkness? Why couldn't the demons or deaths? But once it was golden and shining and rainbows of colors reached out, Jenny didn't hesitate. She didn't look back. She took the next step and slipped into the light, diving into an ocean of radiance.

Once again, she felt the push and pull of the currents around her. The push as she left the world of demons; the massive pull toward the material world. But then, there was that new pull. The pull toward the world of souls. Greens and blues swirled in that direction, and she willed her body toward it, swimming, kicking gently—bracing herself for what she would find. Iblis's mind thrummed somewhere beneath her own, his thoughts and feelings just out of reach.

Breath bubbled away from her lips as the light opened. She emerged head-first, and something wet—she thought it might be water, but it was too thick, too familiar—rushed into her mouth and up her nose, and she sputtered and coughed and choked as she climbed out of the light and splashed into what felt like a thick, viscous river.

It was blood, and for a second, she panicked. All around her was moaning and crying and reaching limbs. Had she waded into the wrong world? Was she back in the world of death, with the blood rain and the ghouls? But then, the notifications surfaced in her thoughts as she tried to find footing.

**Soul (Level 3)**
**Soul (Level 4)**
**Soul (Level 7)**
**Soul (Level 2)**

*"Gah!"* Tearing off her helmet and rubbing her face, spitting, trying not to throw up, Jenny snorted to clear her nose then looked around, breathing hard, blood dripping off her. She froze. *People* were rising from the red waves onto a grassy shore, crawling up the bank, spitting and coughing and crying. Jenny stood amidst them; they didn't even notice her.

The souls were naked, their hair wet and matted. Their skin glistened as blood dripped all over the blades of grass. They were all crawling out of the river as though they were in great pain, none of them looking up until they climbed out of the blood and got onto shore to collapse, breathing hard. Some clutched their chests. Others wailed loudly. Jenny felt Iblis stir with disgust and pity. He didn't say anything, but it was clear: this was unnatural.

Beyond the grassy bank was a dense forest, trees towering over everything. Some souls were wandering into it, but she couldn't see clearly from where she was standing. She would have to climb up the riverbank. Behind Jenny was nothing but the dark-red waves of the river. She wasn't sure how wide it was, but she couldn't see anything on the far side.

Jenny waded up onto the bank, trying not to step on any of the naked, blood-covered bodies crawling around her. They were crying softly; not the desperate crying of happiness that she was used to after saving deaths but a quiet, muffled sob, like they'd been hurt so badly they were afraid to make a sound and be hurt again.

Once the souls got onto the grass, they got to their feet, glancing nervously at one another. Some of them covered their chests and their groins. Some of them didn't seem to care. Some of them fell to their knees, grasping their heads, eyes wide with fear, hyperventilating.

A few of them muttered. Jenny caught the English-speaking ones.

"I'm dead—Why?"

"It was a truck—I didn't see it. Why did this happen to me?"

"An angel? An angel killed me?"

"God sent an angel to take me—I didn't want to die. I want to go back. I messed up, please!"

"Please, someone help me. I don't know what to do. Where am I? Hello?"

But it was an incoherent mess. Everyone was rambling.

A few souls in the lead had begun moving, gathering in small groups and marching together; after a few more bodies got out of the way, Jenny saw why. There was a sign.

### PROCEED THIS WAY FOR JUDGMENT.

It pointed toward a path. Jenny glanced around as the other souls noticed the sign, as they wordlessly followed the souls already walking in that direction. Some looked at her with curious eyes, but each expression was frightened, anxious. They bumped her with their elbows and apologized, and she was worried her armor might hurt their exposed skin.

She didn't know what to say or how to respond, but they felt cold. Ice cold. Cold enough that she could feel them through her armor. Where the deaths had been burning hot, the souls felt like they'd been trapped in the ice with the demons, and Jenny had to suppress a shudder.

But she realized she could camouflage with them. She could follow along and find out what this *judgment* thing was, even though just looking at the pointed sign gave her anxiety; even though the souls followed along as though they had no will of their own.

*I'm going to undress*, she thought to Iblis.

The demon didn't respond, and she felt a silly moment of shyness, undressing while possessed, but then, she figured it didn't matter. The demon had seen the entirety of her life; he was literally inside her mind, and nakedness didn't seem to mean anything when all these other souls were naked as well.

She willed her armor away. Golden light enveloped her, shimmering gently across her silhouette, and then, the dark scales disintegrated. Her helmet vanished, leaving her standing in the moving sea of bodies, her pale skin shining a little too much. She resisted the urge to cover herself. The last to go was her hatchet.

Just to be sure, she willed it back, and it appeared with a flash of light in her hand. At least it was instantaneous. Satisfied, she turned back and stepped back into the river, avoiding the hands and heads of newly surfacing souls, covering herself in blood.

With that, Jenny made her way up the path with the other souls, grimacing each time her body bumped another, each time their coldness felt like a splash of ice water. And now that it was direct skin-to-skin contact, the souls winced too. Some of them even gasped. Did her body feel too warm for them?

She apologized. They apologized too. Nobody really looked at her. Nobody cared that she or anyone else was naked. She knew what was on their mind—the only thing that *could* be on their mind: They were dead. And they were headed for judgment.

And now, so was she.

# CHAPTER TWENTY-SEVEN

# THE TRAIL OF SOULS

Iblis didn't know what judgment meant; Jenny almost didn't want to know, but she figured she'd find out soon enough.

The souls moved at an unbearable pace, one foot in front of the other, shuffling, dragging. They all looked exhausted, frightened, haunting looks frozen on their faces. Some of them were around her age. Some were older. Some younger. She'd even seen a few toddlers waddling around or crawling on all fours, but they reminded her too much of the angel babies that had followed her around the high school, and she couldn't really look at them. A few souls—generally the older ones, with graying hair and wrinkled, sagging bodies—knelt and picked up a few of the babies, but many were left to fend for themselves.

It seemed like everyone who died showed up at this river, emerging from it to walk along this forest path. At least the ground was soft beneath their bare feet. Fresh soil, damp and soft as though it had just rained, curled beneath Jenny's feet. Each step made a soft sound, but there were so many souls that their footsteps sounded like continuous muffled thunder. The only other sounds were the occasional birdcalls overhead, the sighs and muttering of the souls, and the sloshing blood they were leaving behind.

Every once in a while, someone bumped into her and cried out. Jenny winced, too—it was like brushing up against a block of ice, they were so cold, and they looked at her as though she'd burned them. For a moment, they looked shocked or angry, but then, their faces fell, almost as though they forgot, and they carried on, empty.

Thoughts didn't seem to last long in their heads. Jenny wondered if that was because they were dead, or if they just didn't care. Would she care? If she was dead and she was marching toward judgment, would she care about anyone else?

*You're a sinner. All you've ever done is sin.*
*You've never cared for anyone but yourself.*
Iblis's voice crackled from the back of her mind, and she blushed, realizing he'd been present for all her internal, intrusive thoughts.

**Life and death are not about sin. Sin is a concept created for control.**

Jenny chewed on the side of her lip, thinking about that. The nature of sin. What it meant to sin. But then, she bumped into another soul, apologized quickly, and carried on, trying not to think about anything but what she had to do.

Besides. Who would've thought the afterlife was a nature hike?

After a short while, her breath began to cloud in front of her. Not as much as it had in the demon's frozen world, but enough. She was cold, goose bumps were spreading across her limbs, and she was shivering. But she forced herself to keep her arms at her sides, marching forward with the other souls who didn't seem bothered at all by the cooling temperature. Their breaths didn't cloud. She'd have to be more careful; she couldn't stick out.

Another bird cry sounded through the air, ringing shrill and bright, and Jenny glanced up at the branches. Beyond them was something bright that might've been sunlight, but she was sure it wasn't the sun; the light had no warmth to it. What kind of birds would call this place home?

Squinting, she thought she could make out a wing or two, but the birds were too far away to see clearly.

She must've paused when she looked up because someone bumped into her back and cried out.

Jenny whipped around to see an old woman, naked, her sagging skin making her face and body look even sadder than the other souls'. She was carrying a baby, who was sucking on its thumb. The woman muttered something Jenny couldn't understand then walked around her.

Jenny glanced at the others; some of them were looking at her nervously. Turning back, she continued walking, trying not to let the fear thoughts overwhelm her, trying to remember that the souls were too preoccupied to keep track of anything strange.

She made a few mental notes. Poor posture—Check. She was good at that, though her new musculature made that feel strange. But it was easy to remember when everyone around her was hunched over.

She was also glad that people were in various stages of hairy. Some guys were covered in fur: facial hair ranging from stubble to thick manes, hair across their chest, arms, and legs, and thick curls of hair between their legs. Some women were hairy too, with fuzz on their limbs or little bits above their lips. Some people were clean-shaven or trimmed, but ultimately, nobody seemed to care. Nobody even covered themselves anymore. The shame or embarrassment was gone.

Jenny tried not to feel self-conscious of her curls. Of her nudity. And it helped that she hardly recognized her body, like it was someone else's.

Before the survival challenge stuff, she had been far thinner, far less healthy, her skin a dim pale, and her muscles nonexistent. She was firmer now, with a light layer of muscles. She was wider, too, taking up more space, which she tried to relegate to her subconscious, tried not to think about at all. Just walk. Just follow them, moving through an otherworldly forest, nude, with a crowd of other nude people and—

Something swooped down overhead. Wings about as long as Jenny was tall flapped lightly, and enormous white feathers fluttered down.

The souls cried out, covering their heads and cowering. Jenny did the same, squatting down but looking up. What was it? Giant birds? Monsters?

## Harpy (Level 54)

That was all Jenny got. A flash notification in her head. A glimpse of white feathers and what looked like talons, enormous and gruesome and sharp. And then, the enormous, flying thing—a shadowy figure flapping furiously—was gone, arcing back up to the treetops with a high-pitched cry.

**A harpy. I have heard of them. They are meant to be the caretakers of the Garden.**

"What are they?" she whispered under her breath. A man cowering beside Jenny looked at her. She flinched and covered her chest, repositioning her legs, but his eyes were wide with fright, and his gaze didn't linger. He was searching the sky again.

Jenny shuddered and straightened up slowly with the other souls, copying them, moving when they began moving at their slow, fearful pace. Whatever the harpies were, they hadn't done anything. They hadn't attacked anyone. And besides, the souls were already dead. What could the harpies do?

But what if they noticed she wasn't a soul? What if it had noticed a human in the crowd and that was why it'd flown down? She grimaced but kept her steady pace, marching with the others, fighting the urge to watch the skies and make sure nothing would attack her. *I can summon my hatchet back right away*, she told herself. Besides, with Iblis possessing her, she was far stronger. She was confident she could take them.

Comforted by that thought, she continued walking, one foot in front of the other. But looking at naked backs and legs only made her mind wander, and she wondered what the harpies were doing here. What did it mean to be caretakers of the Garden?

Was their job to make sure the souls walked along the path? To keep people from wandering off? On the sides of the road, there were the trees, and Jenny wondered if she might be able to run for it. But the harpies could swoop down from the skies, and they might be all over the forest. She didn't want to get skewered by those ugly talons.

The trail seemed to go on forever. It must've been several hours of walking already; she wasn't sure. Time blurred, and she couldn't tell how long it had been since she'd waded out of that river.

The blood had dried on her skin. Her hair was stuck to her back and shoulders. Dirt clung to her legs nearly up to her knees, and the strange light from the sky was starting to get on her nerves. She was tired of looking at bare shoulder blades and spines, tired of looking at people's backsides. The souls might not notice or care, but Jenny was tired of looking at people's butts.

Just when she thought she might lose it, the forest cleared away, and the sight made her knees go weak. The sun was shining brightly, fiercely; towering over them was a giant stone archway that must've been thousands of feet tall. It looked like the entrance to an ancient city.

Each of the stone blocks was taller than she was, and the top of the arch was so high up she craned her head all the way to see it. She'd walked beneath skyscrapers all the time back home, buildings that seemed to go right up to the clouds, but she was sure they could stack every single one from the city right here and still not reach the top of this archway.

None of the souls were looking up, so she quickly adjusted herself and followed them through into its shade. It was like stepping into a tunnel built inside a mountain, bookended on both sides by brilliant light that illuminated the space. The archway was about a city block thick, the insides lined with the same stone pattern. It was clear that *this* was the entrance to the afterlife. She got another round of goose bumps that had nothing to do with the chill of the souls around her.

As she crossed the length of the archway, her heart pounding, Jenny fought the urge to glance back and see how many people were behind her. The walls seemed to be closing in, too many people crowding her. She resisted an itch in her throat, a tightening in her chest. *Keep moving forward.* But the ground seemed to be shifting, extending and stretching as if hurrying her along.

It was no longer soil. Now, it was stone, and it stung the soles of her feet with every step. The souls didn't make a sound, so she tried not to be too expressive, even as she felt the soles of her feet rubbing away. To her relief, they emerged back into the sunlight on the other end a few minutes later, coming to what looked like a giant corridor or an alleyway between two enormous buildings.

There was a platform raised by several steps, and upon it was a towering set of scales. Two large flat dishes were held up by golden chains; it looked like the kind of scale she'd used in physics class to balance weights. Was this judgment?

# CHAPTER TWENTY-EIGHT

# THE SCALE OF JUDGMENT

The scales moved in tandem. While one tray rose high into the sky, way over their heads, the other dipped down toward the ground, rising and falling like a demented carnival ride. It made her feel so queasy her head spun and her insides twisted, everything inside her *dreading* the scale.

The souls seemed to be responding similarly too, muffled wails spilling from their lips, screaming, all of them crying, pleading, and begging under their breaths. They were terrified, and whatever terror Jenny felt about the scale, they must be feeling it infinitely more. They were the ones who would be judged.

Souls climbed up the steps toward the scale one at a time. When the far scale came down, Jenny saw an enormous white feather resting on it. She squinted at the thing, watching the soul that had just been judged climb off the opposite tray, and then the next soul step on. The scale would balance out till both trays hung equidistant in the air. Then, with a soft chime and the rattling of chains, the trays would move, and the scale would rebalance, passing judgment on the cowering soul.

Everything seemed automated. Shadows flew around, and Jenny wanted to squint at the sky to spot the harpies, but all the other souls kept their heads focused straight ahead, at the towering scale as the trays went up and down, so Jenny did the same despite the pressure building on the back of her neck.

Sometimes, a soul was heavier than the feather, raising it high into the sky. Sometimes, a soul was lighter, and it would sink down toward the ground. The souls would then march away to the left or right depending on how they fared with the scale. If they were lighter than the feather, once the scale brought them back to the ground, they marched to the right. If they were heavier, they were sent off to the left.

How they knew where to go, she couldn't figure out. There was nobody there to usher them. Nobody there to pass judgment. There were no guards. No angels. No one. It was just the feather. But as she climbed the steps, she saw that the feather would turn, its tip pointing in the direction the soul needed to go. And the soul, without crying or screaming or anything, would do as they were told.

Jenny bit her lip and surveyed her new surroundings as she climbed the steps. Judgment took a few minutes or so, so every once in a while, she'd move up another step, along with the line of waiting souls. Beyond the scale were more steps—too many steps—which seemed to lead up into the sky. And in the vast distance, she thought she could spot what looked like another archway.

Walls made of the same enormous stone blocks covered both sides of the scale. From where Jenny and the other souls were standing, there were only three paths they could take: up the steps to the scale and beyond, or the two paths that followed the walls to the right and left.

*Which way do I go?*

Things were moving quickly. A toddler went next, then a young boy with a limp. Then, the old woman with long silvery hair, who had to set down the baby she was carrying. After the baby, it was a balding man with a great big beard, then another child.

Every step took her closer to the giant scales. To the giant feather. To her judgment.

She felt like a kid again, waiting in a long line at a department store because her mom couldn't handle the wait. Her mom would venture into the expensive perfume section like she might buy something, leaving Jenny to hold on to the cart and keep the position in line. And her mom would say she'd be back before Jenny got to the front, but Jenny would count each person ahead, her heart pounding, terrified of what would happen if she got to the checkout and then said she didn't have any money. She was waiting for her mom.

The scale loomed, the soul side coming down like a giant saucer. The golden chains were taut as the soul standing for judgment—a little boy with brown hair—shook, tears glistening on his cheeks. When he was sent toward the right, Jenny realized that all the children—the kids and the toddlers—were sent in the same direction. The older teens and the adults had all been sent to the left.

Her heart pounded as she took the next step; the line had slowed down so much she found herself waiting in between steps, her legs parted, feeling even more naked. But nobody cared; everyone was sniffling or praying or pleading.

Who or what they were praying to at this point, she didn't understand. She didn't care. A part of her wanted to snap at them. It was too late for prayer. They were dead. But she knew that was just her own unease talking.

The pattern never changed. The young were sent to the right. For the adults, the feather always pointed left. That was the way Jenny had to go.

Shivering, she moved close to the man in front of her. Coldness emanated from his broad back. She tried to get as close as possible without touching him, holding her breath, hoping it would work. She'd glanced up to scan the skies and seen there were no harpies around here. No angels. No one standing guard. It was only her and the souls behind her. What was to stop them from getting rowdy? From running away? From refusing to get on the scale?

But she knew the answer to that: It was the scale itself. The weight of their lives. The judgment waiting for them. She wasn't dead, but she could feel this *pull* toward it; it wasn't too different from the pull she'd feel in the Valescent Light when searching for worlds. It was a heavy feeling, like something had weighed down her heart.

The souls probably couldn't even think of anything else, and she wondered if Susan had had to climb these steps too, alone and frightened, with only the memory of Jenny's teeth in her throat and—

When the man in front of her moved forward to step onto the awaiting plate, the opposite side with the feather was raised high, its shadow casting right over Jenny's head. That was Jenny's chance.

Pushing the man slightly with her shoulder, wincing from the cold, she threw herself across the underside of the scale with Instant Acceleration. She was nothing more than a breeze crossing the shadow, and she threw herself down the steps leading down the left side of the scale.

She nearly crashed into a soul, an old woman, who flinched, recoiling as though Jenny was the devil. But she didn't pay the woman any mind. She hurried along, skipping ahead of the line, pushing past the narrow stream of souls, muttering apologies, whispering, "Excuse me." The souls didn't seem to care. If they were forlorn before, they were terrified now, and the further along the corridor they went, the darker it got, as though the sun was setting.

Figuring she'd gone far enough from the enormous scales and nothing had come after her—no harpy or angel or anything else—Jenny slowed down, wiping the sweat from her brow.

She was trying not to breathe too hard, trying to calm down. The souls made it cold, and within minutes, she was shivering again, her teeth chattering. But she'd gotten past the scales. With every step she took, the weight of that fell away, and she focused on the reddening sky ahead.

They were moving downhill, the stone floor at a slight decline, and the souls started muttering.

"No. No, no, no. Please. No." "I don't want to go. I'm sorry. I didn't mean to." "I don't want this. Please. I want to go home. My children need me." "I just wanted someone to hold me." "I'm so scared. I can't breathe." "My mother's sick." "Take me back. I left my wife." "I'm so cold. It's so cold. I didn't want to die—"

Ice-cold water splashed beneath Jenny's feet, and she flinched, looking down. From ahead, faint wails and screams echoed along the walls, and she flashed back to the high school, hiding in a classroom as the echoes of her screaming classmates ricocheted down the halls. She flattened herself against a wall, trying to steady herself as souls wandered past her without sparing her a glance.

The water was only up to her ankle. It was only water this time, not blood, but it was freezing. A soul elbowed her and moved past, a man who didn't look at her twice. He was muttering just like the others: "It's so cold; it's so cold. I'm dead. Why did I sleep with her? Why did I eat pork?"

Jenny rubbed her arms, inhaling as deeply as she could, then exhaling slowly as more souls streamed past her into the water. They splashed effortlessly, hardly making a sound, and Jenny leaned against the wall, too aware of the edges of the blocks against her bare skin.

*Where does this path go?* she wondered. *What was the point of the scales?*

Iblis didn't offer her any answers; he was just as lost as she was, but she got the sense he wanted to know more. They *had* to know more. That would be key to stopping the angels—knowing what was happening to the souls. Shadows flicked by overhead. In the gloomy red light, they seemed even more sinister, and Jenny glanced up to see winged figures flapping away beneath the bruise-colored sky.

Another bloodcurdling scream echoed down the corridor, and Jenny swallowed hard. She was in way over her head. *Maybe I could open a passageway here and get back. I could try again later.*

Jenny could feel it on the tip of her fingers. She could open another one and slip away from this horrible place.

*But then what?*

*Susan.*

"Susan," she repeated. She was so close now. Why would she give up and hide?

How many souls would there be? How would she find Susan? She didn't know, but thinking of her renewed her resolve. Putting another bare foot forward, she splashed into the cold water. A soul bumped past her. She didn't care. Her breathing became shallow and sharp as a horrible cold radiated up her legs. The further she walked, the higher the water became, till it was splashing against her thighs, the spray drenching her all over.

She did her best to keep from crying out. Her increased durability didn't help against the cold, nor her strength, nor her agility. None of it. But she had Ignite. She could create armor.

But she was terrified. It would be a light show, illuminating this entire space. It would be a beacon, drawing all attention to her in the gloomy darkness. And she didn't want the harpies to find her just yet. She didn't want to ask Iblis for any of his fire either; that would just be a waste of resources.

She carried on, clenching her teeth to keep them from chattering, trying to ignore the horrible moans and screams of the souls. The red sky seemed to hang lower and lower, as though it was ready to press down on her, crushing her into the frigid water.

There weren't any clouds, just the redness which reminded her of a setting sun. She couldn't see past all the souls at what was ahead, but another scream blew down the line like a breeze, and Jenny clenched her teeth. Burying her fingers into her palms, she kept going, quietly praying alongside the souls. Their mutterings slipped between her thoughts as her teeth chattered, as her body shook, and she found herself imitating them, whispering out loud, "Please, let me just find her. *Please. Please.* Don't let her be suffering too much. *Please* just let her be okay."

Who was she praying to? She didn't know. She didn't care. Maybe she was trying to will it into being.

A short while later, as she was lost in her thoughts, the corridor split into two different paths. A wall was straight ahead, and the souls seemed to decide on a whim which way they wanted to go. Left or right.

With a sinking feeling, Jenny realized she was inside an enormous maze; all the walls looked the same, made of the same large stones. Above was the sky, and . . . something was perched on the wall. Something was watching her.

**Harpy (Level 77)**

# CHAPTER TWENTY-NINE

# HIT SOMETHING

One of the harpies was perched on top of the wall, far away enough to be obscured by the darkening sky, but Jenny could see the vague outline of a person with wings. Its talons dug into one of the stone blocks, and its wings were tucked behind it. She couldn't see its face clearly, and she didn't know if it had spotted her or if she was just being paranoid.

Jenny kept walking with the flow of souls, hoping it wouldn't notice her in the chaos of the crowd. The sounds of splashing water and people muttering filled the space, the distant, echoing screams only adding to the mess. When the harpy didn't move—Jenny was watching by paying careful attention to any moving shadows—she decided to keep to the left and follow the souls around her, not wanting to make any movement which might attract the harpy's attention.

But where was this corridor headed? Where were any of them going? And why was the screaming getting louder and louder?

The walls changed suddenly. Instead of the neat stone blocks she'd gotten used to, they appeared weathered and stained, the sky growing darker still. A blood-colored glow illuminated the world from above, and Jenny caught glimpses of what looked like a red moon hanging in the sky. But she couldn't stop to look; the souls pushed closer and closer, wading through the water, and then, another scream. This one was closer than before.

The waves were coming up to her navel now so that cold drops splashed against her hips and chest and made it feel heavier to breathe; she was so cold now she thought she would freeze, but surely this had to go some-where? Souls tripped and vanished beneath the water, only to surface again, coughing and sputtering. Other souls stepped right over them, frantic looks on all their faces.

The corridor branched off in different directions every so often, forcing Jenny and the souls to turn. The deeper they went, the more devastated their surroundings became. These walls looked like parts of ancient ruins. Twisted vines of ugly green plants grew out of the water to spread across the broken stones, and in some places, they were the only things holding the crumbling walls together.

Large chunks of stone littered the water, and souls tripped over them, cutting themselves and spilling blood. But within moments, and with sparks of golden light evaporating off their wounds, they healed. They kept crying, but at least they could heal.

**Energy. They are releasing energy every time they heal.**

Jenny walked through collapsed parts of the wall, trying to figure out what was going on, keeping an eye out for any harpies overhead, but stopped when she found a group of souls running frantically.

They were screaming and crying, and behind this new crowd, Jenny spotted a glowing purple form, a hulking silhouette, an enormous creature bounding on all fours through the water.

A notification which made her summon her hatchet without a second thought entered her head.

**Wretched Angel (Level 28)**

She took a step back as souls ran past her, elbowing her, pushing and shoving, screaming in her face. She wasn't going to run; she couldn't run. The angel was looking right at her, its purple exoskeleton shining grossly, like a roach in a dimly lit room. It had smelled her; it knew she wasn't just a soul. Her blood would be richer, more satisfying. It couldn't wait to eat her.

And something equivalent lurched inside her. She felt a dizzying wave of excitement, like a fish leaping out of the water, or like she was standing at the edge of a waterfall looking down at the crashing waters below. All she had to do was jump. And after everything she'd been through with the passageways between the worlds, the deaths in the pillars, and the ghouls . . . she really wanted to hit something.

Jenny adjusted her grip on the hatchet, concentrating on her armor. Golden light responded right away, wrapping her in multiple layers of light, illuminating the ruins and the water and the souls who had fallen. They looked up at her with so much fright she almost apologized, but then, the wretched angel was rushing for her.

Throwing herself out of the way, she winced as the angel stomped on the souls, blood bursting out of the splashing water. It smashed through the wall beside her with ease, and an avalanche of enormous cobblestones crushed another group of souls.

But Jenny was darting away already, trying to get enough space in the tight, crowded corridor, in the rush of naked bodies. At least she wasn't bare anymore; the cold water didn't sap her strength away. The last thing she formed was her helmet, and then she stopped, grasping her hatchet with both hands as she tried to decide how best to attack.

Golden sparks flickered out from the wounded souls as they stood back up, eyes wide with terror. She knew they wouldn't die—couldn't die—but their screams pulled at her heart. She had to keep the wretched angel busy on her, but it had already grabbed three souls with an enormous purple hand, and before Jenny could shout, it brought them to its lips like a bouquet of flowers and bit through their heads.

Blood gushed and rained down, splattering the stones and souls and water beneath the angel. The bodies fell limp, headless, landing with a splash as more blood gushed out of their necks, forming gruesome clouds in the water.

Jenny stared horrified at the headless corpses, at the angel chewing before turning its attention back to her, blood running down its purple chin.

She couldn't get too far away or else it would attack whatever was around. But she knew the wretched angels were smarter than the normal tarnished ones. It wasn't just feeding mindlessly; it was aware that the souls would heal. Right away, light shimmered around the corpses, and they stood again, lifting their faces from the water, gasping for breath, crying and screaming. Before the angel could grab them again, before it could continue eating, Jenny threw her hatchet. *Savage Throw.*

It spun through the air and slammed into the angel's mouth, the obsidian edge cutting into its jaw with a *snap*.

**+200 Energy**

But the angel didn't seem fazed. It grasped the hatchet with both hands, roaring so loudly Jenny almost wanted to cover her ears, but just as the creature yanked the hatchet out of its mouth with another spray of blood, Jenny summoned her weapon back.

The creature's momentum pulled it forward, and Jenny struck again, using Instant Acceleration to close the distance, twisting to avoid its enormous elbows as she swung her hatchet up to catch it on the sternum. She used the speed of Instant Acceleration to generate as much force as possible, but as soon as the hatchet sunk into the angel's crackling exoskeleton, Jenny ducked through the bloody water between the angel's legs, dodging its swinging arms.

**+200 Energy**

She rolled, splashing, until she crashed against the wall, her helmet ringing loudly as it struck a stone. Groaning, she got to her feet, readjusting her helmet as the angel howled in pain. But she'd cracked its exoskeleton. She could see the lines in the purple armor as the creature ripped her hatchet out, heaving for breath, before it dropped to all fours, splashing the water hard enough to send towering waves crashing against Jenny and the wall.

The souls near them had gotten away, but from the corner of her eyes, she could see new groups running over the collapsed walls.

With the screaming echoing all around, Jenny figured there would be even more angels to fight. She couldn't let herself get slowed down now, but why was this angel so strong? It was only a wretched angel. She should have had no problem with that.

**It is the light. There is a distasteful aura to this world that saps your strength and reinforces the tarnished.**

"Well, fuck," she whispered, wiping her lips. It was like she'd been nerfed just by being here, while the angels had a field buff. How was that fair? She almost considered asking to borrow Iblis's power again to have that ridiculous boost in her stats, but she laughed. She didn't need it.

She could kill this thing; she could feel it in her bones. She'd been holding back because of the souls, but as fucked up as it was, she didn't have to. The souls wouldn't die no matter how much they went through.

For a second, she considered killing as many of the souls as she could. Would they give her experience? Energy? She could get stronger and level up, and the souls would just heal.

No. That would be . . . The thought made her stomach twist, and she steeled herself. There would be plenty of angels to cut down. *And what is this one doing?* The wretched angel stayed on all fours, its muscular purple form shining brightly. Jenny summoned her hatchet back and was just about to rush in and attack when a spark of purple light snapped over her head.

Every hair on the back of her neck stood up, and Jenny redirected herself to dive behind a pile of rubble. Whether it was instinct or experience from her fights with the desecrated angel and Miriam, she couldn't tell, but a wave of purple energy blew past her, destroying more of the walls, burning away the vegetation, and sizzling through the water.

"Fuck," she whispered. Her spit tasted like metal. The air smelled heavy. This wouldn't be as easy as she'd hoped.

Water had entered her helmet and was running down her face, but she didn't have a chance to take it off. The angel was splashing toward her, and Jenny turned to face it, swiping at its face and chest before dodging another attempt to grab her. But then, the angel screamed, and electricity sizzled out of its back while an enormous arm swiped from the side.

She had just enough time to brace herself before the blow knocked her away and Jenny crashed into the opposite wall, the stones cracking from the impact with her shoulder. She landed with a splash, her head ringing. Trying to shake it off, Jenny tore off her helmet, refusing to let the water get in the way. The angel was already rushing for her again, its long legs closing the distance quickly, but Jenny was quicker.

With Instant Acceleration, she burst forward before breaking into a slide, using her speed to slip right beneath the angel's legs again and emerge on the other side. It crashed into the wall with a screech, and Jenny threw her hatchet again, striking it right on the back of its head, smashing its face through the wall.

Before it could recover, she leaped onto the angel's back, wrapping her legs around its torso. With a flash of light, she had her hatchet back in her hands, and as the angel screamed in rage, Jenny slammed the weapon into the back of its head again, cutting through exoskeleton and bone, burying the edge in its throat.

It tried to bite down, but she'd cut through the muscles holding its jaw in place. She could feel the desperation in its body now.

Fueled with bloodthirst, Jenny's heart pounding with rage, she twisted around its body to avoid an arm slapping at her as though she were a mosquito and grabbed the hatchet with both hands. Turning, Jenny used Savage Throw while the edge was still in the angel's neck. Screaming, she launched the hatchet through the creature's body. It spun out in a spray of blood as both Jenny and the decapitated angel went limp and crashed to the water.

**You've defeated Wretched Angel (Level 28)!**
**Experience has been awarded.**
**+400 Energy**

**Leveled Up!**
**Jenny Huang, Level 30 → Level 31**
**+ 4 Stat Points**

# CHAPTER THIRTY

# BLOOD IN THE WATER

Jenny pulled herself up and sat in the water, leaning against a block of rubble, breathing hard. Blood and water ran down her face as she stared at the angel's half-sunken body. Its muscular leg lay stretched right next to her, and blood spurted out of its neck, its head floating beside it before the tide pulled it away, its empty eyes staring blankly at her.

She could picture herself summoning her hatchet back and cutting into the angel's leg. There'd probably be another splash of water. A spray of blood. And then, after peeling away the metallic armor with the edge of her hatchet, she would be able to bite through the exposed skin and flesh . . .

She shuddered, her back itching where her tentacles were desperate to escape.

But she would need her strength if she was going to get through this. And who knew what else was waiting? The scent of its blood spreading through the water was so strong . . . So good. So promising.

*And it would be delicious.*

Warm and juicy and tender and brimming with everything she'd ever wanted; even better than Yeshua's flesh. It would fill her insides with warmth and keep away the coldness of the water, and she almost did it, not caring that Iblis was inside her head, that Iblis would see her. His mind felt so distant, so far away . . . And then, she heard splashing. Someone or something was moving toward her, and she turned around, ready to strike. But it wasn't an angel. It was one of the souls; one Jenny *recognized*.

A thin, pale soul with long dark hair. A girl that stood there for a second, naked, a horrible expression on her face, a bizarre mixture of anger and fear and relief.

Jenny almost choked. "Miriam?"

The girl dashed across the water and barreled right into Jenny.

Her ice-cold fist struck Jenny in the face, sending her tumbling back, splashing in the water. Shock and surprise flooded her thoughts, a dizzying mixture of spiking adrenaline, the scent of the angel's blood in her nose, and the look on Miriam's face.

Miriam threw herself into Jenny, dropping her flat onto her back as Miriam scrambled on top, pinning her down. Jenny couldn't fight back, even though she had gotten so much stronger than their previous fight and Miriam was without armor or those creepy wings or anything. It was just a thin, naked girl barreling down on Jenny. The attacks didn't really hurt. Not physically, at least.

Each punch was ice cold and knocked Jenny's head back into the water, submerging her face while Miriam sat on Jenny's chest. She kept punching. Over and over, a battering that Jenny almost didn't want to stop.

She deserved it.

*You deserve this.*

"What-are-you-fucking-doing-here?" screamed Miriam, highlighting each word with a punch. Each one knocked Jenny's head against a wet chunk of wall underneath, and freezing-cold water entered her ears, her nose. She could taste the blood from the decapitated angel. She could taste her own. And she could feel Miriam's cold body—Miriam's soul—on top. The chill seeped through her armor and into her bones.

Eventually, Miriam stopped attacking. She just sat there, straddling Jenny's sides, her hands on Jenny's stinging face, crying. Miriam was crying, her shoulders shaking, her wet hair stuck to her bare chest. "I said I was sorry. And you didn't stop. You didn't stop. Why did you do that to me?"

Jenny tried to speak, but there was a lump in her throat. She didn't feel bad. She shouldn't feel bad. Miriam had done so much worse, and if Jenny hadn't killed her, the girl would've killed everyone else to win. Would've hurt Susan and Oliver and the rest of them. But Jenny didn't have to eat the girl alive. For that, she felt deeply ashamed.

Miriam kept shaking, and Jenny looked away, unable to look the girl in the eyes. She was trying to find the right words. How did you apologize for eating someone? She hadn't expected to run into Miriam here.

She opened her mouth to respond, but Miriam knelt forward and pressed her lips to Jenny's.

It was a kiss. A deep, terrible kiss, with Miriam's fingers digging into Jenny's face and scalp, holding her underwater as though she was simultaneously trying to drown Jenny and resuscitate her with CPR. A wet, slobbering kiss that was a mash of lips and tongues, scraping teeth, and water and blood as Jenny splashed and struggled to push the girl off.

But Miriam held on, wrapping herself around Jenny, repositioning her legs.

"You're so warm!" she moaned. In between kisses, in a feverish rant, she kept going as Jenny inhaled water and blood and felt like she was suffocating. "You're so hot. You owe me! I'm so cold here. So alone. And oh my God, Jenny, you are so, so, so *hot*. Do you know how hot it was when you ate me? How horrible it was? You ate me, and now I have to have some of you. It's only fair. It's only fair! This is what I've always wanted. Someone to . . ." And then, her teeth closed through Jenny's bottom lip. Miriam jerked her head away, tearing the skin down Jenny's jaw.

With a terrible scream, Jenny swung her hatchet and buried it in Miriam's throat.

### Defeated Soul (Level 29)
### + 800 Energy

Miriam's hands wavered, her eyes bloodshot and wide as she gurgled. Blood ran down her chin, and slowly, she looked down at the handle sticking out of her throat, blood spurting from the wound, covering her breasts, her stomach, dripping down her thighs. Jenny shoved the girl off, her bottom lip hanging from her jaw, the stinging burning on her face so terribly that tears spilled from her eyes.

"Valescent Light," she whispered, holding up a shining golden arm as blue-and-purple lights flickered around her fingers. She held her lip up, holding it in place as she healed the burning wound. *Shit.* She should've used a potion or something—she had to save the Valescent Light to open another passageway.

But she shuddered with relief as the stinging pain faded away, chewing gently on her bottom lip to make sure it was intact. Miriam lay in the water, floating like the decapitated angel, the hatchet still in her throat as her lifeless eyes stared up at the red sky.

Her blood smelled even more delicious than the angel's—familiar, nourishing—and Jenny's head spun again. She waded closer to Miriam, swallowing hard as more screaming echoed nearby. She looked back to see more souls running toward them, splashing and stumbling, trampling over one another as a hoard of tarnished angels came after them.

Jenny reached down and grabbed her hatchet's handle, ready to yank it out, but Miriam's fingers closed around Jenny's arm. "Help me," she rasped, the hatchet in her throat making it difficult to speak. "I don't want to be here anymore."

Golden lights sparkled around the edge of the hatchet. Blood swirled away in the water, and Miriam's eyes were so wide and filled with desperation, Jenny didn't know what to say. The tarnished angels were closing in. Souls splashed past them, and Jenny lifted the hatchet even as Miriam hung on, bringing the girl to her feet. Blood continued spilling down her front.

When the hatchet slid out, scraping bone, Miriam stepped back, wheezing as she clutched her throat. But within a few moments, and with sparkling golden light, it was healed. Before Jenny could say anything, the group of tarnished angels leaped onto them.

They moved quicker in this world. Their gleaming white eyes, empty and enraged, their gaunt faces, and their bony bodies were so familiar to Jenny it was almost comforting. They swung at her, and she dodged with ease, lopping off an arm at the elbow, slicing through the palm of another, lodging her hatchet in a third one's hip with a *crack*. Notifications climbed through her thoughts—energy from each attack, from each time she caused pain.

Unlike the souls, the angels couldn't recover, and Miriam threw herself at them too, punching and clawing, biting and screaming, and she was so thin that Jenny sometimes couldn't tell her apart from an angel.

Standing back, Jenny watched as the angels chewed on Miriam's arms and sides, as Miriam bit them right back, pulling on their hair and punching them in the throat, screaming at the top of her lungs. All the while, she was crying, sobbing.

Jenny made short work of the rest of the angels, and their mangled bodies floated in the water around them. More souls ran by, too frightened to stick around. Jenny thought about ditching Miriam. With Instant Acceleration, she could get away and search for Susan, but something held her rooted to the spot. Water splashed the scales on her thighs. She watched Miriam get up.

Why wasn't Miriam like the other souls? Wasn't she supposed to be too frightened to think straight? The rest of them forgot everything almost right away, but Miriam was different.

She watched the girl sitting in the water as it splashed against her healed neck. She was chewing on a severed bony arm, and a limp tarnished angel floated beside her, its hair drifting. Miriam glared at Jenny and swallowed, blood running down her throat.

"You know I don't have to poop anymore?"

Jenny blinked. "What?"

"Because I'm dead, I can just eat and eat. I don't have to throw it back up. I don't have to digest or anything. I don't even know where it goes. But there are no bathrooms here. Nothing."

She got to her feet, swaying, letting go of the dead angel's arm. Another soul, a grown man, ran by, tripping on the floating angel so that he fell into the water. He looked up at Miriam then at Jenny, as though waiting to be admonished, but Miriam only shot him a look of disdain, and Jenny didn't know what to say.

He got up and ran, followed by several more souls—three elderly people and two children. One of them was calling for their mom. Another was looking for her husband. And another kept repeating, "Somebody help me; somebody help me, please."

Miriam pushed one of them. "I tried eating them too. They're like robots now. But"—she opened her mouth to show off her bloodstained teeth—"my teeth won't go through their skin or something."

Jenny held her hatchet at the ready as Miriam approached again, but the girl didn't attack this time. Instead, she stood right in front of Jenny, looking almost shy, her eyes, brown and sparkling, her breath as cold as winter. "Are you really here? Or am I imagining you?"

Jenny didn't know how to respond, but she watched Miriam's eyes flick down. The girl was looking at Jenny's lips as though she wanted another blood kiss; Jenny couldn't help but bite down on her bottom lip defensively. She did not want to feel the pain of having her skin ripped off again. She tapped Miriam on the chest and nudged her back.

"I'm sorry for what I did to you, but I'm looking for someone."

Miriam's face distorted. Her eyes bulged out. Her lips pulled back to show her teeth. "But you're not even fucking real!" she screeched, her voice breaking. She lunged for Jenny again, but this time, Jenny dodged. Miriam stumbled forward and fell face-first into the water, splashing blood. She screamed again, slapping the foaming waves. She slapped the water again, and again, and again, screaming all the while as more souls ran by. One bumped into Jenny, but she hardly noticed.

Miriam was crying. "Didn't I tell you I was sorry?"

Jenny knelt, her hatchet at the ready as she looked Miriam in the eyes. She remembered something Eve had told her once—that everyone experienced suffering. She felt a wave of exhaustion, of pity and heartbreak and world-weariness. "Yeah. You did. And I'm sorry too."

# CHAPTER THIRTY-ONE

# ANOTHER DESECRATED ANGEL

Jenny dashed through the maze of ruined walls, the red sky taunting her from above. She thought she'd glimpsed a moon or a sun, but it kept changing direction. Either that or she was lost.

The walls had fallen apart in this area, the crumbling blocks stained by so much blood that they'd taken on a deep brown color. Jenny jumped across them, fending off angels with quick strikes. She wanted to help souls as angels grabbed them and tore into them in a bloody frenzy, but there were too many, and there was no way she could make a difference. She couldn't protect them all.

Iblis, who'd been quiet for a while in some corner of her subconscious, spoke. He was biding his time, waiting for a serious fight.

**They will have to suffer for now, but we will bring them salvation. Keep to your goals for now. Our forces gather in the other worlds and prepare for war.**

Jenny understood what he was saying, but it still hurt—the blood-curdling screams, the heart-breaking cries for help, the begging and pleading. And there were just too many souls in this horrible labyrinth. Too many souls to search one by one. How was she supposed to ever find Susan in this mess?

*But I found Miriam, of all people.*

Was that just dumb luck? Jenny came to a stop at a corner, breathing hard. She'd spotted two wretched angels—a bright yellow one and an orange-brown one—and along one of the walls ahead glistened a dozen or so sacs. Bile rose to her throat as she remembered the first time she'd seen them, that stairwell on her way up to the third floor, and how the angels had gathered bodies, slowly draining them of blood to feed to their young.

Was that happening here too? She stood close to the corner, scrutinizing the scene, and her heart skipped a beat. Just below the eggs was an even bigger sac, a chrysalis that shone with green light. Jenny knew what was in there before the notification even showed up in her head.

### Desecrated Angel (Level 63)

"Yeah, there are a lot of them here," said a voice behind her. Jenny whipped around to see Miriam standing in the water, one arm crossed shyly over her chest.

"What do you want?" asked Jenny impatiently.

"Nothing," Miriam replied with a shrug. "There's nothing to do here but eat and scream."

"Then why are you following me?" hissed Jenny.

"I just want to know what you're doing here. Maybe I can help."

"I don't want your help."

Miriam scowled, but she didn't say anything. Behind her, there was a trail of wandering souls. They drudged slowly through the water as though they were lost, staring around helplessly, brows furrowing as they looked at cracks on the walls or heard a scream. It reminded Jenny of something she'd heard about goldfish once; that every few seconds, their memories reset.

She didn't know if that was true, but she wondered if the souls were like that. All the ones she'd bumped into had forgotten about her moments after, and they even seemed to forget that angels were constantly feeding on them.

Was that better for them? To forget? Or was forgetting a defense mechanism which helped them deal with the nonstop trauma?

And how come Miriam didn't forget?

Jenny looked at the thin, pale girl again, remembering the white-exoskeleton-covered monster with enormous hand-shaped wings that had wreaked havoc through the high school, that had caused Jenny to snap. But was it fair to blame Miriam for what Jenny had done?

*But it was her fault, wasn't it? She's the reason Susan's dead!*

*No. It was my fault. I did that.*

*I did all of that.*

Jenny suppressed a shudder of rage and squeezed her hatchet tightly. But then, she figured if Miriam was around, maybe they could work together. Miriam wasn't like the other souls; she could still fight, even if she didn't have any weapons or anything. And not being able to die would be helpful in a fight.

"Okay," said Jenny. "I'm trying to find Susan."

Her eyes went wide. "Susan's dead? That girl you liked?"

Jenny grimaced.

"Did you win, then? Is that why you're here? Because you're not dead, right? So how did it end?"

"I don't think anyone won," replied Jenny. "But look, I'll explain that stuff later. I'm trying to find her. And maybe . . ." She bit her lip, eyeing Miriam, who looked so innocent now it almost hurt. Miriam looked helpless and weak, not at all like the demented, bloodthirsty monster she'd been. Jenny wondered if it was alright to fill her in on what they wanted to do. "I'm working with some people who want to stop all this."

"Stop what?" she asked, brows furrowing.

Jenny gestured around her. At the screaming and wailing.

"But why? Isn't this . . . Hell? Isn't this where we're supposed to be?" Miriam looked like she was about to cry. "I deserve to be here."

"I don't know," said Jenny, taking a deep breath, running low on patience. "But something's fucked up about all this, and there's an angel doing all this to us."

"What?" Miriam's eyes narrowed in disbelief, and Jenny was reminded of how she'd found the girl in a closet in the computer lab, and how Miriam hadn't believed Jenny about the angels or the violence or anything.

"Can you help me fight those angels over there?"

Miriam's lip twitched. "I'm just . . . I don't have anything but this. So I don't know. But yeah. I can't die again, can I?"

Jenny was about to ask why Miriam was different from the other souls, but she got the feeling she had no clue. Jenny wondered if it was because Miriam had become wretched before she died. Maybe that warped how someone's soul presented.

That thought wasn't comforting at all. She didn't want to know the answer; she didn't want to wonder what her soul would be like. And she knew what she was asking of Miriam. Without any weapons or anything, the girl would be torn apart by the angels.

Just then, a stranger thought entered Jenny's head as Miriam lowered her hands and stopped covering her chest, a deep blush spreading across Miriam's face. Trying not to remember the horrible kiss from earlier, Jenny thought about using Severed Spirit on the girl, just as she'd used it on the pillars. Would it work? Would it . . . bring out her exoskeleton and give her more of a chance?

Before she could ask, before she could bring up her idea, something swept down in a flutter of wings, and Miriam ducked, her hands over her head. Jenny raised her hatchet, but something sharp raked her arm, drawing sparks against her armor. It clawed at Jenny's face, wings smacking the side of her head, and she went down, splashing into the water, stinging and burning all over from the attack.

Jenny shot back up, swinging her hatchet, but it was too late. The harpy had flown away, back up to the top of the wall, where it landed, a half-human, half-bird silhouette against the red sky.

"What the fuck is that?"

Miriam shook her head, trembling. Water dripped from her face and shoulders. "They're worse than the angels. Harpies."

Jenny readjusted her grip on the hatchet, not taking her eyes off the creature. But the commotion had drawn the attention of several angels, and she grimaced. The angels being more powerful was slowing her down, and now she had to deal with a harpy, too?

## Harpy (Level 49)

It was strong, too. Jenny braced herself, but then, she heard a shout from Miriam. She turned to see the two wretched angels rushing through the water. The orange one was the closest, and Jenny turned to meet it head-on, wondering if she could cut it down quickly.

The harpy swooped down again, and Jenny dashed back with Instant Acceleration, expecting an attack from above. Instead, the harpy landed on the orange wretched angel, its talons piercing the angel's skull right through the eyes and the back of the head. Even Jenny winced as the angel's skull cracked.

Gooey, thick blood oozed down the orange exoskeleton, and the yellow angel—a female that must've been the orange angel's mate—screeched in agony before bounding away, splashing like mad up the corridor, forgetting all about the eggs and the chrysalis.

"No, no, little angels," said the harpy in a singsongy voice. Long white hair framed its astonishingly beautiful face—the face of a gorgeous woman who looked perpetually amused. Its eyebrows rose slightly, its cheeks flushed rosy pink with warmth. It looked at Jenny with a half smile on its plump lips.

The harpy's body was covered in lush white feathers. Instead of arms, it had enormous white, feathery wings. It had a narrow torso, and its thighs gave way to more feathers, but it had the feet of a giant bird, or a dinosaur.

The talons were dark and razor sharp, and they gleamed with blood and other fluids as it remained perched on top of the orange angel. The dead creature stood motionless in the water, looking more like a rock now than the fearsome monster it was.

"What brings you to the Garden?" asked the harpy, its voice like a melody as it cocked its head. Its long white hair flowed gently, and it almost looked serene. "I don't think I've ever tasted a live one before, but I've heard so much about the flavor. The texture."

Jenny glanced at Miriam, who was slinking away, pressing herself up against a wall. She seemed terrified of the creature. The harpy had its sharp stare fixed on Jenny.

What were these harpies? They were supposed to be guardians, but there was a violent ruthlessness to them that Jenny didn't like. A disturbing aura that made her skin crawl. They were intelligent. They could talk. They weren't mindless monsters like the tarnished angels.

**Careful.**

An image flashed through Jenny's mind with Iblis's warning. It was one of blue flames, but she told Iblis to hold on. *Let's see what it's like.*

"Well?" asked the harpy, flapping its wings and lifting the dead angel out of the water. Each wing must've been longer than Jenny was tall.

"I'm just looking for a friend," Jenny replied, bracing herself for its next attack. Blood trickled down her face from the harpy's previous flyby.

The harpy looked curious. "A friend? You came all the way here for a friend?" It blinked and raised its eyebrows as though it couldn't believe what it was hearing. "I wonder what the master would say about this . . ."

"The master?" echoed Jenny, her heart racing. She couldn't tell if that was her anxiety or Iblis's, but she was sure the master the harpy was referring to was Azra'il.

"But that would be such a waste . . ." sang the harpy, pursing its lips. "Your blood smells so sweet."

*Perfect*, thought Jenny. She adjusted her hatchet. "Come and get me, then."

With a shout, she launched her weapon at the harpy, aiming for its beautiful face.

# CHAPTER THIRTY-TWO

# THE HARPY'S TALONS

With a forceful flap of its white wings, the harpy relinquished the angel's corpse and took to the air, a blur of feathery white. The hatchet spun harmlessly through the space where it had just been, and without talons holding it up, the dead angel collapsed forward, falling like a tree.

Just as the angel splashed, the harpy dove with a screech, talons at the ready, its wings tucked. It was too quick. Jenny caught a glimpse of its beautiful white hair trailing behind it, and then she summoned her hatchet back with a flash of light just in time to parry.

Sparks ignited upon contact, the obsidian edge of her hatchet against the harpy's razor-sharp talons. The impact shook her to the bone, but once she knocked the talons to the side, Jenny ducked and rolled through the water.

The harpy flapped its wings hard, generating larger waves as it gained altitude. Jenny's leg bumped against the angel corpse, and from the corner of her eyes, she could see tarnished angels grabbing other souls, making their way toward the eggs on the wall. Now that the wretched angels were gone, some of the tarnished angels were feeding on the eggs like opportunistic scavengers. The sight made Jenny feel sick.

Miriam was still up against the wall, staring up at the sky. When the harpy looped around again, she screamed, "Look out!"

It tucked its wings and dove again for Jenny, coming at her with its talons outstretched. Jenny waited till the last moment, waiting till she knew the harpy wouldn't be able to pull out quickly enough, then flung her hatchet with another Savage Throw.

She saw a flash of worry on the harpy's face, the smug expression vanishing, before the hatchet struck its talons and cut right through one of them before spinning off and leaving a nasty gash in the snow-white wings.

A horrible screech filled the corridor of the labyrinth, high pitched and so shrill Jenny had to clap her hands over her ears. The harpy flapped away awkwardly, spilling droplets of blood as it struggled back up to the tops of the walls. Jenny summoned her hatchet back, then dove into the water where she was sure the long talon had fallen.

Finding it partially buried in the ground, she yanked it out. Black and sleek, the talon looked like a long, rounded dagger that ended in a hooked point; a squishy bit of brain was still stuck to the curved, razor-point edge. She looked at Miriam, who hadn't moved from the wall.

"Here," she said, tossing it over.

Miriam caught it and stared, admiring the length of the cruel talon. Jenny remembered how she'd once given the girl the pink helmet Susan had made. How Miriam had crawled along the hallway floor to escape an angel so long ago. That was all before Miriam had turned into a bloodthirsty monster beyond reason.

She was trusting Miriam with the talon. It would help the girl fight.

*"You filthy mortal wretch!"* came a high-pitched shriek from above the walls. The melodious way of speaking had given way to a nasty screaming voice.

Jenny squinted up, ready to strike again. She suspected that diving was the harpy's best move. They didn't have hands; they couldn't fight up close. Their best attack was to swipe down and strike quickly, and they were too used to fighting souls who couldn't fight back.

"I'm going to peck out your liver and rip all your intestines out like worms and—!"

"Why don't you come down here and say that to my face, you ugly bitch?" shouted Jenny. She had half a mind to use Ignite to roast that harpy and turn her into a bucket of wings.

"WHO ARE YOU CALLING UGLY?!"

The harpy spread its wings, blood freely dripping from its wound, and screeched again, a high-pitched screech that rippled through the air as though the sound waves had force that could push Jenny back. Rubble vibrated; waves splashed Jenny's legs. The sound sent chills of warning through Jenny's body as she turned to see Miriam with her eyes screwed shut, clutching the talon to her chest.

It stopped abruptly, and for a second, there was splashing. Jenny unclenched her jaw, looking up at the harpy, wondering what it'd done. Then, she heard more splashing sounds, loud sloshing, like a crowd of people rushing through a flood.

From both sides of the corridor came angels, tarnished ones as well as wretched. There were maybe twenty or so tarnished, their thin, fragile bodies glistening with wetness, their hisses so loud that it hurt. And then the wretched, large ones with red-and-black stripes, one with a dark-blue exoskeleton, and a third in yellow—the female who had run away from the harpy.

*The harpy must have some control over them*, Jenny realized. The angels were closing in; it would be a mad battle in no time, and all the while, the harpy would be overhead. She looked around for Miriam, trying to figure out how best to deal with the onslaught.

That was when green lightning shot straight up into the sky.

For a second, she'd hoped it was Yeshua and his lightning, and that the light had affected her eyesight and the color of things, but this was different. This bolt sizzled and snapped, lingering in a way that felt unsettling, unnatural, and she knew without looking where it had come from. The green chrysalis she'd spotted earlier.

Before she could confirm her suspicion, the angels fell onto her and Miriam, and everything blurred into splashing water and the red glow of the sky and nails and skin and teeth. Naked and shriveled, they clawed and scraped her armor, slapped and threw themselves at her. The wretched angels struck others down, leaping into them and forcing their heads underwater, gurgling as they clamored to attack Jenny and Miriam.

The striped angel was the first to reach Miriam, who scraped its face with the talon; the weapon proved even more effective than Jenny's hatchet. The sharp point cut almost effortlessly through the exoskeleton, and the wretched angel howled in agony. Meanwhile, Jenny struck down several tarnished angels in one go, barely noticing them, before she stood back-to-back with Miriam.

The wretched angel swung again, clawing at the thin girl. She buried the talon in its wrist as Jenny whipped around and used Savage Throw again. Her hatchet struck the angel right in the gash Miriam had made earlier, bursting into its face. Just before the hatchet ripped through to the other side, Jenny summoned it back to her hand, leaped, and brought it down tomahawk style onto the second wretched angel.

The hatchet's edge struck its yellow skull with a mighty crack. It was weaker and lower leveled, and Jenny managed to cut straight down into its chest, splitting its face and throat in half. The angel was dead before it hit the water.

But there wasn't any time to enjoy the kill, to enjoy the spray of blood that covered her face. Green lightning surged through the water, snapping and hissing, and Miriam and the remaining angels suddenly went rigid, all of them screaming as they burned.

The scent of scorched flesh filled Jenny's nose. She was familiar with the sulfuric odor, but she was puzzled. The lightning hadn't struck her even though she was waist-deep in water.

She looked down to see smoke rising from her scorched armor. Some more of her scales had cracked, but the lightning never made it to her body. She looked back to see Miriam floating face down, her dark hair fanning out. The other angels were floating as well, their flesh bloated and dark red. Bile burned the base of Jenny's throat, but there was another crackle of lightning.

Jenny dashed toward Miriam as the harpy sang above them, and just as the water started to boil, Jenny scooped the girl up and held her up in the air. Jagged green bolts flickered across the surface of the water, sizzling around Jenny's armored legs and burning the angels floating nearby. She held Miriam overhead, the girl's arms and legs dangling, water dripping from every part of her. Before the green lightning faded, there was another screech from above, and the harpy dove again.

"No!" shouted Jenny as talons hooked onto Miriam's frail form and the harpy tore her away.

Blood rained down. Miriam screamed as the harpy flapped higher and higher, but before Jenny had the chance to strike, something large and green slammed into her with enough force to send her rocketing through the pile of floating angels, generating large waves that splashed against the walls. Jenny crashed into a bunch of stone blocks, landing with a splash as loose rubble piled down on top of her.

Wheezing, she forced herself to stand; she had to lean against a stone block. Everything hurt inside. Something was broken—several something's. Maybe her ribs. With golden light, she quickly made a major potion of healing and downed it in one go, dropping the glass as she caught her breath. Something popped and shifted inside her. Steam erupted from her mouth as she healed, and then, she climbed out of the rubble, shifting the collapsed blocks to size up what had attacked her.

### Desecrated Angel (Level 63)

This one was different from the blue armored one in the cafeteria. It wasn't as large, and it was covered in a thin green armor that she knew was ridiculously hard just by how it'd felt during that impact. Several of her scales were cracked, but her enhanced armor had held up.

It was hunched forward, with extra-long arms. Its legs were thicker than the rest of its body, each one almost as wide as Jenny was, and it sort of reminded Jenny of an enormous, monstrous rabbit. Dark, spiky hair shot out of its scalp, and judging by its wider frame and the thing between its powerful legs, it was a male desecrated angel.

Jenny spat blood, readying herself. She thought about running, about using Instant Acceleration through the crowds of souls and angels till she lost this thing or it lost interest, but Miriam's gut-wrenching screams echoed down from the top, and Jenny could see the harpy's silhouette. It was perched on top of the wall, kneeling down and tearing something out of Miriam. Jenny couldn't leave her to that.

She cracked her neck and waded toward the desecrated angel. Its eyes were shut, and its arms swayed as though it was unsteady on its feet. Was it asleep? Jenny slowed down, trying not to make a sound, holding her breath.

*Iblis?* she thought, trying to summon the demon from the back of her mind. *I could really use some—*

Then, she saw what was happening. What the angel was doing. Electricity snapped and fizzed around its thighs, curving from its torso to its arms. The angel was charging up. Little bolts of lightning climbed through its body before it dropped down on all fours with a heavy splash, and enormous bolts flashed toward Jenny, bigger and more powerful than before.

She knew these would do far more damage than the electrical currents before.

# CHAPTER THIRTY-THREE

# GREEN LIGHTNING

The floating bodies burst, exploding like food left too long in the microwave. Their insides splattered the walls, and a huge cloud of steam hid the desecrated angel from view.

Jenny had gotten out of the water a split second before the lightning hit her, jumping as hard as she could and striking one of the walls with her hatchet to hang from it, her legs dangling about a foot over the electrocuted water. As the steam parted, Jenny saw the rest of the carnage.

Even the wretched angels had been blown apart. Their internals must've expanded too rapidly inside their exoskeletons, and they'd popped open, leaving behind a gooey mess in their mostly intact shells. The stench was the worst part; with the water boiling and the bodies superheated, a sour, putrid humidity clogged her nose. It hurt to inhale.

The desecrated angel was still on all fours, its head lowered so that darkgreen hair covered its face. Small bolts of lightning snapped and faded around its back, and now that it was hunched forward, Jenny could see several spikes jutting out from its spine, going all the way down to its bottom, each one about the length of her arm.

She looked up at Miriam, who'd stopped screaming. The harpy was still feeding on the girl, but Miriam was no longer making a sound. Every few seconds, golden light shimmered brightly around them and faded away. They were on top of the opposite wall, across the flooded corridor.

Jenny held on tight to her hatchet, pressing her armored feet against the wall, wondering if she could somehow climb like this. It would be easier to just bring out Iblis, get her wings back, and soar to the top, but she could sense the demon's hesitation.

It would draw even more attention to themselves, bringing more harpies to their location and potentially alerting Azra'il. And if this became a large-scale battle, she would burn out. They were stuck. She had to deal with this herself or open a passageway back to the world of demons.

She wasn't ready to give up. Not yet. There was enough steam lingering in the air to hide her from both the harpy and the angel, she just had to climb now.

Gritting her teeth and digging her fingers into the cracks and grooves between the stones, she yanked her hatchet out of the wall and hung by her fingertips. The strain was already burning her forearms and shoulders, but she could hold on. It wasn't unbearable; she only wished she had more of a hold. All of the strain was on her fingertips, and even with her stats being so high, it was killer.

By pressing her feet against the wall to shift some of her weight, Jenny pulled herself up, swinging with her hatchet to slice into another stone overhead. This way, she kept climbing, higher and higher, as the desecrated angel waded around. Down below, she could see it sniffing the burnt bodies before feasting on some of the exoskeletons with crackling sounds, like someone chewing on hard candy.

Souls wandered into the mess and ran away screaming; the angel didn't pay them any mind. It probably figured they weren't worth the effort, but it seemed to have lost its ferocious drive from earlier. Either that or it hadn't noticed that Jenny had escaped its attack.

Taking advantage of the angel's unawareness, Jenny climbed, her muscles screaming for rest, but she knew if she relaxed, she'd plummet back down to the water, to where the angel was waiting. She'd be at the creature's complete mercy.

Climbing one part of the wall at a time, she tried to be quick before the steam completely dispersed and she lost the element of surprise. The angel's triumphant feasting on charred exoskeletons masked the sounds of her hatchet striking the wall repeatedly, and she kept her mind focused on how the angel moved.

It had some ability that was like her Instant Acceleration. When it'd first attacked, it'd launched itself into her like a rocket. Or maybe it could move so quickly because of its powerful legs. She didn't want to know how high the thing could jump, and as long as it was busy with the carcasses, she didn't care.

At the top, she found that the wall was about three feet in thickness, giving her ample space to stand. The water below seemed so far away it made her dizzy. There was a strange pulling sensation, a tingling in her ankles and feet, as though her body wanted to drop down. She even thought about diving onto the desecrated angel's back and striking it down, but she caught her breath, eyeing the horizon as water and blood dripped from her scales.

There was no moon or star or sun. The sky was simply red, and as far as she could see in every direction, the walls twisted and turned and went on forever; it really was some kind of maze. A labyrinth. Behind her, souls were running along the corridors, crying and moaning as angels gave chase. And across the water in front of her, above where the desecrated angel was still feeding, was the harpy. It had finally noticed Jenny.

Blood dripped from its chin. It wiped its face with one of its oversized wings, and Jenny noticed that the scratch she'd made earlier had healed away. Miriam lay beneath its enormous talons. Unlike the wing, it looked like the talons didn't heal. One of them was still missing.

Miriam was limp on the wall, a leg dangling over the edge. The harpy leaned down and grabbed one of Miriam's hands with its teeth, looking up at Jenny as Miriam cried softly. It wanted Jenny to see. Readjusting its talons, its entire body bobbing like a bird repositioning, it snipped through flesh and wrenched its head, tearing Miriam's arm off at the elbow.

Miriam screamed. Jenny flung her hatchet at the harpy, throwing it so hard she almost lost her balance, but the monster relinquished its hold on Miriam and dove toward the desecrated angel. The hatchet spun over Miriam's body and struck a distant wall with a *thwack*.

*I need a way to cross the distance*, thought Jenny, wishing she could borrow Iblis's wings. She thought about her tentacles for a moment and felt that familiar itch along her spine, but before she could consider bringing them out, the harpy swooped up again, a horrible grin on its porcelain face. Its white hair bounced all around as its wings flapped. In its talons was the green desecrated angel.

The harpy had brought it right up to Jenny.

The angel swiped at Jenny, who blocked its attack with her arms, feeling the scales crack from the blow. She dropped down, hanging off the ledge by her fingers as the angel landed on top with a heavy thud. One of the cobblestones came loose and fell away, landing below with a hefty splash.

Jenny summoned her hatchet back and swung again, trying to climb back on top of the wall. She wished desperately to move quicker, to outmaneuver the harpy and the angel midair.

Like a light bulb going off in her head, a familiar sensation flickered through her limbs, and a notification surfaced.

## Instant Swap (Tier 1)
### Change position with something you've touched within the past five seconds.

And she knew exactly how to use it as the desecrated angel's teeth gnashed, as its claws scraped off the top of the wall, as bolts of green light snapped around it. Jenny let go, falling away, watching the angel drool and spit overhead, watching the harpy flapping even higher up, silhouetted by the red sky. She had only one chance to catch them by surprise, and she wasn't going to mess this up.

Swinging her arm back, Jenny flung her hatchet with Savage Throw.

"You missed me!" sang the harpy as the hatchet spun away, way overhead, shooting straight up into the air. The angel looked up to follow its movement, but the harpy cackled down at Jenny.

Just as she splashed into the water below, she activated the skill. There was a swooping sensation, a feeling in her gut like when she'd be sitting in a car and there'd be a sudden dip, the feeling she imagined would hit if she'd ever had the courage to ride a roller coaster. Her stomach did a flip, and suddenly, she was falling from the sky. Below her were the stretched-out wings of the harpy, white and glistening, and the feathers of its exposed back.

Several thoughts flickered through Jenny's mind in the second or so before she made impact: Crash into the harpy and bring it to the ground. Summon her hatchet and cut through its spine. But then, Jenny thought better of it and righted herself, aiming her armored feet at the harpy as she hurtled down like a meteor. Light flashed to her hand as she summoned her hatchet back, wind blowing past her lips and eyelids, lifting her hair. Her fingers curled around the weapon.

The harpy's cackle was cut short—an abrupt cry. Jenny's feet found the harpy's neck and upper back, and there was a horrible *snap*, followed by something even worse—a very loud *crack* as Jenny brought the hatchet down, swinging it with both arms onto the angel's green head.

Electrical energy crackled around its body. The hatchet's edge sunk through its face, breaking the armor and erupting into a spray of blood. Jenny left the weapon buried in the creature's head as the harpy smashed through the water and into the ground, the impact having sent tremors racing up Jenny's legs and into her hips.

The angel fell a moment later, landing with a splash, its arm slapping Jenny away. She slammed into the wall face-first, bounced off the cobblestones, and collapsed into the water a few feet from the struggling harpy. Its head, its beautiful face, was bent the wrong way. Panic widened those once cool eyes as its wings fluttered uselessly against the water.

The angel, Jenny's hatchet sticking out from its nose and lips, yanked the weapon out and flung it over its shoulder. Lightning snapped and popped around its broken face as it stumbled back, hands struggling with the wound. It was clawing at its own exoskeleton, but then, a cry came from above, a scream, as Miriam also fell from the wall, talon in hand. Had she been clutching that this entire time?

Jenny watched as the girl landed on the desecrated angel, burying the talon through the crack in its metallic exoskeleton, lodging it deep inside its head with a gross, wet sound. Lightning crackled again. The angel twitched. And then, it collapsed on top of a stone block, and Miriam rolled away, her pale arm covered in blood up to the elbow, the talon left buried in the creature's skull.

**You've defeated Desecrated Angel (Level 63)!**

# CHAPTER THIRTY-FOUR

# TRIPLE DIGITS

Jenny wiped her face. She looked at Miriam, who was licking the blood off her arm, then they both looked down at the harpy. It was twitching and struggling in the water, one of its wings impossibly bent, giving the creature a crooked, broken appearance, like a coat hanger twisted out of shape.

Noises came from its spine, its bones cracking and snapping. The harpy was shaking like it had a bad cold. It shut its eyes as its beautiful face sank below the water, and it stopped trying to move, its wings curling back as its white hair trailed in the water.

Miriam stomped forward, a snarl on her blood-smeared face. "I'm going to rip your wings off and make you watch while I—"

But Jenny summoned her hatchet back with a flash and said, "Wait."

"Wait?" snapped Miriam, her eyes flashing with rage. She looked like the enraged Miriam from before, the one hell-bent on eating Jenny. "Do you know what these things do? They snatch us up and eat and eat and eat because"—she slapped her stomach—"we don't die. We just grow back. They can rip us apart as many times as they want. Do you know what that's like?"

"Yeah," Jenny replied, disgust squeezing her insides. It was what had happened to Yeshua. Over and over, healing each wound, healing every time a piece was ripped away. And then, he'd continued letting that happen—by choice, at least—as he fed himself to the deaths.

Why was the afterlife so fucked up? The harpies, the angels . . . This place was torture. She looked down at the harpy. It deserved what Miriam wanted to do to it. The violence was just part of the cycle, after all; Jenny knew it. She knew the harpy deserved far worse, but something was holding her back. Was it guilt?

Was it just because the harpy could talk? Because it wasn't a mindless creature like the angels? Jenny squatted down and grabbed a fistful of wet white hair to look the harpy in its beautiful eyes. Water dripped down its pale face. Its eyes were bloodshot, its mouth open as pained wheezing sounds escaped its throat.

Did she want to spare the creature just because it was beautiful? It looked desperate and angry, and it wasn't speaking anymore; no more laughter, no more threats. No more melodic voice. Jenny didn't want to kill the creature. She got the sense they were stuck here too, trapped in this madness with everyone else. But did that excuse its actions?

Would madness excuse her own?

Besides, the harpy would know things about the world. Maybe it could tell Jenny how to find Susan, what the best place was for an invasion. Something. *Am I just looking for an excuse to not kill it? And if I heal it, and it wants to fight some more . . .*

*I'll roast it alive.*

*I can't just leave it here with a broken neck.* But if she did, the angels would get it, and it wouldn't be on Jenny or Miriam. It would have been the harpy's own actions that led to its death.

Would it even die? What if it was immortal? She didn't know anything about it, and Iblis didn't have an answer to that question either.

"I can heal you," said Jenny finally. Miriam gasped indignantly, protesting.

The harpy's eyes went wide—beautiful, heartbreaking eyes that made Jenny's heart hurt. How could this creature be so cruel? It couldn't be. There had to be hope for it.

Confusion furrowed its brows as its lips curled, and it whispered in a raspy voice. There was no longer any hint of a melody in its voice now. "Why would you do that?"

Jenny licked her lips, dried blood stuck to her cheeks and chin. She squeezed her hatchet. "I need your help. I'm looking for someone, and—"

"I would *never* help a *human*," snarled the harpy, twisting its broken neck, howling from the pain. Its wing flicked Jenny's nose.

But the attack was a pathetic attempt; it didn't hurt at all. The feathers were wet and clumped together, and the harpy looked more like a sickly elderly patient now, thin and small. Its white hair stuck to its scalp and its back and shoulders.

The creature reminded her too much of someone who'd fallen and needed help getting back up.

But then, she felt something else. She saw the harpy's expression change, and it wasn't disgust anymore: it was fear—panic-stricken fear—and a feeling, a strange premonition, like the weighted feeling of the air right before a storm broke loose, right before a downpour. She'd felt it before, the sinking feeling of doom, back in the world of deaths as it rained blood. But what was happening here?

Jenny glanced back at Miriam, who looked blank. She stood stiffly, looking almost paralyzed, staring at the sky. Jenny craned her head up and saw an enormous silhouette descending from the red light. It had wings so large they seemed to blacken the sky.

She didn't need to see him to know who he was: Azra'il. Iblis's rage burned furiously inside her, and the name surfaced in her thoughts almost as if it was a system notification, but then, a notification came anyway, and it only made her feel worse.

### Angel (Level 332)

*Oh fuck.* She wanted to cry out. Triple digits. His level was in the triple digits. He was stronger than Yeshua or Iblis or anyone else she'd met. Jenny had no hope, even if Iblis activated her as a vessel and she had all her stats boosted; she felt that deep down inside, so she looked around, trying to find a place to hide.

She tried to speak to Miriam, but the girl was muttering something, repeating something in Arabic over and over, shaking, tears running down her cheeks. It sounded like a prayer, like she'd given up whatever of her mind she'd held on to and succumbed to the fear just as all the other souls had.

*"Miriam,"* Jenny hissed, but the shadow overhead was closing in, and the harpy was crying softly. It was terrified, shaking, its broken neck almost forgotten as it muttered something about forgiveness, about how sorry it was. Its eyes met Jenny's, and it was almost as if it didn't see Jenny anymore.

*Oh, fuck. I have to hide! I cannot let him find me!*

*Ignite!* she screamed silently in her head, plunging her hands into the water as blue flames erupted from her fingers. Instantly, with a glorious hiss, a cloud of vapor erupted around Jenny, a thick fog hiding them all from view, and she dashed through the water for the collapsed part of the wall, throwing herself behind several large cobblestones.

A moment later, as soon as Jenny sank into the water and leaned against the wall to hide, a furious wind blew away the steam. The ground, the walls, and maybe even the world shook as the enormous angel landed. A wave crashed over the cobblestones and rained down on Jenny, who turned to watch, finding a crack in the stones to peer through.

The angel was *huge*. He was far larger than the desecrated angel, wide and built like the front of an enormous truck. His shoulders were wide and muscular, and each of his arms would've been big enough for Jenny, Miriam, and even the harpy to climb inside. He towered over them all. Jenny couldn't even see his head, but he had to be about half the height of the enormous wall. Around his legs fluttered the horrible loincloth; the one Yeshua had said was cut from the skin of tarnished angels.

"Now, isn't this a curious sight?" His booming voice echoed all around them. "A harpy brought down by a human soul? I knew something smelled promising out here."

Miriam hadn't moved. She stood there in shock, trembling, water dripping down her pale skin, her long dark hair stuck to her face and back. The harpy lay in the water, one of its wings twitching weakly. "Forgive me," it said, its voice melodious again, as though it was singing in prayer. But it was strained. It was in too much pain. "Help me, master. I am hurt."

Azra'il walked over to the harpy, his loincloth flapping between his monstrous thighs as he placed his hands on his knees and knelt, bringing his face into Jenny's view. Dark gray like ancient stone. Eyes that burned with red light, and those horrible snakes with ruby-colored scales that shone slick like blood. Their tongues flicked out to taste the air, and fear clung tightly to Jenny's chest. She couldn't move. If he spotted her, she'd throw her hatchet—

Her hatchet was in the water a bit away from the desecrated angel's corpse. She couldn't risk summoning it back now. She couldn't even risk breathing too loudly. Maybe Instant Acceleration, then. She could dash away, summon the hatchet, throw it over the walls, and then teleport to it and—

Azra'il picked up the dead desecrated angel by its green head, blood gushing from its face, water dripping from its unmoving body. The talon stood out like a demented horn, and Azra'il laughed. "How did a soul break your talon, harpy? Aren't talons supposed to be a harpy's greatest pride?"

The harpy muttered something, and panic struck Jenny's heart like a drum. Would it tell him that Jenny was here? But whatever the harpy had said, Azra'il didn't seem to care. He turned his gaze to Miriam, red eyes sparkling. His voice dropped to a low rumble, and an ugly smile turned the corners of his lips. "My, my. I thought something smelled different . . . Was I just smelling you?" His eyes narrowed, and Jenny got a sick feeling in her stomach.

Miriam must have, too, because she covered herself again. Her face fell. She was too frightened to do or say anything.

"Oh, come on now. You don't have to be shy," Azra'il said in a mock gentle tone. He called her gorgeous for a human, willowy and easy on the eyes. She would taste beautifully. He extended a long, powerful arm. Each finger might've been thicker than Miriam was, and the girl stood there, pale and trembling, not even daring to look up. "I am called Azra'il, the Guide. The Warden. You may call me Master. I am sorry to have not made your acquaintance before."

Miriam didn't move a muscle. She stared at the hand outstretched for her.

And then, Azra'il shouted, causing Miriam to flinch, causing all the waters to crash about and slosh against the walls. His deep, booming voice carried down the corridor like a thunderous train. "IT IS PROPER TO INTRODUCE ONESELF WHEN SPOKEN TO!"

Miriam clapped a hand over her ears. She cried out, and her cry broke Jenny's heart.

Jenny buried her fingers into her palm, wondering what she could do. How she could get them out of here. Should she open a passageway? Here? Could she? She felt rooted to the spot. This was worse than the bursts of fear she'd felt before, when the blue desecrated angel's light had struck her. This was . . . This was far worse.

"Very well," said Azra'il, patting Miriam's head with his hand. He lifted her hair and rubbed his finger against the side of her face. "I deem you beautiful, and I will know your name one way or another." His fingers curled around Miriam's body, picking her up like a doll. She cried out, her fists uselessly striking his enormous hand. He just laughed. "Come. A new princess to add to my collection."

"Master, please . . ." came the choked voice of the harpy, all pretense of melody dropped. "I can tell you something . . ."

Azra'il straightened up, his head disappearing from Jenny's view as he raised Miriam off the ground, water dripping from her dangling feet as she cried softly. "Do not speak to me, harpy. You know what it means to fail me."

Jenny's heart was in her throat.

"*Master, please!*" screeched the harpy, but the response was a heavy, horrible crunch. Azra'il had stomped on the harpy, crushing the creature. The ground shook. Stones fell away from the walls around them, and a wave larger than any before crashed over Jenny's head. She squeezed a hand over her mouth, forcing herself to stay as still as possible.

With a heavy wingbeat, Azra'il flew upward and away, and the suffocating feeling lifted. Jenny waited for a long moment before collapsing.

Iblis roared in her subconscious. Her entire body shook with his rage, and flames spilled out of her eyes.

**He is a monster. He has grown stronger since he conquered my world, my people. We cannot stop him as we are.**

"That's why we're building an army, right?" Jenny let out a long breath as she pulled herself up, water dripping off the cracked scales of her armor. But that creature was what they were up against. An angel so monstrously powerful his very presence was suffocating. At least Azra'il hadn't spotted her. He didn't know she was here, and that made her feel relieved. A relief that only made her feel guiltier.

Disgusted with herself, she kept picturing Miriam's wide eyes looking around for help, kicking and struggling in Azra'il's grip, her feet dangling. What had he said? A new princess for his collection? Was he going to . . . ?

Jenny shuddered with rage and disgust and fear. "I can't let that happen to her. I have to save her too."

*Why did he take Miriam?*

"I have to help her too," whispered Jenny, closing her eyes to try and control the flames. But she couldn't stop shaking. She wasn't sure how much of it was Iblis's rage and how much was the sheer terror she'd felt. Azra'il was a giant. A giant so powerful that—

Iblis cut through Jenny's spiraling thoughts.

**The harpy is still alive.**

"What?" she whispered. But he was right. They could hear the muffled sobs. The harpy was still alive. She felt Iblis pull toward it, felt him leaving her body, streaming out of her eyes and mouth—a fire that she was exhaling.

Before she could ask what he was doing, she saw his sparkling blue light shoot across the water. He brightened the space momentarily, everything shimmering blue, before he descended on the harpy's broken body and all its feathers roared to life with blue flames.

# CHAPTER THIRTY-FIVE

# POSSESSING THE HARPY

Iblis possessed the dying harpy, burning out what was left of its consciousness. Its mangled body rose to its taloned feet, blue flames streaming from its eyes. Its feathers caught fire, and it spread massive, fiery blue wings. Jenny had felt the demon's rage, felt his desire to attack Azra'il—felt the despair in knowing he was too weak. She knew exactly how that felt.

**It's dying. The memories are fading away, but there is a castle. The home of their master.**

Slowly, he raised the harpy's beautiful face and stared at the sky.

**Up there. And there are more souls up there that Azra'il collects. One of them might be your Susan.**

Jenny stood in the water near the possessed harpy. She was still shaking, the presence of that monstrously powerful angel seeming to linger. If there was any solace, it was that Azra'il hadn't spotted her. He didn't know she was here in this world, and that made her relieved. But that relief only pulled on more guilt.

Disgusted with herself, she kept picturing Miriam's wide, frightened eyes looking around for help, kicking and struggling in Azra'il's grip, her feet dangling. What had he said? A new princess for his collection? Was he going to . . . ?

She shuddered with rage and disgust and fear. If Susan was up there, then . . . But she had no choice, even if Susan wasn't there. She had to save Miriam. She couldn't let that monster have her.

On the other end of the corridor, angel eggs had fallen into the water, and tarnished angels were feasting off them. Jenny grimaced, a part of her wanting to save the eggs. The angel babies didn't seem as mindless as the tarnished, but Iblis was right. If they were going to check somewhere, their best bet was this castle.

"We'll have to sneak up there," said Jenny, rightening herself. Golden light formed a flask in her hand, and she downed another potion to heal her body, steam rising from her skin. Iblis lowered its flames, and the harpy body stopped burning before taking a shaky step forward, talons splashing. It was still missing one on its right leg, but its eyes flickered with blue fire, and when Iblis looked at Jenny, she knew exactly what the demon had in mind.

A moment later, wind swirled around Jenny, battering her hair and blowing Iblis's new feathers into her face so that they tickled her nose and mouth. This body was *fast*, rising quickly with each flap of its wings. She looked down to see the walls of the labyrinths that spread all over the ground, as far as she could see in every direction.

Other harpies, their feathery wings outstretched, flew in circles, but a few of them were flapping upward, gaining altitude beside her and Iblis, their levels ranging from the low thirties to the high nineties. They hadn't noticed that Iblis's eyes were burning with blue flames or that Jenny was clinging to his back—they were too preoccupied with the eggs and angels and souls they carried in their talons. One of them was even carrying a chrysalis.

"Why are they doing that?" whispered Jenny. She had to repeat herself with a shout to be heard over the flapping wings and the fierce wind as they rocketed toward the red sky.

**It seems to be a part of their duties. They are tending to the harvest.**

"The harvest?"
Iblis's voice crackled through Jenny's mind.

**They are not proud of this. They are hurt. But they have no choice. No free will.**

Jenny felt the tenseness in the harpy's body; she readjusted her grip, fingers curling through more feathers as the wings flapped right beside her. She saw the ugly wounds, the missing feathers. Why didn't they have free will?

Their breaths began to cloud. The air was thinning out, becoming colder and colder, and then, they burst through a sudden redness—as though the sky had been a massive layer of red clouds—and emerged into bright light. A warm sun shone down on their backs, and Jenny had to squint.

It was blue skies all around, with an enormous castle made of the same stone blocks as the walls of the labyrinth floating up ahead. The ground below was obscured by what looked like an ocean of red water, and Jenny wondered if that redness was supposed to be there. If it had formed due to thousands of years of evaporating blood.

Despite the coldness, the air was easier to breathe. Iblis flapped toward the castle with the other harpies, and Jenny realized they'd have to change things up if they wanted to get through undetected. "Put me in your talons," she whispered to him.

When he acknowledged her words, she let go of his torso, climbing down his powerful legs to the crude talons. He hovered for a moment as Jenny repositioned herself, and once she was safely in his clutches, Iblis flew higher.

The castle was a large, blocky building that looked like something out of a history book; it reminded her of the archway entrance to this world, and as they flew closer, it loomed larger and larger, several city blocks wide.

How could something that large stay afloat?

The entrances—three large arch-shaped openings along the bottom—were massive as well. Harpies flew into the one on the left, while others exited from the right.

None of them glanced at Iblis as they entered. The bright sky vanished, and suddenly, they were in another tunnel, not unlike the walled passageways of the labyrinth. Iblis was still flying; there was more than enough space for his wings to spread wide, flapping gently, some strange wind from behind propelling them forward as the long hallway seemed to stretch forever.

Eventually, the stones gave way, and they came to a large, rectangular chamber filled with an almost fluorescent glow that reminded Jenny of dying light bulbs.

With a hard flap, Iblis banked and shot upward before coming to a stop, hovering in the air. Jenny craned her neck, holding on to his talons. A dozen or so harpies fluttered around them in the dark, gloomy space, their wings spread wide as they circled. All along the ceilings were eggs.

Angel's eggs.

Jenny swallowed hard, staring at their jiggling, softly glowing round forms. And the smell, musty and sweet—somehow a little familiar; somehow a little nostalgic. Then she heard giggling and laughter and looked down.

It was like a nursery. A daycare. Angel babies—pudgy little toddlers—waddled around, crawling or walking on two chubby legs, hands outstretched for balance. And spread between the angel babies were bodies.

Most of them looked like tarnished angels; most of them were half eaten. Babies waddled from one corpse to the other, chewing off bits and pieces, swallowing and burping, gurgling with joy. Thankfully, there weren't any souls up here.

There was a gust of wind, and another harpy flew from behind Iblis. It glanced at Jenny, its beautiful face puzzled, but it didn't say a word. In its talons was a large chrysalis emitting yellow light, and the harpy flew across the room to another wall of enormous archways—a hallway leading to another part of the castle.

"Let's follow," whispered Jenny, not trusting her voice. A part of her was afraid the babies would respond to her here too. Would they, though? Would they have any reason to?

Jenny held on tight as Iblis swooped down. The babies looked up, drool and blood dribbling down their chins, their eyes watching Jenny with intense curiosity. Was that a flicker of recognition or was she imagining it? Some of them even reached for her, their little fingers opening and closing as though they wanted to grab her.

But then, Iblis swung upward, gaining altitude to rush toward the openings at the other end of the chamber, and Jenny told herself the babies just thought she might be food. She must have smelled different than the angels or the harpies or anything else in this world.

As they neared the ceiling, a wretched angel appeared from the shadows. Jenny almost yelped, ready to burst out of Iblis's talons and attack. It had stripes—white-and-yellow stripes across its black exoskeleton. The soft skin of its navel and thighs was exposed, and tendrils floated off from its back.

It hadn't noticed Jenny. Or if it had, the angel didn't pay them any attention. Another harpy had flapped up to the ceiling, and the angel accepted an egg from its talons before turning away, shuffling across the ceiling to find some space for the egg. Jenny turned in Iblis's talons, trying to see. She wanted to watch how it would attach it, but just then, Iblis flew through the next archway.

This time, two harpies were right ahead. One of them carried another glowing chrysalis, this one with a pale white light, and Iblis kept his distance. The hallway curved upward, and Iblis did too.

**The harpy's mind recognizes this place. We are rising to the second stage of the castle. What remains of the Garden.**

Jenny couldn't respond. The wind was battering her, and she was too anxious for what they'd find. Would it be a hatchery for desecrated angels? Would the entire place be crawling with the monsters?

But the next "stage," as Iblis had called it, was wet and grassy. It looked like they'd come outside again, but far overhead was a stone ceiling. A bright light mimicked the sun, and forestry covered the floor. A river cut through the center, winding from one end of the room to the other. The place was so large, it might've been the size of Central Park.

It was a lot more spacious than the angel babies' stage. They flapped away from the archway, trying to take in their surroundings. Other harpies swooped down and affixed chrysalises to giant tree branches. Iblis flew overhead slowly without saying a word.

The forest was dense with lush greenery. On the ground, there was grass, and sometimes she thought she saw little animals zipping by, furry little mammals. If there were desecrated angels here, she couldn't spot them, only their chrysalises, and there must've been thousands of them.

Thousands.

Was this . . . Was this their army? Fear jabbed Jenny in the chest. Were the angels amassing an army of desecrated angels? The one who had attacked her and Miriam in the labyrinth had been much higher level than the one she'd fought in the high school. They must be leveling up quicker in this world, feeding on an infinite source of blood, but then, why were some of them kept up here in the forest?

As Iblis swooped down, Jenny saw some of the babies again, carried in the talons of harpies. They were kicking and struggling, blood dripping from where the talons dug into their little bodies.

"No," she whispered.

Iblis spoke solemnly.

**They are feed. They are an excellent source of nourishment.**

"What the fuck . . ." Jenny watched as a harpy brought a struggling baby to a red chrysalis. The thing opened slightly, and a red-faced desecrated angel's head emerged, gooey liquid dripping away like mucus. She got a notification alerting her to its level—fifty-five. It accepted the kicking and screaming baby with its mouth open, accustomed to feeding like this, and then, Iblis flapped upward, gaining altitude again.

**There is another stage. This harpy has never been there, but it believes the souls we are looking for should be up ahead.**

Jenny's stomach was still twisted from what she'd seen. She wanted to throw up; she kept picturing the little toddlers that had followed her around the high school, the ones who'd listened when she'd instructed them to pro-tect Susan. The ones who must've died carrying out Jenny's order. She vowed to free them too. Somehow. She didn't care what they were or even that they feasted on flesh. She would find a way.

On the other side of the forest, there was the enormous wall of stones, and they found even more archways. Iblis fluttered, slowing down.

**The harpy's mind is frightened. It doesn't want to go there.**

"What if it's . . . Azra'il?" she asked, holding her breath before allowing herself to relax in Iblis's grip. She let her arms and legs dangle, realizing that she'd been tense this entire time. Her hair fluttered in the breeze and whipped her in the face.

*What if it's Susan?*

*What if she's not there?*

Iblis started to respond, but then, he flapped his wings and flew back, flames trailing from his eyes. The movement snapped Jenny around, her vision spinning, and then she saw what he'd dodged.

Three harpies had rocketed up from below to attack, and now they hov-ered in front of them, their brows furrowed, their beautiful faces twisted with anger. White hair of various lengths flopped on their heads.

**Harpy (Level 38)**
**Harpy (Level 21)**
**Harpy (Level 60)**

The harpy in the middle—the largest one and the highest leveled, its wingspan almost double the harpy's that Iblis had possessed—snarled. "And where do you think you're going?" it asked in a scornful, melodic voice that sounded like it was mocking a young child.

# CHAPTER THIRTY-SIX

# CLIMBING UP THE WALL

**Brood mother.**

Iblis spoke in his static voice as flames billowed from his eyes, flapping his wings gently. Jenny moved her hatchet to her hand and hid it behind her back, not taking her eyes off the larger harpy.

The brood mother's eyes were tinged red, the wrinkles on her face deeply set, but she was still eerily beautiful. White, nearly translucent hair framed her face, and her sharp features were distinguished and almost kind. But there was a heaviness to the way she carried herself, a set in her jaw made worse by a scowl. The other two behind her looked much younger, about the same age as the harpy Iblis had possessed.

"You know we are not permitted entrance beyond this stage," said the brood mother. There was a low note in the melody of her voice, a hint of repercussion. Then it squinted at Jenny. "What is that? A soul? Have you brought a *soul* to the Garden?"

Iblis's wings beat rhythmically as he stayed afloat. She could tell he didn't know what to say, so Jenny whispered, "Tell them you're taking me prisoner for Azra'il."

"I found this living human," he said, using the harpy's throat. The voice wasn't as sickly sweet as it had been. There was a rough edge to it. "I wish to bring her to the master."

"A human?" shrieked the brood mother, flapping repeatedly as she flew closer, as her voice got louder. Wind tickled Jenny's forehead. "Is it alive?"

"It is alive," replied Iblis, his voice dripping with disgust. Was that the harpy's voice leaking through? "I defeated it in battle, and I believe Master will have questions on what it wants."

The other harpies flew closer as well. One of them suggested feeding Jenny to the desecrated angels below—she would give a boost to the metamorphosis. Another wondered if they'd get in trouble. But the brood mother shushed them both with a strong beat of her wings. "I will take it. Give the creature to me."

Jenny blinked as Iblis's talons tightened around her, digging slightly into her armor. "But then, I will not be credited for finding it," he said, his voice dropping slightly with uncertainty. "I wish to see the master."

"Credit?" echoed the brood mother. "I will report everything—"

"Forgive me, brood mother, but I am the one who found her. Master will want to see me directly."

"Child, do not disobey me," said the brood mother in a dangerous tone which reminded Jenny all too much of her own mother. She squeezed her hatchet tightly. "Bring the creature over to me right now."

There were more wing beats. Jenny turned her head slightly toward the forest below to see a dozen or so harpies flying up to see what the commotion was. The brood mother flapped closer, her eyes narrowing as she stared at Iblis's eyes.

"I don't—" But then, Iblis flew suddenly to the left. Jenny's head bumped against a talon as someone shouted.

"*A HUMAN HAS TAKEN CONTROL OF OUR SISTER!*" shrieked a shrill, high-pitched voice. More voices joined in, and Jenny knew their gambit was over. But it was almost funny. They thought *she* was the one who'd possessed the harpy. There was no time to correct them—harpies darted in their direction, all of them looking enraged as Iblis flew higher and higher.

Heart pounding, she scanned the forest below, seeing the river. Remembering how she'd created a cloud of steam to hide from Azra'il, she told Iblis to dive for the water.

He fluttered for another second, turning to see even more harpies eyeing Jenny, fear, anger, and disgust twisting their pretty faces like they couldn't stand to see her, like they couldn't stand the thought of a living human being near them. Another dove at Iblis, its talons stretched outward, and Iblis tucked his wings and dropped straight down.

Jenny clung tightly to his legs, her own wrapped around his talons as the forest and river rushed up to meet them. She felt like an airplane falling out of the sky, diving so quickly it must've been faster than Instant Acceleration, and with every passing moment, they only seemed to fall faster. At this rate, they'd hit the river and break every bone in their bodies.

She wanted to look behind them to see if the other harpies were following, but wind violently battered her. She could barely keep her eyes open, could hardly breathe. At the speed they were going, she couldn't even turn her head.

But Iblis spread his wings all of a sudden, catching them like a parachute. The force knocked through Jenny, and she was almost flung from the harpy, dangling from his talons. He'd stopped just a few feet over the water.

Trees surrounded them, and Jenny looked up, blinking away tears to see the other harpies diving as well.

"Fly along the river!" shouted Jenny. Hanging from a talon, she held out her hand as blue flames flared to life on her fingers. Iblis understood what she was trying to do. As they flew, Iblis tipped to the right so that Jenny's burning hand struck the water. The river erupted with a hiss of steam and vapor trailing behind them like a rolling cloud of fog.

"They'll see me as soon as we fly up," said Iblis, still using the harpy's voice. He sounded out of breath. He sounded frantic.

**I am sorry. This might be as far as we go.**

"No," said Jenny, thinking hard as steam and water and wind battered her. "Okay. Fly me as close to the opposite wall as you can. I'll climb. Then, you can fly in the other direction and lead them away, abandon the body, and get back to me."

If Iblis was onboard with her idea, she couldn't tell. But he flapped fiercely as more harpies shrieked above and behind them in the cloud of vapor. Branches hanging over the water swayed in the wind as they flew past. Jenny saw flashes of chrysalises hanging like enormous fruit, but they were flying too quickly for notifications. After a moment, Iblis shouted for her to get off.

Lighting up completely in blue flames, churning up even more steam so that Jenny could hardly see him, he tilted toward the bank, the grassy slope, and flicked Jenny off.

Without missing a beat, he twisted in the air and shot upward as Jenny rolled along the grass, hidden by the dense steam. Guilt filled her chest as he flew toward the sky—he was just a glowing blue beacon, blurred and out of focus, but she knew he'd done that so all the other harpies zeroed in on him.

Before the steam faded away, Jenny used Instant Acceleration and flashed away from the river to hide behind an enormous tree. She watched Iblis and the other harpies turn into distant specks; he was making a beeline for the tunnels they'd entered through, as though he was retreating. Jenny didn't want to waste any of the time he'd gotten for her.

With a flash of light, her hatchet reappeared in her hand. She must've dropped it in the water somewhere during the chase; it was dripping wet. A chrysalis hung above her; a black one. It wriggled grossly. Jenny didn't want to stay here for a fight, so she dashed away from the tree, heading for the wall of cobblestones towering in front of her, then used Savage Throw.

The hatchet cut through small branches and leaves, spinning and rushing away from her, hurling higher and higher before hitting the cobblestone. Using her new skill, Instant Swap, a sense of weightlessness took over as everything shifted. One moment, she was running on the wet grass; the next, she was higher than the treetops and sliding down the wall.

Her stomach did a swoop. Her fingernails searched desperately for anything to grasp onto, scraping against the stone until she found one of the little ledges to catch her. Her head spun with dizziness from the height as she pushed her feet against the wall. In the distance, she could just about make out the other harpies chasing Iblis.

Grabbing onto the stone edges with her fingers, she summoned her hatchet back to her hand.

Taking a deep breath, she threw it again, tossing it over her head with Savage Throw. It slammed into another stone far above her, and Jenny activated Instant Swap.

This time, she felt a tear, as though she were made of Velcro—like something inside of her was being torn and then snapped back together—and popped into existence even higher up along the wall, scrambling for footing. Two of her nails broke. She bit back tears, blood making her fingers slick, but she pressed on.

She summoned her hatchet back. She wouldn't try that trick again; the ability clearly had a limit. Weariness filled her chest. She was out of breath, but her only choice was to climb.

Clenching her teeth and holding on to a tiny ledge, she swung her hatchet upward and struck stone, burying the edge deep into the wall. She pulled herself up, crawling against the wall. *If only there were more holes in this thing*, she thought. Then, not wanting to waste time, she covered her knuckles with her armor and punched through the stone, making her own hand- and footholds.

"Alright," she said with a triumphant laugh. She could keep doing that and save her Instant Swap for when she'd really need it.

Yanking the hatchet out of the wall and swinging upward, Jenny climbed, punching new holes into the stone which became footholds as she kept going. She reminded herself repeatedly not to look down. She'd always been afraid of heights. Or not really afraid, but it would give her a strange feeling in her ankles and legs, and a plunging feeling in her stomach. She didn't want to deal with that. Besides, if she fell now, she could just use Instant Swap to catch herself.

That's why she was saving it, she told herself as her muscles strained. She focused on Susan. She pictured Miriam in Azra'il's hands. She thought about Iblis and the other demons. The deaths. Yeshua. The burning in her muscles was nothing; she could keep climbing, and then she could heal herself. She just had to be quick.

*Iblis!* she called out silently. *Are you there?*

If he abandoned the harpy body and rushed back to her, she could just use the wings and secure the rest of the distance. It would save them so much time. But if he wasn't back yet . . . maybe he was in trouble. Maybe something had gone wrong.

*Stop thinking and climb!*

*Just climb!*

Valescent Light flashed. Her fingernails and muscles healed. She urged herself to keep going, and fell into the pattern: Slam the hatchet into the wall. Punch the wall, pull herself up. Flash the hatchet out. Repeat, over and over, until she could see the dark openings overhead. Relief pounded in her head— or was that a headache? When there was nothing left for her hatchet to sink into, she let out a triumphant cry.

Her fingers found the edge, and she pulled herself up the rest of the way, collapsing on the floor of the archway. She rolled onto her back, laying her hatchet on her chest as a breeze blew into the tunnel, cooling her face. Her feet were still dangling over the side. Now, all she had to do was wait.

She stared at the blue sky, hoping that Iblis was alright. As she stared, wings came into view, bright and wide, almost as wide as the tunnel. For a second, she felt relief. He was alright. Then, she saw the flash of steely white eyes, and her insides went cold.

## Harpy (Level 60)

Jenny rolled away just in time as sharp talons scraped the floor where she'd been lying, sending up a flurry of sparks. It was the brood mother, and her face and feathery body were covered in blood.

# CHAPTER THIRTY-SEVEN

# BROOD MOTHER

The brood mother shrieked as Jenny used Instant Acceleration to escape. She dashed forward, deeper into the tunnel, into the dark space, and ran headfirst into what felt like a wall.

With a crash, she slumped down, everything ringing inside her head. The impact had hurt—not so much that it damaged her but enough that it knocked the air from her lungs and left her dizzy.

The tunnel swerved upward sharply, and she'd accelerated *right* into those large stones. Behind her, she could hear the shrill cries of the brood mother and the flap of her wings. Jenny groaned internally, realizing she'd have to climb again, and this time in the dark. No light shone up ahead.

She needed wings. Could she make wings?

She could grow tentacles, though. Would that work?

Her mind raced, and within moments, the brood mother closed the distance. Her translucent hair seemed to glow in the dark, a shimmer of light around her menacing face as her talons closed in. Jenny threw herself to the side, the clawing, scraping sounds cutting sharply through her ears as sparks erupted from the stones near where Jenny had been standing.

"*HUMAN!*" screamed the brood mother, flapping up to gain altitude, her shrill voice echoing in the tunnel. "*WHY ARE YOU TRESPASSING IN MY GARDEN?*"

"I'm just trying to find my friend!" replied Jenny, staying low to the ground, keeping her eye on those talons. They flashed in what little light came through the archway. As soon as the brood mother dove again, she'd cut them just as she'd cut the other harpy's. She was outmatched in raw strength, but the harpies couldn't maneuver in tight spaces, and Jenny had the advantage in the tunnel.

"A living human has no right to be here," spat the brood mother, flapping overhead. "No right. You are creatures of sin and suffering. This is holy land."

Jenny held her breath. Sin and suffering? Why did the harpies hate humans so much? "How the fuck is this holy land?" she shot back. "All you do is torture people. Everything is horrible. Who the fuck do you think you are?"

"*Who do you think YOU are?!*" screamed the harpy as she tucked her wings and dove again, talons outstretched.

Jenny swung her hatchet, but her weapon bounced off the talons, and the sharp, pointed ends scraped Jenny's chest.

Searing pain burned through Jenny as she stepped back with Instant Acceleration, crashing against the wall behind her. She clutched her chest, breathing hard, coughing. Something wet and hot ran down her armor, and she groaned. Those talons were too wickedly sharp; if she hadn't moved backward, that would've been it for her.

She coughed up blood, her every breath stinging now as she lowered her hand from her chest. The brood mother was far stronger than Iblis's harpy had been, and she was agile and quick, able to maneuver better despite her size.

Jenny summoned her hatchet back. With a quick bit of Valescent Light, her hand shining brightly in the dark tunnel, she healed her chest. She'd wanted to save the light for later, but making a potion and drinking it would give the harpy too much of an opening.

But what did the harpy even want? Why was it so against Jenny being there?

It was almost like a guard dog, protecting something.

"What's up there?" asked Jenny, breathing hard. "Why are you stopping us?"

The harpy flapped again, but she leaned forward midair so that Jenny could see the sneer. "It is of no concern to you. When I kill you and your soul emerges from the blood, maybe then you'll understand humility."

Jenny huffed, trying to steady herself, then threw her hatchet normally. She knew it wasn't fast enough to register as a threat to the harpy, but that was what she was banking on.

The brood mother dodged with a mocking laugh. Jenny used Instant Swap.

Again, it felt as though she was tearing in half, stretching like a rubber band before snapping back into place, but in the next instant, she was on top of the harpy. The brood mother's eyes widened with alarm. She closed her wings, turning midair to try diving out of reach, but there wasn't enough space. Jenny summoned her hatchet back with a flash of light and swung as hard as she could, grasping the handle with both hands.

The edge sliced through one of the wings, cutting away feathers, tearing the skin, and snapping through bone. The brood mother plummeted through the dark and landed in a pile, screaming in pain, her other wing flapping maddeningly. Jenny fell too, rolling away from the harpy's talons.

A bit of torn wing fluttered down like an enormous feather. The breeze blew it around as the harpy cried—from pain or anguish, Jenny didn't know, but the harpy started swearing, her voice changing from singing to screaming and back.

Jenny got to her feet, holding her hatchet, half wanting to charge the creature and cut it down to pieces, to end its onslaught once and for all. To find out what happened to Iblis—to avenge him if she had to. But the brood mother, shaking as she was, got to her talons, her face strained with agony. Blood spurted out of her injured wing. The other one flapped fiercely, but the harpy teetered from side to side as though she couldn't maintain her balance.

"Look," said Jenny, raising her arm, trying to show that she wouldn't attack while the harpy was so weakened. "You're not an angel. You're not a monster. Please. I don't want to hurt you. I just want to—"

For a second, the brood mother's face seemed sad, like she would start pleading, but then, her lips curled into a snarl, and her brows furrowed in anger or pain or something in between. Leaping into the air, she flapped her one wing, tilting her body to keep somewhat steady, her face a mask of pure hatred, and dove without any of the speed of her previous attacks, talons outstretched.

It was a desperate attempt—futile. Just as Jenny was about to answer with her own rage—a fire breath of Ignite—something shot in through the tunnel, a streak of blue flames, and slammed into the old harpy.

A talon sliced through her cheek, another through her ribs, and with an eruption of blood and feathers and fire, the brood mother was slammed against the tunnel wall that Jenny had crashed into earlier.

It was Iblis, pinning her against the wall, his burning wings spread wide as though he was a hawk who'd just caught his prey.

"*Enough!*" he shouted, no pretense of melody in his voice. "The harpies are on the wrong side of this war. Stop this madness now!"

The brood mother cried weakly, her one wing flapping feebly against Iblis's body. "I kept my children safe," she squawked. "I protected them. I . . ."

"You sentenced them to a life of servitude," said Iblis in a dangerous voice. "You stripped them of free will. You succumbed to the angels." He flapped both wings powerfully, lifting him and the brood mother up, dragging her body along the stone. "Now relent, or I will end you."

"Please," she begged, her voice heavy, a wail stuck in her throat. Blood ran down her chin. One of Iblis's talons had pierced her cheek right through to the other side and into the wall; one more was wrapped around her throat, and two others were lodged into her sides.

"I do not wish to kill you," said Iblis, and finally, the brood mother went limp. He flew off her with a beat of his wings, sliding his talons out of her body.

He landed near Jenny, squatting down as he huffed for breath. Blood stained the feathers of his face and body. His wings were torn in several places, and an ugly gash went across his stomach. Intestines hung low, glistening in an ugly way. It must've been a brutal battle with the other harpies, but Jenny was relieved to see him.

The brood mother slumped down to the ground, shaking. She wrapped her one wing around her torso and stared down at the floor. Blood spurted out of the holes in her face and ran down the outside of her wing, staining the feathers. Jenny could see her tongue moving in her mouth.

She almost wanted to heal the old harpy, but she reasoned it would make more sense to heal her on the way back; she had to reserve Valescent Light and her energy as much as she could. Besides, she didn't know if the brood mother would continue to attack them or not.

"What now?" asked Jenny. She couldn't look away from the trembling old harpy, thinking back to her own mother. In her mind, she kept replaying Iblis bursting out of the darkness, talons outstretched. She kept thinking about how she'd wanted to roast the harpy alive.

Iblis flicked the blood off his feathers. A bunch floated away, crumbling into ashes, and Jenny saw that most of that body looked charred.

**I will take her body, and we will continue.**

The brood mother didn't react. She stayed on the ground, looking dejected and forlorn.

Flames spurted as Iblis left the first harpy, who slumped to the ground, looking up, its beautiful face twisted in shock and pain and despair. It looked at Jenny, its lips moving. Then, its eyes rolled to the back of its head and the harpy fell forward, disintegrating just as it hit the floor.

The older harpy slowly lifted her beautiful, wrinkled face, the torn holes of her cheeks glistening grotesquely in Iblis's blue light as his sparkling form shot into her.

# CHAPTER THIRTY-EIGHT

# THE THRONE ROOM

Jenny clung tight to Iblis's new feathers. The brood mother was a much bigger harpy, but their fight had been brutal, and the harpy was broken. Blue-and-orange flames flickered out of its eyes, and the feathers flashed white with every wingbeat. Flames had healed the wing Jenny had torn through. They only needed it to climb to the final stage.

Iblis kept his fire burning, as the tunnel was dark, but even with the flickering glow, they couldn't tell how far they would have to climb. Blood dribbled out from the brood mother's wounds, running past Jenny's face.

Each flap took them higher and higher. The breeze blew Jenny's hair back and stung the scratches on her face. Her legs dangled as she held on tight around Iblis's waist, her armored feet clanging against the sides of the tunnel several times, drawing up sparks and echoes.

After what felt like ages, light appeared overhead, bright and warm and welcoming.

The next moment, Iblis flew right through it, and they emerged into what looked like a palace grand hall; a place where wealthy people might throw a grand ball—something out of a magical fairy tale.

"What the fuck?" whispered Jenny, sliding off Iblis, who'd perched down and buckled as one of his knees gave out. The injured wing fluttered awkwardly as the flames died down, smoke rising from the hole in the brood mother's cheek.

"It looks to be the throne room," he said with that distorted, singsongy voice.

*Throne?* Jenny looked around. The room was draped in enormous violet cloths. Pillars with torches attached led away from the hole they'd emerged from, a purple carpet guiding the way to large stone steps. Above them, slightly raised, was the throne, a giant seat made of black stone that reminded Jenny of the rocks in the world of death. It even glistened similarly in the flickering torchlight—sometimes visible; sometimes invisible.

A cold shudder ran down her spine. She climbed the steps toward the throne, staring at it, dreading the question on her mind. The ceiling was draped with trailing cloths and golden ornaments high up. Past the large stone pillars, she could see two more great archways, one on either side of her, leading into more chambers.

**That must be his throne.**

With a shimmer of orange-and-blue light, he left the harpy behind and floated up. The brood mother crumpled onto the red carpet, blood pooling as singed feathers floated to the top. It cried weakly. Iblis's incorporeal form floated toward the enormous black seat.

"Azra'il? His throne?" asked Jenny in a low voice, feeling every inch of her body on high alert, like something horrible was around every pillar, every shadow. "Why does he need a throne if he's supposed to be serving Adonai?"

**The power hungry often seek the power hungry.**

Jenny followed Iblis up the red carpet, up the steps. The throne towered over her; four of her could've sat side by side with room to spare. The armrests were taller than her, and its back shot up with a curved top like a tombstone. The rock face glistened brightly, but it reminded her too much of the pillars. For a second, she was horrified there would be more deaths in there, trapped in a fucked-up form. She used a tiny bit of fire and held her burning hand against the throne.

To her relief, she found it empty. It turned invisible with the light.

**It is constructed from demon glass. From our cities. From our homes.**

"You shouldn't touch that," said a small voice from somewhere. It echoed from all over, making it impossible to tell where it had come from.

Jenny whipped around, holding up her burning hand. "Who's there?" She glanced at Iblis's blue sparkles then at the trembling brood mother lying beside the hole they'd entered through. From the throne, the hole looked almost like a dark swimming pool.

"That is our master's seat," came another voice. This one was bolder, stronger.

Rushing down the steps, snuffing out her flames, Jenny clutched her hatchet tight and prepared for an attack. Was it more harpies? Something else? They also called the angel "Master."

Shadows moved from behind the pillars, and faces appeared. Men and women, young and dressed in flowing garments of red and purple and pink. Every single one of them had the same notification.

### Soul (Blooded)

One of them, a boy, approached Jenny. He had long blond hair that covered his forehead, and a sharp chin. He squinted at her. "Desecrated . . . human? How?"

"Like the angels?" asked a girl.

"What's wrong with her?"

"Her eyes are so weird . . ."

"Should we get Master?"

Jenny clenched her teeth at their words. She kept her hand on her hatchet, turning in every direction as the souls closed in. They seemed to be gliding across the carpeted floor, their long gowns trailing as though they were at a fancy gala. Were they going to attack? Could they even fight in those dresses?

They weren't at all like the souls she'd met below in the ruins. These souls could speak. They weren't afraid. They weren't crying.

And what was with the *blooded* notification?

Was this where Azra'il had taken Miriam? Was this what he meant by his collection?

"I'm looking for someone," said Jenny, trying to keep her voice even. From the corner of her eyes, she could see Iblis hovering over the souls. They hadn't noticed him, but a few of them wandered over to the harpy, kneeling and poking at it.

"What is this thing? It's such a mess."

"It's one of the harpies!" gasped another.

"Is it dead? I didn't know they could die."

"Yeah, it's dead."

"Did the desecrated girl kill it?"

"No, look, it's moving. It's so pretty."

"Yes," snapped Jenny. These souls, they looked about her age—maybe older—but they sounded like children. A sinking feeling filled her stomach as she realized they didn't have the entirety of their minds. They weren't whole humans. "I'm looking for my friend," she tried again.

"Friend?" asked the nearest soul. A girl, her eyebrows raised. "Who are you looking for? What's her name? I know everyone here."

"Susan," said Jenny, shuddering as she said Susan's name.

The soul frowned. She glanced at a boy near her, draped in pink. He shrugged. "Master brought a new princess not too long ago."

The girl lit up like she'd just remembered. "Yes! Yes, he did. Is that your friend? Susan?"

Jenny shook her head, eyeing the other souls, who looked upset. "No. That's someone else. But I'm looking for her, too. Where does he take them?"

A bunch of souls frowned. "We're not allowed to know. We stay here. And over there." One of them pointed to a large chamber to the right.

But another pointed to the left. "There's another girl in there, I think. But we're not allowed to talk to her."

A few of them grumbled something about master spending too much time with her.

"We don't like her," said another soul. "She's a strange girl who's stuck on something."

"She's being punished."

"She's always screaming."

"She committed a grave sin."

**These souls have had their minds emptied.**

Iblis spoke quietly to her. Jenny agreed. It was like talking to a classroom of absentminded school kids. They seemed innocent and unaware and forgetful, but they looked like adults.

"Master says he doesn't like playing with her," continued another soul. "But he plays with us all the time."

"Plays?" asked Jenny, a sickening feeling rising to her throat. She didn't want to know what they meant, but another soul described it in depth.

"He comes to our chambers and tells us stories and shows us—"

Jenny held up her hand. "Wait. Wait. *Wait.*"

The souls looked at her curiously, like they couldn't understand why she wouldn't want to hear more.

But she was shaking. "Can you tell me where the stuck girl is? The girl your master won't . . . That he keeps away?"

The souls looked shifty. "We're not supposed to go there."

"We are forbidden."

"Master will be furious. Remember when . . . ?"

"Yeah."

"He didn't like it at all. He didn't play with us for so long."

"We shouldn't."

But Jenny didn't want to wait for them to decide. If the chamber to the right led to their bedrooms, then that only left the chamber to the left, where everything seemed dark and hidden away.

She glanced at the black throne, trying not to picture Azra'il sitting there. She'd gotten lucky that he wasn't around. But Miriam wasn't around either. He must be busy with her . . . She tried not to think about that. Tried not to wonder if Miriam would end up as a blooded soul too. What that might mean.

Iblis spoke with his crackling voice.

**There is a girl in that room. I cannot see her face; she is kept in the dark. But there is a cross, as Yeshua was kept on the cross.**

Jenny's heart leapt into her throat. "Excuse me," she said to the souls, moving between them. They didn't flinch away from her touch. They weren't ice cold like the souls she'd met below. They felt warm and alive and soft. And they all looked at her curiously, exchanging nervous glances.

"You can't go there."

"Master has forbidden it."

"Please. We'll get in trouble."

Jenny didn't bother responding to them. She shouldered them aside, and they rushed around her, their faces growing increasingly worried. Some of them tripped over their long, bright gowns.

"*Please!*" Their voices rose in pitch and volume.

"I have to," said Jenny, whose mind was flashing red every time she pictured Susan on the cross. She almost swiped at one of them.

"No!" A soul grabbed Jenny's arm. Fingernails dug into the cracked scales of her arm, but she shook them off. More hands grabbed at her shoulders. Men and women, their faces young and earnest, stared at her.

"You can't go in there. Don't go in there!"

Jenny threw them off and pulled out her hatchet, turning slowly in a circle. "Stay back."

Immediately, the souls gave her space, falling backward, nearly tripping over their flowing gowns. Jenny felt sorry for them, for what they were going through, but she wouldn't let them get in her way. "I need to find her, okay? So stay the fuck back."

The souls looked like they might cry, then one of them broke away, running in the direction of the bedrooms, and the others did the same. A flurry of footsteps. She watched their flowing dresses and bright faces vanish behind pillars and back into the bedchamber. Some of them stayed back, watching Jenny from the shadows, whispering among themselves.

She didn't have time to make sense of their strangeness. Turning around, she marched toward the other room, a weighty feeling gathering in her legs with every beat of her heart, as every step took her closer. A cross . . . Iblis had seen a cross in there.

Would Azra'il show up?

Would these souls be a problem?

Jenny didn't care. Her feet felt heavy as she walked past the pillars. Torchlight flickered overhead, and a horrible, twisting anxiety filled her throat as she neared the opposite end of the throne room.

Iblis fluttered close by. He might've said something, but it didn't register in Jenny's head. Coming to the open doorway, she stared into the dark room. Unlike the rest of the torchlit palace area, this place was too dark for her to see anything, but she could hear the soft sounds of someone's labored breathing.

And then, she heard a voice. A strained, raspy voice full of disbelief and shock and pain.

*"Jenny?"*

# CHAPTER THIRTY-NINE

# BROWN HAIR

Jenny tried to speak, but her words lumped in her throat, each one sticking to the next. She remained at the enormous entrance, the arch so far over her head it didn't really feel like a door, more like the entrance to a separate palace, another world.

The room was dark, but she got the sense it was immense. She could just about make out several silhouettes as her eyes adjusted. The largest was the *T* shape in the center of the room, towering just as Yeshua's cross had in the world of death.

A tremor ran up both of Jenny's legs; suddenly, she felt weak, as though she'd been trapped inside a pillar of salt for ages and ages and all her muscles had atrophied.

"*What are you doing here?*" croaked Susan. Her voice was so strained, so broken, like she'd been screaming or crying for ages. Her breath was loud and raspy.

"I . . ." Jenny's voice broke as well. Hot tears ran down her cheeks, and the more she blinked, the more tears seemed to fall. She didn't know what to say. What was she supposed to say?

The last time Jenny had seen Susan was when she'd held her corpse on the cafeteria floor. Somehow, that felt like so long ago . . . She'd traveled through worlds, fought ghouls and demons and harpies, and . . . none of that changed the fact of what she'd done. The horrible thing she'd done.

*I bit through her throat.*

*I killed her.*

And now, here she was, not with the other souls but separated and nailed to a cross and—why?

*Why is Susan here?*

**The room is empty. The girl is alone. I will keep these souls distracted.**

Jenny swallowed hard, still trying to find words, trying to find the courage to step into the room.

"Stay away from me!" hissed Susan, and Jenny saw the silhouette of a person wriggling on the cross, followed by a muffled cry, as though Susan was screaming but biting her lips, trying to hide her pain. "Go away. You're not real. Just leave me alone. I DON'T KNOW WHAT YOU WANT FROM ME! HOW MANY TIMES DO I HAVE TO TELL YOU? I DONT HAVE IT. I DONT KNOW WHAT YOU—"

"Su—" Jenny tried again, her eyes burning with tears, emotions surging to every part of her face. She couldn't stand hearing Susan screaming like this. Had Azra'il been torturing her?

*"I DONT KNOW WHAT YOU WANT—I DONT KNOW WHAT YOU WANT—I DONT KNOW WHAT YOU WANT!"* Susan kept screaming, kept thrashing against the cross, screaming until her voice broke, and that was more than Jenny could take.

She swept across the room and activated Valescent Light. Golden warmth illuminated the enormous chamber. It was a giant room, cube shaped, with Susan on the cross in the center and heavy curtains on the wall and some other statues or something. Jenny didn't care for anything else. She couldn't take her eyes off Susan.

Susan stopped screaming. She was stuck on the cross, her arms outstretched, nails pushed through her palms. She had one foot over the other, with a third nail driven through them. The cross looked exactly the same as Yeshua's; Susan even had a crown of thorns digging into her forehead.

She looked so much like she had on the cafeteria floor, except the blue was gone from her hair. It was brown again, just as it had been all those years ago when they'd met and Jenny had shyly said hello and Susan had beamed, radiant and wonderful and welcoming.

Tears freely spilled down Jenny's cheeks. Her shoulders shook as she held up her glowing arm, rainbows swirling around her fingers and wrist, the light catching on Susan's face, on Susan's tearstained cheeks, on the blood running down her nose, on the spittle on her chin. She wore a gown too, like the princes and princesses, a purple one that matched the curtains around them. But it was torn in several places, exposing soft skin. And the tearing pattern looked very particular; she'd been whipped.

Whipped and much worse.

She couldn't shop shaking.

"Is that you?" whispered Susan, tears falling from her eyelashes as she leaned her head forward, as she strained against the nails. Her elbows cracked. A hiccup escaped her throat. She kept blinking hard, with her entire face. "Is that really you?"

Snot ran down Jenny's lips. She balled her hands into fists, and when she tried to speak, all she managed was a pained cry. She sniffled and tried again. "Yes, it's me. It's me. I found you."

Susan sobbed. "He told me. He told me everyone's looking for you, and that—and that they were going to destroy you and me, and that—" She broke down crying, softly this time, eyes shut tight, shoulders shaking. "I didn't know what he was talking about. He kept asking me about you. About what we did, and—"

"I'm going to get you down," said Jenny in a small voice, reaching up to touch Susan's feet with Valescent Light.

But the two of them flinched. Susan felt *ice cold* to the touch, and Susan looked as though Jenny had burned her.

"I'm sorry," whispered Jenny, biting her bottom lip and staring at Susan.

Susan blinked away her tears. "It's okay. You didn't hurt me."

Jenny almost laughed. "You don't have to lie to me. I'm sorry . . . for everything." She emphasized the last word, trying to find the courage to say "I'm sorry for killing you."

Susan shook her head and sniffed. More blood ran down her lips and dripped off her chin. "You were . . . I wanted to save you. It was my fault."

"I shouldn't have."

"It doesn't matter," she said with a sound that was half a sob and half a laugh. "I'm just—"

"Yeah." Jenny wiped her eyes and sniffled deeply. Then, she took a shaky breath and tried again. Grasping Susan's feet firmly, she tried to get a good hold on the nail. Susan whimpered several times, but Jenny knew the only way to stop the pain was to set her free, no matter how much that hurt. And she had Valescent Light ready to heal.

Just as she was about to suggest it, Susan said it out loud. "Just rip it off."

Jenny could tell she was trying to sound brave.

"Just rip it off. You have my light thing now, so just . . . Okay?"

Jenny's throat felt like it was collapsing. "I don't know if that works on souls." She blinked several times, trying to go through her memory. "But it looks like souls just heal on their own. You can't die . . . again." Guilt unfurled in her chest.

But Susan was shaking her head. "No. No. He said . . . He told me that the cross was special. It'll keep me here. I'll . . ."

Jenny remembered how Yeshua had been forced back through the worlds, back into the blood storm with all the ghouls. And when she'd returned to find him, she'd found him nailed once again to the cross. There was something about it that completely trapped someone . . . Yeshua had to drag his around. She took another breath.

"It's okay," she said, trying to sound steady. "I met someone else who was crucified. I know what to do."

"Someone else?" whispered Susan. Her eyes fluttered like she was struggling to stay awake. Her shoulders sagged, her arms bent slightly, and she jerked back awake, eyes wide and bloodshot. She looked like she wanted to scream again, glancing around several times before spotting the glowing light of Jenny's arm. When her eyes met Jenny's, she seemed to shrink back. Once again, she asked in a broken voice, "Are you really here?"

Jenny swallowed hard and nodded. "Let me get you off the thing. You'll heal. Or we'll use *something,* okay? And then, we just have to get you out of here before—Wait." She licked her lips and put out the Valescent Light, plunging the room into darkness again. She couldn't see Susan anymore, only the faint outline of the cross and Susan's body. *What if I just open another doorway here?*

Jenny looked around for Iblis. "Where are you?" she called. "Iblis?"

But something had changed. There was a disturbance in the air, like the humidity had gone up, like the room was closing in on them. She was about to reactivate her light or use Ignite to see again, but then, an involuntary shudder ran up her spine.

Susan cried out, *"He's here. He's here. He's back. He's here again. He's going to hurt me again. I knew it. I knew it. You're not real. You're not really here."*

"Who?" whispered Jenny, but she already knew the answer. Her heart was breaking listening to Susan whimper and cry and say the same thing over and over.

"C'mon, c'mon," she muttered under her breath as renewed panic pounded through her thoughts—guilt and anguish and heartbreak and rage—with fear swallowing everything up so that she couldn't think, couldn't breathe. She had to use Severed Spirit. Had to open another doorway. Had to grab Susan and the cross and get out. But where was Iblis?

"I can get us—"

*"The sinner went in there!"* shrieked a loud voice from the entrance hall. "She went to the forbidden room!"

"Punish her!"

"Save us from her sin!"

Susan was shaking so hard, the cross seemed to be rattling. Jenny chewed on her bottom lip, trying to snap herself out of it, but something heavy and awful reverberated through the floor, and she felt that immense, dizzying wave of dread again, like she was standing on the shore and watching a towering ship bearing down on her.

*Why won't this stupid thing just . . .*

She had plenty of heartbreak, plenty of hurt to pull on, so where was it? Where was Severed Spirit? Why couldn't she cut through the air again?

Why couldn't she stop shaking?

Susan's voice had dropped to a rapid, incoherent stammering. Jenny held her breath as the lumbering footsteps drew near, as the suffocating sense of despair sank in. She looked up at Susan in the dark and touched her feet.

"Everything's going to be okay," she whispered to her trembling best friend, knowing fully well that she was lying through her teeth.

# CHAPTER FORTY

# AZRA'IL

Heavy footsteps came to a stop right at the entrance. Jenny was too afraid to turn around. She swallowed hard, wondering if she should just stay in the dark. She flashed back to childhood memories of when the lights would go out and terror would flood her system. She'd lie in bed, clutching the blanket, too afraid to pull it over her head, hoping if she remained as still as possible, whatever was in the dark wouldn't notice her.

But this was the Angel of Death.

Jenny just needed more time. Just a bit more time to open a passageway.

A stench filled the air. Something salty, metallic, like blood and sweat coming in on a musty breeze. The smell of dead things, accompanied by heavy breathing.

"So, we finally meet," said a twisted, rolling voice. Another heavy footstep, and Jenny knew the angel had entered the room. "I thought I sensed something peculiar down there with the filth."

She still couldn't turn around. Susan was crying softly above her, whispering something over and over, "*Please. Please. Please.*"

"Interloper . . ." said Azra'il. Then, with what sounded like a clap of thunder, light illuminated the entire chamber, and Jenny felt utterly exposed. In the clarity of the bright light, the walls turned marble white, the velvet curtains took on a glamorous royal sheen, and she saw that the room was filled with weapons. Swords and axes, great big shields made from steel and emerald and gold hung from the walls, mounted like trophies.

"No wonder my siblings could not find you. A desecrated human sneaking into the afterlife of all things. What brought you here, I wonder."

She looked up at Susan, who'd shut her eyes, screwing up her face and muttering something over and over, her body trembling as though she was freezing. Sweat glistened on her sickly pale skin. The thorns dug into her forehead.

Jenny turned around, trying to swallow the rising fear—it was just like with that desecrated angel she'd fought back in the school. *It's just fear*, she told herself. *Something that triggers fear. Something to make you afraid. Don't be afraid.*

But she was holding her breath. Clenching her insides. And when she turned all the way and faced Azra'il, her legs nearly buckled.

### Angel (Stage VI - Level 332)

He was massive, his head coming nearly to the top of the chamber, and he was so wide he blocked the archway behind him. Contained in the chamber, Jenny felt like a mouse standing up to an elephant.

He was broad chested, the dark-covered skin of his chest and limbs exposed. Instead of hair, vicious red snakes that might've been larger than Jenny snapped from his head. Around his waist was a loincloth made of leather, and from his neck, hanging loosely on his chest, was a necklace made of skulls. His eyebrows were snakes, too, their tongues flickering over his smoldering eyes.

The fancily dressed souls stood around him, mostly behind him, their hands folded over their fronts, each one staring at Jenny with a mixture of pity and disapproval. The tallest of the bunch barely came up to Azra'il's waist. Jenny was sure she could fit a bunch of them into one of the angel's beefy thighs.

He stared at her without saying a word, red eyes glowing brightly. Then, he tilted his head and looked at Susan, and his dark lips twisted into an ugly smile as two of the snakes on his head hissed.

"So, I was right to keep this one. My sister Rafa'el noted you two had a special bond. And when I learned of your ability to cross worlds . . . well . . ." He took a menacing step forward, arms open as though he were coming in for a hug.

Jenny stepped back and bumped into Susan's feet. Susan gasped in pain while Jenny winced. Her hand went to her hatchet.

Azra'il glanced down at it. "You think you can fight me with that? Humans. Why are all of you so hopeful?"

Her mouth had gone dry. Azra'il's booming voice echoed all around the chamber, rumbling from every direction. Her legs were shaking, but she shut her eyes, even as Azra'il took another menacing step closer, even as the chamber shook and the other souls whispered accusatory words.

She forced herself to take a breath.

*He hurt Susan.*

*He hurt Susan's soul.*

Anger unfurled like a roaring beast; she braced herself. She was vastly overpowered, completely and utterly useless in a fight against the towering angel, but what was the point in running now?

*I can't panic. I can't run away. I can't hide from my emotions like I always do.*

*I'm afraid. I'm afraid, but I'm going to protect Susan.*

*I'm going to get her out of this.*

*This is my fault.*

*TAKE RESPONSIBILITY FOR YOURSELF,* screamed a voice inside her, and when she opened her eyes again, she steeled herself, pushing her shoulders back, raising her head, trying to look as defiant as possible. Her legs still shook, she still wanted to pass out from the dizzying aura emanating from Azra'il, but she wasn't going down without a fight. And if Jenny died and had to come back as a soul and fight him again, she would do it as many times as she had to.

She inhaled deeply through her nose as Azra'il cocked one of his serpent eyebrows. A wide grin spread across his face, revealing tombstone-size white teeth.

"Have you gone mad with fear? What hope do you have against me, mortal?" His wings unfurled behind him—four of them, each one curving and hooked like bat wings. The serpents on his head arose, forked tongues aimed at Jenny as they hissed, as they all eyed her down.

Jenny's tentacles burst out of her back with several pops and cracks. Her exoskeleton gushed from her belly button, and she squeezed her hatchet firmly as the gelatinous red substance spread over her armor, covering her from head to toe in a second layer of protection. Around her skull, it formed a helmet with a visor she could see through.

*Iblis, where are you?!* she screamed inside her head. Having the demon's powers added to her own would go a long way, but even then . . . it wouldn't be enough. The angel was just too strong.

What she needed was a distraction, something to catch Azra'il by surprise. Maybe if she attacked the souls hanging by the entrance with their pretentious gowns and their judgmental faces. The angel was just waiting, as though daring her to attack, but if she could get away for just a few minutes, if she could use Severed Spirit and open another passageway—

Azra'il closed the distance between them in a flash. Jenny didn't even have an opportunity to flinch. One second, he was near the entrance; the next, he was right in front of her and Susan, towering over them with his menacing aura. Jenny barely came up to his loincloth, and she had to crane her head to look upward and meet his burning eyes.

Her throat felt tight. Sweat ran down her back. Susan cried out behind her.

"I will offer you one chance, mortal," said Azra'il in his low, rolling voice. "Join my collection, my princes and princesses. Be my living consort, and I will spare you and your beloved."

Jenny blinked. "What?"

Azra'il's lips curved up into an evil smile. A snake hissed and snapped its fangs. "I want a mortal bride, and you are easy on the eyes and clearly powerful. I will even safeguard you from my siblings."

The souls at the entrance whispered loudly; Jenny glanced at them in utter confusion when one cried out in protest. That was when Azra'il struck. He moved so quickly for someone so large, she almost didn't realize what happened. It was her tentacles that picked up on the movement, the shift in the air. In a split second, she used Instant Acceleration, throwing herself out of the way as a fist the size of a semitruck hit the floor.

Instantly, the floor collapsed into a large crater. Jenny rolled away as the entire chamber—maybe even the entire floating castle—shook. Chunks of the floor rose up from the impact, and the weapons on the walls and curtains clattered all around. The cross teetered backward, unstable, before landing with a crash as Susan screamed.

Azra'il turned around, eyes burning. "So, what will it be? That was merely a *taste* of my strength. What hope do you have against destiny, interloper?" Saliva glistened on his chin. Was he drooling? Sneering? "You will be the perfect trophy for all my troubles in His name."

# CHAPTER FORTY-ONE

# BEAT DOWN

Every inch of her tentacles could feel the angel's might; this was nothing like the desecrated angel she'd faced in the cafeteria—that fight felt like it had been years ago. A lifetime ago. She glanced at Susan, feeling her pain, tasting her blood in the air. But her tentacles picked up on something else; a grotesque, ugly sensation. The cloth around Azra'il's waist was different now. It was made from human skin instead of that of the tarnished angels.

Her tentacles shuddered, and mentally, she did a count. She had six. She had all six of them. They'd come out so easily, so readily, she'd almost forgotten she'd been without them for so long.

Azra'il wiped his chin. He picked Susan up by the bottom of the cross, holding her upside down so that her chest fell slightly away from the wood, causing her face to distort in pain as another scream came out of her throat. The sound was wrenching Jenny's heart open.

She took a step forward, anger and hurt clashing like a thunderstorm inside her. "Let her go!" she shouted, knowing it was futile, knowing it was exactly what Azra'il wanted.

The angel grinned again—a big, toothy grin—and shook the cross instead, as though he was trying to flick an insect off a stick. That was more than Jenny could stand.

Stomping forward on one foot, she launched her hatchet with all her might. *Savage Throw!* The obsidian face flashed in the bright light as the hatchet spun faster than it ever had, hurtling toward Susan.

Azra'il raised an arm to block it nonchalantly, as though it was as harmless as a mosquito, but Jenny activated her new skill instead. She only had one chance to make this work.

Flashing to where the hatchet was, the world ripped and came back together around her, placing her inches from Azra'il's enormous body. His serpent eyebrows went up slowly in amused surprise.

Bracing herself with her tentacles and carefully keeping them out of his reach, Jenny roared with Ignite, screaming into the angel's face with a burst of orange-and-blue flame.

He laughed heartily, raising a hand to block the fire. But he wasn't her goal. She bounced off the floor, slapping the stones with her tentacles, and swung again, apologizing silently as she sliced through Susan's ankles.

The hatchet cut through the wood, freeing Susan's legs. Before her severed feet hit the floor, Jenny tossed the hatchet away, to the opposite side of the chamber, and grabbed her best friend by the thighs, by her torso, praying this would work. Susan's face was white with shock, full of tears and spittle and snot, and then, just as Azra'il realized what was happening, Jenny—holding Susan—flashed back to where she'd tossed her hatchet.

Susan's hands tore through the nails, a horrible scream swirling around Jenny, and then, the two of them collapsed on the floor on the other side of the room, littered with polearms and great swords and shields made of sapphire.

It had worked! She could use Instant Swap and take whatever she was holding with her. Susan lay on top of Jenny, bleeding all over—from her torn hands, from the stumps of her legs—shaking and crying while Jenny held her tightly. "I got you. I got you now."

Her heart was pounding. She was banking on Susan's soul to heal itself, just as Miriam's had from being eaten. Just as the other souls had from being torn apart by angels. And a moment later, golden light shimmered across the wounds, repairing the flesh and regrowing her feet. Susan was whole again. All that was left now was opening a passageway and somehow getting Susan and the cross out of this world.

But a deep, ugly laugh rumbled through the chamber. Jenny sat up, holding firmly to Susan, who was resting her head on Jenny's plated chest, both of them breathing hard. Susan's feet had finished growing back, pink flesh expanding from the ankles.

Azra'il hadn't moved. He was still holding the cross, where bits of flesh stuck to the sides. Where the broken bit lay on the floor with Susan's feet still attached.

"Do you really think she can go anywhere?" asked Azra'il with a cackle. He clutched his belly and tilted his head back with a laugh. "She's mine forever. Till the end of time. There is nothing you can do about it!"

Jenny gritted her teeth as Susan shook in her arms. She almost wanted to ask Susan to find some armor and weaponry off the floor to fight with her, but Susan was in no state to fight—and then, she remembered how hungry Yeshua had been after coming off the cross. Did she have to feed Susan? Would Azra'il even allow her to?

Her desecrated flesh wouldn't work, anyway. It had only made Yeshua sicker. All she could do was get back to Yeshua and get some help.

It didn't even seem like Azra'il was taking this fight seriously. So far, all he'd done was laugh and boast and play around, like this was all a big joke to him. He knew that Jenny posed no threat at all.

*He knows I can't do anything to him.*

But the rage . . . the rage burned so hotly inside Jenny, she didn't know what to do. *Kill. Kill. Kill.* She wanted to cut his smug head off. She wanted to rip every single snake from his scalp and tear off his skin and—

A part of her considered what Azra'il had offered. To become his human bride. To play it safe until she could get away.

But the other souls had had their minds warped. They were just like the harpies; their free will had been taken away. They were his playthings. Nothing more.

Revulsion made her stomach twist.

She wouldn't let him do that to her. Or Susan. And if she could find Miriam, then . . . Her tentacles shuddered, all six of them, an ugly realization traveling through their lengths. Her eyes went to Azra'il's loincloth and realized where the skin had come from.

"I will make the offer one more time," came his low voice from the other side of the room. He knelt and picked up the piece of cross that Jenny had cut off. It looked like a broken pencil in his giant hand, but he held it to the rest of the cross, and with a burst of golden light, it reattached itself. The cross was whole again.

He tore the feet from the wood and held them up, eyeing them like they were a snack he'd picked up from a platter. Then, with a red-eyed glance at Jenny and Susan, he popped Susan's old feet into his mouth. Loud crunching noises filled the chamber before he swallowed.

"You can't set her free. Not as you are," he said. "Join me instead. Why fight? What do you hope to achieve?"

Jenny didn't respond.

"You can be my bride instead," he continued. "My princes and princesses will serve you, as you will be their queen. And I will let you keep your toy as well."

"She's not a toy," Jenny hissed between clenched teeth.

Azra'il smiled again, a sickly sweet smile, and raised one of his serpent eyebrows. "But she was my toy all this time."

Heat flashed in front of Jenny's face. She burst forward with Instant Acceleration, anger burning so hot in her body she thought she'd explode—and that's what she did. She used a full-bodied Ignite, blue flames erupting from her chest and arms and head as she smashed into Azra'il's broad chest with all the force she could muster. She felt like a comet colliding with a planet.

And she'd hoped to have just as big of an impact, something cataclysmic. But Azra'il didn't even budge.

She bounced off his chest, her tentacles catching on the floor and her fire sputtering out as she realized he was completely unfazed. An instant later, his foot was above her, and if she hadn't rolled away with her tentacles, she would've been crushed. His heel smashed through the floor.

But he wasn't done. He lunged forward, grabbing two of her tentacles, and swung her against the wall so quickly, so suddenly, she didn't even get to scream. Her exoskeleton-covered head, her back and legs, smashed into the thick wall, burrowing into the stone.

She came to a stop buried halfway through the wall, dust and debris raining down around her, the weight of the castle pressing against her. Before she could inhale, Azra'il's hand—his fingers like enormous worms—dug through the wall and grabbed her.

Jenny activated Ignite again, but the fire didn't faze him one bit, and in the next moment, he'd flung her into the floor.

Another crater blossomed as a scream died in her throat. Blood sprayed out of her mouth, and she collapsed, lying there like a crumpled piece of cloth.

Pain erupted all over Jenny. Her exoskeleton had cracked open, her tentacles flattened against the broken floor.

Azra'il straightened up. He spoke solemnly. "What hope do you have against me? I am the conqueror of mortality. I bent the demons to *His* will. It was *me!*"

He knelt, resting his arms on his knees as Jenny lay in the crater, too hurt to move. He brought his face closer to her so that she could look right into his burning eyes, so that several snakes could dart forward and flick the blood off Jenny's face with their tongues.

"I will have you, interloper. I always get what I want. And when He descends upon the mortal plane, you *will* be by my side, conquered and bent to His will, the pride of the underworld, ready for what is to come."

Jenny couldn't move. Was the fight over so quickly? Her arms and legs felt broken, her ribs snapped inward. Blood was filling her lungs, gushing through like a bursting dam. There was pressure from all around; was she drowning? Every breath sounded raspy; every breath was strained—she couldn't breathe. What was she supposed to do? What was the point of all this bravery if she couldn't fight?

She needed a potion. Several potions. She had so much energy. What could she make to even the odds? What could she do? Her mind raced as Azra'il gloated on top of her. As his snakes licked her face. As he looked into her eyes with a look of maddening glee—like he was so happy, *so happy* to see her broken like this, so happy to take her as his own, to add her to his collection.

Everything inside her recoiled, repulsed. It was too much like the look she'd seen sometimes on her mother's face when Jenny was young, when her mom was so angry, when anything Jenny did was an affront.

A voice crackled through Jenny's mind, and she wheezed for breath.

**You have to open the passageway. NOW. We cannot defeat this angel. I have created a distraction.**

Azra'il's face changed. His nose curled. He looked like he'd smelled something rotten, snorting with flared nostrils. He looked up, sniffing as smoke swirled through the light.

"*Demon scum*," he hissed. "Why do I smell a demon in my halls?"

# CHAPTER FORTY-TWO

# A GENTLE PUSH

Heavy smoke swirled through the light, Azra'il's face a mask of fury as he stomped back toward the entrance. Her neck popped as Jenny turned her head, lying on her side in the cratered floor, watching Azra'il's hulking back ripple, watching his four wings bounce lightly with his every step.

"Demon!" he shouted, his voice booming. The souls were crying out, screaming, flooding into the chamber where Jenny lay broken to escape the heavy smoke. Orange-and-blue light flickered and burned through the dense smoke, and Jenny almost grinned despite the pain. The souls were covered in ash, their fancy garments dirtied.

Iblis must've set the place on fire. Using her tentacles, Jenny willed herself up. Parts of her armor cracked and fell away, revealing bruised skin. She winced from the pain, wanting to use Valescent Light to heal herself, but there was no point. Once she opened the passageway, she would heal as she fell through the light.

She hobbled toward Susan, two of her tentacles dragging behind her, limp and hurt from Azra'il grabbing them. The others swirled, ready to attack if the souls tried anything. They stared at her in disbelief. One or two of them called her disgusting; another called her a monster.

"I've never turned into anything like that."

"She's hideous."

Jenny collapsed on top of Susan, her breathing ragged, her tentacles swirling and swishing, keeping the souls at bay. They didn't know what to do.

"Do we stop her?" asked one.

"She looks broken."

"Why isn't she healing? We always heal after Master hurts us."

"She's not like us."

"Susan . . ." whispered Jenny, looking down at her best friend. Susan had her eyes shut. Blood dribbled down from the thorns in her forehead, and Jenny wanted to rip the crown off, but she barely had the strength to move. Instead, she pressed her palm to the floor as more smoke wafted into the room, as the souls coughed and became more difficult to see. Her tentacles kept track of everything.

"Severed Spirit," she whispered, feeling a sense of relief as the heartbreak came gushing to the surface. It was easy this time. Thinking about how much pain Susan had gone through. What Azra'il must've done to her. How much pain Jenny's body was in, and how sorry she was.

She called mentally for Iblis, but the demon wouldn't respond. Sounds of clashing came from outside the chamber, and the souls cried out as the floor shook, as more things crashed.

Just as Jenny opened the ugly, dark wound in the floor, the darkness gushing out and spreading like liquid, just as Jenny could feel the fabric between worlds, there was a loud boom, and the wall Jenny had been flung into collapsed as a burning figure burst through it.

It landed beside Jenny in a splattering of wings, and she whipped around despite the pain to see Azra'il's silhouette stepping through the smoke. Raising his beefy arms, he clapped them together, and a furious wind slammed Jenny and Susan and Iblis in the brood mother's body against the wall.

The smoke was forced out of the room; even the souls were knocked into the armor and weaponry and curtains. Azra'il's snakes were snapping and hissing as he lunged over the rubble. Jenny reached out with a tentacle, desperately hoping, desperately urging the rainbow light to run down from her chest through its length and into the darkness.

She saw Azra'il's eyes go wide. She felt his anger. His bloodlust. Felt the bodies of everyone in the room, could taste the sweat and blood, could feel the sheer, ugly wrath of Azra'il—and then, the darkness beneath them erupted into golden light. Colors streamed out: reds and greens and oranges. She saw the souls staring wide-eyed; saw Azra'il snarling, startled, one hand raised to block the light as he stared in disbelief. Squinting. Lips curling.

She clutched Susan tightly, wrapped another tentacle around the cross and around Iblis, and sank into the light.

Instantly, the colors, soothing and gentle, began to heal her wounds. Her broken ribs. Her bruised arms. Her face. She clutched tightly onto Susan and Iblis and the cross as they sank deeper and deeper . . .

Just as she was feeling safe, just as she thought they'd gotten away from Azra'il, something tugged on Jenny's tentacles, wrenching her back for a second, like a parachute caught on a breeze. She screamed, bubbles of light erupting from her mouth. Susan's body swung, and then there was a violent sense of pulling and pushing that threatened from all around, like they all might be ripped apart.

Jenny felt wildly around, trying to feel the worlds ahead and above. Below. Which one was the demon world? But colors streamed past her eyes. Colors swirled around her and her tentacles, and then, she saw Azra'il's face bursting into the light, dragging himself after them. A giant. A monster. And the look on his face—he wanted her. He wanted her so badly. But—

The largest pull was from the material world. The center of everything. She pulled Susan close and stared at her limp form. Her brown eyes— surprised and afraid and so full of warmth, the healing light glistening all over.

*I found you*, she wanted to say. *I found you.*

And then, she shoved Susan away with her cross. Her mouth parted in shock—in fear—and Susan tried to swim, tried to hold on to Jenny's tentacle, but Azra'il was closing in. This was the best move; Jenny was sure of it. There was going to be more fighting, and this way, Susan wouldn't be caught in it again. No matter what happened. She couldn't let Azra'il take her again.

She kicked backward into the world of demons as Susan rocketed away through the light and into the material world, vanishing alongside her cross with a sparkle of blue-and-yellow lights. There was a tremor of rage as rivers of blood-red light swished around Azra'il, and then, Jenny fell through the light as well into the demon world, falling from some height.

Cold air stung her right away. Snow stung her exposed skin as she fell through the sky, her limbs and tentacles trailing behind her. Her heart hurt so much she couldn't breathe.

She landed in a heap on the ice and snow. She was back in the world of demons, but the shimmering light of the passageway overhead wouldn't close. It hovered in the air, one of her tentacles reaching back into it, still stuck inside. It was lifting her slightly, keeping her from breaking free. It was Azra'il.

He was inside the light, holding on to her tentacle as though it were a leash, refusing to let go.

With a flash, she summoned her hatchet and cut through her tentacle. Blood spurted out, spraying the ice and snow, and the length of the tentacle snapped back toward the light, vanishing with a spray of blood that rained down on Jenny.

Still, the light didn't close. She couldn't close it. And then, Azra'il's enor-mous, ugly head appeared. He had the other end of Jenny's tentacle in his mouth, and as Jenny struggled to close the passageway, hoping to cut the angel in half, he emerged fully.

The resistance stopped all at once. The passageway closed shut, and Azra'il hovered in the air, wings beating in sequence as he chewed on the tentacle in his mouth.

He spat it out, and it fell to the ground.

"So, this is how you've been evading Rafa'el's eyes," he said loudly. He looked like a celestial object, some kind of moon or satellite taking up too much space in the sky. "And what have you done to that soul?" He spat the words out; Jenny could feel the waves of rage rippling through the air. "A soul in the material world? DO YOU HAVE ANY UNDERSTANDING OF WHAT YOU'VE DONE?"

Jenny shut her eyes. Even the snow seemed to wince from Azra'il's shouting, but Jenny felt a sense of hopeful satisfaction. *I got her away from you.*

The brood mother's body stood, flames leaking from the hole in its cheek, and Iblis whispered something.

Her tentacles picked up motion, vibrations in the icy ground. They weren't too far from where she'd opened the bridge to the world of death, where deaths were marching into this world along with ghouls housing demons. And Yeshua was racing across the ice toward them, his hair and beard flowing in the breeze, stuck with ice and snow, his purple robes billowing. On his face was a look of pure anger as red lightning crackled around him.

"Azra'il!" he roared.

"Failed one," said Azra'il with a laugh before swooping down.

Yeshua leaped into the air, and the two of them collided—an explosion of ice and wind and red lightning crackling all around, hurtling Jenny and Iblis away.

# CHAPTER FORTY-THREE

# FAILED ONE

Jenny tumbled away, her face scraping, her broken exoskeleton crumbling away. The light had healed her body up, all her bruises and broken bones, but it'd left her exoskeleton as it was. It hadn't healed her tentacles either, as though the light was making a statement that this wasn't a part of her.

And now, she only had three tentacles left, the torn one blown in some other direction by the explosive fight between Azra'il and Yeshua, and two others crushed beyond use.

Iblis, in the brood mother's body, stirred, flapping, fire blooming from the torn-up wings, fire leaking out of the holes in the harpy's cheek. Blue flames curled out of the eyes as he stood shakily to his talons and stretched his wings.

Jenny wiped her eyes and stood as well. With a flash, she summoned her hatchet back. Maybe the three of them together could stand a chance.

In the distance, she saw the ghouls, their eyes burning with fire and light—the demons. And she saw the gathering of deaths, so many more of them than when she'd left the world to find Susan.

They had formed miniature armies. They were prepared for war, though she didn't think the deaths would be of much use in battle. But the demons, the ghoul bodies—she felt bolstered by their presence.

"Come on," she said to Iblis. She was trying not to think about pushing Susan through the light, sending her to the material world, and the way Azra'il had responded. Would Susan be alright there? Would she just be a ghost or something?

No, it wasn't helpful to think about that. Susan was out of Azra'il's reach—that was the important thing. Jenny was betting the angel couldn't just go into the material world and take Susan. That had to be why he was so angry.

Red bolts of lightning burst out of the commotion ahead, crackling along the ice and bursting into clouds of steam and vapor. Azra'il was like a mountain hidden by fog, moving in and out of visibility with the wind from the blows exchanged with Yeshua, who darted around the enormous angel, a blur of purple and red light.

Several Yeshuas burst out of him in various directions, striking heavy blows that knocked Azra'il every which way. The angel bellowed in rage, a shout that seemed to shake the entire world, and slammed his fist against the ground.

This time, the world *did* shake, and it was very much like the earthquake Jenny had felt way back when this all began. A huge, ugly fissure cracked through the ice, and Iblis took to the air, flapping with burning wings that were falling apart.

Jenny raced below him, using Ignite to set herself on fire before leaping forward with Instant Acceleration. Azra'il turned to swipe at Iblis, his enormous fingers missing the burning harpy by inches. Yeshua drove a fist into Azra'il's belly while two other Yeshuas grabbed the angel's legs and slowed him down as Jenny rocketed toward the angel's face like a meteor.

She slammed into him with her hatchet, trying to bury the obsidian edge in the angel's face. It caught him on the nose, but instead of slicing, the hatchet bounced off, jerking Jenny backward so that she was horizontal, the momentum robbed.

In a split second, the angel moved. His elbow came crashing down on Jenny's armor and exoskeleton-covered belly, slamming her into the ground. With a cry, she crashed onto one of the Yeshuas, then collapsed on the ice.

Azra'il would've slammed his foot down on top of her, his loincloth flapping against his muscular thighs, but Iblis swooped between his legs, grasped Jenny in his talons, and flew her out of reach as another Yeshua slammed into Azra'il's raised leg from the side. This knocked the angel off-balance, and a Yeshua grabbed Azra'il's head, trying to bring him down.

The wind knocked out of her, Jenny adjusted her ribs with some Valescent Light before she wriggled out of Iblis's talons, the hatchet flashing back to her hand. She couldn't hurt his body, but what about his wings?

With the angel wrestling with two Yeshuas, Jenny dropped down just as she'd done to defeat the first harpy, except this time, she added Instant Acceleration. Her hatchet cut through the webby part of one of Azra'il's wings, slicing through it like she was cutting through fabric.

The other three beat furiously, drumming up a furious wind which slapped her away, but not before she noticed something spraying out. At first, she thought it was blood, but it didn't splatter her face or the snow. It sparkled like the demons did, glittery red and floating before evaporating.

The angel bled with light.

"Well done!" shouted the Yeshuas in unison as Azra'il howled, grasping his torn wing. She'd cut nearly all the way through, and it hung off like a torn page from a book. Azra'il snarled and lunged for her, using that insane burst of speed to catch her just as she landed.

The Yeshuas shouted again. Iblis struck Azra'il in his snake hair with a blast of fire, but his enormous fingers closed around Jenny and raised her so quickly to his face she couldn't help but cry out. Enormous teeth flashed. His burning red eyes were filled with such anger, such malice, and she couldn't help but see her own mother again on his face. A memory from when she was young and she'd done something that kids do.

She'd messed up; she'd broken something, and her mother always took it personally. How could Jenny do that to her? Who did Jenny think she was? And she'd scream, try to scream Jenny's head off, and she knew the angel *would* bite her head off.

She opened her mouth to shout, to hit the angel in the throat with a burst of Ignite, but something blue and feathery streaked past her into Azra'il's open mouth.

"*ARRRRGH!*" shouted the angel, dropping Jenny and slapping at his mouth.

A huge surge of blue flame burst inside, spilling from his nose and ears and even his eyes. Jenny landed hard, everything aching from how hard Azra'il had squeezed her. Smoldering feathers floated down, burning out, and she cried out, "Iblis!"

Azra'il lumbered backward. She saw Yeshua leaping to strike Azra'il in the back, red lightning snapping around his arms. She'd strike too; she'd do something—she threw her hatchet at one of the wings then burst forward with Instant Acceleration, aiming for the flap of human skin he wore, aiming right between his legs.

Again, he screamed as bolts of red lightning pierced his torso, as her hatchet ripped through another wing, as fire roared in his mouth and Jenny struck something soft and squishy between his legs.

Sparks of blue light rushed out of Azra'il's mouth. The angel spun rapidly, throwing off the Yeshuas, and struck out with a foot, kicking Jenny hard in the chest, sending her skidding across the ice as though she'd been shot out of a cannon. When she came to a stop, blinking ice and snow out of her eyelashes—all the breath forced out of her, her entire body aching from the blow—she saw Azra'il ripping something to shreds.

It was the brood mother's burning body. Screaming, ugly screaming, raging like a toddler as he tore it to bits. Alarm flashed through Jenny, and she was about to call out again when the voice flickered through her head.

**Please allow me to possess you again.**

"Yes!" she cried out in relief and resolve. The demon's mind pushed against her own, and blue fire flared to life in her eyes. Warmth spread through her, and new strength flooded into her own. All her stats were boosted again, and she felt the surge in raw power.

The Yeshuas were recovering as well. They swept the hair out of their faces and glanced at Jenny with a nod.

Azra'il dropped what was left of the brood mother's body, a furious scowl on his face. "You pointless mortals," he hissed loudly through his teeth. "You will never change."

He looked like he was about to charge them down, but then, he stopped and took a breath. His snakes hissed and snapped, and he grabbed his two torn wings and ripped them off completely, flinging them away like the sails of a crashed boat. Grabbing his remaining wings, he tore them off too. Red light burst out of his back and flickered away.

He took a loud breath, then in a flash, he turned and grabbed two of the Yeshuas. Before anyone could react, they burst like water balloons in his grip, splattering the snow with blood and chunks of flesh. Blood dripped down from Azra'il's hands, the corpses falling to the ground like burst grapes.

Then, Azra'il leaped for the remaining Yeshua.

# CHAPTER FORTY-FOUR

# BRIGHT BLUE SPARKS

"FALL BACK," shouted the last Yeshua as he caught Azra'il's arms head-on, holding the enormous fists over his strained face. Jenny moved to rush in and attack; she felt superpowered with Iblis's possession coursing through her veins. But Yeshua shot her a look of desperation, his teeth bared, his eyes wide—he was terrified.

"I AM THE CONQUEROR," roared Azra'il, who flung Yeshua around and launched him through the air, the purple robe billowing behind him. "I FUCKED THIS LAND. I FUCKED THESE PEOPLE. I AM THE ONE WHO CONQUERED MORTALITY."

"*YOU CONQUERED NOTHING,*" screamed a hoarse voice from Jenny's throat. "*YOU LIED. YOU STOLE. YOU DAMNED!*"

Azra'il's face twisted with fury. His serpents snapped furiously, growing large, their fangs gleaming, and with an explosion of ice, he stomped toward Jenny, closing in so quickly she only had a split second to defend with her tentacles to take the blows.

She dashed back, bursts of Instant Acceleration on every step, fire spilling from her eyes, blue flames climbing up her tentacles to lash at Azra'il. The only thing keeping him from popping her like the two Yeshuas was Iblis sharing her body. While one of them focused on skipping backward with speed, the other focused on parrying his fists, unable to stop the brute force but able to knock it slightly off course so that the blows didn't land.

Azra'il's teeth gnashed, his eyes burned, and from his back, trails of evaporating light drifted behind him. Jenny swore each of his punches broke the sonic barrier, reminding her of jets causing the air to explode around them as they burst forward. Then, just as she thought Azra'il would catch her, Yeshua flew in from the left and collided against Azra'il with another explosion of snow.

"Go!" he shouted. "Get the deaths, get the demons, and go! And close the passageway; he can't find you without—" A fist knocked him in the head so hard, Yeshua's face and shoulders were buried into the ice, another ugly fissure spreading from the crater. His legs stuck out like a popsicle as his robes fluttered down around his waist.

Jenny was sprinting back to the deaths, who were scrambling to get back through the passageway, colliding with a group of freshly possessed ghouls trying to enter the world of demons.

"Back!" she screamed desperately. "Go back!"

Her thoughts were racing with a plan. She would get everyone back through the passageway, take Yeshua's cross with her, and even as Yeshua held Azra'il back, once the passageway closed, he'd be forced back to them in the world of death, leaving Azra'il here.

Red lightning erupted somewhere behind her, but just as she caught up with the crowd of deaths, Azra'il rushed past her, a mountain blurring by.

He rammed into the crowd, sending the bodies of purple-robed deaths flying, screaming, bursting open the ghouls. Sparks flew away from the broken bodies as Azra'il roared so loudly that it vibrated through the entire world. And then, he reached up. With his fist almost in a cloud, he grabbed something and wrenched it down.

A burst of cold air, colder than any winter air she'd ever felt before, came gushing down from the sky, a hole spreading in the clouds to reveal darkness. Iblis screamed inside her; he recognized this attack. But it was too late. There was nobody who could stop it.

The cold gushed down like a waterfall, cascading around Azra'il's enormous body like a fog rolling down a mountain, enveloping all the deaths and ghouls around him like trees caught in a devastating avalanche.

Jenny sprouted burning wings, her tentacles snapping as she flew above the spreading coldness, watching as the ghouls froze in place, the fire in their eyes dimming to a faint glow, the deaths screaming as glistening dark rock climbed up their legs, enveloping them again in pillars.

Once everything settled, the clouds filled in the hole in the sky once more. Jenny remained fluttering over the field of frozen bodies, the pillars littered between them like strange rocks.

Iblis's hurt ignited inside her, and she almost flew in to attack Azra'il, who stood triumphant over the frozen forms, standing in front of the rippling colorful passageway, the light shining on his enormous body.

"They have done NOTHING to you!" shouted Yeshua from somewhere below her, leaping forward, red lightning propelling his feet as he seemed to take leaping bounds in the air. More lightning sizzled to form a sword in his hands, and with a burst of speed, he collided against Azra'il, the tip of the red lightning sword emerging from the other side of the enormous angel's body.

But Azra'il didn't even flinch. Light trailed up from the wound as his fingers closed around Yeshua's throat, lifting him up.

The sword evaporated inside him, exposing an ugly wound straight through his chest.

Iblis shouted, his static voice louder than ever.

**He needs to be saved! I will give you an opening.**

Jenny wanted to scream, but she understood Iblis's plan; they were sharing the same body. He'd fly into Yeshua's body and attack, while Jenny would grab the cross and burst through the passageway. If she and Yeshua got out of this okay, then they could save the deaths again, could open another passageway and try again. Could come back and revive Iblis again.

She plummeted to the ground, scanning with her tentacles and eyes for the cross until she found it a few feet away, in the midst of frozen ghouls and pillars.

Blue sparkles shot through Yeshua's back. A heartbeat later, blue fire enveloped him, turning purple as red lightning crackled. Yeshua raised a burning fist and struck Azra'il in the face with a blow so powerful it kicked up a fierce wind, and for the first time, Azra'il stumbled back from an attack.

Jenny ran for the cross, grasping it with three tentacles. She tried to snap forward with Instant Acceleration, make a break for the glowing passageway, but it hardly budged. It was heavy—insanely heavy, so much heavier than Susan's.

What was wrong with this cross? Or did she have to be holding Yeshua too?

The cross and the crucified had to be held together? Was that it?

She ground her teeth, looking desperately at the burning Yeshua exchanging blows with Azra'il. One of the wings Azra'il had torn out blew past Jenny, and she took a step forward, dragging the cross with her tentacles, guiding it through the pillars and frozen ghouls, her heart aching for the deaths and demons frozen inside. She could see their lights, their dim flames like distant stars, but there was nothing she could do for them right now.

*We'll come back for you. I promise.*

"BEGONE FROM HIM," came a cruel shout, and Jenny looked up to see Yeshua plummeting. Blue sparks erupted upward—it was Iblis, forced out of Yeshua the same way Yeshua had once forced the demon out of Jenny.

Then, Azra'il's hand shot out and closed around the hovering blue sparks. There was a blinding flash of light—brighter than anything Jenny had ever seen before, so bright that it seared her vision—and she collapsed on the ground, letting go of the cross. And she knew. She just knew.

Iblis was dead.

The ground rumbled. Heavy footsteps approached her, and she looked up, tears streaming down her face, freezing on her cheeks, to find Azra'il towering over her, a look of pity and disgust on his face. One of his hands was scorched black, burnt and crumbling. In the other, he held Yeshua, whom he dropped on the ice in front of Jenny.

Then, as Jenny watched, the black rock of a pillar grew along Yeshua's body, forcing him upright, contorting and twisting his body as he stared at her, blood running down his face, his eyes still wide with fright, his lips trembling. He turned his eyes toward the sky as though in prayer. Then, rock grew upward, covering his throat, and then his face, sealing itself over his head.

They had lost.

# CHAPTER FORTY-FIVE

# JENNY AND HER DEATH

Jenny didn't have the strength to even cry out. Azra'il picked her up like a rag doll before grabbing the cross. For him, it didn't seem heavy at all. Her head swung, her hair and tentacles blowing in the cold breeze as Azra'il paused in front of the passageway she'd opened.

"The world of the damned," he said with a laugh. "What hope did you have, my beautiful little interloper?"

She was too hurt to respond. She'd failed. They'd failed. They'd lost. If there was any solace, it was that Azra'il didn't have Susan still. Susan had gotten away.

"A soul in the material world . . ." he said. Then, he took a step into the passageway, and the world of snow and ice, the world of frozen demons, and the world where Yeshua and hundreds of deaths were stuck in pillars made of salt vanished.

Light bent around her. Greens swirled and chased purples by her face; she shut her eyes. Tears bubbled up from behind her eyelids and slipped away. She felt the light seeping through her body, healing her insides. But what did it matter? She knew what was coming. What Azra'il would do to her.

She'd always known she would be punished. And she deserved it. She'd known that ever since she was a kid.

*But Susan got away. Susan got away.*

*I got her away from him.*

The light snapped shut, and Jenny was thrown onto wet ground with a splash. It was thick and hot and disgusting, the metallic stench clogging her nose and lungs immediately. She opened her eyes, feeling her insides clenched with fear as Azra'il towered over her in the dark world, blood raining down his enormous form and running down his limbs. In his burnt hand, he held the cross.

"You were trying to save him, weren't you?" he asked solemnly, almost understandingly. "I pity you. The Failed One has corrupted your mind, but fear not." With a lumbering step, he raised the cross and plunged it into the world, as though he was sticking a dagger into the ground.

The rain stopped immediately. There weren't any ghouls swimming around, and the deaths and demons had done a great deal of work clearing much of the land. The nearest pillars were quite a distance away, and Jenny scanned the area, trying to spot any demons or deaths who'd gotten through the passageway when the order for retreat was called. Were they hiding? Had Azra'il's power reached through the passageway? There was nobody in sight.

She tried to get to her feet, but her arms gave out. Something inside her felt broken; she was exhausted, completely drained. Reaching down, Azra'il grabbed her head with two meaty fingers and held her up, pressure squeezing the sides of her temples as his broad grin came into view. The blood rain had stopped, but a few drops slithered down the side of his nose and ran down his lips. Her tentacles hung uselessly.

"I almost bit your head off in my rage," he said. "And what a shame that would have been." His tongue came out, jet black and larger than Jenny, and before she could even scream, he'd licked her from her toes to her forehead.

Her exoskeleton, or what was left of it, burned away. Her armor dissolved, and she cried out as she was left naked and bare.

"Imagine I had killed you," he whispered, eyeing her greedily. He looked like he wanted to lick her again, but it was his snakes that snapped forward and flicked her body with their tongues all over: her arms, her hips, her thighs, her ankles.

"*Fuck you*," she managed to spit, even though she was trembling, even though she was terrified he'd pop her head like a grape.

His lips curled into a sinister grin. "I love a human with spirit. That is why I have decided you will be my bride. My queen. The queen of the underworld. And this way . . ." He moved her away from his face, pressing her back against something hard. Something wooden. She couldn't help but whimper. "This way, I can keep you here. On the Failed One's cross. Until it is time."

"No," gasped Jenny, wanting to protest, wanting to beg, a part of her ready to be his bride if it would mean being spared. But then, she remembered finding Susan in that chamber, finding Yeshua in this world, losing their minds with pain.

She wasn't going to beg. She bit her bottom lip till blood ran down her chin.

"What spirit," laughed Azra'il. He waved his burnt hand, and three points of golden light appeared, spiraling and spinning until they solidified into three gruesome-looking nails, each one as thick as Jenny's arm.

*Don't scream*, she told herself. *Don't scream. Don't scream. Don't give him the satisfaction.*

*Don't scream!*

With a flick of his fingers, the nails darted forward. Her arms were slapped back against the cross, spreading them wide—she bit her lip so hard she bit right through it. The nails shot through her palms, through her feet, and dug into the wood with a loud, horrible *snap*.

Blood dripped down her hands. Blood streamed down her feet. Blood ran down her chin, her chest, her navel, and down below.

Azra'il released her head and admired his work as she hung from the cross. "Now you cannot harm destiny. I am certain the holy tablet has changed. That my sister has secured His plan."

All Jenny managed was a pained whimper, red tinging her vision, the pain so much she could hardly breathe.

"I will inform my siblings I have detained you, interloper. They were so concerned. But now, destiny will proceed as planned."

He laughed, a deep, cruel laugh that shook his entire body, and then, he brought his face close to her own. The snakes licked at her lips. At her chest. There was another burst of golden light, and a circle of thorns appeared. Gently, almost lovingly, he placed it on top of her head, and she shut her eyes, trying not to make a sound as the sharp spikes dug into her skin, into her hair, settling into place.

"I will come back for you once the work is done. Once all the worlds bask in His glory. Then, I will claim you—my bride—and we will preside over death for as long as He deems fitting." He held his fingers to her belly. Something *moved* from his flesh—his meaty, hot flesh—and pushed into her belly button, squeezing through her insides and into her. "Now, you can heal too, like the souls, like the Failed One. You will stay here, perfect until we are bound in matrimony. And the womb who birthed the Antithesis will be conquered."

Jenny's mind was numb. Something *wriggled* inside her stomach, worming its way through her chest. Her mouth hung open. Every breath hurt. What was he saying?

His words almost sounded far away, muted, like she was dreaming. Everything hurt so much. What the fuck was he talking about? Matrimony? Why did he want her so bad? The Antithesis?

She blinked, breathing deeply, ignoring how each slight movement pulled against the nails, ignoring whatever was wriggling in her belly.

"You're pathetic," she said, her voice hoarse. Every breath ignited a new round of pain in her hands and feet. She so badly wanted to use Severed Spirit again, to no longer feel any of this, but she was already desecrated. What could she do?

"What did you say?" snapped Azra'il. That fury flashed in his eyes again.

*That's right. Get angry. Kill me.*

*You want to die. You want the pain to end. You want to be free of this. Then your soul can go find Susan and—*

*What delusion are you convincing yourself—*

"How dare you," said Azra'il, curling his lips. "I'm not pathetic. You mortals are the pathetic ones, thinking you can fight against your creators. Rebellion against He who created you." He leaned in close, his mouth opening wide to reveal his teeth, and then he screamed, his hot breath billowing over her body. "WHY DON'T YOU JUST ACCEPT YOUR PLACE IN THE WORLDS?"

Jenny hawked up some phlegm, as much as she could—it was easy with how badly she wanted to cry, with all the snot in her nose—and spat right into his open mouth.

"ARRRGH!" he screamed, and he looked ready to pummel her, to punch her with his truck-size fist and end her right then and there, but he composed himself. He stood straight. "I will return once the material world has fallen. And believe me," he snarled, "I will find your friend. And I will add her to my collection. And she will hang from my palace, and every time you refuse to do as I ask, if you do not satisfy my every desire, I WILL take it out on her."

"FUCK YOU!" screamed Jenny, but Azra'il stepped back into a pool of darkness opening beneath his enormous feet. It was just like the liquid she'd found on the cafeteria floor from where the angels had crawled through. Just like the darkness that opened up when Jenny used Severed Spirit on the worlds.

And he was gone, leaving Jenny alone in the dark, empty world she'd found herself in after leaving the survival challenge. After leaving Susan's corpse.

It was quiet. It was quiet, and she was alone, hanging from a cross, refusing to cry as pain wracked every inch of her body, as the stillness of the world seemed to threaten her from every side, as the dark, heavy clouds above seemed to mock her. As Azra'il's voice rang through her head over and over; what he might do to Susan.

Unable to stop herself, knowing it wouldn't help, she sucked in a deep, painful breath and screamed at the top of her lungs. The thing in her stomach pushed against her skin, and she whimpered, stifling her scream. It wriggled again, a bump rising past her rib cage, and she couldn't hold back anymore.

She shut her eyes and screamed and screamed and screamed, fire bursting out of her throat, fire catching all over her skin, unable to do anything to the wood that bound her in place. Fury burned inside her, coiling around the pain and fueling her fire. *I WILL KILL HIM!*

*I WILL KILL HIM!*

*I WILL KILL HIM!*

"Who are you going to kill?" asked a small voice, and Jenny stopped screaming. Tears blurring her vision, she looked down at the ground, where a boy stood in front of her, a stricken look on his face. He couldn't have been older than eight or nine.

## Death (Level 0)

She blinked away the tears, squinting, wondering if she was finally losing her mind. The boy looked familiar—too familiar. He looked just like she had as a child: the same round, pale face, the same dark hair. The same sad look in the eyes. He wore a purple robe, and beyond him, she could see a large gathering of many, many deaths.

Yeshua and the others must've freed so many while she'd been in the world of souls. They must've been hiding here. Or they had gone through the passage . . . Were there any demons? She couldn't see.

And who was the boy? But even before she asked her question, she knew who he was.

"Who are you?" Jenny took a deep, shuddering breath, blood running down the side of her face.

"I think I'm your death," said the boy, raising his hand and waving slowly. "Hi."

# ABOUT THE AUTHOR

Tess C. Foxes has haunted New York City all of her life. She loves beaches on rainy days, reading stories until four in the morning, and munching on too many hazelnut snacks. She dreams of living in a cabin on a seaside cliff one day, but for now, she jots down all of her anxieties and wishful thoughts as best she can.

# RESPAWN YOUR CURIOSITY

*follow us on our socials*

 podiumentertainment.com

 @podiumentertainment

 /podiumentertainment

 @podium_ent

 @podiumentertainment